The Lion's Paw

Stephen England

Also by Stephen England

Sword of Neamha

<u>Lion of God</u>
Lion of God: The Original Trilogy
The Lion's Paw

<u>Shadow Warriors Series</u>
NIGHTSHADE
Pandora's Grave
Day of Reckoning
TALISMAN
LODESTONE
Embrace the Fire
QUICKSAND
ARKHANGEL
Presence of Mine Enemies
WINDBREAK

To the victims of the Assad regime, past, present, and yes, sadly, now future—this book is respectfully dedicated. May your sacrifices for democracy be remembered and may those you leave behind one day know the freedom you were so cruelly denied.

"With our soul, with our blood, we sacrifice ourselves for you, O Bashar!"

~ A chant taught to Syrian schoolchildren

"They make it a desolation and they call it peace."

~ Calgacus, chieftain of the Caledonians

Prologue

The battered Toyota Hilux jounced out of one shell crater and over the lip of another as it rumbled down the road—catching the young fighter on the *Dushka* off-balance, the muzzle of the big Soviet-made machine gun mounted in the technical's bed swinging wildly as the teenager struggled to regain his balance.

Off to their northeast, in the fading twilight, one could hear the ceaseless chatter of automatic weapons fire—a long line of tracers arcing out through the semi-darkness.

An unearthly sound seemed suddenly to fill the air above their heads, like a freight train roaring past overhead.

Mohamed Taferi raised his head above the bullet-pocked side of the Hilux to see a Southern Front T-72 silhouetted on the skyline to the west, the muzzle of the tank's 125mm main gun belching fire as it engaged Hezbollah positions farther east, out toward Jadieh.

"Allahu akbar!" the teenager screamed, pumping a fist to

1

the sky as yet another heavy shell flew by above. *"Allahu akbar!"*

God is great.

Indeed He is, Mohamed mused ironically, his dark eyes scanning the horizon—his hand on the grip of his Glock G19, riding there in its holster on his hip, just below his plate carrier. *But what do you know of Him?*

The Hilux turned back down a side road, toward the Israeli border—lying just a scant dozen or so kilometers to their west, the heights of the Golan looming there in the gathering darkness.

The buildings on either side of the road were little more than rubble, pulverized by fighting that had gone on now in the governorate for half a decade. Up ahead, the shelled-out, spectral hulk of a house rose two stories against the setting sun, all but one wall blown out and that seeming to cling to life by a thread, a breath away from crumbling down into the dust all around.

Mohamed looked across into the eyes of another young fighter sitting in the bed of the truck across from him—a black bandanna wound round his forehead, soaked dark with sweat, a wild grin on his face, the last dying rays of sun reflected in his eyes. Blood-red streaks of fire among the gray clouds.

He couldn't have been much more than seventeen. The old Chinese-made Type 56 assault rifle cradled loosely in the kid's hands, its wooden furniture battered and scarred, was at least three times as old as its owner. *Had he even hit puberty when all this began?*

A childhood lost to war.

Another technical swung out from a side road, its wheels

grinding the remains of concrete rubble into powder—the dusty, begrimed fighters in its bed raising a throaty cheer of *"Allahu akbar!"* as they came alongside.

Fursan Tahrir al-Sham, he thought, noting the recognition in the eyes of the fighters surrounding him in the truck. Their brothers, the "Knights for the Liberation of *Sham*"—that amorphous region of Greater Syria which embraced all that an English speaker would have known as the Levant, including the country out on the other side of that border which Mohamed had called home since his earliest years. He was on his way to meet with their commander, Abu Ahmed al-Golani, the briefcase clutched in his right hand a gift for the rebel leader. *Gift?* Better to call it for what it was. *Payment.*

A heavily bearded fighter stared back at Mohamed from the adjacent Hilux as the men called out back and forth, his single eye shining with a vicious intensity which more than compensated for its neighboring socket, raw and empty, the left half of his face nearly destroyed.

Knights they might be, but there was no shining armor here. With any of them. . .or with him, however he might have wished to see it otherwise. War did not suffer delusions.

Half of these men would kill him where he stood if they fully grasped who—*what*—he was, the Israeli realized, gripping the side of the truck as they swung into a turn, the camp visible just ahead. Al-Golani might have chosen to look the other way—to shake hands with the devil to keep himself and his men alive. *In the fight.* But the rank and file wouldn't take such a long view of things.

The success of his mission—his very survival—rested in being able to keep his head down, keep to the shadows.

3

Move unnoticed and unremarked. As his people had been doing for a thousand years.

A wry, sardonic grimace played at Mohamed Taferi's lips. Hiding in plain sight came naturally to the Druze. . .

Chapter 1

6:46 A.M., Israel Standard Time, December 10th
Caesarea National Park
Caesarea, Haifa District
Israel

Overhead, the shrill cries of a gull wheeling and turning through the sky heralded the dawn, the sun's glow creeping slowly above the Judean hills to the east.

It was a cold and unusually clear December morning, though it had rained the night before and would, if the reddening eastern sky were any gauge, likely storm again before nightfall.

David Shafron shoved his hands deeper into the pockets of his coat, gazing steadfastly out to sea, the roar of the breakers filling his ears. Their white foam just visible in the growing half-light, the Mediterranean dashing itself to pieces against the rocks of the Reef Palace as it had done for more than two thousand years.

He was standing among the upper seats of Caesarea's Roman theater, another of the relics of that long-ago occupation, the sea breeze rippling across his close-cropped dark hair.

The haircut, like the smoldering cigarette held between the thumb and forefinger of his right hand, was a legacy of his military service—a service which had lasted far longer than the compulsory three years which had been standard for IDF conscripts in his day.

"Where are they?" he heard Shaul Litman murmur from a few feet behind him, a note of disgruntlement in the security officer's voice.

"Patience, Shaul," Shafron responded calmly, raising the Camel to his lips and taking another long drag. The Americans were late, but they would arrive when they pleased, and not before—as they always did.

The price of doing business with a superpower, as you came to accept over time. *Reality.*

But accepting realities of that nature took maturity, and Litman was still young and a bit of a hothead at moments. Like he'd been at one time, Shafron reflected with a touch of amusement—back in his twenties, transitioning from the regular military into first *Sayeret Duvdevan* and then into the *Kidon* units of the Mossad. Back when most of the people around him had known him as "Ariel." *The Lion of God.*

No one had called him that for a very long time.

"They're on their way in, David," Shimon Ben-David, the senior member of his security team, announced, touching his earpiece—his coat open to reveal the Jericho 941 holstered there on his hip. Shafron just nodded. Their lookout would have picked up Keifer's people about three kilometers out, along the road. It always paid to have eyes out, even when it came to your allies. Perhaps *especially* when it came to your allies.

He'd quit smoking more than once, back then—striving

6

for the peak of physical condition to keep up with his unit, to *excel* in the field.

But then had come Iraq, a dark night in the desert which had cost him dearly—two of his men dead, a pair of bullets smashing into his left arm and shoulder blade. It had marked the beginning of the end for his career with the *Kidon*, and he'd only gone back out into the field a handful of times in the more than decade and a half since.

A flicker of headlight beams off to the north caught Shafron's eye in the semi-darkness and he glanced out to see a small convoy of three black SUVs turning into the park off Road 6511.

"Here they are."

12:04 A.M. Eastern Standard Time
An apartment
Washington, D.C.

The television news was on in the background, but the man in the wheelchair had tuned it out long before, the knife in his hand sinking deep into the ripe flesh of the apple on the cutting block before him.

It was another report from the Philippines, the subject of the Braley kidnapping consuming media attention—and most of his own focus, these days.

Most. Bernard Kranemeyer set the knife aside and popped a slice of apple into his mouth, glancing at his wristwatch. Keifer should be meeting with the Israelis any moment now. He needed his sleep, with the ongoing crisis, but he'd wait for the call all the same. Wait to see if they went for it.

He wasn't sure he would have, if he'd been in their position. It was a high-stakes gambit with considerable potential for blowback if it went the wrong way, which was why they had decided to approach Mossad in the first place. No way the President would have signed off on cross-border authorization.

But if you could convince an ally to do the work for you, arrange some kind of acceptable *quid pro quo* between intelligence partners, you wouldn't *need* the President's signature. That was the beauty of this—*if* Shafron went along with it.

David Shafron. Kranemeyer picked up the plate of sliced apple and placed it in his lap, wheeling back into the living room of his small apartment and reaching over for the TV remote. He knew the man well, back to a particularly dark night in Iraq, well before the war, when Kranemeyer—then an Army NCO with 1st Special Forces Operational Detachment-Delta—had been attached to Shafron's *Kidon* team to call in air support for a mission which had been blacker than black, the kind of thing no one ever talked about after the fact.

Like this.

They had both come a long way since that night, Kranemeyer thought with a grim smile—their field careers both abbreviated by injury, Shafron's during that very op, his own several years later, on a dusty street in Tikrit, an IED mangling his right leg below the knee. Fortunes of war.

A war they continued to wage, Kranemeyer now as director of the CIA's Clandestine Service, Shafron as the right hand of Mossad director Avi ben Shoham, serving as—according to the CIA's best intel reports—head of MEGIDDO, one of the

Mossad's more recent and nebulously-defined departments.

Warriors for whom there would always be a war, even if it had now fallen to their lot to send other men to fight it.

"There's no difference between one's killing and making decisions that will send others to kill." Kranemeyer remembered the words of Golda Meir, the wizened Iron Lady of the Jewish state, and a woman with more than enough blood on her own hands.

The smile had vanished from his face, his coal-black eyes seeming to grow somehow even darker in the soft glow of the television screen as he recalled the rest of the quote.

"It's exactly the same thing. . .or even worse."

7:06 A.M. Israel Standard Time
Caesarea National Park
Caesarea, Haifa District
Israel

"You're serious about this," David Shafron heard himself ask, looking up from the satellite printouts into the face of his counterpart.

They were standing in the desolate ruins of the Reef Palace now, just the two of them, their respective security details abandoned fifty meters back, as the dawn came up over the eastern hills, a bloody streak carving its way through the clouds like a gaping wound. *An omen?*

"Dead serious." Paul Keifer was a short, stockily built man with an unremarkable face and a rough shock of hair which had been blond in the earliest Mossad file photos, but which was now almost completely turned to gray. "We don't know how long they'll be deployed at Khmeimim, but right now, they're exposed. This is *opportunity*, David, and it's knocking."

There was raw excitement in the voice of the CIA station chief, an enthusiasm even the crash of the breakers failed to drown out.

It was a conversation they'd never had, but Keifer was of an age to have grown up in the twilight years of the Cold War, engrossed by stories of high-stakes espionage between the great powers—defections, double agents, and the ever-present arms race between East and West.

He glanced back at the satellite printout in his hand, marking the distinctive, blended-wing bodies of the parked aircraft, and shook his head. This was certainly feeling entirely too much like a Clancy novel.

"It's something like that," he acknowledged slowly, looking the American in the eye. He'd always had a good working relationship with Keifer, since the American had first arrived to take over Station Tel Aviv early in the year, but that didn't mean he actually trusted the man. A good intelligence officer would use you with a smile. "If it's opportunity, why aren't you taking advantage of it? Latakia's right on the coast, just a few kilometers in-land. Well within the striking distance, if your Navy SEALs were to lock out of an *Ohio*-class."

He allowed himself a quiet internal smile at the look of discomfort which flickered across Keifer's face for a brief moment before disappearing. No doubt that idea had come up.

"It's not that simple, David. We—"

"It never is," Shafron replied coolly, handing back the printouts. "So, what are you offering?"

"Look, you guys don't like Russia in Syria any better than we do. They're an adversary of the state of Israel, every bit as much as they are of the US of A. Those tanks that came pouring across your borders back in '73? Every last one of them, Russian-made."

"I wasn't around then." He smiled, refusing to take the bait. "Times change and we change with them, Paul. You Americans saw off the Soviet Union when I was in high school. We talk with our Russian counterparts regularly about Syria through our deconfliction channel, and cooperate on counterterrorism in the region, where we can. Prime Minister Shamir himself made a state visit to Moscow earlier this year."

None of which altered the reality that Russia continued to be a thorn in their side. Without the frenzied efforts of the Kremlin, the regime of Bashar Assad would have been consigned to the dustbin of history years before, and Russian support for Iranian meddling in the country remained as unabashed as ever. Keifer wasn't wrong, just. . .self-interested, like any spook worth his salt.

And playing his hand entirely too close to the vest for Shafron's liking.

An exasperated curse escaped the American's lips as he shook his head, glancing out to sea for a brief moment. "You're not planning to make this easy, are you?"

Another smile. "No reason to. That's not how this business works, you know that. Particularly not now, when anything we share here this morning might well find its way to the desk of your President, to be shared with his counterparts in Moscow as he sees fit."

The American's face flushed red-hot. That story had just

hit the Israeli media within the previous few weeks, but Mossad had known for much longer. That intelligence they'd shared with their US counterparts had been passed along by the American President in an Oval Office meeting with the Russian foreign minister over the summer, resulting in the compromise of a Mossad asset. A knowledge which had precipitated an angry flurry of phone calls between his boss and Keifer's.

The man was still missing, Shafron reflected grimly, his smile vanishing. Likely dead. Just another of the hundreds of thousands who had died in the civil war still devastating Syria, but he had been theirs.

"Look, David, I don't know how to. . ." Keifer's voice trailed off there, as if he'd changed his mind mid-sentence, a curiously determined look crossing his face. "That's exactly why we need your help. This can't go to Norton's desk, and as long as we're not directly involved. . .it won't need to. We can make it worth Mossad's while."

"I'm listening."

11:34 A.M. Syria Standard Time
Khmeimim Air Base
Latakia Governorate, Syria

Thirty-one days, Andriy Makarenko thought, his pale grey eyes scanning the assembled crowd as the twin-engine Russian Federation Tupolev Tu-214SR taxied to a halt just across the tarmac from where he stood at the edge of the gathered crowd of military and security personnel. That was how much longer he had in this godforsaken country—just another month before he could return home, rotating out of his position as the GU's head of security here at Khmeimim.

A lieutenant colonel—*podpolkóvnik*—in the Main Directorate of the General Staff of the Armed Forces of the Russian Federation, the GU—still more commonly known by its Soviet-era designation of "GRU," Makarenko had spent the better part of the last year in Syria, overseeing security for the hundreds of Russian military personnel garrisoned at the airbase.

A hard, arduous task with the airfield coming under sporadic attack by rebel groups probing their perimeter, lobbing mortar shells at the airfield. The realities of war, never far from anyone's mind even here, in the heart of what was supposed to be Assad country, the surrounding population dominated by the Alawites who formed a distinct minority in the rest of Syria.

His fiancée had given birth two months after he'd left Russia, and he'd first met his newborn daughter through video chat, watching her progress, her growth, from afar. He'd be back together with them soon.

First, though, he had to get through today—a day which had been a source of elevated stress ever since he'd learned of the surprise visit a week before, the news filtering down from his superiors in Moscow. *Get ready. Don't embarrass yourself—or* us.

Makarenko glanced back, making out the tall, angular figure of Syrian president Bashar al-Assad approaching across the tarmac from back toward the hangars. Shaking hands with General Kovpak's command staff as he made his way to the forefront of the waiting crowd, surrounded by his own security team—Alawites like the president himself to a man, many of them the sons and grandsons of long-time retainers of the Assad family.

That was what had been giving him an ulcer. There were far too many guns he didn't control on this piece of real estate just now with Assad's security present in force—far too many chances of something going awry. And he would bear full responsibility, even if in the final accounting it might be clear that it had all been out of his control. *Helpless.*

Twenty meters away, uniformed Russian Air Force personnel rolled ramp stairs bearing the livery of *Syrian Air* into position at the door of the Tupolev, security personnel from the SBP—the Presidential Security Service—emerging from within the airliner and hurrying down the stairs to take up positions at its foot.

More men with guns who didn't answer to him, though he had briefed extensively with General Semenyakin's staff prior to this visit. They were singing off the same sheet music, at least.

And then the slight figure of the Russian President appeared in the doorway, seeming to hesitate for a moment before descending the stairs, his thinning grey hair tousled by the brisk December breeze which cut across the runway from the northeast.

Were the rumors true? Makarenko found himself asking, watching the man as he descended, the military guard lined up to receive him—the roar of jet engines increasing in volume from the distance as a pair of Sukhoi Su-57 stealth fighters, the pride of the Russian Air Force, blazed in out of the north, flashing past in the backdrop, barely a thousand feet off the deck, before pulling straight up into the clear blue sky. *A display of power.*

It was dangerous to even think the murmurings might be

accurate, he reflected, watching as General Kovpak marched stiff-legged toward the President, the stocky base commander drawing himself into a smart salute as he bellowed out his official welcome to the base. The nearby Russia Today news crew catching all of it on camera.

More dangerous to dismiss them and be caught flat-footed when change came—on the wrong side of whomever would manage to fill the vacuum. *Mironov?*

He would have to find a way to survive, no matter who it was. For Zinaida. . .*and Natalyushka.*

Makarenko thrust those doubts aside with an effort, forcing a smile to his face as he moved forward—watching as the President reached out, embracing the much taller Bashar Assad, the two men exchanging warm greetings.

And then the President of the Russian Federation stood before him.

12:09 P.M. Israel Standard Time
Mossad Headquarters, Glilot Junction
Tel Aviv-Yafo, Israel

". . .here in Syria, far from home, you are doing exactly that—you are protecting our Fatherland. We will never forget. . ."

"Do you think there's anything to the reports?" Avi ben Shoham asked, turning his chair away from his computer as the Russian president continued speaking from Khmeimim Air Base, the video of his surprise visit to Syria live-streamed by RT.

"That he has months to live?" David Shafron shook his head, arms folded across his chest as he stood in his boss' office, eyeing the livestream critically. "You wouldn't know it to look at him."

The former IDF general reached up to adjust his necktie, a grimace passing across his weary face. A combat veteran who *had* served in the Golan during the Yom Kippur War, Shoham had spent nearly two decades in the IDF before ever coming to "the Office," as Mossad was known to its familiars, and few could have predicted just how thoroughly the former tanker would adapt himself to the far more shadowy world of intelligence and special operations.

Nearly twenty years Shafron's senior, Avi ben Shoham was now the Office's *memuneh*—"the one in charge"—and it had been under his directives that MEGIDDO had been stood up several years prior, with Shafron tapped to head its operations, answering directly to Shoham's office. But their professional history went back so much further. To the early days of the Second Intifada.

"That's cancer for you," the Mossad chief observed grimly. If that's what it was, really—no one knew for sure, and the Kremlin certainly wasn't saying anything, officially. "My father was a leathery old kibbutznik—never knew him to be sick a day in his life, until one day they realized he had stage four liver cancer. He didn't last the year."

David winced. He hadn't spoken with his own father in the last twenty-two years of his life, and when he'd passed, five years earlier, a sense of relief had warred with the guilt.

"The Americans' timing is impeccable, though, I must admit," Shoham said, gesturing toward the computer screen. "Did they know about this visit?"

"Keifer didn't say." David shrugged. "We didn't—I checked with Rosenblatt before coming up."

That was the way of the business. You did your best to know everyone's secrets, but here and there, one got through. And as intelligence misses went, the itinerary of the Russian president was a minor oversight.

"There's no way I ask Eli to put *Sayeret Matkal* on the ground in Syria against the Russians," Shoham said firmly, referencing Prime Minister Eli Shamir, the expression on his face that of a man lost in thought. "But Keifer's not wrong—this is an opportunity. You saw the planes yourself in the livestream."

He waved a hand at the screen, where the Russian president was concluding his brief remarks. "As ever in the past, anything the Russians field now could be fielded against us in the future by Syria—or Iran. If they're making advances in stealth technology, that's something we need to understand *now*, not when it's streaking south over the Golan at Mach 2."

The scars of '73, Shafron thought, watching the older man closely. Israel had ridden a high of invulnerability in the wake of the Six Days of 1967, the lightning campaign in which they had crushed all opposition before them, the Arab armies crumbling to dust beneath the treads of their tanks.

And then had come the crash, as ever following an addict's high. A scant six years later, as those despised Arab powers came roaring back, their tank divisions pouring across the Suez Canal and the Golan, shattering the surprised and understrength Israeli defenders.

Those who had survived—like Shoham—had emerged traumatized and determined never to allow it or anything like it to ever happen again. *No matter the cost.*

It could be a blind spot of its own, at times.

"So you think this is worth pursuing." It wasn't a question, not really—he could see the answer in Shoham's eyes.

A nod. "*Ken*. Without question. The value of the intelligence in itself would justify the risk, but having even partial access to the American intelligence on the Astana talks. . .we have our own sources, of course, but it would be useful to know what they know."

In more ways than one. The Syrian peace process had dragged on for years, with the shift of venue to the Kazakh capital seemingly accomplishing precious little. Israel was not a party to the talks, but that didn't mean they weren't interested.

"The question is how to accomplish it. Our fingerprints can't be on this, David," Shoham said, looking his subordinate in the eye, "any more than the Americans'. Not in any way Moscow can prove, at least."

"Understood," Shafron replied, his mind already turning over the possibilities. As dangerous as this was, it was the sort of operation MEGIDDO had been established to carry out. "There are groups we have supported in Syria, in the fight against the Hizballah militias. . .Latakia isn't exactly home turf for any of them, but one or more might be capable of undertaking the operation. The problem would be getting the intelligence back."

A snort from Shoham. The Syrian rebels weren't exactly trained intelligence officers. An operation of this delicacy— well, it was far easier to trust them to break things than it was to rely on them to recognize or secure highly sensitive technological intelligence.

"If, however, we were to send along one of our own, accompanying the rebel fighters. . ."

"You have someone in mind?" the Mossad director asked, glancing shrewdly over at Shafron.

"I do."

5:07 P.M.
Beit Jann
Northern District, Israel

The night air was cold and crisp as Mohamed Taferi stepped out onto the flat roof of the small house, steam rising from the glass of tea in his callused right hand.

Below, further down the slopes of Mount Meron, the village of Beit Jann spread out before him, lights glowing from half a hundred houses in the gathering darkness. *Home*.

This small village, clinging to the mountainside, had been his home for the first eighteen years of his life—right up until the moment he'd left to begin his mandatory thirty-six months of service to the state of Israel. It had been the home for his people for at least seven centuries—ever since a pair of Druze hunters out for hyraxes had stumbled across an ancient cistern filled with clear, cold water. Or at least that was the local legend.

He wondered at moments if he had been here then, perhaps even one of those hunters. Certainly, he had to have passed through this village more than once or twice over the centuries.

Mohamed lifted the steaming glass to his lips, the sweet fruity tang of sugar and lemon strong against his tongue as he heard the door open and close behind him, his mother's soft footsteps against the concrete of the roof.

Memories of those past lives came only in the most fleeting

of moments, triggered by some familiar scene or happenstance, but he knew he must have lived them. Every Druze was the reincarnation of some past Druze, down through time—the male Druze finding themselves reincarnated as men, the women in like manner. Dying to be reborn in the body of a Druze child being born at the same time.

Perhaps once he had fought the Teutonic Knights in these very hills, their citadel of Montfort barely sixteen kilometers the other side of the mountain. Or perhaps. . .his lips curled in a wry smile. Perhaps he had just been a shepherd, all those hundreds of years. A simple man, out there tending his sheep on the hillsides of Palestine. *Wouldn't that have been ironic?*

But in this part of the world, sometimes even the shepherds had to fight.

"Your father will be so glad to see you when he returns home tomorrow," Fatin Taferi announced, the white shawl draped about her face seeming to glow in the darkness. She had been a beautiful woman in her day, and there remained a quiet nobility in the lines of her weathered face. "It's been too long, Mohamed."

"It has," the Mossad intelligence officer replied simply, unable to dispute his mother's statement. He hadn't even been in the country for most of the last year, but that was something he couldn't tell her, and it would only have worried her in any case. "I've been busy. Didn't know father would be away, just now."

Not that it was that uncommon—a graduate of the inaugural class of Talpiot, the elite IDF training program for academic over-achievers, Jassan Taferi had gone on to put his talents—and his extensive network of contacts among

20

fellow Talpiot alumni—to work in Israel's tech sector. His trips to Silicon Valley were nearly as frequent as his son's trips to the Bekaa.

"He's very proud, you know," his mother went on after a long moment. "He speaks of you frequently."

"To me," she added quickly, catching his look of alarm. Beyond his parents, the rest of his community understood simply that he worked for the government, some office job in Tel Aviv, presumably. "Mossad" was not a word he allowed to leave his lips outside the headquarters of the Office itself.

Still, *pride*. . .that was something of a sea change. His father had long believed that his son would follow in his footsteps, as his older brother had done, and turn to the private sector to make his fortune after paying his dues to Israel. Twelve years on, perhaps his dad was starting to get the idea. Even if he wasn't himself sure why he kept at it.

Mohamed lifted the glass to his lips and drained the rest of the tea, a slight grimace crossing his face. He preferred herbal teas over the almost candied fruit *halitot*, but his mother was a traditionalist. In this, as so much else. She would be asking if he'd found a nice Druze girl next, if this conversation ran its usual course.

"You are being careful, aren't you?" she asked instead, resting a single hand on the parapet of the roof as she looked up into his face. "I see things, on the news. . .I think of you, and it worries me."

"Na'am," he replied. *Yes.* "Of course, mama. I'm always careful."

And so he was, though he doubted it would meet her definition of the word. It wasn't five days since he'd been

21

neck-deep in a firefight over there across that border, out in the darkness nearly fifty kilometers to the east—a surprise attack by Iranian-backed militias taking the rebel fighters off-guard. Mortar shells falling all around as they scrambled for their weapons, Mohamed reaching for his own M4, though, as so often, he'd never ended up firing it. Shrapnel tearing through the leg of one young fighter, laying him open from ankle to thigh.

The kid had laid there, helpless, in the blood-damp dust, screaming and cursing and calling out for God. *And his mother.*

No, it wouldn't have met her definition of *careful* at all.

"I saw there were aid workers kidnapped by rebels in Syria only last week," she continued, her voice sounding strained. "You haven't been there, have you?"

"La," he said quickly—too quickly—shaking his head. Deception was his business, but he was never comfortable lying to her—those dark brown eyes, seemingly able to look straight through him. He couldn't see them now, in the darkness, but he could feel the skepticism radiating from their depths. She wasn't buying it, not for a moment.

"I pray for you, every day," his mother went on after a long moment, "that you will know the protection of Allah, wherever you are."

"Shukran, mama." *Thank you.* "I am always—"

His cellphone began to pulse in that moment, his voice breaking off as he checked the screen. *Work.*

"Yes?" He listened for a long moment, then nodded, feeling her eyes on him. Knowing just how disappointed she would be. "I'll be in first thing in the morning. . ."

Chapter 2

9:07 A.M., December 11th
Mossad Headquarters, Glilot Junction
Tel Aviv-Yafo, Israel

Mohamed Taferi was thirty-one, according to his personnel file, David Shafron reflected, and had been recruited by the Office near the close of his term of conscription in the IDF. That gave him just under a decade as an intelligence officer, and it was a decade he had turned to good effect, distinguishing himself in more than a few operations just during Mirit Refaeli's tenure as department head for Metsada, the Office's operations branch. Most of them in southwestern Syria, where Taferi's Druze heritage gave him the ability to fade into the background, unremarked and unnoticed.

He had been among the officers Shafron had handpicked when MEGIDDO had first been stood up, but Mirit had proven unwilling to let go of him, and Shafron had lost that particular bureaucratic turf battle. A smile touched his lips at the memory.

Ten years his own senior, Mirit Refaeli was a fourth-generation Sabra whose father had fought in the Palmach as a teenager at the dawn of the Jewish state, and whose grandfather had been left a cripple by an Arab mob in the attack on the kibbutz of Mishmar HaEmek back in 1929. Hard as the land itself, she ran Metsada with a rod of iron and defended her department with a fierce tenacity belied by her grandmotherly looks.

Not even Shoham crossed her lightly, or so it was rumored. He hadn't stood a chance.

"We're targeting the Russians." It wasn't a question, but the surprise was still visible in Mohamed Taferi's eyes as he looked up from the briefing folder Shafron had handed him.

A nod.

"Deliberately."

Another nod. It wasn't that they hadn't already clashed, more than once. Syria was like that—you often didn't quite know who you were shooting at until it was over, and Russia's aggressive deployment of the ostensibly private Wagner Group had led to a number of violent confrontations with Israeli and Israeli-backed forces in the war-ridden country. Still, Taferi was right—this *was* different.

"The Sukhoi Su-57 is the newest jet in the Russian lineup," Shafron announced, rising from his office chair and moving around to the front of his desk. "A fifth-generation stealth fighter designed to compete with the Americans' F-22 Raptor and replace the Russian Federation's current fleet of MiG-29s and Su-27s."

And Israel didn't have F-22s to counter it, he thought grimly, courtesy of a now-septuagenarian American congressman from Wisconsin who had decided back in the late '90s that exporting America's new stealth fighter—then barely making its first test flights—posed an unacceptable security risk. It was a decision which had ultimately cost the American program dear, but it had severely hamstrung the IAF up until the arrival of the F-35, which was just now entering service—and with future deliveries only expected to bring their total to a couple dozen.

"Our intelligence on the Su-57—which our NATO partners have cleverly dubbed the 'Felon'—is spotty beyond the general specifications. If we're to have a reliable chance of countering it, we need more."

Which was to say nothing of the American willingness to trade intel. But that *quid pro quo* was above Taferi's paygrade.

"And they've parked a pair of them at Khmeimim."

"For the moment," Shafron replied. "They flew in from Russia three days ago. We don't know just how long this window will remain open, but while it's open, we're going through it. That's where you come in."

That got Taferi's attention. "What do you need me to do?"

"Our fingerprints can't be on this one—not with the risk of Russian casualties. We need a proxy, a cat's paw if you will." A part of him wondered if they might not themselves be the paw in this scenario. *For the Americans.*

But this was a decision which had already been made, above him—Shamir's government signing off on Avi's proposal the previous night. They were doing this.

"Fursan Tahrir al-Sham," he went on after a moment's pause. "I want you to go back into Syria—and reach out to Abu Ahmed al-Golani."

1:36 P.M. Syria Standard Time
Quneitra Governorate
Southwestern Syria

Yunus was dead. He had fought beside the older boy for two years, shared his food and even his blankets when the desert grew cold at night—the chill night breeze sweeping through the bombed-out buildings in which they so often took shelter. They'd been as close as brothers, though they'd never met before the war had thrown them together—lost souls adrift.

But Nassif found he had no tears for him now, as the teenager pawed through his dead friend's pockets—the mostly-empty pouches on the chest rig beneath his jacket, his fingers closing around a pair of magazines for the battle-scarred Type 56 Yunus had carried, transferring them to the pockets of his own jeans. They'd work equally well for his own rifle, and every last round was precious.

He wanted the jacket too, but a bullet cracked by over Nassif's head before he could strip his friend's arms out of the sleeves and he nearly dropped his rifle as he scrambled back over the rocks, seeking the cover of a nearby shell crater. The screams of another wounded fighter ringing in his ears.

He couldn't remember the last time he had cried. . .for anyone, the years at war seeming to drain all the emotion out of the boy, hollowing him out until all that remained was a brittle shell. His parents had died in a barrel bombing years before, along with his little sister—he'd found her body, or at least he'd thought it was hers, lying in the street of their Damascus suburb, missing a head and most of her right leg. Perhaps he'd cried then, he couldn't remember—

all the loss blurring the memories together.

Nassif and his brother Talha had fled after that, drifting south through the fighting, surviving however they could. A brutal, hardscrabble existence, but they *had* survived.

His brother was out there, somewhere, Nassif thought—off to his left in the rubble—trading fire with the Hizballah fighters they'd ambushed five hours before. The Knights had rolled out of their camp, back ten kilometers to the southwest, under the cover of darkness, more than forty *mujahideen* in a small, scrapped-together convoy of vehicles, moving to ambush their Iranian-backed opponents, cut their supply lines.

It was all supposed to have been over by now, the Knights melting back across the lines toward their camp—but there had been more of the militiamen than they'd expected, and the Iranians had fought back aggressively, turning the ambush back on their attackers. And they'd started taking casualties.

"Allahu akbar!" he heard someone chant from a few yards away to his right, the words punctuated by a long, ragged burst of gunfire, and he pushed himself up above the lip of the crater, his fingers closing tightly around the stock of his Yugoslavian Kalashnikov—his eyes searching wildly for targets.

Combat wasn't the way you saw it on television—in the Western action movies he and his brother had watched as children. Most of the time, you only got flickering glimpses of your enemy—flashes of movement, off in the distance. If you were lucky, that's all they'd see of you, too.

He saw movement there to his front, maybe eighty meters out beyond the muzzle of his rifle—a figure moving forward, ducking from cover to cover. Maybe trying to recover their wounded, maybe moving to a better firing position. A strange green smoke drifted lazily up into the sky not far from the moving figure.

The AK's trigger broke beneath his finger, a wild cry escaping his lips as the rifle bucked back against his shoulder, its muzzle climbing wildly as he struggled to control it. *"Takbir!"* he heard someone call out from off to his right, the answering cry of *"Allahu akbar!"* breaking from his own throat, swelling all around him.

Little jets of dirt seemed to spurt from the earth in front of him as the magazine emptied, his mind realizing belatedly that it was incoming fire—a round smacking into the crumbling concrete of the wall at the edge of the crater.

He dropped, fumbling for one of Yunus' mags in the pocket of his ragged jeans as he rolled onto his back, hitting the mag release. Hearing the *boom* of a recoilless rifle somewhere far off to his left—theirs, the enemy's, it was impossible to tell at this distance.

And then Talha was there, his older brother collapsing into the crater beside him—out of breath, his plaid shirt torn and smudged with dirt and what looked like blood. The tan leather hiking boots he'd taken off a dead Hizballah fighter a week before, now caked with mud and dirt.

"Alhamdullilah, bro—you're alive," he gasped out, reaching out to pat Nassif affectionately on the shoulder. "Abu Muin has given the order to fall back," he said after a moment, referencing one of Abu Ahmed's lieutenants, the man who had led the ambush party. "Everyone, back to the trucks—quick as you can. I'm to pass the word along."

Talha picked his own rifle back up and was gone again,

as quick as he'd come—running and ducking his way along through the rubble to the north as Nassif finished reloading, jacking the AK's charging handle back to chamber a round.

Time to leave. To cut their losses, and—he heard them then, that deathly, familiar sound sweeping over the battlefield from the north, low and fast. *Helicopters.*

Two of them, ugly and bug-like, grim as death—a chainsaw seeming to rip apart the sky as the Gatling mounted beneath the chin of the lead helicopter opened up, rounds slamming into the ground. Hot magnesium flares falling away from the helicopter to cascade down from the heavens, sparkling and burning brightly. And then rockets flashed from beneath its stubby wings. . .

The boy flattened himself against the sloped side of the crater, trying to make himself small—to disappear—the AK's receiver deathly cold against his fingers, his eyes squeezed shut as the explosions hammered his eardrums, rubble falling all around him.

He felt something heavier hit the ground just beside him and opened his eyes—his ears ringing—to see the mangled lower half of a man's leg laying not six inches from his hand.

And attached to the leg. . .a dirty hiking boot that once had been tan.

1:45 P.M.

"We smoked them," Senior Lieutenant Oleg Kurbatov heard his weapons systems officer exclaim triumphantly from the compartment in front, the man's voice coming clear over his earpiece as he punched the countermeasures button once again, flares fluttering from their dispensers in the wake of the Mi-24D *"Galya"* helicopter gunship as it banked low over the rubble-strewn battlefield.

So they had, the Russian Air Force pilot thought, eyeing the drifting pillar of green smoke marking the position of the Hizballah militias they were here to support—but there was no sense in getting reckless. He had no intention of dying in this desolate waste.

The four-barreled 12.7-mm Yak-B Gatling in the Mi-24's chin turret opened back up as Kurbatov brought the gunship around for another low pass, keeping a careful eye on his fuel gauge. *Wouldn't do to linger.*

Maksim was in his element, a battered old Toyota below exploding into flames from the impact of a rocket, rebels running in every direction—a delighted chortle from the weps officer reaching Kurbatov's ears along with the renewed rattle of the Gatling.

The pilot shook his head, unable to share in his friend's delight. This was a job, nothing more—a job he'd be just as glad to have over. The President's announcement, the day before, coming as welcome news—his country was drawing down their military commitment to Syria, and though he still had a few months left, he *would* be going home. So long as he managed to stay alive.

He saw an RPG-7 stab up into the sky at him from out to the west, far off his left wingtip, rocketing off uselessly into oblivion—but close enough to send a cold chill rippling down his spine. One of those, well, the *Galya* might have inherited the "flying tank" tradition of the *Shturmovik* from the Great Patriotic War, but those RPGs had been designed to *destroy* tanks.

A burst of static over his headset as he banked the Mi-24

into another turn and he heard the voice of his wingman, announcing they were out of rockets, running low on ammunition. Time to call it a day, then. *Return to base.*

First to refuel at Al-Dumayr, and then. . .back to Khmeimim.

4:03 P.M. Israel Standard Time
Mossad Headquarters, Glilot Junction
Tel Aviv-Yafo, Israel

"He won't be expecting me," Mohamed Taferi mused, twisting the pen back and forth between his fingers as he glanced up from his hand-scribbled notes. His tea was growing cold in the Styrofoam cup before him, but he had lost interest. He looked around at the team of officers assembled in the windowless, sound-proofed conference room deep inside the Headquarters Building. "It's more than three weeks away from our next scheduled meet. I don't want to spook him."

They had taken a physically hands-off approach to their liaison operations in Syria from the very beginning. Too many trips across the border, too many comings-and-goings. . .simply put, it was the pitcher and the well. Sooner or later, you were bound to get broken.

It wouldn't do for the rank-and-file of the rebel groups to start piecing together that some of their leaders were taking money from the Jews. That they were, in fact, as Shafron had said, a cat's paw. *A* lion's *paw*, he thought with an ironic smile, reflecting on his department head.

A few people around headquarters still referred to Shafron as "the Lion of God," though almost never in his presence, apparently some reference back to his days in the field as an operations officer. "When was our last actual contact with Abu Ahmed, Nika?"

"Six days ago," Nikahywot Mengashe replied from her seat on the other side of the conference table. A couple years his senior, the Mossad staff officer had been born in Gondar, Ethiopia before making *aliyah* with her parents at the age of five. A quiet, incisive woman, she had been among the first officers tapped by Shafron for the new department, and she was responsible for coordinating MEGIDDO's ongoing operations with the Syrian rebels. "He asked for more weapons."

That was a perennial request, and one they fulfilled, to the extent it was considered judicious. One day, things would settle in Syria. And which way would those guns be turned then?

"Do we have any more recent confirmation that he's still alive?" Mohamed asked, getting to the heart of the issue. Never mind the natural attrition of the Syrian Civil War, they had other problems.

It had taken them the better part of two months to recognize the pattern of assassinations and establish more or less what was going on, but al-Qaeda had had a busy fall.

More than eighteen opposition leaders across southwestern Syria, including three they had been working with—all of them leaders of groups that had failed to toe the Salafist jihadist line, at least openly—had died since August, in a bloody purge that was leaving their surviving networks increasingly shaky.

"There have been no reports of his death, at least not that we've received," Nika replied cautiously, gesturing up the table to Yoram Ben Yitzhak, one of Leonard Rosenblatt's people from Collections, working the Syria desk. She had been one of the first to pick up on the trend—the lights being turned out, all across the map.

Yoram nodded his agreement, leaning forward. "We've been monitoring the chatter and social media traffic closely. If he'd been taken out, we would have seen *something*."

He supposed the analyst was right, but it was *his* neck that would be out there on the line if the intel was bad—if he linked up with *Fursan Tahrir al-Sham* only to find out Abu Ahmed was six feet under and some AQ stooge had taken his place.

"We have to sort out what he's going to want," Nika went on, sorting the briefing papers in front of her. "The Knights' operational strength is only about a hundred and seventy to a hundred and ninety fighters, according to our latest intel—and we're asking him to take more than a third of those fighters off the line and shift them nearly three hundred kilometers to the northwest. He's going to squeeze us, and you need to know your parameters going in. How far you can go."

Mohamed grimaced. She wasn't wrong. Making this request of Al-Golani was far from ideal, but they'd lost their last serious leverage in the north when a rebel commander on their payroll around Homs had gotten himself vaporized by a VBIED back in late July. Another AQ assassination.

There was the YPG, of course, but the Kurdish *peshmerga* were coming under increasingly heavy pressure from the Turks and likely wouldn't be in the mood to piss off the Russians too.

Shafron arrived in that moment, taking his seat at the

head of the table, everyone looking up from their notes at his entrance.

"David," Nika Mengashe began, a smile crossing her face, "your timing is impeccable."

8:09 P.M.
Mount Scopus
Jerusalem, Israel

Night had fallen over the Old City as Paul Keifer stood looking out from the observation plaza down the slopes of Mount Scopus toward the Temple Mount off to the southwest, the Dome of the Rock gleaming brightly in the lights. The small, muted-gray dome of the *Masjid al-Aqsa* just visible in the background, fading as ever into the shadow of its gaudier cousin.

It seemed hard to believe that more than a year had already passed since the attack on that holy site, an attack which had brought this region so very close to the brink of war.

An attack the CIA had been involved in stopping, though Keifer didn't know the details. He'd only arrived in-country the following January, and by that time, a tight veil of secrecy had been dropped over the whole affair—from both the American and Israeli ends. He didn't have need to know, even as chief of station—which spoke volumes of just how dire the situation must have been.

He could sense David Shafron's presence there in the half-darkness behind him—his security team having alerted him to the Israeli's arrival five minutes before.

"So," he began without turning, "we doing this?"

"We are," the Mossad intelligence officer replied, coming forward to rest his hand on the stone parapet bearing the engraved names of Nancy and Lawrence Glick, the Chicago philanthropists who had given their name to the observation deck. "But I need to know what more you're prepared to offer."

It was hard to see Shafron's face in the dim light, but there was no mistaking the hardness in those eyes. They'd both been field officers once, before the years and their respective climbs up the bureaucratic ladder had landed them behind desks. But Shafron. . .well, no one in the intelligence business cared for the word "assassin," but that was essentially what he'd been. A dangerous man, even now.

"I already explained our terms, David," he said carefully, turning to lean back against the parapet as he looked the Israeli in the face. "What we're willing to give you, in exchange for benefitting from the fruits of this operation— the intel on the talks in Astana, insight into the deals being cut there. We can't—"

The Israeli held up a hand. "Not to us. To pull this off, we're going to need to reach out to an opposition group in Syria itself—use them for the heavy hitting."

"You're going to send Syrian rebels after highly sensitive technological intelligence?" Keifer couldn't quite believe his ears. "And you really think it won't just get lost or sold off to the highest bidder? Come on, David, have you thought this through?"

"There's a plan," Shafron replied evenly. "Either trust me with it, or go get your president to sign off on your own op."

Well, *that* wasn't happening. Kranemeyer had made that much perfectly clear. The CIA station chief subsided reluctantly, his eyes never leaving Shafron's face.

"The opposition leader is going to need an incentive to put his men into the line of fire," the Israeli continued, "probably more than we can offer. That's where you come in—you have assets on the ground in Syria already, military and Agency both."

Keifer grimaced. This hadn't been a part of the deal. "We're talking about a moderate, right?"

Shafron just looked at him.

The CIA man swore loudly, shaking his head. "Look, David, this *matters*. The President may have already moved on, but you and I both know the threat didn't go away when Raqqa fell. And the administration has always been squeamish about who we find ourselves in bed with. We can't run the risk of strengthening groups who could later turn against us."

"I assure you, Paul," the Israeli officer replied quietly, "I'm more worried about than you are."

Fair enough. He nodded his understanding, recognizing that there was no moving his counterpart. Nothing to do but make the best of it. "I'll reach out to Langley, find out what latitude they'll give me. But, David, for the love of God, get this show on the road. We don't know how long the jets are going to be in-theater."

Chapter 3

"This is as far as I go," Nika Mengashe announced, putting the SEAT Tarraco into park, the headlights going out as she shut off the engine, plunging their surroundings into darkness. "Be careful out there."

Two hundred meters ahead lay the border crossing itself, the "A-Gate" as it was known. Controlled by IDF soldiers as it had been for the last several years, Israel moving into the vacuum left after the "Blue Helmets" of the UNDOF—United Nations Disengagement Observer Force—had abandoned their declared buffer zone in the face of mounting casualties.

Mohamed could see them down there now, shadowy figures moving back and forth behind the floodlights. The blacked-out guard tower rising over the gates.

Kids. Conscripts, just like he'd been once—young boys and girls barely out of school. Serving out their mandatory enlistments, marking time, little more.

The stern old patriotism you read about in the histories

of the state of Israel was largely a thing of the past, replaced by a sort of cultural malaise, never more obvious than among the young. The soldiers down there would fight, and they might even die—but their heart wasn't in it.

Still, they would have his back until he crossed that line, and he had to respect that.

"Of course," he replied then, looking over at his colleague in the darkened car. "Always am."

He could feel the pressure of the Glock against his hip, in its inside-the-waistband holster—its bulk strangely comforting. But the comfort was an illusion, as he knew well. It wouldn't be enough to save him, out across that border, if anything went wrong.

"We've had a good working relationship with Abu Ahmed," Nika went on after a moment, the strain audible in her voice, "and I know you've met with him any number of times over the last two years. But never allow yourself to forget that the relationship is a transactional one—from our side, *and* his. If he feels that it's in his interest to betray you. . ."

Then that's exactly what Al-Golani would do. She wasn't telling him anything he didn't know, but that she felt the need to *say* it. . .that was telling.

"If you believe the mission has been compromised, if you believe that you are in danger of being betrayed—you need to abort the mission."

He was in danger of being betrayed just crossing through those gates, but he simply nodded by way of acknowledgment, his hand on the door of the vehicle.

"The last thing anyone needs is for you to be taken over there, to be used as a bargaining chip by one faction or another. If you sense that the situation's getting out of your control—bail." Israel didn't need to find itself in the position of freeing another thousand terrorists in exchange for a single intelligence officer. *Message received.*

"Good luck."

Mohamed acknowledged her words with a brief nod, shoving open the door and stepping from the midsize SUV. Reaching back in for his backpack and slinging it over his shoulder.

Time to do this.

The gravel crunched beneath his hiking boots as he walked down the hill toward the gate, many of the buildings surrounding the gate still bearing the *UN* lettering of their previous owners—razor wire strung along the top of the gates and the border fence, stretching out into the darkness beyond the lights in either direction. His contact would be waiting for him on the highway out on the Syrian side of the line. And from there, well, he'd go meet Abu Ahmed. Come what may.

Blue-and-white signs in Hebrew, Arabic, and English loomed out of the darkness as he approached the gate, admonishing him to *"Have a safe journey."*

Yeah.

2:21 A.M.
Mossad Headquarters, Glilot Junction
Tel Aviv-Yafo, Israel

From thirty thousand feet above, the infrared cameras of the 210 Squadron IAI Eitan UAV picked out the lone figure crossing the desolate highway out beyond the B-Gate on the

Syrian side of the border.

Another hundred and fifty meters ahead, a car waited—an old Opel, from the look of it, its single occupant still behind the wheel, where he'd been since arriving thirty minutes earlier.

The drone had launched from Tel Nof hours before, arriving on-station just before sundown—giving them persistent surveillance over the site of the meet. There was no one with the driver, no one lying in ambush. They were as prepared as they could be.

But all the tech in the world couldn't give them the intent of the man behind the wheel.

David Shafron took another sip of coffee, his eyes fixed on the screens as he watched the spectral figure of Mohamed Taferi walk toward the car, moving steadily, never breaking stride.

The man had nerve, he had to give him that—he could remember what moments like these were like, out in the field, the strange mix of fear and euphoria, the feeling of being so very *alive* in every passing moment, poised there on the edge of death itself.

If he were to be honest with himself, he missed it.

He'd moved on with his life, moved up in the world, as most would have seen it—become a department head, a husband, and a father. But he'd never found anything that compared with those moments.

The figure moved to the passenger-side door of the Opel, pulled it open—and disappeared inside. The car, lurching into motion a moment later as it described a slow U-turn on the deserted highway before turning back northeast toward Quneitra.

No signs of a disturbance, no indication that anything had gone amiss. The cameras of the Eitan continuing to track the vehicle as the 210 Squadron operators down at Tel Nof manipulated their controls, taking the UAV out of its orbit and bringing it about toward Quneitra.

He could hear a sigh of relief go up around the room from the gathered personnel—looked over to see his own deputy, Abram Sorkin, standing there a few feet away, the dimmed lights of the operations room glistening off the man's shaven scalp.

"That went smoothly," Sorkin announced, giving him a tight smile. A few years younger than himself, and a career officer from the intelligence side of the house—not ops—Sorkin had been born in Belorussia back when it had still been a part of the USSR and had made *aliyah* with his parents when Gorbachev had thrown open the borders, allowing Jews to leave the country. "He should be with Abu Ahmed in time for breakfast. And then we'll have our answers."

Something like that, Shafron thought. Or he would be explaining to Mirit what he had done with one of her people.

"Go home, David," Sorkin said after a moment, "and get some sleep. We'll keep the 210 boys on him as long as we can, and I'll let you know if anything important comes in."

3:41 A.M. Syria Standard Time
Khmeimim Air Base
Latakia Governorate, Syria

The pair of young soldiers had been taken off-guard, their conversation falling silent at their commanding officer's sudden appearance in the guard tower out on the southern perimeter of the air base, but Andriy Makarenko hadn't been able to sleep—a strange restlessness seeming to possess his body, forcing him out of his quarters and into the night.

He was calmer now, taking a long drag of a cigarette he had bummed from one of the soldiers—his eyes searching the darkness out beyond the lights as he listened to the soldiers' conversation. He'd quit smoking a year ago, at Zinaida's insistence, but it still nagged at him.

It had taken the soldiers the better part of half an hour to loosen up in the lieutenant colonel's presence, but they were talking now. The younger one, Artyom, was twenty-one and had been born in Soligalich, on the banks of the Kostroma River—conscripted into the army straight out of school, but he'd stayed in after his twelve months were up. *A patriot, perhaps?* More likely he'd just needed the job.

He had a girlfriend back there in Soligalich, but he hadn't spoken to her in a week—thought she was cheating on him, his voice nearly cracking with the admission.

"Of course she is," his buddy replied with a sneer and an unsympathetic chuckle. "They all do."

Makarenko grimaced. That wasn't true, or at least he wouldn't allow himself to accept that it could be. Zinaida had always been true to him—they had a child together now, for God's sake. *And yet.*

He shook off the doubt, suppressing his anger at the sound of the soldier's laugh. There was a reason their American allies in the Great Patriotic War had used such propaganda to eat away at the morale of the Germans— suggesting their wives, their girlfriends, were betraying them even as they fought and died. It distracted a man, sapped his strength.

A low noise, building out of the night, broke in upon his thoughts, and he looked up—his hand on the parapet of the guard tower, his eyes straining as he searched the sky—the whine of jet engines becoming clearer until finally the distinctive shape of the Su-57 broke into view just ahead of them, on final approach to Khmeimim's runway, its landing gear already extended.

He watched as it roared past the tower, a haze-gray ghost against the darkness, settling down on the runway behind them. Another mission, brought to an end.

It was a magnificent sight, there was no denying that. But he would be glad when they were gone.

6:17 A.M. Israel Standard Time
A country residence
Beit Shemesh, Jerusalem District
Israel

He was in the garden when she found him, in the shadow of a shesek tree, staring out toward the hills of Judea toward the west. Their neighbor's vineyards, stretching out across those gentle, rolling slopes, just visible in the half-light of the early morning.

It was good wine, David Shafron thought—they had a bottle of it in the house, a delicately fruity syrah with notes of oak. A favorite of his wife's.

He didn't know how long he had been in the garden, but he knew he still hadn't slept—arriving home from headquarters around four to find the house asleep, his wife and children long gone to bed. He'd missed the second night of Chanukah, as he had the first, his oldest son's childish voice reciting the blessings before lighting another candle of the family menorah. *"Baruch Atah Adonai, Elohenu Melech Haolam. . ."*

Blessed are You, Lord our G-d, King of the Universe. . .

The words were still there, as he had recited them in his own childhood—his Haredi parents looking on, beaming with pride. *Had he believed them, even then?*

He'd joined his wife in bed, only to slip back out after lying there restlessly for an hour or more—finding himself at last in the garden, looking out on the hills as a new day broke.

After all the hours, he still had no answer for his unease—it was far from his first time sending men into the field, and Mohamed Taferi had spent much of the last year in Syria. This was just another mission, like all the rest.

But something felt different about this one.

He felt his wife's arms wrap around him from behind and he leaned silently back into her soft warmth, just standing there, the two of them, as the growing light cast their faces in shadow.

"What's wrong, David?" he heard her ask, her voice not much above a whisper. "I heard you come in. . .and then you left."

"Nothing," he responded quickly—more quickly than he intended, knowing even as he spoke that she wouldn't believe him.

Rahel Baruchi Shafron had been married to him for eleven years and had borne him two sons. He had his secrets—such was the nature of his work—but there was no lying to her.

"I'm afraid," he admitted after a moment, still not looking at her.

"Of what?"

"That I may have just sent a man to his death."

6:49 A.M. Syria Standard Time
Quneitra
Quneitra Governorate, Syria

It still didn't quite seem real, as if he found himself wandering, lost in a hellish dreamscape of rubble and fire. *Alone.*

Nassif picked absently at the small, chipped bowl of cold lentils which formed his only breakfast, unable to muster much appetite, yet possessed by the certain knowledge that if he didn't eat, he would weaken. If he weakened, for even a moment, he would die.

Like Talha and Yunus, the both of them gone in a single hour, leaving only mangled flesh behind.

The Syrian teenager lifted his eyes up above the crumbling wall of the shelled-out storefront to their east, watching as the sun's first rays came streaming through the broken windows and gaping holes in the walls. Pungent tendrils of smoke drifted upward from another squad's cooking fire, another ten meters out on their right flank, toward the road.

He had run out into the open, desperately searching for his brother's body—but all he'd found was the blast crater formed by the Russian 80mm rocket, the earth blackened and still smoking, littered with scraps of smoldering meat.

The moments which had followed were hazy, indistinct—a blur across his memory. He remembered only the hands on his shoulders, one of Abu Muin's men

45

screaming at him to get down—the strange, palpable silence that followed a wild, frenzied burst of gunfire, pulling the trigger of his empty rifle uselessly as it shook in his hands, still aimed toward the sky.

The long ride back along broken, shell-cratered roads toward Quneitra, huddled in the back of the technical, his knees clasped tight to his chest.

The lentils seemed to turn to sand in his mouth at the memory, and he set the bowl to one side, barely able to choke them down—listening to the idle talk and laughter of the men around the fire, weapons slung over their shoulders as they chatted, pushing away the last remnants of sleep, preparing for a new day.

They had lost seven men out there yesterday, their ambush of the Iranians turned back against them at a terrible cost. *Yunus. Talha. . .*

But this was *Sham*. Where life was nothing if not cheap.

A white Toyota Hilux rumbled in off the road just then, an older fighter he knew named Abdul Latif on the quad-barreled Russian anti-aircraft gun in the truck's bed. A battered Renault sedan, its red paint faded and chipped, pulling in just behind it.

He saw Abdul Latif jump down easily from the back of the technical, striding over to the fire and greeting one of the other fighters with a fierce hug before kissing him on both cheeks.

The passenger door of the Renault came open, creaking in protest. The movement and sound drawing Nassif's attention as a man extricated himself from within, tossing a heavy backpack over his shoulder as he straightened.

He was of average height for an Arab, his face cloaked by

a close-cropped black beard, the hair of his head rippling in the cold December breeze. But it was his bearing which struck Nassif—the way his dark eyes flickered around the courtyard, ever alert, searching for threats. Even for someone who had spent years at war, with death waiting at every hand. . .it was noticeable. Something curiously analytic in the man's gaze.

"*Salaam alaikum,*" the stranger began, glancing around him. *Blessings and peace be upon you.* "I understood that it was here I could find Abu Ahmed."

"He's in the church," Abdul Latif said, the big man's words muffled by the lentils he had just crammed into his mouth. He wiped his lips with the back of a grimy hand, gesturing out toward the bullet-scarred façade of the Greek Orthodox church another fifty meters to their north, on the other side of the low courtyard wall—which Abu Ahmed had commandeered as his headquarters a month before, after driving out the rival commander of a smaller faction. "I'll take you to him."

Chapter 4

"I lost seven men yesterday," Abu Ahmed al-Golani announced quietly, his face and eyes betraying his weariness. "Seven men, and here you show up this morning, asking me to take my men and send them north, all the way to Latakia, three hundred kilometers through hostile territory, with no guarantee that they'll ever return."

He leaned back into his plastic chair, going silent as he stared across the flimsy wooden table which served as his desk, regarding his guest with a peculiar expression somewhere between animosity and self-loathing.

"Do you know," he began, his low, soft voice sounding ominously loud in the small room, "what those men out there would do if they had any idea who you are? What you *represent*?"

Mohamed Taferi nodded slowly. He did, all too well. His legend identified him as the representative of a businessman from Qatar, and his passport would indicate that he had

48

slipped across the border from Iraq after entering the country at Umm Qasr. But Abu Ahmed knew better, and if anyone else caught wind. . .

The sacristy of the old Greek Orthodox church had been taken over by Al-Golani for use as his makeshift office/sleeping quarters, rubble still strewn across the floor—daylight just visible high over the militia commander's head where an artillery shell had left a hole in the outer wall of the church.

Escorted through the nave of the church back toward Abu Ahmed's private quarters by Abdul Latif, Mohamed had been struck by the scale of the devastation—half the roof of the church blown away, the icons of their saints torn down and defaced, bullet scars pocking the walls of the sanctuary, Arabic graffiti littering what pillars remained. The remnants of a campfire before the altar itself.

This war left nothing untouched, no matter how holy. It didn't matter how misguided he believed these people to have been in their faith—you didn't spend nine centuries as a religious minority without understanding what it felt like.

"Likely the same thing they would do to you if they knew where the money for their weapons was really coming from," he replied quietly, turning Abu Ahmed's implied threat back on him. *If they knew you'd sold out to the Jews.* "We're not asking for all your men. Fifty or sixty, at most. You command nearly two hundred, according to our intelligence reports."

Al-Golani snorted incredulously, shaking his head. "Once, perhaps. A hundred and thirty now, on a good day. Yesterday was not a good day."

The news was unfortunate, on a lot of levels, if completely unsurprising. That was the intelligence business for you, never as tidy as policy-makers wanted it to be—and he had expressed skepticism more than once through the months, concerning headquarters' strength estimates for the militias they had chosen to back. They'd seemed. . .inflated, beyond what he could see in the field. It was no satisfaction to be right.

"Even so, the kind of aid we're offering could tip the scales in your favor," he countered, his eyes never leaving Abu Ahmed's face. This wasn't a difficult calculus—power came from the barrel of a gun here, as so many places around the world, and the man who could put guns—more of them, and better guns—in the hands of his followers was going to be a leader with great *wasta*, that wonderful Arab concept that could perhaps be translated best into Western thought as "clout." "If the Americans were to support your efforts here in the Golan with training, perhaps even the occasional airstrike. . ."

"Be careful what you promise," Shafron had warned, *"the Americans are dragging their feet."*

That was typical. Leave it to Langley to get a ball rolling downhill and then get tangled up in meetings over which way it should roll after it was already in motion.

But in this case, it didn't matter—Abu Ahmed's face growing darker as he mentioned the Americans, shaking his head even as Mohamed finished.

"La," he spat, his voice growing lower as he leaned across the table toward the Mossad intelligence officer. *No.* "I can't be seen to be openly cooperating with them, any more than with *you.* Do you know how many leaders in my position have been killed these last few months? *Do you?"*

His voice trembled as he spoke the words, his eyes no longer weary—flashing now with anger and fear. You could almost smell it.

And Mohamed did know, all too well. He'd known

several of them personally. If more of those men had been alive. . .well, he might not be here, dealing with Al-Golani. He wouldn't have been anyone's first choice.

"I do. But if you don't want our offer, then I'll have to look elsewhere." He pushed back his chair and rose, reaching for his backpack. You always had to be prepared to walk away in this business—walk away and hope you had read your mark properly. *"Wa alaikum as-salaam,* Abu Ahmed."

"La!" The rebel commander exclaimed, starting to his own feet, and moving as if to block his exit from the room. Mohamed shifted the backpack to his left hand, easing his right closer to the holstered Glock beneath his field jacket. *Careful.* "I did not say that what you asked was impossible. We could work together. But what you're offering. . ."

"How much more?" he asked, his eyes narrowing. Shafron had given him considerable latitude when it came to the financing of this op, but every last *agorot* would have to be accounted for. Headquarters always made sure of that.

"It's not the money. What I need is—"

The door of the sacristy burst open in that moment, Al-Golani's hand half-way to his own pistol before he recognized Abdul Latif in the entry, a laptop gripped carelessly in one of the fighter's big hands. "Abu Ahmed!" he exclaimed, shoving the computer toward his commander. "The Iranians are launching an attack."

Mohamed caught a glimpse of streaming footage playing across the laptop screen, jerking and buffering over the poor Internet connection. *A surveillance drone?*

The Syrian opposition was using drones, they knew that much, for surveillance *and* attacks—small hobbyist models and cruder, homemade variants cobbled together from various kits and spare parts. Few quite as large as the drones a Belgian jihadist group had used in an attack on the *Stade de France* in August, but even so. . .

The laptop's screen shifted as Al-Golani took it, and he got a better look—making out a column of trucks moving forward, through the ruins of one of the deserted villages out to their northeast, toward Jabah, the resolution clear enough to make out the individual figures riding in their beds.

Clear enough to see a Hizballah fighter riding in the foremost truck suddenly raise his weapon—fire sparkling from the muzzle.

The drone seemed to stagger then, veering off-course—the video cutting in and out until the screen went dark completely, eliciting an angry curse from Al-Golani. "How long do we have?"

Abdul Latif shook his head. "They'll hit the outposts in five minutes. They're—"

The explosion outside drowned out whatever the big man had been about to say, seeming to shake the very walls of the church—dust and bits of plaster raining down upon the three men.

Mohamed heard shouts—men running—and then another explosion, even closer than the first. *Mortars.*

9:18 A.M. Israel Standard Time
Tel Aviv Station
The Embassy of the United States
Tel Aviv-Yafo, Israel

". . .something like this, we'd be more likely to run through our SF teams on the ground, since they'd ultimately be the ones tasked with liaison ops. Have you talked with JSOC yet?"

Paul Keifer shook his head, grimacing as he glanced into the camera lens, eyeing the image of Baghdad's deputy chief of station, Jerry Simoulis, on the screen at the other end of the small conference room. "No, no we haven't. We need to keep our involvement in this off the radar, Jerry. Blacker than black. Don't bring in DoD unless we have to, and even then. . .handle them like mushrooms."

Kept in the dark and fed horse crap.

"Right," Simoulis replied, his facial expression conveying his lack of enthusiasm. A former DIA intelligence officer who had been "loaned" to the Agency in the early days of the Iraq War and never ended up going back, Simoulis had come to Baghdad Station along with Denny Hamrick when the latter had taken over as COS from the outgoing Rebecca Petras. And with many of the Agency's operations in Syria being run out of Baghdad following the closure of Damascus Station along with the embassy early on in the Syrian Civil War, Simoulis had found himself with a full plate. "I can reach out to some of our people at al-Tanf, see what they can offer. This guy we're talking about—you say he's a moderate?"

"The Israelis are doing business with him." That was still the limit of his knowledge about the commander Shafron had referenced. He didn't have a name, even, though Langley had provided a short list of a dozen commanders they considered possibles, several of whom might no longer be living.

Simoulis cursed, shaking his head. "Come on, Paul, you know that doesn't mean jack squat."

Yeah. The Israeli approach to Syria was nothing if not pragmatic, an attempt to keep Damascus and its Iranian partners on the back foot by any means necessary. The American position was strangely more delicate—the distance giving them the freedom to pick and choose their partners, while imposing the burden of doing so "responsibly," whatever that meant in practical, on-the-ground realities.

"We're going to need more. I'll reach out to Gulotta, see what assets he can shake loose if it comes right down to it." Simoulis looked up at the camera, the light catching the dark circles around the deputy's eyes. "Just what has headquarters gotten us into, Paul?"

9:47 A.M. Syria Standard Time
Quneitra
Quneitra Governorate, Syria

Shots echoed down the long-abandoned streets of the ghost city as Nassif sprinted forward, the crossed bandoliers of linked ammunition weighing heavily on his thin shoulders. Just ahead of him, a gaunt, one-eyed fighter he knew only as Mamdouh bobbed and weaved among the rubble, carrying an old Soviet RPD light machine gun—another pair of fighters armed with rifles moving with them, more rounds cracking high above their heads.

The Iranians were close now, within the city limits— *Fursan Tahrir al-Sham*'s outposts either pushed back or overrun in the suddenness of the morning's attack.

They pushed forward across the street toward the ruins of a collapsed building to the northwest, ducking low as they ran, the sudden movement drawing fire—closer now.

The element they'd been ordered to link up with had to be close—somewhere just ahead in the maze of half-ruined buildings and undergrowth which had risen up to claim the city in the decades since its destruction. *If they were still alive.*

Out of breath and panting after crossing the open street, Nassif looked up to see men in camouflage fatigues moving among the ruins not a hundred meters to their west. A cry of alarm escaping his lips as rounds smashed into the concrete wall a meter above his head. He instinctively fell to one knee, seeking shelter in the rubble as the group of Hizballah militiamen opened up on them.

Mamdouh let out a savage scream of defiance, getting off a ragged burst with the RPD, firing the machine gun from the hip, rounds going everywhere—hot brass raining down on Nassif's neck as the belt jerked spasmodically.

He cursed in frustration and pain, bringing his own rifle up as Mamdouh dropped into the ruins of the collapsed building beside him—reaching forward to extend the machine gun's bipod before triggering another long burst.

More rounds slammed into the aged concrete all around them, chewing the half-standing wall to powder. Nassif shrugged one of the ammo belts off his shoulders, glancing over to see one of the riflemen still standing in the open, exposed, firing his rifle down the street.

"Allahu akbar!" the man cried out exuberantly, a wild light shining in his eyes as he emptied the Kalashnikov, ejecting the magazine and reaching for a spare in his chest rig. *"Allahu ak—"*

The round went straight in through his forehead, exploding out the back in a rain of brains and gore. More bullets stitching his chest as his legs went out from under him, dropping him into the dust of the street.

Nassif reached up, wiping the man's blood from his face with the back of his hand, his ears ringing with the throaty chatter of the RPD. Another life, another death—no meaning to any of it, only the chaos enfolding them all.

A hand struck him on the shoulder and he realized someone was screaming at him—looking over to see Mamdouh half-raised on one elbow, an empty belt dangling from the RPD's feed tray, its barrel all but smoking. "Another belt! *Yalla!*"

10:03 A.M. Israel Standard Time
Mossad Headquarters, Glilot Junction
Tel Aviv-Yafo, Israel

"All right, have we had any comms with Taferi at all?" David Shafron asked, glancing around at his team. He'd come back in to work half an hour before, still unable to sleep—to shake the feeling of restlessness which possessed him.

"Not since I dropped him off at the crossing," Nika Mengashe replied, shaking her head. It certainly wasn't the longest they'd ever gone without hearing from an officer in the field, but they had *expected* Taferi to make contact by now.

Abram Sorkin cleared his throat, reaching up a hand to scratch at his scalp. "210 Squadron tracked him into Quneitra but lost him in the city around 0345 hours. We believe he may have changed vehicles, perhaps more than once—before being taken to Abu Ahmed."

"We have, though, received intel reports via Northern Command from Captain Etzioni," Mengashe interjected, concern in her dark eyes, "commanding the troops at the crossing, reporting heavy small-arms fire and artillery in the last hour from the direction of Quneitra. We don't have sat coverage just yet, but it's very possible that the Iranians have launched another offensive."

Shafron grimaced. And there it was, the reality that made Syria such an operational challenge. You did your best to protect your people, to safeguard them as best you could against compromise and betrayal—but you were still dropping them into the middle of a *war*, where Death claimed people at random every single day.

Nothing to be done for it.

"Let me know the moment we have sat coverage," he replied, closing the folder before him and laying it to one side. "Now, about Vienna. . ."

10:13 A.M. Syria Standard Time
Quneitra
Quneitra Governorate, Syria

"Allahu akbar! Allahu akbar!" Mohamed Taferi heard one of the Knights chant, his mantra—and the sharper crackle of small-arms fire off in the distance—drowned out by the crash of the gun as another rebel fighter pulled the lanyard on the old American M40 recoilless rifle mounted in the back of a surplus Willys Jeep, sending another 106mm high-explosive round screaming down-range.

The M40 had been designed—almost seventy years before—as a direct-fire weapon, but Al-Golani's men were taking a more. . .unorthodox approach, elevating the gun's barrel to fire over the rooftops to the northeast.

Hard to say what they were hitting, if anything, without

a forward observer or any way to mark the fall of the shells. *Hopefully not their own men.* He'd been infantry in his own time with the IDF, but there were some things you couldn't just trust to blind luck—or Allah.

Mortar rounds were still falling all around, another explosion not thirty meters distant forcing Mohamed to duck back beneath the eaves of the battered church, but the Knights were holding their own, near as he could tell— blunting the Iranian militias' assault.

Behind him, in the narthex of the church, he heard Al-Golani's voice, tense and urgent, issuing orders over the radio. Trying to maintain some form of command and control, while rallying other rebel groups to his aid. With nearly sixty factions forming its ranks, the neatly-labeled "Southern Front" had never been anything more than a ragtag alliance, held together only—barely—by a common enemy.

He had a rifle now—a Chinese-built Type 56 Kalashnikov knock-off—which he had taken from a fighter injured in the initial mortar bombardment while helping drag the man to safety. His ammo carried in the pouches of a plate carrier he'd stripped off the body of another fallen fighter who had been drilled through the head by a Hizballah sniper. The armor, failing to save him in the end.

This wasn't Mohamed's fight, but if it came down to it, if Abu Ahmed's fighters broke and ran, well. . .he had no plans to die alone.

He heard the gravelly rumble of a tank engine from somewhere behind them as a teenaged fighter in a faded blue tracksuit ran forward to slam another shell into the smoking breech of the M40—turning to find a rebel T-55 crawling down the street behind them, its armor scored and smoke-blackened from previous battle damage, the barrel of its long 100mm rifled gun leading the way—a single fighter perched aright in the open hatch, his ears protected against the cold by a maroon stocking cap, a rifle in his hands as he seemed to shout down guidance to the driver.

Mohamed shook his head at the recklessness of it all, shifting the rifle to his off hand as he moved from the doorway, stalking out across the open courtyard toward the shattered building off to the north, the ruined entrance to its basement seeming to offer the best shelter just now. He wouldn't be able to continue negotiations with Al-Golani for hours, and if the Iranian militias had the opposition commander's headquarters pinpointed for their own artillery or even Russian airstrikes. . .best to be elsewhere.

He was half-way there when he heard another mortar shell come shrieking in behind him—instinctively throwing himself into the shelter offered by the wheel of a parked technical. The explosion dying away to the sound of screams, forcing him to look out once more.

The man sitting in the open hatch of the T-55 was still there, but he'd dropped his rifle, holding desperately onto the blood-slick remains of his intestines with both hands as gravity pulled them slithering away from his body, the shrapnel of the blast all but disemboweling him.

He fought the battle against pain and shock for a moment that seemed to last an eternity before pitching slowly forward, gore and viscera spilling out over the tank's forward glacis as he bled out.

Mohamed grimaced, passing a hand across his face as he picked up his rifle once again. This promised to be an exceedingly long day.

Chapter 5

Every muscle in Nassif's body ached, a dull, throbbing pain that concentrated into a single razor-sharp point lancing down the length of his arm every time he shifted position—a piece of shrapnel having laid his left bicep open half-way to the bone.

It was bandaged now, as best as they could manage here in the field, but they had nothing for the pain—and there were worse casualties, even if they had, like Mustafa, who had taken a pair of rounds to the abdomen, just beneath the plate of his body armor, and who now lay just five feet off to Nassif's left in the fast-falling darkness, moaning softly in pain.

But the fighting hadn't stopped, only ebbed and flowed throughout the day as the sun marched relentlessly across the sky above, their ammunition running low right along with their will to keep fighting.

The RPD had gone silent hours before, the last of

Nassif's belts of ammunition finally exhausted, Mamdouh carrying on fighting with Mustafa's rifle. Russian fighter jets screaming by overhead at one point early in the afternoon, the sound of their bombs, falling deeper in the city, beating a lethal tattoo against the earth.

In the end, they'd only held out because they were pinned down, unable to advance or fall back. Only the encroaching dusk saving them from being overrun.

They were still out there somewhere, Nassif thought, feeling a cold chill run through his body with the night breeze as he stared out from behind the half-collapsed second floor of the building in which they'd taken shelter, his eyes struggling and failing to pierce the darkness—his rifle propped up against the rubble where he could lift and point it with one hand. The firing, dying down to a desultory scattering of shots—just enough to keep a man on edge. *Jumpy.*

"We need to fall back," Mamdouh announced, a raw edge of fear creeping into the one-eyed man's voice—that single eye glittering in the gloom as he turned to look at Nassif. It was just the two of them, now, still able to fight. The rest of their little group, dead or incapacitated. They'd never linked up with the forward element they had been sent to join.

The teenager didn't respond for a long moment, listening to Mustafa's low moans. He was out of it, delirious—no way he had heard or understood. "What about him?"

There was no way he could carry much more than his rifle, and he questioned whether he would be able to fire it on the move. Helping carry a person. . .

"What about him?" Mamdouh challenged, his disfigured

face twisting into a hard scowl as he picked up his rifle, rising to one knee. "He's going to die. So you can stay here and die with him, or you can come with me."

7:03 P.M.
The church in Quneitra
Quneitra Governorate, Syria

The Iranians were falling back, or so Abu Ahmed's scouts claimed, reporting in by radio, the last of his drones grounded by the coming of the night. He'd lost two that day, best as Mohamed Taferi had been able to determine— both of them blown out of the sky by the Iranian-backed militiamen after straying too close to the fray.

Now Al-Golani sat once more in the small sacristy of the shelled church, the opposition commander stripped to the waist to reveal a sunken chest and the paunch of an encroaching middle age, a small, somehow almost fragile figure, his pale skin nearly glowing in the glare of the utility lights. His arm extended out over the small card table as a bearded young fighter nervously picked small scraps of shrapnel from the flesh of his right shoulder, trying to clean the wound with hands that. . .weren't.

Mohamed stood in the doorway, looking on—his purloined rifle still slung over his shoulder. No one had taken it from him, not yet—or the body armor—though it was possible that it just hadn't occurred to anyone. The nave of the church was filled with wounded, most of them neglected and crying out with pain—not enough men to go around.

And there were hard-eyed fighters from *Jaysh Khalid ibn*

Walid—formerly the Yarmouk Martyrs Brigade—present now, one of the rare southern rebel groups to have pledged *bayah* to the Islamic State at the height of its powers. They had rolled into town in the late afternoon, flying the black flag of jihad—spilling out of technicals and old Syrian Army trucks to noisily join the fighting just as it wound down to a close.

"Go, just go," Abu Ahmed ordered brusquely as the man finished, wrapping a sweat-stained rag around the shoulder to help stop the bleeding. "Leave us."

He looked over at Mohamed then, the first he had acknowledged the Israeli's presence since he had waved him in past his bodyguards earlier. "Close the door and have a seat."

The opposition commander produced a small, dark brown bottle and a pair of glasses from somewhere, awkwardly unscrewing the cap with his left hand. "Join me?"

"La, shukran," Mohamed replied, watching as translucent spirit spilled into the glass. *No thanks.* Like most observant Druze, he didn't drink. Arak was made of grapes and aniseed—the latter giving it its distinctive licorice taste—and coming in at nearly 190 proof for homebrewed arak, which this was, almost certainly, was typically cut with water. Taking it neat. . .Abu Ahmed wasn't going to be feeling any pain.

"Better not let Al-Refai's boys catch you with that," he joked as Al-Golani drained the glass, referencing the *Khalid ibn Walid* commander. Like most other Salafist groups, JKIW enforced strict *sharia* within their zone of control, punishing offenders harshly.

His host glared at him for a long moment before leaning over to spit onto the floor, unleashing a stream of obscene and extremely descriptive Arabic detailing exactly what Al-Refai was welcome to do with his prohibitions and his mother and. . .dogs.

Al-Golani reached up, wiping his mouth with the back of his hand before pouring himself another small glass.

"You'll have your men," he said quietly then, his hand trembling ever so slightly as he replaced the bottle.

Really? If that had seemed unlikely this morning, it seemed all the more so now, hours later, in the wake of the casualties the Knights had suffered—the likelihood that the Iranians would be back, if not tomorrow, *soon*.

But he wasn't here to run Al-Golani's war for him.

"And in return?" he asked, watching the opposition commander carefully.

"I want sanctuary," Abu Ahmed replied, tilting back the glass and draining it in a single swallow. "Somewhere far from here—away from all of this. California would be nice—you know John Wayne, right? I've always wanted to see where they filmed *Red River*."

"It's not in my power to make that deal," Mohamed replied slowly, his mind racing. Everything they had planned for, every possibility for which they had made contingencies. . .but Syria never lost its ability to surprise, and the look in the commander's eyes assured him that he was deadly serious. "But I will place some calls."

"See that you do." Al-Golani took a deep, shuddering breath, setting the glass to one side. "Or else the *takfiris* will kill me, like they have so many others. Sooner or later, if not this week, the next—or the next after that—I will be dead."

It was hard to argue that point, after the bloody swath the Salafists had cut through the upper echelons of the

Southern Front since summer. And now, with the arrival of *Jaysh Khalid ibn Walid*, Al-Golani had them in his own camp. Still. . .

"What about your men?"

A shrug, that twisted into a grimace of pain as the movement aggravated his shoulder wound. The Syrian reached over for the bottle of arak. "What about them? You see them out there, lying dead and wounded. I'm not leading them to victory. There will be no triumph in Damascus, for any of us."

The translucent spirit splashed once more into the glass. "After I am gone, they will find someone else. *Insh'allah.*"

7:34 P.M. Israel Standard Time
The Shafron residence
Beit Shemesh
Jerusalem District, Israel

". . .*Adonai Elohenu, Melech Haolam sheasa nisim laavotenu bayamim hahem bizman hazeh.*"

Lord our G-d, David Shafron thought, a quiet smile crossing his face as he handed over his Bic lighter to his oldest son, *King of the Universe, who performed miracles for our forefathers in those days, at this season.*

They were lighting the menorah late, as they tended to do—his wife's job at the Ministry of Justice lent itself to long hours, if more predictable than his own, and he had stopped to pick up jellied doughnuts for Chanukah on the way home. It took seven-year-old Aaron several attempts before flame spurted from the end of the lighter and he then reached up to the menorah in the window, touching it to the end of the *shammash* candle before using that candle to light the rest, from left to right, beginning with the new one.

Each wick, bursting into fiery life—lights, reflected in the glass of the window, wavering in his son's shallow breath, shining bravely out against the darkness. *Holding it back.*

Perhaps that's all anyone could do—keep it at bay, out there beyond the reach of the light. The darkness was never *gone*, never defeated. . .not once and for all, but for well over two thousand years, it had failed to overwhelm the light.

He retrieved his lighter from Aaron, briefly tousling his son's tawny hair before turning to find his own mother standing behind him, stooped down, speaking softly to his younger son, Shmuel.

"*Barukh haba*, mother," he said, forcing a smile. *Blessed be the one who comes.*

"*Barukh nimza,*" she replied, straightening and reaching up to brush a loose strand of silver hair back beneath her muted blue headscarf. *Blessed be the one already present.*

In her late sixties, Miriam Shafron remained a striking woman, a strangely regal beauty written in the lines of her careworn face and accentuated somehow by the austerity of her dress. He only rarely remembered her without the headscarf, even as a child, within the privacy of their home—as if, somehow, she were vying with the priests' mother from the Talmud, the walls of whose home had never seen the braids of her hair. *Well, he was no priest. . .*

It had taken him two years after the death of his father to reach out to her, and months more had passed before she'd darkened the doors of his home, meeting her grandchildren for the first time in their lives. The breach he had left in his family when he'd turned his back on his Haredi upbringing to become a soldier, still not completely healed, even after all these years.

But at least she was admitting he was alive. That was progress.

"It's good to have you join us, mother," he began, the words coming awkwardly as Rahel disappeared into the kitchen to tend to what remained of the meal prep. "I am glad that you were—"

His cell phone began to buzz just then, and he caught his mother's sharp look of disapproval as he broke off to check the screen. *Headquarters.*

"Forgive me, I have to take this." Shafron left the living room and went into his home office, closing the door behind him. "Yes?"

He listened for a couple minutes before replying, "All right, reach out to Tel Aviv Station and set up a meet with Keifer. Yes, Abram, tonight, if possible, usual spot—I don't want to leave our man exposed over there any longer than we have to. Have Litman and Ben-David meet me in the city."

Signing off curtly, he slipped the phone back into his pocket, stooping down by his safe and punching in the combination to retrieve his holstered Jericho 941. Well, he had been with his family for the lighting of the menorah at least.

But the darkness was still out there.

8:27 P.M. Syria Standard Time
Khmeimim Air Base
Latakia Governorate, Syria

"She rolled over on her stomach today," Andriy Makarenko heard his fiancée Zinaida announce, her voice only slightly distorted over the poor Internet connection, the video buffering in that moment, freezing the image as she leaned over little Nataly, dandling the little girl on her bare knee.

"Chudesno," he replied, a smile creasing his face as he leaned back into the folding chair that sat beside the small table which served as a desk in his cramped quarters, feeling the chill of the metal seep through his thin undershirt. *Marvelous.* "Did you get video?"

A shake of the head, coming through clearly this time, as Zinaida reached up to adjust the camera, brushing hair back from her eyes. She looked tired, he realized—as though the long nights up with Nataly were taking their toll. "The little rascal waited until I was out of the room."

He had never thought that she would be bearing that burden alone, that he would be missing. . .all of this. But then the GRU had intervened—its massive bureaucracy, unknowing and uncaring. He was used to it by now, and one day—one day this career would ensure a much brighter future for them all.

"Say hello to your daddy," he heard Zinaida say, reaching down to pull one of Nataly's hands up and waving it at the camera. But the little girl seemed interested in looking everywhere and anywhere else, her eyes wandering distractedly around the room as she fussed on her mother's lap.

"Natalyushka," he began softly, leaning closer to the tablet, knowing that she had begun to recognize her name. "Can you look—"

He broke off in mid-sentence, a clearly audible explosive *thump* somewhere in the distance arresting his attention. *Mortars?*

"Andriy," he heard his fiancée ask, the note of worry clearly audible in her voice. "What is it? Is everything okay?"

"Nichevo," he replied. *It's nothing.* It was strange how quickly you got used to being under fire, how something that would have sent you racing for cover in your first few weeks in Syria, now was just another night. Mortar attacks were far too common to get excited about.

Unless it got significantly worse than this. . .

As if in answer to the unspoken thought, another series of muffled *thumps* reverberated through the barracks, closer this time—the light flickering above his head. Followed a moment later by an urgent pounding on his door.

"I'm sorry, *kroshka*," he said before Zinaida could say anything else. "I have to go."

Across the runway from the barracks, angry flames flickered from within a half-finished revetment as Makarenko emerged from the building, his body armor hastily thrown on over his undershirt, the pistol belt holding his issue MP-443 Grach buckled hastily around his waist, his ears ringing with the concussion of yet another nearby explosion.

Sirens were going off now, adding to the cacophony—searchlights from the guard towers stabbing out through the darkness surrounding the base, shadows flitting across the airfield as soldiers and firefighting crews raced to their battle stations.

He stumbled toward the cover of the nearest bomb shelter, hearing the whine of another falling shell—his brain struggling to filter and process the sensations bombarding his mind. This—this went well beyond the normal sporadic attacks on the base, beyond anything he could remember in the last year. *This was bad.*

Makarenko made it into cover, shaking his head as if to clear it. He raised his radio to his lips, keying the mike. He needed a sitrep on Major Kulik's QRF, needed to sort out where the fire was coming from—how to fight back—but he could barely make out the sound of his own voice, another explosion reverberating across the airfield in that moment.

And when he looked out, it was to see a parked strike aircraft burst into flames. . .

11:04 P.M. Israel Standard Time
The observation plaza
Mount Scopus, Israel

"He wants *what*?" The look on Paul Keifer's face was pure incredulity, the American turning away to pace across the observation plaza toward the stone parapet, looking out over the city. "This wasn't part of the deal, David—wasn't part of the deal at all."

Yeah, well Al-Golani hadn't gone for *their* deal. That was the beauty and the stress of dealing with assets—they could surprise you, as he knew Keifer was well aware.

If you looked closely, you could make out the lit menorahs sparkling in the windows of houses below, all across the city—the miracle of the light made visible to the world, here at the heart of the Jewish faith. A thousand such *Chanukahs*, down through the long centuries of exile. *Next year, in Jerusalem.* And here they were, at long last.

"It's his price, Paul. What he wants—the *only* thing he wants—in exchange."

"Can you do it?" the CIA chief of station asked, turning to face him. "Get him out?"

A nod. It could prove tricky, but they were going to need to devote assets to exfiltrating Taferi after the op—no real reason he couldn't bring along a friend.

Keifer grimaced as if he'd hoped the answer would be something else entirely. "God, that's going to be such a mess. We'd need to bring in State, the FBI—DHS, probably. Any chance he would take Canada?"

Shafron chuckled at that, shaking his head. "You'd rather bring a *third* government into this menagerie than involve your own bureaucracy?"

A rueful smile. "You don't know the half of it. But you're probably right. Look, David, I'll see what I can do. No promises."

No promises, the Mossad officer thought, hearing Keifer's footsteps fade as he walked away, disappearing into the darkness at the edge of the observation plaza. *Well, that went double.*

It might be past time to discuss contingency plans with the *memuneh*. In case the Americans got cold feet. . .

Chapter 6

In the morning light, the mortar shells no longer falling, the fires long out, it was easier to take in the scope of the damage. Six aircraft either disabled or completely destroyed, including three Su-24 bombers and an An-72 transport which had only flown in from Taganrog the night before, hours before its destruction.

At least the Air Force's prized new stealth fighters had somehow escaped the shelling, Andriy Makarenko thought, his head still ringing painfully as he walked among the wreckage of the damaged aircraft, supervising the ongoing clean-up. But that had itself been a near thing, an ammunition depot going up in a sympathetic detonation not two hundred meters from one of the parked Su-57s. Two personnel dead, in addition to more than a dozen injured in the bombardment.

It had taken their QRF a full twenty minutes to mobilize and roll out through the darkness toward the low hills rising to the east of Khmeimim, infantry supported by BTR-82s and a pair of T-90 main battle tanks. An Mi-24 attack helicopter which had managed to take off through the barrage flying top cover.

The firing had stopped soon after, but they could only claim three kills for the effort—a rebel mortar crew caught packing up and sent to meet Allah by the Mi-24's rockets.

Everyone else had simply vanished ahead of the sweep, melting back into the countryside. *The way they always did.*

He'd tried to liaise with the local pro-government militias, early in his posting to Khmeimim, but had given it up after months of failed effort, finding their commanders little more than petty warlords and smugglers, interested only in turning a profit—and who saw Russia as a fresh mark ripe for exploitation. When they'd been forcibly disbanded, he'd breathed a sigh of relief, but coordinating with the local Syrian Army commanders was only marginally less infuriating, and they remained as blind as ever.

Makarenko shook his head, uttering a curse of frustration as he rubbed his temples, fighting against the pain. Moscow was going to make someone answer for this. . .

8:23 A.M.
Quneitra
Quneitra Governorate, Syria

Nassif gritted his teeth, struggling not to cry out as Mamdouh peeled the dirty bandages back from the wound—pain shooting through his arm and up his shoulder as the soiled cloth came away from his torn flesh. "Hold still there."

He bit back an angry retort, his eyes closed, squeezed shut so tightly that tears began to flow from between their lids—the pain finally forcing a gasped curse from his lips.

It had taken them hours to pick their way back through the dead city, dodging patrols and isolated units, both theirs—they thought—and the enemy's. In the dark, it was all the same and a "friendly" bullet would kill you quick as a hostile one, everyone on edge—jumpy.

"Do you want a hand with that?" he heard a strange voice ask and he felt Mamdouh's rough, callused fingers pause in their work. The boy blinked back the tears, looking up and over his right shoulder into the face of the stranger he had seen arrive the previous morning. Standing there over him—a rifle slung over his shoulder, his face dirty with grime and sweat, a plate carrier visible beneath his open jacket. His Arabic was clear and fluent, but Nassif couldn't place the accent. . .the man wasn't from anywhere he had ever been, of that alone he was certain.

He heard Mamdouh's fiercely protective *"La,"* but shook his own head, biting back the pain. "No. . .let him."

2:49 P.M. Israel Standard Time
Mossad Headquarters, Glilot Junction
Tel Aviv-Yafo, Israel

"So, what are the hard facts, near as we can determine them?" David Shafron demanded, closing the conference room door behind him, and taking his seat at the head of the table.

The looks he saw traded told him as clear as words that hard facts weren't something they had in abundance, just yet. Ever the limitations of intelligence work. You always needed more than you had, sooner than you had it.

Sorkin was the first to speak, clearing his throat. "Significant damage was visible in the imagery from Khmeimim during the first TecSAR overpass this morning, some cratering around the runway, a building previously identified as an ammunition depot now in rubble, the wreckage of at least two planes still being cleared away—Rosenblatt's IMINT analysts are saying the damage is commensurate with a mortar attack."

The timing couldn't have been worse, Shafron grimaced. With the Americans dragging their feet, the last thing they needed was for the Russians to get spooked. "The Su-57 'Felons,'" he began, glancing from face to face, "were they damaged in the attack?"

"We were able to identify at least one of the two still on the runway, apparently undamaged. The other one remains unaccounted for—possibly tucked away in one of the hangars on-base."

Or among the wreckage, he thought. And if it wasn't, it might have been—a fact which was sure not to escape Moscow.

"Earlier this morning," Nika Mengashe spoke up, "the website for the Russian daily *Kommersant* acknowledged the attack, claiming that five planes were destroyed and ten personnel injured in the incident—no fatalities. That report has already been denied by the Russian MoD, which acknowledged both the attack and the casualties, while denying that any aircraft were destroyed."

"They *look* destroyed," Sorkin observed ironically, shaking his head as he used a fob remote to bring up the imagery on the screen at the end of the conference room. That was the Russians for you, as they all knew well—the kid with his hand in the cookie jar, chocolate smeared around his mouth, denying that he had ever so much as *heard* of cookies.

Shafron chuckled to himself, thinking of his own sons. Shmuel would do something like that.

"Make sure the Americans are seeing this," he said heavily, the humor fading as quick as it came. "Let them know it's time to stop dragging their feet. Now, where are we with our plans to extract Abu Ahmed, if it comes to that?"

"Khmeimim is less than three kilometers in from the Mediterranean," Nika replied, consulting her notes. "Metsada has access to a Palestinian fishing trawler the Navy confiscated off the coast of Gaza last year, and we've reached out to Mirit's people. . ."

3:16 P.M.
Jaffa Port
Jaffa, Tel Aviv-Yafo, Israel

The beauty of the *Tachash* lay in its ugliness, Avigdor Barad thought, wiping grease from his rough, callused hands with a dirty rag as he straightened, uncurling himself from within the cramped engine compartment of the fishing trawler. No one gave an ugly ship a second glance—particularly one as ugly and seemingly broken down as the *Tachash*.

No doubt it had once been some Palestinian fisherman's pride and joy, but maintenance often proved lacking in Gaza and it had suffered further after its confiscation by the Israeli Navy, lying abandoned for nearly nine months before the

Office had come knocking.

When he'd first gotten his hands on her, her engine had completely seized up, refusing to start, and it had taken several months to make her seaworthy again. They hadn't done a thing about the aesthetics, though. . .that suited their purposes just fine.

A former Navy man himself, Avigdor had served out his conscription on the then-newly-commissioned *Sa'ar 4.5*-class missile boat INS *Tarshish* in the late '90s and gone on to spend another twelve years in the service. He'd been at the tail-end of a failed marriage by that point and had gotten out of the Navy with the intention of salvaging what remained of the wreck.

But Mossad had come calling instead, and so here he was five years on, in his mid-forties the unofficial captain of the *Tachash*—and he still loved no woman quite as much as the sea.

He laid the rag aside and levered himself up onto the deck—running a grimy hand through his thinning, salt-and-pepper hair as he glanced out across the harbor. The *Tachash* fit in here, in the port of Old Jaffa among the fishing fleet, both weather-beaten commercial boats and smaller, snappier sports vessels—masts dotting the skyline over on the far side of the port, where yachts rode at anchor and small boats made their way in and out under sail.

Men had set sail from Jaffa for near as long as men had gone to sea, and you could still feel the history in this place— see it in the face of the old man sitting cross-legged on the deck of a nearby seiner, mending his nets like men had done along these shores for thousands of years.

His boat might well have belonged here, Avigdor realized

with a grimace, but he didn't. He had spent so much of his life at sea, but it wasn't enough, not to truly experience it in the way these men did, to be at one with it. He was an imposter, playing a part. Like the rest of his crew.

And if the call he'd received earlier was any indication. . . they were due back out on center stage.

5:03 P.M. Moscow Standard Time
GU Headquarters, Khodynka Aerodrome
Moscow
Moscow Oblast, Russia

". . .but if you are unable to provide security for the planes while they're in-theater, I'm afraid to say that we will—"

"You deployed them into a *war*, Maxim," Colonel General Yegor Khudobin, the Director of the Main Directorate of the General Staff—GU—growled in exasperation, his impatience finally bleeding through the civil veneer as the videoconference wore on. "That choice came with risks, risks you accepted."

"In the full confidence that your people at Khmeimim were *competent!*" the Russian Air Force general fired back, his face on-screen purpling with barely suppressed anger beneath the thick shock of snow-white hair. It was impotent wrath. Khudobin outranked the man, and—what counted for more—was closer to the President.

At seventy-six, Lieutenant General Maxim Knyzhov wasn't quite old enough to remember the Great Patriotic War, but he remained a relic of a previous age—his appointment as Commander-in-Chief of the Russian Air Force more a tactical move to sideline more politically ambitious candidates than a reflection of either his influence or his competence.

"They are," Khudobin replied, adding contemptuously, "unlike some I could name."

In truth, it was far too soon to say. It was possible that the GU's man on the ground in Latakia, Lieutenant Colonel. . .he checked his notes—*Makarenko*, had made mistakes in providing for the security of the airbase, and he would certainly see that there was a full investigation into the man's conduct. But that didn't mean he was going to sit here and listen while this old buffoon disparaged his directorate.

"Gentlemen, please," Ruslan Sadyrin exclaimed, exasperation in the Defence Minister's voice as he leaned forward into the camera, "my time is far too valuable to be wasted listening to you bicker. General Knyzhov, how much longer do you require for your in-theater testing of the Su-57?"

The older man seemed flustered by the sudden question, uncertainty spreading across his face as he looked away, his microphone picking up a frantic shuffling of papers.

"The first round of testing was scheduled to be over by this Friday," Knyzhov replied finally, seeming to collect himself. "With work on the part of the pilots, I believe we could wrap up in the next two days. But before the planes can return to Syria, I will need assurances from—"

"The matter is being handled," Khudobin announced, cutting him off. "An hour ago, a military transport lifted off from Tolyatti, en route to Latakia, carrying personnel from the 501st Special Purpose Detachment. Minister, I give you my word. Khmeimim *will* be secured."

8:47 P.M. Syria Standard Time
Quneitra
Quneitra Governorate, Syria

". . .the Americans have finally come around, and agreed to the deal with Al-Golani." There was a sense of weary relief in Shafron's voice, Mohamed Taferi thought, but they both knew this was only the beginning of this road. Not the end.

He glanced back toward the flickering fires in and among the clusters of ruined buildings around which Abu Ahmed's men were gathered, warming their hands against the cold, and turned away once more, the Thuraya satellite phone pressed to his ear. *Far from the end.*

And just how many of those men would still be alive when they reached it? Mohamed mused, thinking of the teenager whose wound he'd helped treat earlier in the morning. A brittle, hollow shell of a boy, too young for all this—old beyond his years, having suffered more loss than most men would in a lifetime.

A cat's paw—*lion's* paw, he reminded himself with a bitter smile—was nothing if not expendable.

But Shafron wasn't done. "Relay all this to Abu Ahmed, and impress upon him the urgency with which this operation needs to be executed. If we don't get what we need, when we need it. . .there's no California waiting for him."

"Understood."

"And get transportation back across the border, as soon as it can be arranged. I'll meet you in Galilee to relay your final mission instructions."

11:56 P.M.
Khmeimim Air Base
Latakia Governorate, Syria

The roar of the Antonov An-26's twin turboprops filled the night as the Russian Air Force transport taxied to a stop, silhouetted against the runway lights.

They'd be going dark in another couple minutes, denying the enemy any excess illumination of their targets. Andriy Makarenko shot a glance off to the hills to the east, finding himself ill at ease out here in the open. *Exposed.* There'd been no further mortar attacks, but a sniper had fired a handful of shots at the airfield just before dusk—hitting nothing.

The cargo ramp of the Antonov went down just then, its aging hydraulics groaning in protest. A short, stocky man in full battle rattle appearing in the opening—backlit by the aircraft's interior lights. An AK-104 carbine carried loosely in his left hand as he walked down the ramp.

He spotted Makarenko then and walked over, offering his hand even as more soldiers began to disembark from the bowels of the Antonov behind him. He didn't salute—it wasn't advisable in a warzone—but the smile on his face was anything but friendly. *Insolent*, almost.

"Captain Valeriy Egorov, 501st Special Purpose Detachment, 3rd Guards Spetsnaz Brigade, reporting for duty. Colonel Makarenko, I presume?"

Makarenko nodded, taken off-guard by the Spetsnaz officer's self-assurance—the runway lights going out in that moment, plunging them back into the pitch darkness of the night, the moon obscured by low-hanging clouds.

"Welcome to Khmeimim."

Chapter 7

The kibbutz was waking, David Shafron realized, glancing across the road toward the main gate of Ein Zivan—picking up signs of life behind the security fence which enclosed the entire perimeter of the settlement.

Ein Zivan was among the oldest of the Golan settlements—all of them judged "illegal" in the eyes of the outside world, places where Jewish families had lived, worked, and raised their children for nearly fifty years. He'd been here in the spring and walked through the orchards— some of the largest in Israel—bought chocolates and a bottle of wine for Rahel. And wondered all the time how many more years could pass before they might well find themselves coming for these settlements as they had those in Gaza. Bulldozing it all to the ground in the name of peace.

They make it a desert. . .

But these were their own people, their blood and their flesh—as much as the settlers could themselves prove a thorn

82

in the side of the security services.

"Our security estimates at Khmeimim are still holding firm?" he heard Mohamed Taferi ask, the words breaking in on his reverie.

He nodded. The two men were standing in a grove of trees as the morning sun filtered down upon them through the branches—his security team taking up positions farther back toward the road. Behind them, deeper into the grove among the rocks, the rusting hulk of an M4 Sherman tank sat in mute silence—a stone marker identifying it as a memorial to the fallen of *Gdud Siyor 134,* an IDF recon battalion which had, back in '73, been savaged in the defense of these heights, losing thirty-five men killed in action. *The sacrifices we have made. . .*

"They have accommodations for a thousand personnel on-base—we believe their actual strength to be more like seven hundred, of which only an estimated hundred and fifty are combat troops, infantry and armor support. Base security is under the command of a GRU lieutenant colonel, given their SIGINT station at the airport. That's your secondary objective, believed to be located in this building along the runway. Grab what you can, *if* you can, but do not jeopardize the primary mission to do so. Their defenses are likely to be on elevated alert after yesterday's mortar attacks from rebels in the region, and they *will* respond to the incursion, if you give them enough time. Don't stick around."

Taferi nodded, running a hand across his bearded chin. "Of course. And afterward?"

There was no sugar-coating any of this, Shafron thought, regarding the younger officer closely, no concealing just how long these odds were. This stood a very good chance of being their last meeting. *Ever.*

"You take Abu Ahmed and run. Escape and evade. It's not much more than two and a half kilometers to the Mediterranean—*Metsada* will have a boat there, waiting. Your comms kit is set up with the frequencies."

"What about the rest?" The Druze officer's eyes seemed strangely shadowed, a note of uncertainty entering his voice. "The fighters we take with us to Latakia."

"That's Al-Golani's responsibility—something he'll have to arrange with his subordinates."

"And if he doesn't?" Taferi shook his head. "I've talked with him—he's paranoid, defeated, on the brink of giving up. He's not thinking beyond his own survival, at this point."

And that's why they could *use* him. He refused to patronize the younger man by stating the obvious—Taferi had been at this long enough to know how it worked, hard as it was to ever get used to.

"That's still not on you," Shafron replied, looking him in the eye. "You'll have enough to do, getting out yourself."

He paused, choosing his words carefully—loathing himself in this moment. *The burden of command.* He'd spent an hour in the *memuneh*'s office the previous night, arguing over it with Shoham. Without changing the result.

"If you should be taken prisoner en route to Latakia, we will of course do everything in our power to obtain your return."

A nod. They both knew just how unlikely that would be to do any good. But the hard part was yet to come.

"But if anything happens in the assault itself, or

immediately thereafter," he continued, "through your contact with Russian security forces—then we will be left with no choice but to wash our hands of the whole affair. There'll be no help coming."

8:03 A.M. Syria Standard Time
Khmeimim Air Base
Latakia Governorate, Syria

"So you found mortars here, here—and here," Captain Egorov asked, glancing critically across the map, the locations marked in grease pencil. "What type of mortars did your men recover?"

Makarenko gestured for Major Kulik to take the question, the army officer taking a step closer to the table. "We only recovered one mortar in our sweep, right. . .here, two and a half kilometers out. It was an 82mm, a PM-37."

One of ours, the GU lieutenant colonel thought ironically, as with a lot of military equipment in this part of the world—the Soviet Union selling off its surplus stocks to the Arab world all through the Cold War.

It would probably continue to be true another fifty years on, in the wake of this conflict and the weapons Moscow was selling to its allies in Damascus—and the Iranian-backed militias supporting them.

"Some of the blast craters, though," Kulik continued, "we estimate to have been from a 120mm piece, and indeed, we recovered bombs for such a mortar in a cache—here." He extended a hand for an aide to pass him a grease pencil and quickly circled the spot, in between two of the other marks, the stocky Spetsnaz officer nodding his head as he scanned the map, clearly picking out the nearby villages—noting landmarks.

"We'll go out there tonight, then," he announced abruptly, looking up.

Makarenko nodded. "Major Kulik will be happy to provide you with whatever support and extra personnel you may require. I—"

"Just my men, Colonel," Egorov replied with a tight smile, taking Makarenko by surprise. He had only brought twenty troopers with him—a much smaller unit than Makarenko had expected when the Aquarium had informed him they were dispatching reinforcements. "Though you're welcome to come along. . ."

10:07 A.M. Syria Standard Time
Quneitra
Quneitra Governorate, Syria

"Come on," Mamdouh bellowed impatiently, light flashing from his lone remaining eye as Nassif struggled clumsily to untangle the belts of ammunition for the RPD with his good hand. Automatic weapons fire crackled around them as men ran up the shell-torn berm at the far side of the road, emptying their rifles toward the Iranian positions off in the distance. "There's no time for this—*yalla, yalla!*"

A sniper round cracked into the single still-standing wall of the house behind them, high above their heads, but both men ducked anyway—Nassif nearly dropping the belts.

His left arm was still in a makeshift sling, and hurt whenever he moved it incautiously, even though the stranger had given him a small handful of pain pills after bandaging the wound the previous morning. He was rationing them out, trying to make them last, even if it meant gritting his teeth against blinding pain—the stranger had disappeared once again overnight, and if anyone knew where he had gone, or who he was, they weren't saying.

Mohammed. He had identified himself only by the name of the Prophet, *alayhi as-salaam*—Allah only knew if the name were really his, or only a *kunya*, as so many fighters used. If the man were a fighter, which. . .he didn't seem to be. But he had known what he was doing in bandaging his arm.

Mamdouh's curses rang in his ears as he untangled the linked rounds, straightening the belt as the older fighter brought the RPD to his shoulder. The war waited for no one.

"Hold it there, hold it right there, don't let it tangle again," he admonished, taking a few running steps before charging up the berm—Nassif stooped at his side. *"Allahu akbar! Allahu akbar!"*

The RPD bucked and jerked in Mamdouh's weathered hands as he held down the trigger, holding it up above his head, spraying rounds down-range—brass flying everywhere as flame spouted from the machine gun's barrel.

"Allahu akbar!" Nassif screamed, finding himself swept up in it by a savage fury, hearing guns open up on either side of them as rebels ran up the berm and fired off into the distance. *"Allahu—"*

The RPD went silent, a bullet slamming into the berm in front of him in that moment, burying itself in the earth and spraying clods of dirt into his face. Mamdouh stumbled off the mound, choking and sputtering curses—nearly dropping the gun.

They both collapsed against the sheltered side of the

berm, Nassif blinking and rubbing at his eyes to clear them of dust—Mamdouh cursing and struggling with the RPD's charging handle to clear a jam.

He leaned back into the dirt, hearing bullets whistle through the air above their heads—glancing over to see one of the dark-bearded *Jaysh Khalid ibn Walid* fighters kneeling a few feet away, the black flag of jihad draped across the man's back as he reloaded his rifle.

The jihadist seemed to feel his stare and looked up, his face twisting into a scowl, rocking the mag into the empty well of his AK with a forceful motion.

Nassif held his gaze for only a moment before looking away, turning his attention back to Mamdouh's efforts to clear the gun. Even in the nightmare that was war-ravaged Syria, the black-flagged fighters exuded a special darkness, humorless and fiercely intolerant of the slightest deviation from what they deemed the true path.

Two years before, southeast toward Dara'a, he'd seen one of Talha's friends beaten nearly senseless by a pair of foreign *takfiris* for smoking a cigarette—six months later, he'd been standing nearby when one shot a younger man dead for the boots he was wearing.

He'd seen them fight, and when they fought, they could fight like devils—but he mostly remembered them as bullies, preying on the already weak, the vulnerable. Dark jackals, prowling the battlefield, picking their way through the bodies of the dying and the already dead. And flying above it all, that death-black flag. *La ilaha illa Allah. . .*

It was a creed he had learned from his mother as a child, one he still believed, even to this day. *There is no God but God. . .*

The ending she had taught him, though, had been different—and it seemed hard to think of these men as having anything to do with Allah.

He heard a voice barking out orders then, along with the growl of a vehicle engine, glancing over to see Abu Muin—one of Abu Ahmed's lieutenants—waving a heavy flatbed truck into position just down the street, perhaps a hundred meters off.

There was an anti-aircraft gun mounted in the open bed, a twin-barreled Russian autocannon—a bearded rebel in a green tracksuit in the gunner's seat, his legs straddling the gun, yelling instructions at the driver as the truck lurched forward once again before stopping. The barrels of the gun swaying with the movement as he brought them back onto their target—triggering a long, extended burst.

Even from a hundred meters out, he could see the disintegrating links and shell casings fly—the whole truck shuddering with the impact of the recoil on the suspension. A thunderous, ripping sound filling the air as the gunner slowly traversed the gun from left to right, raking the Hizballah positions downrange.

Ignoring Mamdouh's shout of protest, Nassif pushed himself to his feet—his rifle slung loosely over one shoulder as he trotted closer to get a better look, another burst rippling out from the gun.

Half-way down the street, in the shadow of a half-collapsed building, he ran across Abdul Latif—a rifle in one hand, a cellphone in the other, its camera aimed at the technical, filming the action. A feral grin on the big man's face as the gunner cut loose once again.

"We've got them now," he exclaimed, catching sight of

Nassif standing there. "That's going to chew right through the Iranian devils. *Allahu akbar!*"

Nassif nodded, a tight smile creasing the teenager's face—the sound of the cannon ringing in his ears.

And then he heard it, a deeper, throbbing sound that seemed to pulsate through the very earth. His reply to Abdul Latif dying in his throat as he saw a helicopter sweep into view over the buildings to the north, followed almost immediately by a second.

Abdul Latif swore, dropping the phone—screaming a warning that went unheard as the anti-aircraft gun on the back of the truck opened up again, clouds of dust visible off in the distance beyond the berm as shells slammed into the Iranian lines.

A rocket lanced out from the helicopter's wings, streaking over their heads and striking the berm another thirty meters down the street—smoke and dust rising up from the blast.

Nassif glanced back, looking for Mamdouh, but there was no sign of him—and the gunner on the cannon was reacting now, desperately traversing the gun as the helicopters flashed past above.

Too slow, too late. . .

10:13 A.M.

"They've got a flak piece on a truck," Oleg Kurbatov heard over his headset from the forward compartment, an unaccustomed note of fear creeping into Maksim's voice. "Bring us around, Olezhik! *Bring us around!*"

A cold prickle raced down his own spine, his head

craning around, searching the street below for the gun as he manipulated the stick—the heavy helicopter responding sluggishly, its airspeed falling rapidly as he brought it about. "*Sokol-2, Sokol* Lead," he began, keeping his voice even with a mighty effort. "We're dealing with enemy AA—do you have a visual?"

A moment's pause, seeming to hang for eternity as the Mi-24 came back around toward the north, before his headset crackled with static, the other pilot replying, *"Nyet."*

Men scattered in all directions across the street below, a few firing back desperately—foolishly—bullets beginning to ping harmlessly off the attack helicopter's armored fuselage. *But if they got hit by that gun. . .*

Kurbatov felt the sweat bead on his forehead beneath the helmet, his eyes once more scanning the street. *It had to be—* and then he saw it, the big autocannon in the back of the flatbed, its twin barrels slowly rising toward the sky.

He saw those muzzles come almost even with their low-flying helicopter as they swept in—heard the chatter of Maksim's chin turret as it opened up, glimpsed the truck through his PKV sight—thought almost that he could make out the look of panic on the gunner's face in the second before he squeezed the trigger, rockets shooting out from beneath their wings.

The shock wave of the resulting explosion rocked the Mi-24 as it passed overhead, Maksim's savage, euphoric scream of exultation filling Kurbatov's headset as he glanced back to see flames leaping from the destroyed truck. *Yes!* They were still alive.

1:27 P.M. Israel Standard Time
Jaffa Port
Jaffa, Tel Aviv-Yafo, Israel

Through the apartment's open window, you could hear the sounds of the street two stories below—the chatter of tourists, sailors calling to one another from one boat to another. Off in the distance, the murmuring hubbub of Jaffa's flea market. If Avigdor Barad had taken two steps to his right, he could have glimpsed the *Tachash* through the window, riding at anchor.

But his attention, like that of everyone else gathered in the apartment's small kitchen, was on the printouts strewn across the island, liberally papering its granite surface.

"So, when are we actually doing this?" he heard Reuven Aharoni demand, leaning back into the counter—arms folded assertively across his broad chest. The former *Shayetet-13* operator was a decade younger than Barad and had a swimmer's physique, lean and wiry—still in the peak of condition despite having left the unit for Mossad five years before.

"We don't know just yet," Nikahywot Mengashe replied, half-turning toward Aharoni, seeming unfazed by his attitude. "Sometime within the next week."

"That's it?" He glanced from the Ethiopian woman to Barad and back again. "You're kidding me, right?"

"No." Her voice was clear and even, only the faintest trace of irritation visible in her dark face. "We're working with the Syrian opposition, after all. That doesn't allow for certainty. Why, Reuven?"

He glanced across at the other former *Shayetet-13* man in

the room, Omri Tishman, cursing softly. "You want to tell her, Omri, or should I?"

A shrug from his old partner. Omri was the quiet sort—Reuven's polar opposite, which might have been one reason they worked so well together.

Certainly the team couldn't have taken two Reuvens, Barad thought, watching Aharoni closely. The younger man was brash and assertive, in the best of times. And he didn't seem to like Mengashe very much. Whether they had a history, or whether he—like more than a few in Israeli society—simply struggled to see Ethiopians as fully "Jewish," was impossible to say. And not particularly relevant, unless it affected the mission.

"It changes *everything*," Aharoni spat, his voice rising. "If it gets pushed past Friday, we're going to be inserting with an increasingly full moon. We'll be lit up out there on the water bringing the boat in. Do we have depth charts for that far down the coast from Tartus?"

"We do," Mengashe replied, her own tones now as cold as ice. "And you'll keep your voice down unless you want all of Jaffa read in on this op."

"He raises a good point, though," Barad said quietly, intervening. "We're going to be awfully exposed out there once things kick off. With a full moon. . ."

The fourth member of his crew nodded his assent. A veteran of the war in Lebanon and close to Barad's own age, Marc Harel had served with the *Hiluz* branch of the IDF's combat search and rescue outfit, Unit 669. A more than competent fighter in his own right, his medical training would come in handy if worst came to worst and they found themselves dealing with casualties.

God forbid.

Mengashe pursed her lips, reaching forward to shuffle through the papers on the island. "We have no intelligence indicating Syrian or Russian naval patrols in the immediate area. . .if we can free up a Navy patrol boat to support you, have it stand off just out of territorial waters—I'll talk with Shafron."

Barad grimaced. That was a long shot, and even so, a patrol boat twenty kilometers away wasn't likely to do them much good. Still, he was sure everyone else—including Mengashe—knew that as well as he did, so he left those thoughts unsaid.

"Make what contingency plans you can," she said after another moment, "and stand by. You'll have the depth charts by tonight."

4:57 P.M. Syria Standard Time
Quneitra
Quneitra Governorate, Syria

Outside the church, the sun was disappearing beneath the mountains to the west, tinging the heavy, low-hanging clouds an angry shade of purple.

Inside, the low moans of the wounded still disturbed the desecrated sanctity of the nave—ringing in Mohamed Taferi's ears as he sat there, knees drawn up in front of him, leaning against the interior wall. A solitary figure, shrouded in shadow. *Anonymous*, once again.

He could hear voices from within the sacristy, rising and falling in the heat of argument. Al-Golani had called a meeting of his lieutenants, to announce and discuss the proposed strike on Khmeimim, with the morning's attack by Russian helicopters on *Fursan Tahrir al-Sham*'s forward positions serving as handy pretext.

Abu Muin, a heavily-bearded al-Na'ime tribal elder who was the oldest and most irascible of Abu Ahmed's subordinates, had been the last to arrive—stalking in past where Mohamed sat only minutes before. And it was his voice that he now heard raised in angry protest, snatches of Arabic filtering out through the battered stone walls of the church.

". . .*you would have us simply walk away, abandon our homes—our families? For* what?"

Abu Ahmed's response was unintelligible, and the Israeli intelligence officer leaned wearily back into the stone. He had known this wouldn't be easy—they all had, except perhaps the Americans.

Americans were slow to see the difficulty in anything, slower still to believe that money couldn't solve whatever problems cropped up.

Al-Golani's own tribal background was unclear, but despite his *kunya*, Mossad's best intelligence indicated that he was a native of Dara'a, off to the southeast, likely a member of the al-Zou'bi tribe. Not one of the traditional elders, or even a government sheikh, but a native son who had served in the Syrian Army—as an officer, or so he was known to claim—and returned home to the tribes when revolution came.

But *here*—Quneitra—this wasn't home for him, something Abu Muin was no doubt reminding him of just now. *Not one of us.* Tribalism, at its most elemental.

"*Every day. . .those helicopter gunships. . .you see the wounded,*" Abu Ahmed said, his own voice rising above the dull murmur of his subordinates.

So that's how he's selling the strike, Mohamed thought, grimacing as a wounded fighter moaned in pain not three meters away, obscuring the commander's next words. *Retaliation.* For their own dead.

The opposition driver bringing him back from the border crossing had dropped him off at the church at almost the exact moment the casualties began streaming in from the front—victims of the latest gunship attack.

He'd helped hold one of the wounded down as he writhed on the makeshift operating table—a weary, blood-spattered Southern Front doctor who had been a surgeon in Damascus before the war removing the mangled remains of the young man's right leg above the knee with a saw that would have looked more at home in an American Civil War field hospital. Mohamed's fingers digging into the fighter's thin, bony shoulders as he struggled.

When the struggling had stopped, he'd almost felt a sense of relief—until the doctor reached over, groping with bloody fingers for a pulse, a weary look of resignation spreading across his face as both men realized the patient was gone, dead from shock and loss of blood.

Just another of the many.

He had seen the boy, Nassif, straggle back in, still among the living—clambering down out of a truck bed with Abdul Latif, the big fighter he remembered from his first day back here.

The sight of the kid he'd helped filling him with an irrational sense of satisfaction—it was impossible not to know that his odds of surviving this war were vanishingly small, but for this moment, he was still in one piece.

". . .we chose you, to lead our fighters. To help us win. " Abu Muin's voice again, clearer and louder than before. *"But this is madness. You've lost, you believe our cause is lost, and this is how you want to end it all. But you won't do so through the lives of my men."*

The door of the sacristy came open in that moment, banging back against the stone as Abu Muin stormed back out, his face dark as he passed Mohamed in the dim light of the nave.

A couple of Abu Ahmed's other lieutenants not far behind him, as though they had waited to follow the older man's lead. Someone shut the door then, and he heard Al-Golani say something unintelligible, presumably to his remaining subordinates.

It was another half hour before they, too, left, more quietly than those who had gone before, and when they did, Mohamed rose from the shadows and moved to the open door, finding Abu Ahmed already opening his bottle of arak, pouring the spirit into a dirty glass.

The Syrian commander lifted it to his lips, his face twisting into a grimace as he swallowed—catching sight then of the Israeli standing in the doorway. He set the glass back down, an air of defeat seeming to cling to him as he shook his head slowly. *No.*

Chapter 8

They had made out the truck more than an hour before, making its way furtively, lights out, along the roads twisting through the low hills which rose up from the Mediterranean coastline—the small Honda and its handful of occupants picked up on the cameras of the pair of Orlan-10 surveillance drones they had in orbit above.

Makarenko shifted his position restlessly on the hard, cold ground, his Kalashnikov slung over his back, binoculars in his hands as he scanned the ground below them. It shouldn't be long now.

The Honda had stopped in a village three kilometers to the northeast—the one, in fact, which Kulik had pointed out on his maps at the morning briefing—something large and heavy being loaded from an equipment shed into the bed of the pick-up before they proceeded.

The leaves of the *shamouti* orange trees above Makarenko's head rustled in the chill breeze, seeming to whisper like ghosts in the night. They were positioned on the edge of one of Latakia's countless citrus orchards, maintaining an overwatch position on the road which ran along below the ridgeline, perhaps a hundred and fifty meters to the south. He glanced over to his left, making out the figure of one of Egorov's designated marksmen, posted up on a limestone outcropping at the very crest of the ridge, prone on his belly—the outline of his venerable Dragunov SVD sniper rifle just visible in the darkness. The Dragunov had been in service since the '60s, and its replacement, the SVCh Chukavin—a Kalashnikov design, like so many other Russian small arms—was only now making its way into production. It would be another several years before the GU's Spetsnaz outfits got their hands on them.

He stole a glance at the tablet in Egorov's hands, its glow shielded by the Spetsnaz officer's jacket. Stripped to his shirtsleeves, his rifle laying on the ground beside him, Egorov seemed not to feel the cold—his breath steaming into the night air as he looked up to meet Makarenko's gaze.

"Are you ready, *tovarisch podpolkóvnik*?" the man asked with a broad smile, his teeth bared—his expression seeming nearly feral. He was enjoying himself, Makarenko realized, something inside him seeming to shrink away from the Spetsnaz officer. "They're almost here."

"*Da*," Makarenko replied slowly, reaching back and unslinging his own rifle from his shoulders. "I'm ready."

Egorov smiled in amusement at the sight. "You won't need that, *tovarisch*—they will all be dead, very soon."

He closed the tablet and rose to his feet, rifle in hand, moving quietly among his men, issuing hushed orders. Makarenko brought his night-vision binoculars back up to his eyes, making out the truck, just now coming into view over the crest of a hill to the east.

The lieutenant colonel found himself holding his breath as it crept closer, the noise of its engine audible now—its silhouette standing out against the dark green haze of the background in his night-vision.

He'd been in the military for well over a decade, had come under fire a score of times since his deployment to Syria, but this was the closest he'd ever come to *combat*, and he felt his pulse quicken at the thought.

As the range closed, he laid aside the binoculars, reaching up to his helmet to flip down the mounted PN21K night-vision monocular, bringing the truck into focus. *Any moment now. . .*

The two rifle shots rang out as one without warning, shattering the night and the tension right along with it—Makarenko almost coming out of his skin with the report, keeping his own finger off the trigger with a mighty effort.

The truck seemed to lurch sideways, steam rising from its engine block—men spilling out of cab and bed alike as it came to a stop.

He saw muzzle flashes—heard the distinctive chatter of multiple Kalashnikovs going off on full-auto as the Syrian rebels reacted to the ambush, firing wildly in all directions. *Death blossom*, he'd read the Americans called it in Iraq—that uncontrollable, undisciplined response to coming under attack.

It wasn't going to save them—the rest of Egorov's Spetsnaz opening up a moment later, from their positions lower down the slope, the designated marksmen continuing to engage targets with remorseless precision. He saw one man throw down his weapon and take off running—a bullet catching him in the back of the neck and dropping him in his tracks.

Another man cowering behind the engine block of the truck, poking his head up to stare around in confusion and bewilderment at the unfolding carnage—until one of the marksmen blew half of his skull away with a 7.62x54R round.

And then it was all over, quiet falling once again over the Syrian hillside—not more than forty-five seconds from first shot to last. *Death, now reigning supreme.*

Makarenko pushed himself to his feet to join Egorov's men as they descended to the road, leaving a small contingent to maintain overwatch. Joking and laughing as they moved, rough exultation in their voices. The rebels hadn't stood a chance.

The moans of the dying assaulted their ears as they closed in on the truck and he saw one of the commandos stop by the prostrate form of a rebel, taking out his pistol and executing the wounded man with a bullet to the back of the head.

Egorov strode around to the back of the truck, a savage, triumphal smile playing at his lips as he tore away the ragged, bullet-riddled tarpaulin to reveal the familiar shape of a *Samovar*—an M1943 120mm mortar—broken down for transport into barrel, bipod, and baseplate.

"Rig it to blow, Anatoliy," he ordered one of his Spetsnaz, turning to Makarenko. "Good hunting, isn't it, *tovarisch?*"

1:08 A.M. Israel Standard Time
The apartment
Jaffa Port
Jaffa, Tel Aviv-Yafo, Israel

Nika Mengashe had come through with the charts, and they were now spread across the floor of the apartment's living room, pieced together to form a comprehensive picture of the Syrian coastline off Latakia. The exceptional weakness of Mediterranean tides was going to play to their favor, Avigdor Barad reflected, bending down from his chair to scan the charts—no more than a few centimeters of difference between high and low tides.

The Red Sea was a very different story, as he knew from hard-earned experience. There, particularly in the south, toward the Gulf of Aden, the difference could be as much as a meter—more than enough to play havoc with your op if you hadn't allowed for that, going in.

Across from him, down on one knee on the floor, Reuven Aharoni took a long pull on his bottle of Maccabee lager, setting the beer to one side on the carpet.

"We'll take the Zodiac in here," he announced, indicating a small inlet just southwest of the Russian airbase, about two and a half kilometers from the perimeter, and only a couple kilometers up the coast from Jableh. Not much of a beach, according to their IMINT, but it would have to do. "Cut the engine, paddle in the last two klicks. Avigdor, you can handle the fishing boat yourself, can't you?"

Barad nodded. It wasn't ideal, but. . .if they were unlucky enough to be stopped by a Syrian naval patrol, it wouldn't make much difference if there was one or two of them.

"Good. All right then, Marc, I want you with us in the Zodiac. If they've taken casualties, you'll be right at hand. If they're still in contact, we'll have the extra gun. If fortune smiles and we come away clean. . ."

"From your lips to God's ears," Barad smiled grimly, reaching for his own beer. Sometimes you got lucky, and operations went just that smoothly. *Sometimes.*

"The road's right there, right off the beach," Omri spoke up, comparing Reuven's depth charts to the satellite imagery. "We'll be exposed."

There wasn't much getting around that. Latakia was a densely-populated part of Syria, particularly along the coast—row upon row of greenhouses dotting the landscape between the airbase and the beach in the photos from the TecSAR spy sat.

"How long do you think we can give them?" Barad asked, his eyes flickering over the maps. As much as he might find Reuven's personality insufferable at times, his own background wasn't in ops, and he deferred to the younger man on those decisions. He was going to be keeping the *Tachash* several kilometers off the coast, after all—it wasn't going to be his butt hanging out there in the wind on that beach.

Reuven grimaced, trading a look with his partner. "Ninety minutes, tops. If we have to go in under a full moon. . .a lot less. Making an approach lit up to anyone who happens to be looking out to sea—even thirty minutes will be pushing it."

4:49 A.M. Syria Standard Time
The church in Quneitra
Quneitra Governorate, Syria

Outside, one could hear the camp beginning to stir—the sound of a vehicle engine starting up somewhere off in the distance audible through the ancient stone, a low murmur of voices as men gathered around their cooking fires, stirring the coals back to life. The pathetic, moaning cries of the wounded from the nave—though those had never stopped, all through the night.

One man in particular, seeming to cry out despairingly every few minutes until he finally lost his voice. Or perhaps someone had lost patience and smothered him—that seemed equally likely.

And then there was the snoring. Mohamed Taferi opened one eye with painful reluctance, forcing himself awake—every muscle in his body stiff and sore from the night spent sleeping in a plastic chair. The snoring continued, seeming to grow louder, if anything—the sound poking at his brain with a sharp stick.

Its source, Abu Ahmed al-Golani, half lay, half sat a few feet away, still sound asleep—his upper body sprawled across the card table, its frail structure improbably supporting his weight, the half-empty bottle of arak perched recklessly near his outstretched hand as he snored on, his glass already knocked over a few inches from his fingers.

Mohamed had lost track of just how many times that glass had been emptied and refilled as they'd talked, deeper and deeper into the night, the rebel commander growing progressively drunker—roaring back at one of his subordinates with such a fury when they knocked that they'd backed hastily from the room. Wrath changing in moments to sorrow as Al-Golani wept helplessly into his drink.

"I no longer have my men," he'd said finally, shaking his head in frustration and despair. *"I can do nothing for you now."*

That was another thing the Americans were slow to grasp, Mohamed reflected now, regarding the snoring opposition leader with a mixture of disgust and pity. *No wonder the Prophet prohibited our use of alcohol.*

Americans understood military operations through a Western prism—an extremely *modern* Western prism—a hierarchical command structure, orders filtering down the chain of command from the brass above to the grunts below, executed by disciplined subordinates who were expected to exercise their own judgment and initiative without unduly questioning the overall mission.

Here in Syria, particularly among the tribes. . .things remained far more feudal, the command hierarchy an incomprehensibly complex web of personal and tribal fealties which would have put medieval Europe to shame.

Even calling Al-Golani a "commander" was something of a misnomer. He was in command until he wasn't—until the men he led decided to no longer follow.

"Perhaps we don't need Abu Muin's fighters," he'd suggested, the germ of an idea forming in his mind as Al-Golani regarded him through increasingly bleary eyes. *"Perhaps we don't need that many men at all. All we truly need, Abu Ahmed, is a* diversion.*"*

The door of the sacristy came open in that moment, Abdul Latif standing in the entryway, the big man's face darkening as his eyes fell on Mohamed sitting there in the chair opposite his unconscious leader.

"What have you done to him?"

"Nothing he didn't do to himself," Mohamed replied calmly, grimacing as he rose from the chair—his muscles protesting against the sudden exertion. He moved over to stand in front of the rebel fighter, looking up into his face. "And I'm not your problem here. . .you need to get him sobered up before one of our boys in black pokes their head in and finds him like this."

7:04 A.M.
A village
The foothills of Jabal an-Nusayriyah
Latakia Governorate, Syria

"Vykhodite!" Makarenko heard Valeriy Egorov bellow, standing there in the center of the small Syrian village, rifle in hand—his short, stocky frame casting an unnaturally long shadow in the morning sun. *Come out.* "Come out and see your dead."

Behind the *Spetsnaz* officer, his commandos threw the bodies of the slain militants from the bed of a KamAZ light cargo truck, pitching them unceremoniously into the dust of the street.

One body landed not far from Makarenko's feet, the dead weight striking the earth with a sickeningly dull *thud*—stiffening arms and legs somehow twisted together, one eye gazing out sightlessly to meet the dawn.

The GRU lieutenant colonel suppressed a shudder, gripping his rifle more tightly as his gaze flickered among the austere stone and concrete-block buildings scattered around them, separated by tight alleys—electrical wires crisscrossing over their heads, in places forming a nearly impenetrable web.

They were exposed here, sweat forming in Makarenko's armpits, cold and damp beneath his kit.

"How many of these dead men belong to you?" Egorov continued, his bellowing voice ringing out across the otherwise ghostly village, seemingly heedless of the average Syrian villager's ignorance of Russian. "How many are your sons, your husbands, your *fathers?*"

Makarenko thought he caught a glimpse of movement out of the corner of his eye, a shadow passing across the second-story window of a nearby house, but it was gone by the time he'd focused on it—his finger playing uneasily with the safety of his Kalashnikov.

He'd urged against this expedition to "return" the corpses of the rebels they'd ambushed, argued that at least they should call in back-up from Kulik's QRF detachment before proceeding, but Egorov had laughed it off, his actions making it clear that—as far as he was concerned—the chain of command didn't exist beyond the perimeter of the base.

And now even their small force was split, one of the Spetsnaz NCOs peeling off with a squad to find that equipment shed where the rebels' mortar had apparently been cached.

"These men raised their hands against their government— against the Russian forces who have come to bring stability to your country," the Spetsnaz captain continued, seeming to reach the climax of his monologue, his voice echoing off the outer wall of a distant house, "and now they're dead. Come out and bury them, and know that if you think to join them, you should dig an extra grave for yourself."

Silence fell as he stopped talking, no movement from the houses—no one responding to his offer. Makarenko edged closer to him, about to open his mouth and suggest they call an end to this charade, return to base before they ran out their luck, when he saw Egorov turn to one side, pressing a hand to his ear. "Good, good," he said, his face lighting up with a smile. "*Da*, blow it."

A moment later, the earth trembled beneath their feet, smoke and fire rising into the morning sky a few hundred meters to the west. Clearly, Egorov's men had found the cache.

"Come on, *tovarisch*," the captain grinned, "let's get out of here. Our work for the night is done."

It was only ten minutes later, as the small Russian convoy drove back west out of the village, a pall of smoke still lingering against the dawn, the sun filtering through the gnarled branches of the olive trees bordering the road, that Makarenko heard it, through the open window of the lead vehicle: the anguished, heart-wrenching sound of women wailing.

Heard it, and looked over to see Egorov smile.

10:04 A.M.
The church in Quneitra
Quneitra Governorate, Syria

One could still hear the dull, percussive *thump* of falling shells far off to the northeast, but things seemed somehow calmer in the *Fursan Tahrir al-Sham* encampment this morning, men gathered around the cooking fires, warming their hands against the morning cold—their weapons laid off to the side.

Perhaps this was as calm as it got in Syria, Mohamed Taferi thought, glancing up at the clear, cold skies above—hardly a cloud in sight. A beautiful morning, the kind of day that could almost make a man forget he was in the middle of a war.

He ducked into the door of the church, his eyes adjusting to the semi-darkness of the interior, and was immediately brought back to reality—the soft, pitiful moans of the wounded swelling up from around him, a weary-eyed, bloodstained rebel slowly drawing the remnants of a bedsheet over the face of a man lying just within the door.

Abdul Latif stood guard by the door to the sacristy, scowling at Mohamed's approach, but he waved him on through without a word. Everyone in the opposition's ranks knew how important Qatari money was to their continued survival, to their ability to keep fighting, and so long as his cover held. . .

He found Abu Ahmed stripped to the waist, bent over the washbasin in one corner of the small room, splashing cold water over his face. At least he wasn't drinking again, Mohamed thought—trying to chase one hangover away with another.

The opposition commander seemed to sense his presence, and his hand stole out toward his Glock as he turned, his bloodshot, bleary eyes seeming to slowly recognize Mohamed as he stood there, water dripping from his haggard face, the pistol clutched loosely in his right hand.

"What are you still doing here?" he asked, his voice thick

and still slightly slurred. Just as well it was calm outside—he was in no shape to command, or even be seen by his jihadi allies. "I told you, last night. There's nothing more for you here. Nothing I can do to help you."

There was grief and despair in his voice, a hopelessness exacerbated by the hangover. A man staring into the abyss.

"You don't remember?" the Druze intelligence officer asked, taking a step closer. "We talked about this—about the drones."

Chapter 9

"No." Mirit Refaeli's voice was clear and cold, the look on her face absolutely unequivocal as she glanced back and forth between David Shafron and Nika Mengashe. "I can't sign off on a request like that to the Navy. Absolutely not."

"Barad specifically raised the issue of naval support for his crew's end of the operation," Mengashe protested, her eyes betraying her discomfort with how this meeting was going. "They're going to be exposed off the Latakia coastline for hours, the least we can give them is some back-up in the case of all this going sideways."

"If all this goes sideways," the Metsada department chief responded icily, brushing a short lock of slate-gray hair back from her forehead, "we want to be as far away from it as possible. We are launching a paramilitary operation against a *Russian* military base, and the last thing we need is the Kremlin being able to point to an Israeli warship parked offshore at the time of the attack. We're taking enough of a risk with the *Tachash*."

That was hard logic to argue against, Shafron reflected, leaning back in his seat. As he'd made clear to Taferi, deniability was essential to this operation. He could go over Mirit's head, file his own request with Shoham, but. . .

"It's your assets on the line, Mirit," he said instead, choosing not to fight this particular battle, "your call on managing their exposure. We—"

"Yes, David, they are my assets," Mirit replied, folding her arms across her chest, a hard set in the lines of her face as she stared across her desk at him, ignoring Nika for the moment. "You would do well to remember that, both now and in the future."

It seemed hardly likely that she would allow him to forget, if truth be told. A tall, elegant woman with a deceptively maternal mien which belied the steel hidden just beneath the surface, Mirit Refaeli had fought against the creation of MEGIDDO from the beginning, arguing—not without reason—that it encroached on the operational turf of her own Metsada. Having lost that particular bureaucratic battle, she'd then proceeded to demand that it be incorporated into the existing Metsada operational structure under her direct authority, like CAESAREA and RAINBOW.

But an independent unit, answering directly to Shoham's office, had been the point of the reshuffle, and the *memuneh* had stuck to his guns, ultimately carrying the day, albeit with a much-reduced budget.

A handicap which often landed him here, in Mirit's office, like he was today, hat in hand—forced to fall back on Metsada's superior resources and accept the strings which came attached to them. Because with Mirit, there would *always* be strings.

"Noted," he replied coolly, refusing to take the bait as he rose to leave. Just because their relationship had been contentious over the years, going back to his own time as an operator in the *Kidon*, didn't mean she was wrong on this. "We'll leave the Navy out of it. Just make sure your people are in place for the extract, Mirit."

"They will be."

3:24 P.M. Syria Standard Time
Quneitra
Quneitra Governorate, Syria

The shadows were lengthening over the ruined, desolate city as Nassif picked his way forward, through the rubble of a half-destroyed house, his rifle in his hand. The rough skirmish line of militants surrounding the boy all but silent as they moved, communicating only in gestures and the most hushed of whispers, the fading sunlight glinting off the brass cartridges in the bandoliers crisscrossing Mamdouh's chest as he advanced with the RPD. The one-eyed man was sporting a fresh, raw scar across the destroyed half of his face, the old scar tissue ripped apart by shrapnel from the previous day's gunship attack, but he seemed oblivious to the injury—hefting the machine gun in weathered hands as he kept pace on their flank.

One of their quadcopter UAVs had picked up Hizballah infiltrators slipping into the city from the northeast, circumventing their scattered positions, and it had fallen to Abu Muin's fighters to move out and engage them—lock them down, before night fell and left them exposed. *Vulnerable.*

They were somewhere ahead, now—in the last several blocks of crumbling houses, shops, and apartment buildings before one reached the open desert. They didn't have the Iranians' exact position—the quadcopter had taken fire and its operator had brought it back rather than risk losing it. But it couldn't be far now.

Movement, *something*—drew Nassif's eye across the city street, but it was only a worn piece of cloth in the window of a burnt-out technical, rustled by the bitter December breeze. *Nothing.*

Calm down, the boy told himself, cursing beneath his breath as his eyes lingered on the charred wreck for another moment before moving on. Talha had always teased him about being jumpy, told him he was a coward. Maybe he was, but he was still here, still alive, and his brother was—

A rough metallic *klatch* struck his ears, the distinctive noise resounding through the stillness of the deserted street—a curse escaping Mamdouh's lips as he recognized it, too, the RPD's long barrel coming up.

Nassif's eyes flickered back across the street and *up*, this time—to the open, second-story window of a mostly-intact house just behind the charred technical. A figure there, in the shadows of a darkened room—the glint of a rifle barrel.

His mouth opened to scream a warning, but a tsunami of automatic weapons fire drowned out the words, and men began to fall—bullets lashing the street. He saw Abu Muin himself go down, the front of the tribal elder's combat fatigues stained dark with blood—saw Mamdouh down on one knee, the machine gun raised in both hands, the RPD biting chunks out of the concrete face of the building across the street, the chaos of battle swirling all around him.

He found himself on his belly without realizing how he'd gotten there, pressing himself into the dirt until he could taste it against his teeth, the safety of his rifle still on—cowering, praying for it all to go away.

And he could hear his brother, somewhere, mocking him. *Coward.*

4:13 P.M.
Khmeimim Air Base
Latakia Governorate, Syria

Russian ground crews were busy at work painting the newly arrived Su-34 fighter-bombers, stripping away the characteristic camouflage scheme and painting over the red stars of the Russian Federation on each wingtip and the twin tail fins, as Andriy Makarenko walked across the tarmac toward the GRU listening station located in a squat, nondescript building on the western side of the base just across from the terminal serving Bassel al-Assad International.

It was about deniability, he knew that much, though he'd been careful to ask no questions. The aircraft were bound elsewhere, Libya, most likely, where Wagner's contractors were in need of close air support.

Officially, they had never been here, a conceit he found more than mildly ridiculous, given the near-certainty that American spy satellites were watching the whole process from above—their Navy's spy planes out in the Med, keeping their distance, and careful watch.

The guards acknowledged their lieutenant colonel's approach with the briefest of nods, nothing that would have marked him as an officer to anyone out there with a scope and a good rifle, but Makarenko barely noticed, walking in past them without a word of greeting. His face a brittle mask, the morning's events in the village still replaying themselves over and again through his mind. Egorov unnerved him—he couldn't get away from that, no matter how he tried. *That mocking smile.*

It was more than the satisfaction of a professional over their work—far more. It was a pleasure that bordered on sadism, if, indeed, it didn't cross that line entirely.

He would be glad when the Su-57s were gone—another day, if that, and then God willing, he could say good-bye to Captain Egorov too.

The building was dark and cool, shielded by several feet of reinforced concrete—its central area lit by the pale glow of several hundred screens. It was perhaps the single most strategic aspect of the Russian presence here at Khmeimim, enabling them to monitor communications all across the Middle East, as they slowly re-established the regional dominance they had lost with the fall of the Soviet Union. They were back, and the Americans were too distracted, too *divided,* to throw them back out this time.

"You had something for me, *tovarisch leytenánt?*" he asked, rounding the edge of a workstation to find a sallow-faced young SIGINT officer sitting there bent unhealthily over his keyboard.

"Da, da," the younger man replied, seeming startled by Makarenko's sudden appearance. "We've picked up an intercept from—"

The building seemed to tremble inexplicably in that moment, the SIGINT officer's words breaking off suddenly.

The walls were too thick for them to hear anything from without, but a moment later the klaxons began to ring throughout the listening post.

They were under attack. . .

4:51 P.M.
The church in Quneitra
Quneitra Governorate, Syria

He'd been at the church when word of the ambush had first started trickling in over the radio, and now Mohamed Taferi stood in the courtyard as darkness fell, the trucks rolling in with the wounded, armed men spilling out of their beds, gesturing wildly with their weapons—angry shouts filling the air as Al-Golani's headquarters personnel hurried forward to help move the casualties.

The rebel leader had, fortunately, been sober enough by the time the emergency calls started streaming in to organize a fairly rapid response, at least by opposition standards, bringing more forces to bear to flank the Iranians, applying pressure on them from the rear—forcing them to break off the engagement.

But Abu Muin's fighters had still been badly mauled, all the same—Mohamed's breath catching in his throat as he recognized the figure of Abu Muin himself being unloaded from the back of a Hilux, one fighter supporting his head and shoulders, the other carrying his feet, his body hanging limply between them, head lolling lifelessly to one side.

And he understood the shouts, then, the anger written in the faces of the men. A thirst for vengeance. He saw the boy, Nassif, clamber awkwardly from the bed of a battered

Honda, his rifle slung across his back, the wound in his shoulder still evidently paining him—turning to take the machine gun from the hands of his one-eyed companion.

"Mohammed bin Ammar?" a voice asked from behind him, using the name of his Qatari legend.

"Yes?" he replied, turning to find a heavily bearded jihadist clad all in black standing there in the semi-darkness. Likely one of the *Jaysh Khalid ibn Walid* fighters. "Who asks?"

"Salaam alaikum," the man replied, offering his hand. If he smiled, it was impossible to tell through the thicket of beard, and the Islamists weren't known for smiling. "Anas ibn Nadhar."

One of the companions of the Prophet, peace be upon him, Mohamed thought, recognizing the name for what it was— a *nom de guerre.* And something of a prideful one—Ibn Nadhar had been among the most gallant of Muhammad's *sahabi,* and had found martyrdom at the Battle of Uhud, defending his prophet. When they'd found his body on the battlefield after the defeat of the polytheists, it had been pierced by more than eighty wounds, cut nearly to pieces— surrounded by enemy slain. *"Among the believers are men true to what they promised Allah. . ."*

But this man appeared to be quite intact.

"Wa alaikum as-salaam," he replied, regarding the man keenly as he took his hand.

"I understand you are looking for men," the jihadist said then—and this time he *did* smile, teeth visible through the coal-black scruff, "for an attack on the airbase of the Russian infidel."

5:34 P.M.
Khmeimim Air Base
Latakia Governorate, Syria

The shelling had only lasted for eight minutes, an utterly ineffectual rain of mortar rounds falling wildly around the base, injuring no one and doing little damage.

But it had enraged Valeriy Egorov, and Makarenko knew why. The Spetsnaz captain had stood in his office that very morning, borrowing his phone for a conference call with the Aquarium and the Defence Ministry, assuring them that there was no need for any interruption in the Su-57's testing. That Khmeimim was now secure.

Subsequent events had put the lie to that arrogant boast, secretly to the delight of the GRU lieutenant colonel—though in truth, it was as much his problem as Egorov's. Syria wasn't a place that rewarded rash optimism.

Even before the barrage had stopped, the Spetsnaz had been out of the gates, racing into the foothills ahead of Kulik's armored QRF—the Orlan-10s scouting ahead. But all they'd found was the abandoned firing position, two and a half kilometers to the east, a handful of shells laying scattered about, and Egorov had returned to base in a towering fury.

"We're going back out there," he said now, punctuating his words with a snarled obscenity as he glared around at the gathered officers, including the just-arrived General Yury Kovpak, the overall commander of Russian forces at Khmeimim. "Tonight."

"And what do you think you'll accomplish, *tovarisch kapitán*?" Makarenko demanded, casting a sidelong glance at the general. Kovpak was a career soldier with a ruthless edge he'd demonstrated more than once, to allies and enemies alike, since arriving in Syria, but he was no sadist—and he had already heard out Makarenko's complaints concerning the Spetsnaz captain. "Dump a few more dead bodies in the arms of freshly-made widows? Do you even have a target? A plan? Of any kind?"

"We destroyed materiel last night," Egorov spat, anger in his dark eyes. "We killed armed rebels, and we made an example of them."

"An example no one seems to have heeded, *tovarisch*," Major Kulik interjected. He and Makarenko had had a long talk earlier, after Makarenko's return from the raid—over a samovar of tea in Kulik's quarters.

"Then these savages need a better example," came Egorov's ominous rejoinder. "It's not as though your methods have had any better success, in all your months here."

Makarenko shook his head, looking over at Kulik. "I am the GU's ranking officer here, and I will not authorize your men going out without clear, actionable intel. We do not want this population turning against us through your recklessness. We've all seen what happened to the Americans in Afghanistan and Iraq. Our Syrian partners—"

"We are not the Americans, *tovarisch podpolkóvnik*," General Kovpak said quietly but firmly, his next words taking Makarenko completely off-guard. "We are not afraid to use a firm hand, when necessary. And our Syrian partners owe their existence to our support. I think *Kapitán* Egorov is right."

9:34 P.M. Israel Standard Time
Mossad Headquarters, Glilot Junction Tel Aviv-Yafo, Israel

The elevator ride up to Avi ben Shoham's office had been long and uncomfortable, Mirit's very silence seeming to build in volume the longer it continued. Now, sitting there on the couch opposite the Metsada chief, waiting for the *memuneh* to finish going over his briefing notes, David Shafron felt as though the slightest breath might trigger an explosion.

The lights of Tel Aviv sparkled in the distance through the one-way glass of the office windows—a city which never slept, pulsating to the beat of its scores of nightclubs.

"This is a problem," Avi ben Shoham announced, his gift for understatement never more vividly on display as he took off his reading glasses, staring across the desk at his subordinates.

Shafron nodded, only too aware of the truth of the *memuneh*'s words. He'd been at home when the call came in, Chanukah festivities over for the night, his sons gathered around him on the couch to watch *Galis: The Journey to Astra* for what seemed like the fiftieth time, Aaron and Shmuel fighting over the right to sit in his lap as Rahel looked on in amusement.

But there would be other nights for he and his family—if not, he feared, for the man he had sent into the field.

"Dealing with *Fursan Tahrir al-Sham* was one thing," Shoham went on. "We all know their rank-and-file would probably take our officer's head if they knew he worked for Israel, but they're not extremists. JKIW? They're outright jihadists—on the US State Department's list of Specially

Designated Global Terrorist organizations. They've sworn *bayah* to the Islamic State."

"If *Jaysh* found out through the jihadist grapevine, the Russians likely already know," Mirit observed coldly from the couch across from Shafron. She, too, had presumably been at home when they'd heard from Taferi, but in contrast to Shafron's jeans and rumpled polo, she was back in her dove-gray pantsuit, the stark white turtleneck beneath giving just the right note of austerity to the outfit. "We need to cut our losses. Pull Taferi out of there before this gets any messier. Before this misbegotten operation stumbles past the point of no return. The Ameri—"

"You're assuming it hasn't already, Mirit," Shafron interjected, cutting her off. "That we even *can* exfiltrate him without bringing this whole house of cards crashing down, on everyone beneath."

Chapter 10

Jet engines glowed bright against the darkness of the Syrian night as the pair of Su-57 stealth fighters taxied out onto the runway, their distinctive silhouettes visible in the runway lights.

Andriy Makarenko stood in the shadow of a BMP-3, the throbbing roar of the infantry fighting vehicle's diesel engine drowning out all else, its hull painted in the mottled desert camouflage Russian forces had been forced to adopt ad hoc since their deployment—many of their vehicles had arrived in-theater still dark woodland green.

Fine camouflage, he supposed, if one planned to storm through the Fulda Gap—but in Syria's harsher landscape, it just painted a target on your back.

The first Su-57 accelerated down the runway, its screaming whine penetrating through the engine noise surrounding him as the convoy formed up at the base gates.

Makarenko shifted his rifle to his off-hand, watching

123

them go—the second taking off nearly on the heels of the first. Watching as they turned north, fading away toward the dark horizon. *Heading home.*

In another few weeks, he would join them. See Zinaida once again—and finally meet his daughter, for the first time. In the meantime, he hoped he had seen the last of the Air Force's pride and joy.

Let them finalize their testing on somebody else's watch—he'd gotten his bellyful of the responsibility.

He looked up to see Valeriy Egorov walking down the line of vehicles toward him, pausing for a moment to hail the commander of the T-90 positioned mid-column, standing upright in the open hatch of his ponderous main battle tank.

Then he was standing before him, Egorov's face cold and unsmiling beneath the greasepaint. "We're ready to move out, *tovarisch podpolkóvnik*. Do try not to get in the way out there."

12:57 A.M.
The church in Quneitra
Quneitra Governorate

With six men packed into the narrow confines of the sacristy, the room was crowded and almost hot. At least Abu Ahmed had made away with the arak before receiving visitors, Mohamed Taferi thought, spreading out the commercial geosat images on the table as everyone gathered around.

It seemed as though he could still *smell* it, though, the pungent aroma of the anise spirit somehow persisting through the dominant odor of sweat and unwashed bodies. Perhaps it was just his imagination—nerves—for none of the new arrivals, mercifully, seemed to pick up on it.

Anas ibn Nadhar—or whatever the jihadist's name actually was—stood across from him, his beard parting occasionally to reveal a smile devoid of congeniality. To his left was another JKIW man, introduced only as Musa'b ibn Zayd, while on his right stood Mohammad al-Refai himself, *Jaysh Khalid ibn Walid's* commander, stroking his own long, graying beard as he stared at the images spread out before them.

It would be just his luck for the Americans to launch a drone strike on the church just now, Mohamed thought ironically, keeping his face neutral with an effort. He knew Al-Refai was in their target deck, as he was Tel Aviv's.

Abdul Latif stood glowering by the door, a pistol prominently displayed on his hip—the only armed man in the room, or so they all hoped. Mohamed had seen the frisking the JKIW men had been given, and it wouldn't have passed muster in his days with the IDF. He had himself been allowed to keep his knife, though perhaps Abdul Latif had viewed the small four-inch folder as more a utility tool than a weapon.

"The airbase has come under repeated mortar attack over the last few months," he went on, gesturing to the images showing Khmeimim's runways, "but it has had no perceptible effect on Russian air operations. Any craters are filled in, any damaged equipment simply repaired or replaced. And they continue to harass our operations here, against the Persian apostates. An all-out attack, though. . ."

He was taking a huge risk here, sharing this much

without authorization from headquarters—but he'd had little choice in the matter. Any reticence, he'd realized from his very first conversation with Anas, could well raise the jihadists' suspicions—his presumptive Qatari masters certainly would have had no such misgivings—and there was only one way that ended. An orange jumpsuit and an unwelcome appearance on the Israeli nightly news.

"A truck bomb, at the gates," Al-Refai proposed, looking up, "could force our entrance. Our *mujahideen* could be inside the wire before they'd had a chance to recover."

"It could," Mohamed responded, shuffling his sheets, "but look here—at the gate, the maze of barriers leading up to the checkpoint. Snipers in the towers, most likely, here and here—they'll take out your truck with a shot through the engine block before you get anywhere close."

The Russians had taken a page out of the American playbook in Iraq and Afghanistan, erecting a complex labyrinth of Jersey barriers on the main approach road. To negotiate them, any vehicle would have to slow to a crawl, leaving it exposed. Vulnerable.

Al-Refai looked impressed. "You've had training. Joint Special Forces? *Lekhwiya*?"

"My employers prefer that all be left out of this," Mohamed replied, unsmiling, recognizing Al-Refai's references to the Qatari spec-ops units, "but yes, I have had training."

He tucked the geosat image of the gate back into the pile, spreading out another set of images. "This building here, near the terminal, we believe to be a GRU listening station, from which they monitor all communications in the region, including your own un-encrypted battlefield comms. If you wonder why the Iranians know which way you're going to move before you do, this building right here is why. And you shouldn't imagine even your encrypted communications to be totally secure. That's why the details of what we are planning here—even our target, must stay in this room."

If that particular horse hadn't already left the stable, none of them would be standing here, he thought, watching the jihadists trade glances. But it was worth stressing, on the off chance they *weren't* already blown.

"That building is our primary target," he continued, now that he had their attention. "Everything else is a diversion."

"So, you have a plan?"

He nodded, glancing at Al-Golani, who stood off to one side, his eyes ringed in shadow from lack of sleep, seeming nervous in the presence of the Islamists—no doubt craving a drink. But that was going to have to wait. "We do. We're going to kick off our attack with a drone swarm. . ."

1:23 A.M.
A village
The foothills of Jabal an-Nusayriyah
Latakia Governorate, Syria

A woman's shriek rent the night, a shrill, desperate sound rising above the crackling flames, her fists beating uselessly on the backs of Egorov's commandos as they dragged her husband from the doorway of their home.

As Makarenko watched, standing in the hulking shadow of the BMP now parked in the center of the Syrian village, one of the Spetsnaz troopers seemed to lose his patience, turning for a moment and slamming the buttstock of his carbine square into the woman's chest.

She went down hard into the dust of the street, her husband wresting away from the commando holding him just in time to take a rifle butt to the face, the dull *thud* audible across the street.

The GRU lieutenant colonel shook his head, looking on helplessly—surely this wasn't what Kovpak had intended, at all. *It couldn't be.* They had encountered no resistance, sweeping into the town in force, backed by both elements of Kulik's QRF and a Syrian Army contingent assigned to the base, the latter throwing out a cordon to encircle the village as the Russians entered and began to rip people from their beds.

Another explosion resounded from somewhere deeper into the village, glass blowing out across the street—no resistance, but they *had* found more weapons caches, and Egorov was insistent on blowing them in place. *Make an example.*

More than one house had already caught fire, its flames fanned into hellish fury by the December wind.

His eyes narrowed as he saw another of Egorov's Spetsnaz emerge from the house, dragging after him a young teenage girl, his tactical-gloved fingers dug deep into her forearm. Stepping over the prostrate, gasping form of her mother in the street.

Makarenko heard the girl's wail of despair, heard and looked back and forth down the street—his eyes searching for Valeriy Egorov, scarce able to say whether he was hoping to find him or not.

Another explosion—followed by a sudden flurry of shots and distant orders barked in Russian from off toward the outskirts of the village, and when Makarenko looked back, the soldier and the girl had both disappeared, the darkness of a nearby alley beckoning to him.

He murmured an obscenity beneath his breath, letting the Kalashnikov hang from its sling across his chest as he plucked a tactical flashlight from his vest and pulled his MP443 Grach from its holster, moving toward the trash-littered alley.

It didn't take long to confirm he'd gone the right direction, the girl's sobbing cries becoming louder as the darkness closed around him, the echoing sound of an open hand meeting flesh. He hit the light's switch, a strobing light pulsing out into the darkness—illuminating the soldier down on the ground, on top of the girl, struggling to hold her down with one hand as he tugged at his belt buckle with the other.

"*Stoyat'!* Get off her!" Makarenko spat, bringing up the pistol even with the light—his fury boiling over in that moment. He had a daughter, a daughter he hadn't even seen yet, and this man... "You're a Russian soldier, not an animal—get off!"

He heard an angry curse, saw the commando straighten, fumbling with his belt. He thought the man was zipping himself back up, but then he saw a glint of steel in the light—*knife.*

The movement of his finger was instinctive, no thought—no *time* for thought, the Grach's double-action trigger breaking roughly as the sound of first one, then a second, gunshot hammered his eardrums, the pistol bucking back against his palm.

And he saw the knife drop, the soldier's eyes turning

glassy in the pulsing beam of the light. He took another faltering step toward Makarenko, a horrid gasping, choking sound coming from his throat. Then his legs seemed to give way and he followed the knife down into the dirt. . .

2:03 A.M.
The church in Quneitra
Quneitra Governorate, Syria

"They are going to kill you if they find out who you are," Abu Ahmed al-Golani observed softly, his hand trembling as he poured out the last few drops of the arak into the glass. He paused, seeming to consider it for a moment before reaching across the table for a half-empty bottle of tepid water and pouring in perhaps a quarter of what remained— the clear spirit reacting to the water, turning the white and cloudy color which had given it the nickname of "lion's milk" in Israel.

"They won't," Mohamed Taferi replied, pushing back the chair and rising to his feet, wishing that he felt half the conviction in his voice. There was no way to be that certain. No way for either of them—but he didn't need Al-Golani getting cold feet. Or worse, thinking of betraying him. "And you need to make sure they don't, Abu Ahmed—because I *will* take you down with me if I fall. I swear it by Allah."

He took his leave then, closing the door of the sacristy behind him and walking out through the nave of the church, stepping carefully among the wounded.

The burgeoning crescent moon and stars above shone down out of a cold, clear sky and Mohamed pulled his jacket closer about him, a chill running through his body. The border was out there, to the west, only a handful of kilometers past the outskirts of this ghost city, ruined so long ago by Israeli artillery and bombs. He could still run, but if he ran, he was certain he would die. Al-Refai's men would be watching for that.

He was equally certain he would be hearing from the Office in a few hours. But these dice. . .had already been cast.

Time to get some sleep.

2:13 A.M.
The Jaysh Khalid ibn Walid encampment
Two kilometers southeast of Quneitra, toward Al Qataniah

The weathered, dust-grimed Kia Cerato pulled to a stop outside the small cluster of buildings which JKIW had commandeered from another group of rebels two weeks prior—Al-Refai shoving open the door as his bodyguard and driver emerged from the front seats.

It might have been thought natural that his bodyguard would have opened his door, but Al-Refai believed clinging to the trappings of one's power was the surest way to attract attention, "like a British officer on the Western Front waving a sword," he had once told Anas ibn Nadhar. And attracting attention was, in its turn, the surest way to end up on the receiving end of an American Hellfire.

Like the previous JKIW commander, Abu Mohammad al-Maqdisi, not that many months before, or even the entire senior command structure of the Islamic State's *Wilayat Sayna*, which had perished in a drone strike in the north Sinai early the previous summer.

Ibn Nadhar scrambled out of the Cerato behind his leader, closing the car's door behind them, his finger catching on the jagged metal where a bullet had left its hole, a week prior, scarring the faded electric-blue paint.

"Reach out to Abu Tayem," Al-Refai said, zipping up his jacket against the cold as he turned back toward Ibn Nadhar, his face grave in the faint moonlight. "Tell him I've authorized you to take forty of his best fighters for a special operation, to depart tomorrow night. Then—"

"Sheikh, you honor me," Ibn Nadhar exclaimed, unable to help himself—stopping short as he saw the expression on al-Refai's countenance.

"I hadn't finished. Then contact Abu Khatab, have him reach out to our friends in State Security in Doha and make inquiries about this man, this. . .Mohammed bin Ammar."

Chapter 11

"He made his morning comms window," Nika Mengashe announced, knocking on the open door of David Shafron's office. "No distress codes were employed."

Proof of life. That was something at least. Even if he wasn't able to break free and call, Taferi sent at least one or more texts to his "family" in Qatar every morning and evening, the cellular number re-routed back here to headquarters. If he'd been compromised, it would be there in the text. If he was dead. . .

Then again, he wasn't calling it off.

"Good," Shafron replied simply. He'd spent the night at headquarters, crashed out on the couch in his office, after his meeting with Shoham and Refaeli ran into the wee hours, the *memuneh* finally expelling them both from his office to finish their argument in the elevator.

"We're taking a terrible risk here," Mengashe said, her brow furrowing as she stepped into his office. "He's out there alone, totally unsupported. And we're making the

133

same mistake with Barad and the crew of the *Tachash*. You know that, David, as well as I do."

"I know that with *Jaysh* involved we need to be even more concerned about staying clear of the fall-out. Taferi knows the score here—*has* known it, long before he ended up on the other side of that border." As he had known it in his own days in the field, the MEGIDDO department head reflected. His work with Caesarea's *Kidon* teams, every bit as deniable as any of this. And it never meant you stopped hoping for the cavalry to come when things got tight.

Sometimes he thought it had been easier out there, making the moment-by-moment, split-second decisions that could save an operation or doom it to failure—easier than sitting here, calmly and deliberatively making decisions which could consign men to their graves.

But someone had to make those decisions, every bit as much as the ones in the field. And for now, at least, that someone was him.

"But he isn't totally unsupported. He has us, and we're going to do everything in our power to give him what he needs. To bring him back, if we can do so without compromise." He closed the folder laying in front of him on his desk and handed it across to her, followed by two more. "I had Gal Levi send these over from the Syria Desk at Research. Mohammad al-Refai, the latest of *Jaysh Khalid ibn Walid*'s string of commanders. Abu Tayem, their military emir. Abu Khatab, the new security emir. Bring your team up to speed."

8:46 A.M. Syria Standard Time
Khmeimim Air Base
Latakia Governorate, Syria

"I killed him." Makarenko could still remember the shock and disbelief in Valeriy Egorov's eyes when he'd spoken the words—shock rapidly turning to smoldering fury.

It had taken the Spetsnaz nearly thirty minutes to come across the body of their comrade—the traumatized girl long since fled back within her ransacked house, clutching her torn pajamas tight to her body. *Safe once more*, at least for the time—if *anyone* could consider themselves safe here.

Egorov had ordered the village razed to the ground when he found out one of his commandos had been killed, an order even Kulik's men had balked at following, despite how many houses were already on fire.

And then Makarenko had stepped forward to make that brutally calm announcement, shocking everyone surrounding the command vehicle into silence.

Now, confined to quarters on Kovpak's orders, he sat upright in his chair, a military rigidity in his posture as he stared into the webcam, the videoconferencing software connecting him with Moscow—with his, no, make that *their*—superiors back at the Aquarium.

In the top right frame of the quadrisected window, his own boss, *Generál-mayór* Gennady Zheleznyak, the deputy chief of the Sixth Directorate—electronic intelligence—leaned forward into the camera, seeming to jar it as he did so, his glowering visage blurring for the briefest of moments.

On the top left, much to Makarenko's satisfaction, he could see *Polkóvnik* Vasily Yarovoy, the section head of

Third Direction, Second Directorate, in charge of directing the GRU's Spetsnaz deployments. *Egorov's boss.*

And in the bottom left, Egorov himself—sequestered somewhere else in the barracks, his face betraying that he knew the reality as well as Makarenko did. He and his boss were both outranked.

"And do you mean to tell me that you find this acceptable behavior on the part of your men, *tovarisch kapitán?*" Zheleznyak demanded, his eyes dark and shadowed as he reached up, adjusting the webcam. "The rape of a young girl? The. . .the. . .*sack* of a rural Syrian village? It is true enough that if not for our intervention, Bashar Assad's head would have ended up a football in the streets of Damascus—and he knows it. But that is *now*, there are no guarantees for the future, and we are talking about a part of the world with very long memories. My directorate's listening station at Khmeimim represents the restoration of capacity lost to the Russian Federation since the fall of the USSR, and it is a capacity we will *not* retain long-term without Syrian goodwill."

"The village was storing arms for the rebels, *tovarisch generál-mayór,*" Egorov put in quietly when the general finally stopped speaking. "We destroyed eight weapons caches. I know nothing of any rape."

"Then you acknowledge that you did not have your men under control?"

Egorov colored, clearly recognizing the trap he'd just walked into. Yarovoy remained quiet, as he had for much of the call, refusing to come to his defense. "I acknowledge nothing of the sort, *tovarisch generál-mayór.* I merely—"

"This has wasted quite enough of my time this morning.

Vasily, ensure that your people understand the GU's chain of command at Khmeimim runs through the Sixth Directorate. I want *Kapitán* Egorov's Spetsnaz kept on a tight leash, and that leash, for the duration of their deployment, will repose in the hands of *Tovarisch Podpolkóvnik* Makarenko, with any appeal to be directed to my office. I want no more of these incendiary incidents."

"Da, tovarisch generál-mayór," came Yarovoy's quiet, almost sullen response.

"Tovarisch generál-mayór," Egorov began once again, his voice rising in a protest, "the raid on the village was undertaken with authorization from *Generál-mayór* Kovpak. We acted with his—"

"However the army blunders about is their business, *tovarisch kapitán*," Zheleznyak replied icily, crushing the protest with all the casual disinterest of a man squashing a bug. "You answer to the GU. And Kovpak was not in Afghanistan. I was."

11:04 A.M. Arabian Standard Time
State Security Bureau
Doha, Qatar

The air-conditioning was running strong in the sixth-floor conference room of the Ministry of Interior building in the heart of Doha, but the back of Ibraheem Saleh al-Murrah's dress shirt was damp with sweat, clinging moistly to his skin beneath the suit jacket as the middle-aged bureaucrat played with his stylus, pretending to examine the notes on the touchscreen of his iPad as his department head carried on with the briefing, oblivious.

Or at least so he wanted to convince himself—he knew he had reacted upon hearing the name. Knew it had to have shown on his face, if only for a moment.

Mohammed bin Ammar, aka Mohammed ibn Mansour al-Amrah. A name he had never expected, in a thousand years, to hear come up in an office meeting. The name of a man he had. . .well, "created" sounded blasphemous, but it was hard to find another way to describe it.

He hadn't known he was working for the Israelis, not in the beginning at least. They'd approached him through cut-outs, offering money for his cooperation, not long after his wife had been passed over for an expected promotion at her job with Ahli Bank QSC, constricting a family income which had already found itself under strain, the two of them living at the edge of their means, for too long.

The Americans, he had told himself in the beginning—either because he'd believed it, or needed to in order to salve his conscience, he couldn't say which, looking back. And surely, passing information to the Americans wasn't so bad—they were an ally. In fact, he drove past the headquarters of their Central Command at Al Udeid twice a week on his way out to visit his aging parents. If his government could take billions from them, surely he could take a few thousand dollars here and there, just enough to keep himself afloat. *Savings*, he told his wife, when she'd expressed surprise.

By the time he'd begun to realize, from the assembled nature of the various intelligence requests—piecing together a mosaic like the analyst he'd been before working his way up into the low levels of management—that his masters far more likely resided in Tel Aviv, Israel than Langley, Virginia, he'd been in way too deep to back out.

And it had all remained quite innocuous, for a time. Until one day, more than a year before, when they'd asked him to slip a name into the personnel rosters of the Joint Special Forces. . .

2:30 P.M. Syria Standard Time
The church in Quneitra
Quneitra Governorate, Syria

Nassif grimaced, a jolt of pain stabbing through his shoulder as Abdul Latif loaded another box into his arms, adding to the stack he was already holding. "Go on," the big man said then, gesturing him out with a shoo-ing motion, "carry them out to the truck. *Yalla!*"

There had to be seven or eight of the rectangular cardboard boxes already loaded into the back of the rearmost truck, the boy thought, staggering out of the crumbling, concrete-block structure just across the street southeast of the church which served the rebels as a storage depot, the afternoon sun striking him full in the face—each of the boxes in the bed of the Nissan holding one of *Fursan Tahrir al-Sham*'s UAVs, almost all of them assembled from commercial kits and used for both aerial reconnaissance and attack, after someone had figured out how to modify them to drop hand grenades from the sky.

Mamdouh knelt not far from the truck, untangling belts of ammunition for his RPD, his single remaining eye darting quickly along the links, an inventive flurry of obscenities escaping his lips as he pulled and tugged fruitlessly.

If one listened, one could hear the sound of artillery off

to the northeast, way out beyond the city limits, but it was largely quiet today—or would have been, except for the sudden stream of orders emanating from Abu Ahmed.

A contingent of Abu Muin's men had left at dawn, carrying the body of their fallen tribal elder home for a rapid burial, in accordance with Islamic law, and Abu Ahmed had responded by immediately calling on volunteers from the dead man's remaining fighters—more than a few of them, like Mamdouh and Nassif themselves, drifters with no actual tribal affiliation to Abu Muin—to join him in what was only being described as a "special strike" against the enemy.

No details, except that the picked men would be gone the better part of a week, perhaps longer—farther down the street, they were already loading food and supplies into the backs of several military trucks. And the strike, whatever it was, apparently required the deployment of nearly their entire inventory of UAVs.

The Qatari was involved somehow, Nassif mused, setting the boxes down on the tailgate of the Nissan and reaching up to massage his slowly-healing shoulder—unable to truly determine what he thought of the outsider. He always seemed to be around Abu Ahmed, these days. A part of him resented the thought of an outsider coming in, meddling, helping direct a fight that wasn't his own. But he had to admit that his shoulder might well have become infected without—

He turned to go back inside for another load, coming to a sudden stop as he realized the object of his thoughts was standing directly across the street, near the corner of the church courtyard's half-demolished wall—the Qatari's eyes invisible behind the expensive Western sunglasses he typically wore.

He knew, Nassif felt with a sudden, unnaturally strong conviction, pausing only a moment before turning away. The stranger knew where they were going—and what they were intended to do when they got there.

Mohamed Taferi watched until the boy disappeared back inside, a quiet smile passing across his face. He liked the kid, though he still wasn't sure exactly why. There was a fragile resilience about him, a defiance lingering in the face of overwhelming loss. Perhaps as a Druze, it was impossible not to feel some empathy for the underdog.

He'd finally made contact with the Office a couple hours before—a brief, cryptic conversation with David Shafron which had ended with the MEGIDDO department head giving a grudging, cautious go-ahead, but only after Mohamed had delivered a terse, brutally honest assessment of his own chances of walking away at this juncture.

There were too many eyes on him now and pulling out would compromise everything. Not just this operation—the disclosure that an Israeli agent had been involved in funding *Fursan Tahrir al-Sham* would cause a ripple effect across the Southern Front, dominoes collapsing into each other as the militias tore each other apart in the kind of internal witch hunt which would make James Jesus Angleton's corpse turn green from envy.

Under other circumstances, that might have even been welcome—like FTS, more than a few of the Southern Front militias weren't exactly pro-Israeli, while lacking the outright extremism of JKIW. But with Tehran knocking at the door. . .

No, they—*he*—had to play this out, come what may.

They were too far committed now.

Going forward, there would be no more calls to Tel Aviv, no more conversations with David Shafron or the rest of the MEGIDDO support staff. Everything routed through Doha, to ensure operational security, his twice-daily texts back to "family" in Qatar serving as ongoing proof of life.

They'd maintain that up until the attack itself went live, when he'd establish encrypted radio comms on an as-needed basis with the Metsada support craft offshore, and—through them—with the American ISR platform providing overwatch.

A technical rumbled past toward the front, a couple of young fighters from the Lions of Sunna Brigade leaning against the cab, carrying on an unremitting conversation in rapid-fire Arabic. *More grist for the mill.* Soon to be ground to powder.

He saw the one-eyed man straighten, coiling long bandoliers of ammunition for the machine gun around his shoulders—sunlight glinting off the brass cartridges. Saw him look over, his one eye meeting Mohamed's for a long moment in a strangely unreadable gaze before the Israeli turned away, returning to the courtyard and the church.

Time to field-strip and clean his own weapons, make sure they were ready for action and the road. Make sure Abu Ahmed was sober and sticking to the plan.

A few more hours, and they'd find out whether the jihadists intended to hold up their end of the bargain.

5:09 P.M. Israel Standard Time
Mossad Headquarters, Glilot Junction
Tel Aviv-Yafo, Israel

It was already growing quieter in the headquarters building, many of the staff clearing up their desks to head home and join their families for the sixth night of Chanukah. The conference room door opened and shut, admitting Abram Sorkin, the click of its latch as it closed, seeming to resound in the stillness of the room.

Shafron's second-in-command paused, glancing about him at the solemn faces of the assembled MEGIDDO team. "What's going on?"

"Have a seat, Abram." David Shafron took a deep breath, weighing out his words. It had been *his* decision—his thoughts earlier, during his conversation with Nika, now returning to haunt him. Someone had had to make it.

But the problem with being the one sitting in this seat was that you could never have all the information you truly *needed* to make those decisions—not here, not in the field. You were just liable to end up with a higher body count, sitting here.

"An hour ago," he began heavily, avoiding Nika Mengashe's eyes as Sorkin took his seat at the table, "we heard from DROR."

He saw recognition flash across Sorkin's face and nodded. "DROR" was the codename for a senior Mossad intelligence officer working in Doha under non-official cover, running their Qatari networks under his legend as an American Arab businessman. Another of Mirit's people. He was also handling the physical aspects of that end of Taferi's comms set-up.

"Earlier today, he received an urgent message from AGUR—our man in the Security Bureau there in Doha." Recruited by DROR, albeit through a cut-out, the recruitment of the well-placed Qatari bureaucrat had been one of the biggest coups of DROR's placement in Doha, giving them a truly unique ability to monitor the Gulf state's involvement in Syria. And do. . .other things, too. "Someone is checking up on Taferi's legend."

Sorkin murmured an obscenity beneath his breath. "Will it hold?"

"We don't know," Nika Mengashe answered for him, before he could speak, the dour expression on her ebony face expressing her feelings more clearly than words. "AGUR was tasked with working him into the Joint Special Forces' personnel roster when Metsada first sent him across the border into Syria to liaise with the opposition groups last year. He altered the databases, giving Mohammed ibn Mansour al-Amrah—Taferi's Qatari legend—a complete enlistment history with their military on paper, but Qatari spec-ops is a very small community. If they're satisfied with the official record, we should be fine. If they start asking around, talking with people he should have served with. . ."

7:01 P.M. Syria Standard Time
The church in Quneitra
Quneitra Governorate, Syria

Night had fallen by the time *Jaysh Khalid ibn Walid*'s *mujahideen* showed up, rolling in heavy with four technicals, a pair of purloined Syrian army trucks, and a blacked-out fourth-generation Toyota 4Runner.

They were going to outnumber and outgun the patchwork force Abu Ahmed had been able to pull together, Mohamed Taferi realized grimly, walking out to greet them—the familiar figure of Anas ibn Nadhar emerging from the passenger seat of the 4Runner.

"Salaam alaikum," the jihadist greeted, reaching out to draw Mohamed into a close embrace, kissing him on both cheeks.

"Wa alaikum as-salaam," the Israeli intelligence officer replied, forcing a smile to his face as he returned the gesture, feeling the scraggly black hairs of Ibn Nadhar's beard against his lips, the smell of onions and garlic hot on the man's breath. "Welcome, brother."

"Is everything in readiness?" Ibn Nadhar asked, taking a step back and glancing around the courtyard in the darkness— nearly deserted except for the men bustling around the church itself, the vehicles lined up at the gate. Abu Ahmed had deliberately put every other available man out on the front lines, to reduce the number of spectators to their departure.

That left only a handful of guards, those tending the wounded in the church, and the couple dozen fighters Al-Golani had scrounged together for the expedition north.

"Insh'allah," Mohamed replied, smiling righteously. *As God wills.* "We only awaited your arrival."

"Then let us wait no longer, *akhi,*" the jihadist replied, his teeth showing from beneath the beard in what was no doubt intended to be a smile. *Brother.* "Let us go strike a blow in the struggle of God. *Allahu akbar!*"

The Israeli nodded, his own voice raised with the rest as the fighters in the vehicles behind Ibn Nadhar began to take up the cry. *"Allahu akbar! Allahu akbar!"*

Chapter 12

On a good day, with good roads, the drive from Quneitra to Khmeimim could be covered in just under six hours. Syria hadn't known any good days in a long while, and as for the roads. . .

Mohamed Taferi leaned back into the threadbare backseat of the old second-generation Kia Sportage, listening to the utility vehicle's worn shocks groan with every bump and dip in the uneven ground.

Wargaming it out with Abu Ahmed days earlier, the Israeli had estimated it would take four days—minimum— traveling only at night, avoiding main roads whenever possible, heading straight across the desert itself when, as now, it was necessary.

Night wouldn't provide any real cover from the Americans or the Russians—he knew that—but it would give them some margin against the dozens of other groups fighting along the civil war's amorphous, ever-shifting front, most of which, in the tradition of Arab armies since time immemorial, tended to avoid night fighting due to lack of training and equipment.

Outside his window, he could make out a JKIW gun truck keeping pace with them as they rolled north through the flat, barren desert, the black flag of jihad unfurled from its bed—the sinuous white lettering of its Arabic script against the dark field just visible in the faint moonlight, curling and uncurling, snapping in the wind. *There is no God but God. . .*

He glanced over to his left, making out the dark figure of Al-Golani across from him on the seat, the beads of the man's *tasbih* twisting relentlessly through his fingers as he stared out the window.

It was impossible to tell whether the opposition commander's lips were moving, whether he was reciting the hundred names of Allah beneath his breath, or whether the restless fingering of the beads was just nerves—most likely the latter.

Abu Ahmed had sought and received permission from his Southern Front superiors to move his contingent north, ostensibly to support another group engaged in heavy fighting with the Syrian Army itself around Beit Jinn.

But once they had passed beyond the Southern Front lines, they would be on their own. A bad place to be, in this war.

Having *Jaysh* with them could actually prove an asset, as they moved east into Ghouta, where their Islamist counterparts of *Jaysh al-Islam* and *Hayat Tahrir al-Sham* were as thick on the ground as the remnants of the Free Syrian Army—though there was as much infighting among the various Islamist factions on that front as any other—but then there were other groups in the same beleaguered pocket less sympathetic to their cause, and he hoped Ibn Nadhar's boys had the good sense to furl that black flag when they needed to.

Counting on the good sense of jihadists, Mohamed mused ironically—feeling the holstered pistol dig into his hip as he shifted position on the thin seat cushions—now that was betting against the house.

3:32 A.M. Israel Standard Time
The Shafron residence
Beit Shemesh
Jerusalem District, Israel

All was quiet in the house, the hum of the refrigerator the kitchen's loudest sound as David Shafron sat there alone at the table, drinking a cup of hot milk.

He'd arrived home well after midnight, looking in on both of his boys as they slept—marveling as so many times before at the *peace* on their faces, their innocence, so unspoiled by age and the world—before lying down beside his sleeping wife, staring up at the ceiling as the battle to go to sleep began.

He'd fought it out restlessly for the better part of two hours before hanging out the white flag, rising and coming out into the kitchen. For a brief moment, glancing wearily about him as he heated up the milk, he'd considered making *sachlev*—but there was something about the sweetness of the drink which repelled him this night.

"Taferi knows the score," he'd told Nika, standing in his

148

office not twenty-four hours before. Well, yes, and so had he—or thought he had. Thought he'd understood the burden even in Metsada, well before the stand-up of MEGIDDO. After leaving Caesarea's *Kidon* unit in the wake of the Iraq op—so long ago, it seemed now—he'd spent years training others like himself as Israel reeled from a ceaseless stream of suicide attacks and the Second Intifada roared to its fullest fury. Knowing that if he let his trainees down, if he failed to be at the top of his game—if he, as their teacher, somehow failed to give them what they needed—those young men and women wouldn't be coming back.

More than a few of them hadn't.

"David?" Shafron heard his wife ask, her voice still thick with sleep—looking up to see Rahel standing there in the doorway of the kitchen, a long housecoat wrapped around her body, her eyes bleary and unfocused.

"I woke you," he said, feeling a fresh rush of recrimination wash over him. "My restlessness, the light—*ani mitnatzel.*" I'm sorry.

Her job didn't benefit from lack of sleep any more than his did.

She shook her head, drawing out a chair and sitting down across from him, reaching out to cover his hand with hers. "David, what's wrong?"

He just looked at her, helpless to respond. There was so little he could share with her of his work, so little way to put it in terms she—anyone—could understand. They had both accepted that reality long ago, but it made it no easier to deal with.

"You wish it was still you, don't you?" she asked after a long moment, gently caressing the back of his hand with the tips of her fingers.

Her words took him off-guard, and he found himself once more struck by her perception. They'd met not long after he'd finally pulled himself away from the training officer billet, securing permission from his superiors to head up a small team liaising with Shin Bet in the territories, countering attempts by the Arab states to stoke the ongoing Intifada. Back out in the field, on that razor's edge. Doing what he did best.

He'd given it up, for the life he had now. For a home—a wife, two sons whom he loved more than life itself. Traded hell for paradise. *And yet.*

He didn't meet her eyes, a reluctant, painfully slow nod serving as answer to her question, and he heard her sigh heavily, her fingers entwining with his own and holding on tight. As if she expected him to slip away. . .

6:34 A.M. Syria Standard Time
Beit Jinn
Rif Dimashq Governorate, Syria

Looking out from the shell-damaged minaret of the mosque over the trees, the shallow belt of woods that girdled Beit Jinn on the east, south, and west, the Syrian Army seemed practically within spitting distance—tanks and infantry visible, moving into position a couple kilometers east of the town, out toward the prominent, rebel-controlled hilltop of Tal al-Ahmar.

Even as Mohamed Taferi watched them through the narrow lens of his monocular, he saw the burning trail of an anti-tank guided missile—a CIA-supplied TOW-2A or Konkurs, most likely—streak in from the south, exploding harmlessly ten meters from the nearest government tank.

Harmlessly, at least, as far as the tank's crew was concerned—as the dust cleared, he saw a Syrian infantryman dragging himself away from the impact zone, one of his legs seeming to trail limply behind him. Another pair of soldiers staggering out, limping, arms around each other's shoulders—until a sniper's bullet took one of them in the throat and they both collapsed helplessly together.

Hayat Tahrir al-Sham had retaken the hillside from pro-Assad forces not two days prior as the front descended into a maelstrom of heavy fighting and it was clear that the jihadists intended to make the government pay a blood price for taking it back.

Another missile lanced in just then, detonating against the hull armor of a ponderous Syrian Arab Army T-90 main battle tank, the resultant explosion so blinding that Mohamed looked away from the lens for a moment, blinking it away.

But when he got back on the glass, the armored monster was crawling inexorably out of the smoke, seemingly undamaged—its reactive armor apparently neutralizing the warhead.

"We'll lose the hill by nightfall," he heard Captain Musa Alwan announce from behind him, the dour observation followed by a curse from Abu Ahmed.

He tucked the monocular back in his pocket, turning to face the Rahman Legion officer, standing there in the twilit shadows alongside Al-Golani. Standing no more than 5' 4", and nearly twenty-five years Mohamed's senior, Alwan had the look of a man who had once carried a great deal of weight—and his body hadn't quite known what to do with itself once he no longer did, refusing obstinately to shrink back inward, the now-empty skin seeming to hang from his face in folds.

A beard might have helped, but most of the Rahman Legion officers avoided the heavy beards of their jihadist brethren, and the thick mustache adorning Alwan's upper lip did little for him.

"I want your men to move into position out to the west, alongside Abu Abbad's company," the Rahman Legion officer went on, glancing between Al-Golani and Taferi. The Legion took much of its own funding from Qatar, and he had been welcomed with open arms when they rolled in a couple hours before. "Rest your fighters, get something to eat—we'll be launching a counter-offensive toward Maghar al-Mir at noon."

A Druze village, Mohamed thought, glancing back to the north and west toward the slopes of Mount Hermon, the first rays of the dawn striking its snowy summit just visible through the scattered clouds, straddling the borders of Israel, Syria, and Lebanon.

This was home for him, for his people—though few remained, now, scattered by war. Some, on the other side.

There was no way to tell Captain Alwan that, whatever role they might play in reinforcing his afternoon offensive, they would be gone from his lines by nightfall, slipping out past the Syrian Arab Army lines in an effort to link up with *Ahrar al-Sham* fighters deeper in the East Ghouta pocket. With any luck, they might even make Harasta, a shattered, rebel-controlled suburb on the northeastern side of Damascus, by the next daybreak.

But in the meantime, they'd earn their keep.

"As for the jihadists who came with you. . ." the Rahman Legion captain let out a sigh, shaking his head wearily. "I'm not prepared to turn away any man with a rifle, at this point. But keep them on a short leash, as best you can."

Insh'allah.

6:39 A.M. Israel Standard Time
The Tachash
Five kilometers off the coast of Ashkelon

He heard them long before he could even make out the glistening white wake of the Zodiac's outboard against the dark-blue sea, the boat itself all but invisible in the early-morning twilight.

Water conducted sound like little else, Avigdor Barad thought grimly, a full-size Glock 17 riding in a holster on the sailor's hip as he stood at the *Tachash*'s wheel, the weapon covered by his loose shirt. Even the smallest noises—voices, even—had nearly unfathomable range.

It was the reason Reuven and Omri would cut the motor for the last leg of their trip in to the beach, minimizing their sound profile and their chances of detection.

As long as the moon didn't betray them, Barad reflected, glancing out of the small wheelhouse to mark the position of the growing orb as it descended toward the distant horizon. It would be even larger tomorrow night, and the night after that. . .

A pair of Kalashnikovs, an AKM and a Romanian-built Model 63, were stashed beneath oilcloths in the wheelhouse, rounding out the boat's armament.

A far cry from the *Tarshish*, or the big INS *Lahav*, one of the last Navy ships he had served on before leaving the service for Metsada.

The engine noise grew louder as the Zodiac came alongside, Barad stepping briefly from the wheelhouse to heave over the rope boarding ladder—recognizing the greasepaint-blackened faces of the men below.

Reuven Aharoni was the first up the ladder as Omri and Marc unshipped the outboard, preparing to deflate the Zodiac and bring it aboard. "Seventy-three minutes on the inbound leg," he reported, taking a drink from his canteen. "Outbound, it's gonna depend. We have to come out hot? Six-seven mikes."

Barad nodded as Reuven turned back to help the other men with the boat. They couldn't ask for much more, if it came to that. He hoped it wouldn't. . .

9:32 A.M.
Tel Aviv Station
The Embassy of the United States
Tel Aviv-Yafo, Israel

The truth was right there, in the high-resolution satellite imagery scattered across the surface of Paul Keifer's already-cluttered desk. Right there for anyone to see, if they chose to look.

And he would have rather not.

"They're gone," he announced finally—reluctantly—looking up to where Steve Bollinger, his deputy chief, stood in front of his desk, hands shoved into the pockets of his dress pants.

Bollinger grimaced. "So it would seem. That's our

second KH-13 overpass over Khmeimim not to pick up the Su-57s in their usual revetments."

"Is it possible that they were simply out on sorties both times?" Keifer demanded, reaching for the remnants of his half-eaten challa and popping the chocolate-smeared roll into his mouth. He had, improbably, put on weight since coming to Tel Aviv, despite his best efforts at the gym.

A shrug from his deputy chief. "Look, Paul, you know how this game goes. . .anything's possible. But it doesn't fit in with the pattern of life we'd established from earlier reconnaissance."

And that said it all. They both knew that. "Even after the mortar attacks," Bollinger went on, relentlessly, "we knew where they'd put them. Could verify they were still on-site. Not now."

"Okay, Steve, okay, I get it," Keifer said, the last bite of challa seeming to stick in his throat as he swallowed, wiping his mouth with the back of his hand. He had gambled so much personal capital on this operation, on convincing the Mossad to go through with it, despite the risks. And now. . .

"We need to tell the Israelis."

He shook his head. "Not yet. Give it another day, at least. Then, if their own surveillance hasn't already picked it up, we'll reach out to them."

He saw Bollinger's look of disapproval and leaned back, hands resting on both arms of his office chair. "Look, we don't know anything yet other than they haven't shown up on two sat windows. They were ferrying planes through Khmeimim to Libya yesterday—a pair of Flankers buzzed a Navy P-8 out in the Med, for God's sake—it may have messed with their normal air ops."

His deputy chief's expression told him that he was no more convinced by the argument than he was himself. But it was a straw to cling to. "Another day."

". . .so that's where we are with Dubai," Abram Sorkin announced, closing the folder in front of him. David Shafron nodded quietly, his mind still half on the night before as Sorkin finished his report. The Office's networks in the city had been largely scorched by the successful unmasking by local police of Metsada's Caesarea officers in 2011, following the assassination of Mahmoud al-Mabhouh.

It had been one of the most humiliating reverses in Mossad's long history of direct action and from what he understood, Mirit's resignation letter had gone to the desk of the Prime Minister before it was all over.

It hadn't been accepted, but there were long-term Mossad assets still rotting in Dubai prisons after the sweep which had followed. Which was, he had no doubt, inconvenient for the assets, but it had also left the Office blind.

Part of MEGIDDO's tasking had been to rebuild those networks from the ground up, without relying on the compromised architecture put in place previously—a task which was consuming a great deal of their time and resources.

"The Syrian Arab Army renewed its offensive in Western Ghouta this morning," Nika Mengashe said, the stress lines clearly visible on her face as she glanced Shafron's way, "pressing in around Beit Jinn from the north and east. Twitter accounts linked to *Hayat Tahrir al-Sham* and the Rahman Legion are blowing up, and we've begun assembling a rough order of battle for the government side. The 4th Armoured is there, we know, along with elements of the 7th Mechanized, various Druze militias, and embedded contingents from the al-Imam al-Hussein Brigades, including their so-called 'Death Battalion.'"

That had the potential to make life difficult, David Shafron thought, acknowledging her words with a nod. They weren't privy to the exact route *Fursan Tahrir al-Sham* had intended to take to Latakia, but it only made sense that they would hook around the east of Damascus, leapfrogging from one rebel pocket to another as they attempted to make their way through the hostile Syrian countryside.

And now one of those pockets was about to be extinguished. . .

2:09 P.M. Syria Standard Time
Beit Jinn
Rif Dimashq Governorate, Syria

Men spilled from the back of the army truck as a salvo of IRAMs came screaming in, shredding through the canopy of trees eighty meters to their rear, the Improvised Rocket-Assisted Munitions tearing apart trees and men below.

Mohamed Taferi lifted his gaze from where he lay, pressed flat against the ash-strewn earth, his hand gripping the stamped receiver of his Type 56, the metal cold even through his gloves. His ears ringing with the force of the explosion. *The screams.*

They seemed to rise out of the very earth, ghastly, otherworldly shrieks of fear and pain. There was no gallantry, no nobility in death—not here, not now, men turned to reeking piles of meat by shrapnel, whistling through the trees in every direction. And they were the lucky ones.

The Rahman Legion's counter-offensive had kicked off late, predictably for this part of the world, and immediately run into stiff opposition—artillery and rockets raining down on them before they'd made it even halfway to Maghar al-Mir.

They wouldn't be retaking it, not today—possibly not ever. Mohamed grimaced, pushing himself up on one elbow, bringing his weapon to bear as he scanned the remaining band of shattered woodland, catching the occasional muzzle flash out there beyond the trees, a random figure here and there, flitting from cover to cover. A machine gun opening up off to their left, raking the woods with long, extended bursts of fire.

He had warned Al-Golani to keep his men back, to avoid taking unnecessary risks, insofar as it was possible to do so without raising the suspicions of their hosts. None of that did much good when you were under bombardment.

A body stirred to his right, and he glanced over, realizing it was Nassif lying there in the shell-torn earth beneath the trees—the teenager's knuckles white around the receiver of his rifle.

His mouth was open, and his breath was coming fast and shallow, dark eyes darting back and forth. "Take heart, *habibi*," Mohamed said, placing a firm hand on the boy's shoulder. "Allah will be your strength."

"This was my village." He thought for a moment he hadn't heard the teenager aright, a ragged burst of fire coming from their left as a Rahman Legion NCO got a fire section in motion. *But that would mean. . .*

He reached out reflexively, like a striking snake, seizing the boy's wrist—Nassif's face turning suddenly toward him, startled eyes boring into his own. "Then," he began, "you too are one of the *Muwahhidun*." The people of monotheism. *The Druze.*

The boy just looked at him, uncertainty playing across his countenance for a long moment as machine-gun fire crackled across the front, bullets whining through the trees above their heads. Then, in a soft voice almost lost in the chaos, "Do they plant the seeds of *halalij* in your country?"

A smile. "*Na'am.* They are planted in the hearts of the believers."

He saw the hesitancy turn to surprise, a flurry of emotions roiling across the teenager's usually impassive face—opened his own mouth to offer some words of reassurance. Knowledge could be a dangerous thing in this place, and the Druze had always survived by keeping a low profile.

But then Abdul Latif was there, before he could speak, an AK clutched like a toy in the big man's hand. "Get up and move," he bellowed, kicking men to their feet when they hesitated. "Move, or by Allah, I will end your cowardice myself. *Yalla, yalla!*"

And another volley of rockets came shrieking in on their right.

3:23 P.M.
Khmeimim Air Base
Latakia Governorate, Syria

"'. . .with the Knights for the Freedom of Sham.' The next part, *tovarisch podpolkóvnik*, is unintelligible due to the poor quality of the audio," the young GRU SIGINT specialist said apologetically, glancing over at Andriy Makarenko, "but the speakers, both confirmed members of the Khalid ibn Walid Army, then clearly mention 'delivering a gift' to 'the Russians' and the base here at 'Khmeimim.' The language of the attackers is veiled, but we've seen all this before, sir. They're talking about an attack."

"Who are these 'Knights'?" Makarenko heard Valeriy Egorov demand, a derisive edge to the Spetsnaz captain's voice as he stood there in the listening station's SCIF, hands poised on his hips.

"Fursan Tahrir al-Sham, tovarisch kapitan," he replied, turning to look at the man. That he had only learned of their existence thirty minutes prior wasn't going to keep him from savoring this moment of superiority. "They're a Southern Front-aligned terrorist group in the Quneitra Governorate, along the Syria-Israel border. The Khalid ibn Walid Army is a Daesh-affiliated group from the same area."

"Quneitra?" The Spetsnaz captain looked incredulous. "That has to be. . .what, two hundred and fifty kilometers away?"

"Closer to three hundred." *And war-torn country, all of it,* Makarenko thought skeptically. Much of it now controlled, however loosely, by forces loyal to Bashar Assad.

"That's ridiculous," he heard Egorov pronounce, mirroring his own thoughts. *But was it?*

8:37 P.M.
Beit Jinn
Rif Dimashq Governorate, Syria

Tracers flickered out through the night to the south, a rebel machine gunner somewhere back toward Beit Jinn itself lashing the crest of Tal al-Ahmar with a fiery whip. They had lost the hill, as Captain Alwan had predicted, after a day of bloody fighting that had apparently come down to nearly hand-to-hand combat in *Hayat Tahrir al-Sham*'s fighting positions on the reverse slope, a suicide bomber charging a Syrian Arab Army T-72, shot dead more than fifteen meters from the tank—before he could trigger his explosives.

Mohamed Taferi hadn't seen much of it, his field of view narrowed by the trees and the smoke from burning buildings in Maghar al-Mir drifting across the battlefield. Their advance had stalled out on the very outskirts of the village, the first few compounds and sturdy stone houses of the region's characteristic black basalt acting as a tarpit—a deadly maelstrom of intersecting fields of fire stopping them cold.

There were bullet holes in his jacket that hadn't been there when he'd slept in it that morning, the Israeli thought grimly, stalking back through the mutilated trees toward their vehicles, moving past small knots of clustered men, more than a few sporting bandaged wounds.

Easily the heaviest fighting he'd personally taken part in, well. . .ever. Gaza as an IDF conscript in the waning days of the Second Intifada hadn't held a candle.

Back then, of course, he'd been on the side with the tanks.

He found Abu Ahmed where he'd expected to find him, leaning up against the side of the Kia Sportage, its door propped open, a stray bullet hole through the window, spider veins streaking through the glass in all directions.

He hadn't expected to glimpse a bottle in his hand as he came up, Al-Golani turning half away as if to conceal it—the guilt written ever so plainly on his face.

Mohamed swore, shaking his head in disbelief and anger. "Are you serious?" he demanded, moving in close enough to Abu Ahmed to smell the fruity odor of the arak on his breath. "You brought it *with* you? Do you *know* what Ibn Nadhar will do if he catches you with that? They'll flay the skin from your back."

"We're all going to die out there anyway," Al-Golani replied sullenly, refusing to meet his eyes, even as he tucked the bottle within a pocket of his jacket.

"Well, you can die," the Israeli intelligence officer snarled, "or you can die screaming. Your choice, but throw *that* away."

"Brothers," he heard a familiar voice hail from out of the darkness. *Anas ibn Nadhar.* He saw the sullen look vanish from Al-Golani's face, replaced by alarm—his hand reflexively patting the pocket where he'd secreted the arak.

A child could have taken Abu Ahmed to the cleaners playing poker, that much was clear, Mohamed thought wearily—turning to see the jihadist approaching the trucks, flanked by two of his men, both clad in a mix of civilian clothes and camouflage fatigues, rifles slung over their shoulders.

"Captain Alwan is on his way out from the town to take a look at the apostate government's lines," Ibn Nadhar said breathlessly, favoring Al-Golani with a curious glance before addressing himself to the Israeli. "He's supposed to spend most of the night out here."

Mohamed traded a glance with Abu Ahmed. They'd wanted to give it another few hours, to let the fighting settle, to relax the vigilance of the sentries the Rahman Legion—and the Syrian Arab Army, for that matter—would have thrown out. But now. . .

Anas ibn Nadhar spoke the words before Mohamed could utter them. "We need to be gone before he arrives."

Chapter 13

The night chill bit into Nassif's exposed cheeks as he sat in the back of the Toyota Hilux, one bare hand holding onto the bullet-scored metal side of the technical's bed for stability, the other wrapped around the receiver of his Yugo AK.

The bulk of the dual-mounted PKMs loomed above the heads of the huddled men in the darkness, a strangely comforting presence—every jolt of the vehicle transferring itself through the boy's body as they rolled northwest toward Damascus over broken roads.

The burnt-out hulk of a sedan littered the roadside as they rolled through a small rural village, the stark, blackened skeleton reminding Nassif somehow of a car his father had once owned. The buildings on either side of the road were desolate, abandoned, as if the war had passed through the countryside of rural Damascus like a giant broom, sweeping all before it. He wondered where they all were now. . .pressed into the teeming refugee camps of Jordan and Lebanon? Turkey? Escaped to the

West? He had a second cousin who had made it to Germany with his family, but that had been in the early days.

Or were they dead, like his parents and little sister. Like—like Talha, lying blown apart in some shell crater.

Mamdouh sat beside him, a blanket drawn over his broad, gaunt shoulders for warmth—that single eye glittering out from his destroyed face.

Across from him sat the, the. . .*Qatari*, the teenager thought, marking the foreigner's alert posture, his rifle clasped in both gloved hands. Except he *wasn't* a Qatari, he knew that now—what he *was*, less certain. They held each other's secrets now, and with them. . .each other's lives.

Nassif's eyes drifted back to the JKIW gun truck following in their wake, the gunner on the big *Dushka* in its bed just visible in the faint moonlight filtering through the clouds.

He knew little of his own faith—he only remembered his mother telling him over and again as a kid that *they*, and they alone, truly believed in the unity, the *oneness*, of God, no matter what their Muslim neighbors might have claimed.

That had made little to no sense to him at the time. He'd been taught the same creed, *There is no God but God*—but it didn't matter—he'd been born a Druze and that alone was enough to place him in mortal jeopardy with the *takfiris*.

But why was the man *here*, Nassif asked himself again—releasing a deep, shuddering breath, steaming out into the night. The object of his thoughts looked up then, as if he could feel the boy's eyes on him, his expression unreadable. No hostility. . .but precious little warmth, either. He knew his danger, as well as Nassif's own. He—

The truck ground to a halt then, the unexpected

deceleration taking Nassif off-balance and throwing him into Mamdouh, provoking an exasperated string of curses from the older fighter—the brake lights of the vehicle just ahead glowing red in the night, shouts ringing out. *A challenge.*

Mamdouh shoved him roughly to the bed of the truck, threw off the blanket and was on the PKMs in a heartbeat, the machine guns' twin muzzles training out over the Toyota's cab, his eye searching the darkness. The stranger vaulted over the side of the truck and stalked off toward the front of the convoy, rifle in hand.

Nassif pushed himself up by the truck's cab, watching until he had disappeared into the night—the teenager's hands wrapped around the receiver of his rifle, listening as the shouts continued. Listening and waiting.

Mohamed Taferi slipped off the safety of his Kalashnikov as he advanced, moving up past the Kia Sportage which served as Abu Ahmed's command vehicle toward the gun truck at the head of the column, making out the lights lancing through the night—men shouting.

They had been prepared to blow through Syrian Arab Army checkpoints if necessary, but aside from one Hizballah patrol just outside Maghar al-Mir which had gone down in a hail of bullets from a JKIW technical, the rest of the Shiite militants scrambling for cover, they had managed to elude detection, slipping around the lines inexorably wrapping themselves around Beit Jinn like fingers around a throat.

At one point, rolling across the desert with their lights out, they had made out a column of tanks off to the east, rolling south, hulking dark shapes against the night. The fall of the pocket was only a matter of time now, everyone they had left behind, doomed to annihilation.

Death waiting for them, forward or back.

"You're going to have to turn around," he heard someone say in Arabic as he came up, making out the muscular figure of a bearded fighter standing there before the lead truck, a flashlight in one hand and an M4 carbine in the other. More men spread out behind him in the scattered rubble of the half-destroyed building to the right of the road, rifles at the low ready. Darkened vehicles farther back, a checkpoint clearly.

"What's the problem?" he asked, coming up on the truck's dismounts, noting the concern, the tension written on the men's faces.

"It's the Rahman Legion," someone said. Well, that explained why the lead vehicle hadn't opened fire. They must have broken through, reached the next beleaguered enclave of opposition. *If they could gain admittance.*

"Are you in command here?" the man with the M4 asked then, playing his flashlight over the group, his question catching Mohamed off-guard. He didn't see Abu Ahmed anywhere, had no idea where he was. It was more than possible that he had polished off the rest of the arak and was crashed out drunk in the back of the Kia.

"La," he replied, shaking his head in the negative, looking around for support, and failing to find it. "We escaped the Beit Jinn pocket before it could be cut off—they took Tal al-Ahmar before nightfall."

"So we heard," the man replied with a dark scowl, spitting on the ground. "And now you've come here."

"That's right," Anas ibn Nadhar interjected, materializing

suddenly from the night, backed by two of his jihadis, not a smile to be found among the three of them. His appearance, somehow more unwelcome than Al-Golani's would have been, given the at-times adversarial relationship between the Legion and their more blatantly jihadist counterparts, but perhaps more effective, depending on the condition of the latter opposition commander. "The struggle of God continues, even if Beit Jinn falls. I have orders to continue the fight alongside *Jaish al-Islam's* forces holding Douma. Now please. . .stand aside."

7:21 P.M. Eastern Standard Time, December 18th
Quill at the Jefferson
Washington, D.C.

"Look, if we were talking about a leader US forces had worked directly with. . ." Jordan Sorbello's soft voice trailed off, as he spread his hands in a gesture that endeavored to communicate both sympathy and helplessness and succeeded at neither. "As it is, Olivia, and given the stance the POTUS has taken toward immigration from Muslim countries in general, and Syria in *particular*. . .I don't see how we can make this happen."

Olivia Voss lifted the small high ball glass, the taste of the rum sweet on her lips as she drained the last of her Nor'easter, smooth jazz from a tinny piano filtering through the lounge around them.

She hated smooth jazz.

"The POTUS," she began finally, setting the tumbler to one side as she folded her hands, staring directly into the eyes of the Deputy Assistant Secretary, Bureau of Population,

Refugees, and Migration—State Department, "has come, and one day he will go. And you and I, Jordan, will still be here, working together."

The comparative permanence of the civil service, ensuring some level of continuity, of sanity, in American government no matter how rocky the electoral landscape became.

These were the relationships that really mattered in this town and the man sitting across from her, nervously twisting the thin stem of the martini glass between his thick fingers, knew it.

"Look, what's your interest in this Abu Ahmed al-Golani anyway?" Sorbello countered, taking a furtive sip of his cocktail before trying another tack. "Most of our efforts have been focused up north, around Raqqa. I couldn't find any evidence that we've had dealings with him, and his group. . .you know what, that's not a question I want the answer to."

Olivia Voss allowed herself a quiet smile, her eyes never leaving Sorbello's face. The relationship between State and CIA, where she served as the Clandestine Service's deputy director, had always been contentious—despite, or perhaps because of, the reality that the majority of the Agency's overseas personnel operated under official cover with Foggy Bottom.

"Don't you all have your hands rather full just now?" he asked then, the question almost plaintive as he glanced back toward the television over the bar. She followed his gaze and grimaced—the ongoing hostage situation in the Philippines was once again headlining the news cycle, with the discovery of yet another of the hostages dead. And yes, they *did* have their hands full.

"We can walk and chew gum at the same time, Jordan. And our hands haven't been empty since 9/11."

She had herself joined the Agency just a couple years before the attacks, at a time when many had wondered aloud whether the intelligence community could find a new purpose absent the clearly defined great power competitions of the Cold War, in what politicians and pundits had taken to calling a "unipolar" world.

All that seemed quaint now, looking back, proving nothing so much as the reality that whatever else they were at Langley, they weren't prophets.

And here they were, in a world that had never looked much less unipolar, once again stealing sensitive tech from the Russians. Or trying to.

She had the feeling that Sorbello wouldn't have wanted to know that, either.

"Fair," he acknowledged, emptying the remainder of his cocktail and pushing the glass to one side. "I'll talk with some contacts at DHS, see what I can do. Look, all I'm saying is that given the competing equities, bringing this guy over is a really hard sell."

Voss favored him with her best smile, pushing back her chair and reaching for her coat as she rose, patting Sorbello on the shoulder. "If it were easy, Jordan, anyone could do it. . .and we wouldn't need you."

8:09 A.M. Syria Standard Time, December 19th
Douma, Eastern Ghouta—the suburbs of Damascus
Rif Dimashq Governorate, Syria

Getting in to the Ghouta pocket had been difficult—having required, at the last, rousting a sleepy but thankfully *not* visibly inebriated Abu Ahmed al-Golani from the back seat of the Kia to talk some measure of sense into the Rahman Legion non-com.

Getting *out* promised to be an order of magnitude more so, Mohamed Taferi reflected, turning his attention from Abu Ahmed's worried face to gaze out toward the horizon as armed *Jaish al-Islam* fighters hurried them toward a nearby alley, half-destroyed tower blocks still rising into the slate-gray winter sky, their blown-out, paneless windows hollow black squares, the barren, snow-dusted slopes of *Jabal Qāsiyūn* forming the backdrop, looming over the city.

He could remember having dinner up there once, with his parents, years before, at one of the many restaurants crowded with Western tourists which had once graced the mountain's summit—gazing down on the lights of Damascus, sparkling in the night like a galaxy of a million stars.

This had been a modern city, once. Now, it was rubble.

And there were government artillery pieces dug in on those slopes, where Western tourists had once dined.

He saw children playing in the rubble fields out toward the towers, a pair of boys chasing each other up and down the unstable, ruinous inclines, shouting and. . .laughing, inexplicably, in the midst of the wasteland.

There were still civilians here, as improbable as it seemed, some seventy thousand of them, imprisoned by the government's blockade of the city, by the rebel leaders' own refusal to let them leave. As long as they had the people, the desperate pretense that they were fighting for anyone beyond themselves could be sustained for a little while longer.

The once-glorious attempt to end the murderous oppression of the Assad regime, ending now—as revolutions tended to—in an oppression as immediate and cruel as anything Bashar Assad could have ever dreamed of, the horrors of a besieged city visiting themselves upon Ghouta in ways that wouldn't have been at all foreign to the inhabitants of Leningrad—or Jerusalem, two millennia prior.

And now it looked equally likely that they might not be allowed to leave either, their men and weapons pressed into the forlorn fight for the beleaguered enclave.

The bitter wind bit into his bearded cheeks as they ducked in between the buildings, picking their way over rubble and the detritus of war, the narrow alley seeming to function as a wind tunnel. Five *Jaish al-Islam* fighters served as their party's escort, two of them leading the way, another three bringing up the rear. Anas ibn Nadhar strode confidently ahead, flanked by a pair of his own bodyguards, with Mohamed and Abu Ahmed following behind, accompanied by Abdul Latif.

The Israeli's Kalashnikov was slung over his shoulder, the Glock 19 on his hip beneath the jacket—displaying his weapons openly, like any of the rest of them. You didn't simply walk around Ghouta without weapons, not if you expected to stay anywhere close to the top of the food chain, and no one had insisted on disarming them—*yet*.

Somewhere off in the distance, an artillery shell arced into the city, followed by another and another, a series of long, piercing whines borne to them upon the wind, followed by the distinctive muted *crumps* of explosions.

The resultant silence followed, minutes later, by sirens, as an ambulance from one of eastern Ghouta's few surviving hospitals responded to the shelling.

"How much farther is it?" he heard Ibn Nadhar demand anxiously, the wind nearly whipping away the Islamists' response. *Two more blocks.*

9:37 A.M.
The foothills of Jabal an-Nusayriyah
Latakia Governorate, Syria

The Russian BMP-2 crawled down the desolate village street, its diesel engine emitting a steady growl, the main gun turret trained forward, like a giant proboscis, sniffing danger—its commander standing upright in the hatch, exposed, his eyes scanning for threats.

Syrian soldiers loyal—one hoped—to the Assad regime patrolled nearly fifty meters out from the vehicles, spread out, weapons at the ready, inner security being provided by Kulik's infantrymen.

Andriy Makarenko leaned back into the seat of the GAZ Tigr military utility vehicle twenty meters back from the armored personnel carrier, his gloved right hand wrapped around the pistol grip of his Kalashnikov, the carbine's muzzle pointed down, between his feet.

This was routine—what the Americans in Iraq and Afghanistan had called a "presence patrol," a way of establishing oneself in occupied territory, making a show of force. It was a theory the American military had brought with it from the law enforcement sphere, and like many such Western ideas, had proven less analogous to armed conflict than its acolytes had hoped.

That wasn't the Russian way of war. But here in Latakia, in the ostensibly loyal Alawite heartland of the Assads, their hands were more tied than in other parts of the Syrian conflict, and after the first mortar attacks, Kulik had taken to these patrols as a way of showing the flag—demonstrating Russia's military might to anyone who might think to challenge it.

The more cynical among the lower ranks saw it as a way to get shot at—and they weren't wrong, such patrols had been fired on.

But so far today. . .Makarenko glanced out through the heavy glass of the vehicle's windscreen, searching in vain for any sign of life in the village which surrounded them, the only sounds those of vehicle engines and the typically obscene banter of on-the-edge infantry the world over, in both Russian and Arabic.

It was more difficult to show the flag if there was no one to show it to, though he felt reasonably certain that there were people shut up in those squat concrete-block and adobe compounds, behind the shuttered windows and closed doors.

Valeriy Egorov was quieter this morning than he had been three days prior, he thought, glancing into the back seat of the GAZ, when they'd shot up that mortar truck not four kilometers from here and dumped the bodies at another village, two kilometers to the southeast.

Now, chastened and smoldering after Zheleznyak's stern rebuke, the Spetsnaz captain sat in the back of the vehicle, seemingly absorbed in the terrain map on his comms tablet. It wasn't usual for either of them to be out here, on one of Kulik's patrols, but the signals intercepts the day before had left Makarenko on edge. An attack from so far away seemed improbable, but even so, if a concerted effort were made, would they be ready for it? What form would it take? Who would lend the attackers aid?

Glancing about him at the shuttered houses as the utility vehicle rolled slowly after the lumbering BMP, he suspected he knew the answer to at least that final question.

10:19 P.M. Israel Standard Time
The Tel Aviv Museum of Art
Tel Aviv-Yafo, Israel

He found the American standing in front of an orange mirror-polished stainless-steel sculpture which resembled nothing so much as, well. . .a balloon dog, like the one an entertainer had made for Aaron at a friend's birthday party, a couple years before. It had lasted maybe four days, long enough to be named "Rexie" and to break his son's heart when he developed a leak.

This one appeared to be made of sterner stuff.

"What do you suppose the purpose of this is, David?" Paul Keifer asked, not looking back, his eyes on the orange metal balloon dog. Beyond him, an Asian woman slipped into one of the diagonal corridors beyond the exhibit. A tourist, or perhaps a member of Keifer's security team. "In a museum, I mean. Is it a commentary on life? On fate?"

David Shafron shook his head. The artist was an American, so Keifer presumably knew as much as he did. "Sometimes a balloon dog is just a balloon dog, whether of latex or steel. How long have you known, Paul?"

The CIA chief of station drew in a heavy breath through his nose, the sound telling Shafron everything he needed to know. His face tightened, an unspoken curse rising to his lips.

Never trust the Americans—one of the oldest watchwords of their business.

"This isn't a *game*, Paul," he spat, when the American hesitated a moment longer.

"Yesterday," Keifer replied then, still refusing to look at him. The hesitancy telling him that, too, was almost certainly a lie. Their own TecSAR bird had sent back imagery in its pass the previous night, indicating the absence of the Russian fighters quite clearly.

There were a lot of planes on the ground, some of them quite clearly in the process of being repainted, likely en route to the Wagner Group in Libya, but the new Sukhois were nowhere to be found.

"Yesterday, Paul, I could have still sent in a team," Shafron snarled, anger bleeding into his voice as he glared at his American counterpart, "extracted my people from this operation. Today, I can't."

"We didn't *know*, not for sure, we thought maybe they'd been moved—were out on a sortie during our satellite overpass."

It was a palpably weak excuse, given the persistence of American surveillance off the coast, but Shafron suppressed the obscenity which sprang to his lips with an effort.

"Your people—where are they now?"

"Damascus."

10:58 A.M. Syria Standard Time
Douma, Eastern Ghouta—the suburbs of Damascus
Rif Dimashq Governorate, Syria

"We understand, though," Anas ibn Nadhar said, a rare, ingratiating smile spreading itself across the jihadist's face, "that you have tunnels by which you can still smuggle fighters and supplies in and out of the city."

"*Insh'allah.* Suppose we do," Mohsen Abdul Aziz al-Shaykh, the *Jaish al-Islam* sector commander known popularly among the opposition as "Abu Firas," conceded grudgingly, glancing at his deputies, "what concern is it of yours?"

"None," Ibn Nadhar replied, his smile seeming to irritate Abu Firas almost as much as it did Mohamed. "But if you can bring supplies in, we should be able to get out—to be on our way north, to Idlib."

They'd had that talk before leaving Beit Jinn—Idlib was now their purported destination, a goal of linking up with the jihadist remnants in the north serving as veil for their genuine objectives at Khmeimim.

"Why?" was the flat response. Ibn Nadhar was becoming more of a liability by the moment, Mohamed feared, the empty holster on his hip feeling conspicuously light. They'd all finally been disarmed before ascending the five flights of rubble-littered stairs to Abu Firas' headquarters in the middle of the crumbling tower block.

The JKIW lieutenant had nearly gotten them shot, name-dropping *Jaish al-Islam* leaders at the Rahman Legion checkpoint the previous night—the two factions having gone to war with each other here in Ghouta not eight months prior, tearing the enclave apart even as government forces closed in—and now even here, among his own, his help was proving anything but.

"If those tunnels are discovered," Abu Firas went on in that same emotionless monotone, his left hand idly playing with the graying fringes of his long beard, "if they are closed and the apostate regime succeeds in cutting off our supplies,

Ghouta will fall. Why should I run such a risk for strangers? For men who won't even stay and lend their arms to our defense?"

"The will of God is not to be—" Ibn Nadhar began, but Abu Firas cut him off, indicating quite clearly that the only will which mattered in this room was his own.

"*Khalaas!* Abu Zuhair will show you out," he said brusquely, gesturing to one of the younger men who stood by the door, "and give you back your weapons. If you choose to stay and fight, ammunition and food are both available, if you have the money to pay for them. If you still choose, though, to leave Ghouta, you are welcome to do so the way you came—on your own. Your trucks and heavy weapons, though, will stay here in Douma, to be used, by better men, in the defense you've spurned."

Mohamed heard Abdul Latif curse, saw Ibn Nadhar color in anger beneath the beard, Abu Ahmed stepping forward to offer a protest of his own, but Abu Firas cut them all off with a wave of a hand that indicated more clearly than words—this meeting was *over.*

The younger deputy led them back out, the *Jaish al-Islam* sector commander's bodyguards shepherding them out with their carbines at the ready.

Wind whistled down the corridor as they made their way to the nearest stairs, a desolate, howling sound—the north face of the abandoned apartment tower half-destroyed by artillery fire, daylight visible through the shattered door of a stripped apartment, the draft cold enough to take one's breath away.

He saw firewood stacked haphazardly in one of the open apartments, a few neatly split chunks of wood mixed in with bedframes and dressers clearly taken apart with an axe. Anything to stay warm, as the siege entered yet another long winter—the poor quality of the kindling bearing stark testament to how difficult it was for even a man of Abu Firas' stature to supply his own most basic needs.

Their weapons were, God be praised, waiting for them on the ground floor, a stone-faced young jihadist handing Mohamed back his Kalashnikov and Glock.

He shoved the pistol back into its holster beneath his jacket, lifting the rifle and depressing the mag release, hefting the steel mag as it fell into his hand. *As he'd suspected.*

The weight was off—the magazine more than half-empty. He let out a heavy sigh, meeting the young man's gaze. "The rest of the ammunition, *min fadlak.* And the knife." *Please.*

"I don't know what you're talking about," the man replied, meeting Mohamed's unblinking gaze, bold as brass.

Abu Zuhair cuffed the younger man across the ear with the back of his hand, cursing him in Arabic. "Give the man what he wants—you know the penalty Allah has ordained for thieves, don't you?"

The man shoved a reluctant hand into his ruck and came back out with a fistful of cartridges, dumping them into Mohamed's outstretched palm, a mix of 7.62x39 and 9mm, demonstrating that the Glock's mag had been pilfered too.

"The knife," he repeated with icy calm, holding the man's gaze until he produced the small folder, handing it over grudgingly.

"Shukran," Mohamed smiled, inclining his head to Abu Zuhair before tucking the knife into the inner pocket of his jacket. The rest of the party beginning to check their own weapons.

"Maa fi mushkil," the jihadist replied genially. *No problem.*

He glanced over Mohamed's shoulder, seeming to wait until everyone else was absorbed in recovering their stolen ammunition before stepping in to slip a small cellphone into the pocket of the Israeli's jacket, patting him familiarly on the shoulder.

"I can help. . .call me."

Chapter 14

". . .and we've had eyes on for the last five hours. People have come and gone, including one large group which finally departed not long after 1100 hours local, 0900 Zulu. But no known targets identified, and no sign of the primary."

The last words came out in a weary sigh as the UAV pilot with the captain's bars on the collar of his uniform blouse reached up, kneading his forehead with his fingers.

"I got this, Marc," Captain Cole Haskins said, clapping his old friend on the shoulder and squeezing it affectionately as he moved past him to take his seat at the controls of the Reaper UAV. "Go home and give Samantha a hug—get some sleep. The target deck won't go anywhere while you're gone."

That observation brought an ironic obscenity to his fellow officer's lips as he turned to leave, a blast of raw air buffeting Haskins as the door of the trailer opened and closed. No, the target deck never went anywhere. . .more names added to it faster than they could ever be knocked off.

A look of regret passed across Haskins' face as the door closed on the captain and he picked up the headphones, exchanging a curt nod with his sensor operator, a tall black sergeant from Baton Rouge named Joe Villemont. "I have the bird."

He'd known Marc Fuentes for a couple years, since he'd first transferred into Creech, and the last six months, it felt like he was watching the man come apart before his eyes, the stress of this job eating away at him.

Haskins didn't know what had precipitated the decline, and it would have been as much as Fuentes' clearance was worth to have discussed the details with anyone who hadn't been read-in on the specific mission, but rumor around Creech said the younger captain had been on the watch during the infamous, much-publicized strike in the Sinai back over the summer.

The one that had blown up in the faces of everyone from the POTUS all the way down to General Lowenthal, the Air Force brigadier who oversaw UAV operations at Creech, when it came out in the media that civilian casualties had been heavy, while the main target of the strike was revealed to have survived unscathed.

That was a lot to weigh on any man's conscience, and if Marc had been the trigger-puller, well. . .it didn't matter how reasonably you could shift responsibility, point to the chain of the command, the intel—it was still a burden you took home with *you* every night. And it got no lighter, he found, over the years. He'd have recommended Fuentes see a therapist, but he knew from his own experience how little good most of them did, and it was a bad thing to have in one's file. For all the lip-service paid to mental health by the brass, the military wasn't that progressive, not yet.

He scanned the array of screens in front of him to orient himself, each of them displaying the view from another of the MQ-9's cameras—"flying" a UAV was so different than a plane that it took constant readjustment for someone who had come up in the old Air Force, as Haskins had.

The Reaper was flying unfamiliar skies this morning, orbiting the Syrian rebel enclave of East Ghouta at fifty thousand feet ASL—its cameras aimed down at the wasteland of destruction below.

He'd run endless support missions for the final push on Raqqa, and even so, the scope of the devastation here took Haskins off-guard. It was as though someone—a giant, or perhaps a god, had reached down and simply *flattened* the city with a single blow from a clenched fist, leaving destruction everywhere one chose to look.

And yet still the rebels fought on. It was impossible not to admire that level of determination, and yet. . .there was a reason they were braving the danger of Syrian or even Russian anti-aircraft defenses around the capital of Damascus itself to fly this mission.

Mohsen Abdul Aziz "Abu Firas" al-Shaykh. He glanced at the image on the screen of the laptop propped up beside his flight controls, marking the visage of an unsmiling middle-aged man with a long, heavy beard which extended down out of frame, and was sprinkled with far more salt than pepper.

He didn't know what he had done to end up in their target deck, how he differed from any one of a hundred ragheads running around Syria, wreaking havoc on their own war-torn country. Perhaps someone up there had just flipped a coin. *Your lucky day, pal.*

Haskins leaned back in his chair, retrieving his Starbucks as he eyed the monitors. It was getting dark over there, the sun visibly declining on the western horizon out beyond the Reaper's cameras as the great ungainly bird continued to circle, on autopilot.

They'd stay on-station regardless—for the next twelve hours—but the darkness would make visual PID difficult.

Come on, he thought, reaching forward to tap al-Shaykh's image on the screen of the laptop. *Come on out and play. . .*

4:36 P.M.
Douma, Eastern Ghouta—the suburbs of Damascus
Rif Dimashq Governorate, Syria

The truck slowed to negotiate its way around the fresh-fallen rubble of a half-collapsed building, the heavily bearded driver cursing vociferously in Arabic as a scrawny teenager pushing a wheelbarrow took advantage of the lull to cross the street in front of him, a desperately thin shadow wavering in the vehicle lights.

Mohamed Taferi leaned back into the seat, wincing as a spring poked through the threadbare cushion, gouging insistently at his back. His gloved right hand was on the foregrip of his Type 56, holding it upright at his side as the truck lurched into motion once again—the muffled *crump* of artillery fire echoing through the night off to the north.

He'd called the single number listed on the phone's SIM within two hours of their abortive meeting with Abu Firas, reaching, as he'd expected, a singularly cryptic Abu Zuhair.

"There will be a truck to pick you up, Mohammed bin Ammar, in a few hours. Go with the driver—you, and only you. I can help your friends, but this is not something we should discuss over the phone. Trust me."

Trust. Mohamed snorted at the memory, drawing a look of incomprehension from his driver. There was no question of trust, not here, not now—not with the likes of Abu Zuhair. But their options were growing fewer by the hour, their position increasingly untenable, so he'd ultimately agreed to the jihadist's conditions.

He had no intention of staying on to die in this pocket when it fell, whatever else came. If Death was to come for him here, might as well get it over with.

5:03 P.M. Israel Standard Time
Mossad Headquarters, Glilot Junction
Tel Aviv-Yafo, Israel

"I hope you're satisfied with yourself."

The look on Mirit Refaeli's face indicated quite clearly that she hoped for nothing of the sort, but the *memuneh* cut in before David Shafron could formulate an appropriate response.

"The decision to proceed with the Syria op was mine, Mirit, not David's," Avi ben Shoham said heavily, a warning light in his dark eyes as he glanced between his subordinates. "The risks inherent in an operation of this nature were weighed against the potential for success—what that would *mean*—and were deemed justifiable."

"Until the Americans pulled the rug out from under you, as they do."

It was very hard to disagree with her there. Whatever the political landscape in the United States looked like at any given moment—and, riding to victory on the enthusiastic coattails of America's evangelical community, her current POTUS had claimed to be the finest friend Israel could have ever asked for—the relationship between Mossad and their counterparts at Langley was ever tenuous, with the Americans' insisting on the driver's seat in almost any partnership—and driving from the backseat when they didn't.

"Give me another forty-eight hours, Avi," Shafron said, studiously ignoring Mirit as he focused his attention on his boss. "Let things play out, at least that much longer. It would take us more than that long to lay on an exfiltration from eastern Ghouta anyway."

"What did you have in mind, David?" Avi ben Shoham asked, before Mirit could interrupt, the former general's hands tented on the desk before him.

"We need a look at the adversary's cards. I had a chat with Mordechai, earlier, on the secure line." Mordechai Eichler was the Mossad's Chief of Station in Moscow, an old Russia hand who had been working the beat of the old USSR since the Wild West days of the '90s.

"And?"

"And the secure line wasn't secure enough," Shafron replied evenly. "I'll be flying out of Ben Gurion in a few hours for Helsinki, by way of Warsaw. Mordechai will meet me there."

"It sounds as though you have it all arranged. And in the meantime, Taferi will be told. . .what?" Mirit demanded, leaning back into the cushions of the sofa across from him, arms folded deliberately across her chest. "Anything? Anything at all?"

"Mohamed Taferi will be apprised of everything that is necessary for him to know," Shafron replied coolly, "which, at the moment, is, in fact, nothing. He's not alone in eastern Ghouta—he has an objective, and allies who have signed on to help accomplish it. If he wavers, if he shows hesitancy, his fellow travelers will begin questioning his real purpose in all of this. The moment they do that, Mirit, he's dead. And there'll be no getting back so much as a body."

5:07 P.M. Syria Standard Time
Douma, Eastern Ghouta—the suburbs of Damascus
Rif Dimashq Governorate, Syria

The tower block loomed ahead of them in the inconstant moonlight, a forbidding monolith—the beam of the driver's flashlight playing across scattered rubble as he took point, leading the way through the detritus of crushed buildings.

A sudden noise, the abrasive, creaking rasp of metal on metal and Mohamed flicked his own light off to the side, searching for the source of the disturbance, the muzzle of his Glock coming up to cover the light.

The wide eyes of a young Syrian boy, no more than perhaps nine or ten, stared back at him—the metallic creaking coming from a manual water pump atop a well sunk there amidst the ruins, no doubt the donation of some aid organization. The boy was just barely tall enough to reach its long, sweeping metal handle at its highest extension, but water gushed out every time he pulled it down, flooding into a bucket almost as big as he was that he'd placed beneath the spigot.

As Mohamed watched, the boy dropped the handle and grabbed up his bucket—darting laboriously off with it into the night, water sloshing at his heels.

"Come on," his driver said, adding a few curses for emphasis when he looked back to find that he had stopped. *"Yalla!"*

Terror, the Israeli intelligence officer thought, switching off his light as he fell in once more behind his jihadi escort. That's what had been written in those dark, hunted eyes, old far beyond their years. The kind of fear that was less a momentary alarm, and more a state of being, for a child likely not old enough to remember anything but a world at war.

The approach to the tower block led through a narrow alley, electrical wires hanging uselessly in gnarled, tangled bundles above their heads, appearing like some sort of ghastly spider's web in the pale moonlight.

Up close, it looked as though this tower had taken even more direct damage than the one in which they'd met Abu Firas, one entire corner of the block torn apart and crumbling into what had once been the street below, and it was straight up that cascading slope of rubble that his escort led the way, the broken scree shifting uneasily beneath their feet as they climbed. The steady pounding of artillery off in the distance providing an ominous backbeat, their shells falling to the north and west, explosions briefly flaring in the night.

A voice called out a challenge as they reached what had been the third floor, a figure carrying a rifle emerging from the shadows of a half-destroyed apartment as Mohamed's escort answered.

"Abu Zuhair is waiting for you," the young fighter told him, extending a hand for his rifle. Mohamed unslung it from his shoulder, handing it over with palpable reluctance, even as another salvo of artillery thundered forth from the slopes of *Jabal Qāsiyūn*. "Go on in."

5:14 P.M.
Elsewhere in Douma

"They brought us here to die." The large head of pale cabbage in Mamdouh's hands seemed to almost glow in the moonlight as they hurried down the street, the one-eyed man in the lead, rifle slung over his shoulder, his head swiveling from side to side as explosions sounded off in the distance.

Vegetables had been few and far between, but they'd managed to get some coarse barley bread from a dealer camped out in a half-destroyed building about three kilometers from their own bivouac, along with half a dozen eggs, paying more than fifteen thousand *lira* for the food.

Nassif hurried to keep up, clutching a liter of fuel in his left hand, and the bread in his right. The fuel had cost them another thirty-six hundred *lira*, and it wasn't even real gasoline—just plastic, melted down.

"What are you talking about?" It wasn't so much that he disputed the man's premise—that they *were* going to die seemed foreordained, walking the streets of this devastated city—but the note of paranoia in Mamdouh's voice was impossible to miss.

The one-eyed man turned on heel, his voice descending to a low hiss as he looked Nassif in the eye. "We've been sold out to the *takfiris* by Abu Ahmed and all the rest, your Qatari 'friend'—brought here to fight their jihad for them. And if we stay, if we don't find a way to slip off. . .this is where we will die."

5:16 P.M.
The tower block

"This is some kind of trap." An icy draft seemed to sweep through the room at that moment, bellying out the dark tarpaulins which covered the tower apartment's long-shattered windows for a brief moment before snapping them back against the concrete with a loud *pop* which served to punctuate Mohamed Taferi's words.

"La, la," Abu Zuhair protested, shaking his head earnestly. "I swear it by Allah."

An oath which almost certainly meant nothing, as they both knew. "And by the life of my mother," the jihadist added, inclining his head back toward the old woman, swathed in black from head to foot, just disappearing into the next room.

"She's not your mother," Mohamed replied coldly, taking a sip of the hot tea the woman had poured for them only a few moments before, using up precious fuel to heat the water.

Abu Zuhair laughed at that, a genial smile breaking apart the black beard. "You are right, *akhi*. My mother is nowhere near this city of the damned, Allah be praised. I sent her from the country many years ago—to safety, with family in the West."

"Alhamdullilah," Mohamed replied ironically, the vision

of the boy at the well still haunting him. Men like Abu Zuhair had sent their own families away, while imprisoning so many thousands of others. . .for *what*, save their own desperate sense of legitimacy? Once they might have been accused of sheltering behind civilians, using the innocent as human shields, but neither Russia nor the Assad regime demonstrated any sign of caring who was beneath their falling bombs or shells, as attested by the pounding artillery fire in the distance.

"I understand your skepticism, my friend," Abu Zuhair said then, his face lit by the glow of the electric lantern on the table between them as he leaned forward, hands clasped before him. "But what I have heard of you. . .your background in the Special Forces in Qatar, the aid you've provided to the opposition here in *Sham*, all convinces me that if anyone can kill Mohsen Abdul Aziz al-Shaykh, it's you."

"Perhaps," Mohamed replied noncommittally, "but why should I?"

"Isn't it obvious? Because he stands in your way—and mine. Remove him, and I will clear the way for you and your friends to leave the city for Idlib. . .or wherever you intend to go."

What did he know? The Druze officer thought, his eyes narrowing at the insinuation in Abu Zuhair's words, another icy draft sweeping into the room and seeming to cut through his coat like a knife. This was dangerous ground.

"And what's to prevent you from turning on us, once he is dead? The oath you swore on the life of your mother, safely removed to the West?"

A smile. "Very little, my friend. Very little indeed, but

your options, in truth, are so very limited. Or you would never have come to me at all."

He had never liked the man less than in that moment, a terrible coldness in that smile. But he was right.

"If I were to accept this proposition," he said cautiously, his eyes never leaving Abu Zuhair's face, "could you get me in close enough to do it?"

"As a member of Abu Firas' trusted inner circle," Abu Zuhair smiled, "I can get you in anywhere you. . ."

A low roar struck Mohamed's ears in that moment, building out of the north—the jihadist's face changing and his voice trailing off as he heard it, too. A shout of warning from the young guard without.

"Russian bombers," Abu Zuhair hissed, grabbing for the lantern and plunging the room into darkness. "We must get to the basement."

Chapter 15

7:42 A.M., Central European Standard Time, December 20th
Warsaw Chopin Airport
Włochy District, Warsaw
Poland

". . .passengers, we would like to remind you not to leave bags unattended. Please report any suspicious bags to the airport security service. . ."

A little boy not much older than his own Shmuel rode up the elevator just ahead, the white pom-pom on his Santa hat bouncing relentlessly about his shoulders as he chattered away, tugging at his mother's hand. His own boys would be in school, David Shafron thought, smiling at the sight—his wife, off to work at the Ministry of Justice. Everything in life, proceeding as normal, despite his own absence.

The way life did, as he had learned so long ago. *With you or without you.*

The name on the passport in his pocket identified him as Mark Bernstein, a Canadian citizen and resident of Montreal, a businessman in the IT sector who had flown into Tel Aviv only a week before and would be meeting with counterparts in Helsinki before returning to Canada by way of Belgium. That was the legend, as he had memorized it in the hurried hours before his departure—all the small personal details, including his second cousin, David, who was the cantor at a Montreal synagogue.

A Christmas tree towered toward the ceiling, shimmering with lights as he reached the top of the escalator, taking a sip from the coffee he'd just secured from the Costa Coffee on the first level. The signs of the Christian holiday, everywhere he looked—balls of sparkling light hanging from the ceiling all across the terminal. And the little boy with the Santa hat was not alone—it seemed as though every child in sight had one on, along with a handful of the adults.

The Turkish Airways flight out of Ben Gurion had taken the better part of five hours, and he'd spent most of it asleep—except when they'd run into a patch of rough weather over Romania. That disturbance had killed any further thoughts of sleep—he'd once managed to sleep soundly amid the cacophony of an IAF Hercules en route to a combat jump, but he'd been a much younger man then. With, he supposed, a much clearer conscience.

The Israeli fell in with a pair of young college women pulling rolling luggage cases, keeping pace behind them as they crossed the upper level. Off to one side, a sign in English reading "Heritage Highlights" admonished him to "discover Poland's 'Monuments of History'," and Shafron wondered darkly if those monuments included Auschwitz and Treblinka.

His own mother had been born in *Eretz Yisrael*, in 1947, but her parents had been survivors of the camps—turned in to the Nazi occupiers by their Polish neighbors. He knew, intellectually, that that hadn't been true for all—that some Poles had, in fact, risked their lives to hide the Jews, but it didn't change the betrayal his own grandparents had known. And with the dark turn that Polish politics had been taking in recent years, along with those of much of the rest of Europe. . .well, Europe had always been a place more interested in self-absolution than atonement, the darker evils of its history to be swept under the rug at the earliest possible moment.

He had another hour to kill before boarding his FinnAir flight for Helsinki, and then, in a few more hours, he'd have an answer—or the beginnings of one.

9:03 A.M. Syria Standard Time
Douma, Eastern Ghouta—the suburbs of Damascus
Rif Dimashq Governorate, Syria

Dust from the previous night's bombardment still hung in the air, half-obscuring the sun as Mohamed Taferi stalked down the street, ducking into a small shop set up in the alcove of a half-destroyed office building, metal shelves covered with everything from scavenged tools to auto parts to food and fuel. A bin in the corner stuffed with wood, the chopped-up remains of furniture, now being sold to feed the cooking fires of Ghouta's starving.

The contents of the shop would have been of scanty value, under any normal circumstances, but Mohamed could feel the eyes of the proprietor—a gaunt, grey-bearded man in a black knit cap and threadbare jacket—following him around the room as he browsed, the man's rifle, an old bolt-action of indeterminate make and model, only too prominently displayed at his side.

He'd barely slept, his eyes bloodshot and gritty with dust—the Russian bombers had passed them by, to strike targets deeper in the city to the south and east, but they'd spent the better part of three hours hunkered down in the crude bomb shelter of the tower block's basement, all the same—huddled in the dark along with several dozen civilians and a handful of Abu Zuhair's fighters. Mothers ineffectually hushing frightened children, men alternately cursing the darkness and crying out to God, tension crackling through the confined space.

He'd never been a man given to claustrophobia, but it had gotten to him, down there—feeling the vibration through the concrete as bombs fell to the earth kilometers distant. The civilian beside him had kept twisting the beads of his *tasbih* through bony, aged fingers, repeating the hundred names of God over and over again all through the night in high-pitched, whining Arabic until Mohamed had been sorely tempted to slap them from his hands and shake him until he shut up and gave them a moment's peace.

God would have understood, of that he was sure. As He would surely understand what he was to do this day. He'd told Abu Zuhair *"yes,"* in the end—before they'd parted ways as dawn broke. In a perfect world, he'd have reached out to Tel Aviv, sought their authorization, but he was in the middle of a war, and one fewer jihadist in this world would upset no one—even if it enabled another's rise to power. And maybe—just maybe—Abu Zuhair wasn't playing them. It was a gamble he had to take.

"Uncle," he heard a young voice call out, a small boy not

yet in his teens entering the shop, carrying a heavy box, and setting it down on the metal desk in front of the proprietor, which served as a makeshift counter, "I have things to sell you."

Mohamed took an onion from the shelf, listening distractedly as the boy extolled the virtues of cappuccino powder as a replacement for coffee with a cheerfulness that was astonishing for someone who had also, like as not, spent his night underground. Perhaps he was still young enough not to need coffee.

"I'll take them," he announced suddenly, peeling off hundred-*lira* notes from his roll as he turned back toward the boy, who was still standing there with the packets of powder in his hand, haggling with the proprietor.

If he was going to kill a man, he might as well be awake for it.

3:04 A.M. Eastern Standard Time
CIA Headquarters
Langley, Virginia

Olivia Voss closed the folder before her and leaned back in her office chair, glancing wearily at the row of digital clocks on the opposite wall, contrasting local time with the times in other major world cities. At the moment, Manila and Damascus. It was late morning in the latter, late afternoon in the former, thirteen hours away on the far side of the world.

Too late, wherever you were in the world. And she had been up too long. She'd known what it would mean when her boss, Bernard Kranemeyer, had approached her with the offer of the deputy's post—the late nights and long days it would mean. The *responsibility*, most of all—because the CIA had always been a place for odd hours, no matter your rank. But she'd taken it anyway, because she'd been here far too long—devoted far too much of her life to the Agency—not to do so. The confidence he had placed in her, naming her to the post, a trust she couldn't betray.

So she was here, and her ex was taking the kids to Disneyland in her stead. Those were the breaks.

They'd had a FLASH-Traffic from Manila Station two hours before—Manila's COS, Darren Lukasik, updating Langley on the latest development in the ongoing Braley hostage crisis: the arrival in the Philippines of a third party, a former Agency officer now freelancing for a private mil/intel firm, presumably there to negotiate a ransom with Abu Sayyaf.

Because what a situation this complex needed was the private sector sticking their oar in.

She reached for her cappuccino, realizing she was already well over her caffeine limit for the night, turning her attention back to the folder. Ten years before, such a drone strike would have been a major process, involving multiple agencies and undergoing interminable review. *Now?* Well, unlike the hoops they'd had to jump through the previous summer in the Sinai, Syria was a war zone, and she was rather surprised DoD had possessed the courtesy to even let them know in advance.

Mohsen Abdul Aziz al-Shaykh had been on their radar for some time, ever since his early days as a field commander with *Jabhat al-Nusra*, Syria's official licensed al-Qaeda franchise. That he had jumped ship to *Jaish* in the years since mattered little, in the final reckoning—he had blood on his hands.

Which was why there was currently a Reaper in orbit over eastern Ghouta, awaiting the final launch order. . .

1:03 P.M. Eastern European Standard Time
Suomenlinna
Helsinki, Finland

At the foot of the shallow cliffs, waves crashed into the rocks, sending salt spray dashing up toward the sky—the sonorous bellow of a ferry's horn resounding from off to the north and east, back toward the city.

The day was clear and cold, the sun burning feebly down upon the snow which covered the ground, its melted and refrozen crust brittle beneath the feet, the pathway back toward the gate of the fortress slick with ice.

A bitter wind bit at David Shafron's cheeks as he glanced back along the battlements of the ancient Swedish island fortress once known as Sveaborg, snow resting incongruously in the gaping steel-black muzzles of the Russian coastal artillery pieces still sitting in their stone emplacements, pointing seaward as they had done for a hundred years or more, still guarding a harbor faithfully for masters which had long since faded into history.

"So you're telling me that you can't acquire the intel?" he asked then, turning to the man at his side, his tall, spare figure cloaked by a heavy coat, a sixpenny hat perched atop his graying hair, dark eyes piercing out through his thick glasses with seemingly undiminished intensity.

"That's not what I said, David," was Mordechai Eichler's testy reply, glancing sharply at Shafron. "I said it would be difficult. WILLOW was our highest-placed source on the General Staff. What would have been child's play for him to have obtained, for others will be. . .challenging, and potentially dangerous."

But WILLOW—the Mossad codename for Colonel Vadim Kalugin, a headquarters apparatchik within the Russian military's General Staff—had, as they'd learned to their sorrow the previous summer, been a British asset as well, betraying his country to both Israel and the UK—selling secrets, it seemed, to the highest bidder.

A promising career in disloyalty which had ended abruptly when Colonel Kalugin had taken a completely accidental header from the balcony of his lover's St. Petersburg apartment to splatter against the pavement below, and rumors spread like wildfire through the underworld of intelligence that the UK's Moscow network was being rolled up. *All of it.* Every last agent.

The reasons for all that remained unclear—it had somehow, miraculously, stayed out of the cable news cycle, but it had been a disaster. A disaster which was now impacting his own operation, as unlikely as that might once have seemed.

"The stakes here are worth taking a few risks," he replied, half-turning to face Eichler. They were alone here on the cliffside, few tourists braving the cold and snow to visit the old fortress at this time of year—a single sail out to sea, white against the pale blue horizon, marking some hardy soul out braving the chop.

Eichler bristled visibly, reminding him of his own father in that moment—fifteen years Shafron's senior and a thirty-five-year veteran of the Office's Collections Department who had put in his time at postings all across the former

Soviet Republics, he clearly resented receiving this kind of tasking from an officer so much his junior, even though it had all been cleared through proper channels with Rosenblatt, the head of Collections. Well, he could resent it all he liked, so long as he came through in the end.

"Moscow Station's assets," he said finally, his voice so low it was almost obscured by the breakers, "take 'a few risks' every time they make contact with one of my officers. I realize this may be hard for someone of your operational background to fully understand, David, but we're not dealing with Arabs here, arrogant and overconfident in their own limited abilities—we're operating in one of the most denied spaces in the world, second only to Beijing, up against antagonists with a long tradition of counter-intelligence work. *Smyert shpionam.*"

The Russian syllables came out in a growled hiss, Eichler's eyes cold and hard. *Death to spies.*

"But I will see what I can do," he said then, relenting with grudging reluctance, seeming to sink deeper into his coat as he turned back toward the gun casements and the icy path leading west to the ferry terminal. "And if our assets can determine whether the Russians intend to redeploy their new stealth toys back to Syria. . .you'll be the first to know."

4:35 A.M. Pacific Standard Time
Creech Air Force Base
Las Vegas, Nevada

They'd been in the air for nine hours—he'd been on the watch for the last six, monitoring the screens as the MQ-9 Reaper continued its long slow orbit, loitering above Eastern Ghouta.

Cole Haskins leaned back into the stadium chair he'd long ago started bringing with him to replace the uncomfortable Air Force-issue seat installed in the trailer, taking another careful sip of his coffee, rationing it out.

Staying alert was the hardest part of this job—particularly this far into an op. Alert, despite the boredom that inevitably set in. He had learned long ago that the personal lives of terrorists made for no more riveting television than his own.

All the footage would be reviewed by others, passed over to intel analysts attempting to identify new faces, establish "patterns of life" for their myriad targets.

But if there was anything that would affect the trajectory of his mission in real-time, the Air Force captain couldn't allow it to escape his attention.

He reached into the pocket of his uniform blouse, withdrawing a packet of gum and unwrapping a piece. *Spearmint*, he thought, making a face as the taste began to pervade his mouth. He'd bummed the pack off his wife on the way out the door, forgetting her preferences in gum. With a full payload, they'd only be at this for another five hours, but the Reaper was flying light today, with only six Hellfires mounted beneath its wings instead of its full complement of fourteen, extending their loiter time.

"We've got movement," he heard Villemont announce, an edge creeping into the sensor operator's voice. Haskins stopped chewing, his eyes focusing in on the topmost screen, the UAV camera aimed at the main entrance of the tower block. *Abu Firas' front door.*

And the SUV which had just pulled up outside, a faded blue Kia which looked very much the worse for the war. It was like looking through a telephoto lens from across the street—the Reaper's cameras delivering an incredibly crisp picture from its orbit at thirty-five thousand feet. If the SUV had had plates, they could have read them.

A handful of armed men emerged from the building to greet the new arrival, spreading out toward their own vehicles, but the mood was relaxed—most of the men's rifles were still slung over their shoulders. Men laughing and joking as they moved. It almost felt as though you could *hear* the banter, as ridiculous as that seemed.

He'd almost relaxed when a second, smaller knot of men emerged from the door, clustered around a tall man in Western jeans and a winter jacket, a solid black knit cap drawn down tightly over his ears.

It took him a moment to focus in on the face, the heavy, graying beard straying down over the collar of the coat. But it was him.

"Pass the word up the chain," he ordered, glancing over at Villemont. "That's our man."

2:43 P.M. Syria Standard Time
Douma, Eastern Ghouta—the suburbs of Damascus
Rif Dimashq Governorate, Syria

"Whatever happens, follow my lead." Mohamed Taferi pushed open the passenger door of the Sportage and stepped out, trading a brief glance with Abdul Latif as the big man turned off the engine. Praying to God that he remembered his admonition on the drive over.

Getting the all-clear from Abu Ahmed and Ibn Nadhar to go treat with Abu Firas alone had proven harder than setting up the actual meeting, though Abu Zuhair had facilitated all of that with the *Jaish* field commander, as promised.

Ibn Nadhar had been set on giving the uniquely persuasive charms of his fanatical rhetoric another go, and Al-Golani had felt that as leader of this expedition, he should be the one to negotiate with Abu Firas.

Only his reminder of the influence his Qatari employers had with *Jaish* had served to quell the raging egos, and even then, Al-Golani had insisted that Abdul Latif accompany him as. . .*bodyguard?* Minder? Likely both—he'd been unclear on that point, and Ibn Nadhar had immediately put forth his own lieutenant, an al-Hariri tribesman from near Dara'a known by the *kunya* of Abu Basir, a move which had threatened to swell his retinue beyond any reasonable limit. In the end, it was Al-Golani who had won that particular round.

"*Salaam alaikum*, Abu Firas," Mohamed said, feeling the bulge of the Glock hard against the small of his back as he touched his hand to his heart, bowing slightly at the waist. *Blessings and peace be upon you.*

"You're late," the *Jaish* commander scowled, pulling up short before finally offering a grudging "*wa alaikum as-salaam.*"

And unto you.

Being late had been the point, Abu Zuhair's words still echoing in his head. "*Have him bring you to me. My own men are loyal to me, and they'll protect you—once he is dead.*"

"Leave your vehicle, no one will touch it," Abu Firas ordered then, seeming to make up his mind suddenly. "You'll ride with me."

Mohamed traded a look with Abdul Latif. *This wasn't the plan*—not that the big man actually knew that. Still, he seemed to recognize that something was going wrong, his expression betraying the unease that Mohamed had successfully masked.

He started to shake his head, but Abu Firas wasn't taking no for an answer. *"Khalaas,"* he said brusquely, clapping his meaty hands together with a crack which sounded like a pistol shot. "We're wasting time."

"You," he ordered, looking right at Mohamed, "will ride up-front with my driver. You"—a fat finger shot in the direction of Abdul Latif—"in the truck behind. Leave your rifles with my men."

4:58 A.M. Pacific Standard Time
Creech Air Force Base
Las Vegas, Nevada

Third vic. Cole Haskins pushed the controller's stick forward delicately, keeping the Reaper's cameras focused in on the small convoy as it threaded its way through the wreckage and rubble littering the streets of Ghouta. Mohsen Abdul Aziz al-Shaykh—Abu Firas—had gotten in the third vehicle back from the front, a silver late-model Hyundai SUV. They had him on the cameras, waving one of the newcomers into the front to ride shotgun before pulling open his own rear door.

Come on now, he whispered silently, feeling the sweat build on his palms, despite the chill of the hangar. Command was watching the same screens they were now—whoever they had roped in to make the call at this hour. But the decision wasn't coming. Perhaps they were trying to establish the identities of the new arrivals, though it was a safe bet that anyone with Abu Firas was no friend of theirs.

He wanted to do this and get out—there was no telling where the convoy might stop, and Abu Firas disappear into the warren of collapsed buildings and underground tunnels that honeycombed the destroyed city. And they were taking risks here, flying in contested airspace like this.

They'd gone unchallenged, so far, but Haskins had no illusions—the longer they kept this up, the longer their odds got. And he had no desire to be the one holding the bag when a sixteen-*million*-dollar Reaper got blown out of the sky by a Russian fighter.

When his earpiece crackled with static, it was a woman's voice over the comms network. "Haskins, this is Valerie Dixon. Do you have Abu Firas' location in the target vehicle?"

Lieutenant Colonel Valerie Dixon, the 432d Wing's executive officer. Well, that answered the question of whom they'd brought in. "Yes, ma'am. He's in the back seat, driver's side." *As usual,* he didn't add. Therein lay the value of establishing "patterns of life." Men were creatures of habit, and even hunted men found habits hard to shake. "Do I have target authorization?"

"Pending, Captain. Your feed is up on our screens, and we have IMINT analysts surveying the images for further targets. We get one shot at this, and we need to make it count. But Abu Firas dies today."

3:09 P.M. Syria Standard Time
The convoy
Douma, Eastern Ghouta—the suburbs of Damascus
Rif Dimashq Governorate, Syria

". . .am not able to help you, as I have already made clear. I do not know why I agreed to this meeting."

The heaters of the Hyundai Santa Fe were turned up, blasting hot air in Mohamed Taferi's face as he turned uncomfortably back to face Abu Firas, sitting behind him in the back. It was awkward carrying on a conversation like this, and he suspected the jihadist field commander knew it—knew it and had *intended* it—every lurch of the SUV as the convoy rumbled over rubble and through shallow shell craters taking him off-guard. "Because you know how much the support of my employers means to your cause here in Ghouta. And because I have conveyed to you the importance of our mission, to them."

Because you recognize the consequences of disappointing your backers, he chose not to say. He might have deployed a line like that had they been alone, but here, in front of Abu Firas' own subordinates—the risks of insult were too great.

"Then put me on the phone with your 'employers,'" the jihadist sneered, stroking his long, grey beard as he gazed out the window at the devastation. "I have many friends in Qatar, and perhaps some of them even know those you represent. But all I have just now is you—a messenger, without authority."

He turned back, his dark eyes boring into Mohamed's from above the thicket of beard. "I want to talk with someone in charge."

"My instructions were to treat with you myself," Mohamed replied, his mind racing as he looked the man in the eye, the bulk of his holstered Glock biting into his flesh. Knowing what he had intended to do, weighing the uncertainty of Abu Zuhair's promises against the potential of working with Abu Firas, after all. "But it's not impossible that something could be arranged."

4:12 A.M. Pacific Standard Time
Creech Air Force Base
Las Vegas, Nevada

It seemed as though an eternity had come and gone since the *Jaish al-Islam* convoy had first rolled out from the tower block that Abu Firas called his headquarters, the gum in the corner of Cole Haskins' mouth long since reduced to a tasteless wad of paste, nearly bitten in two.

The tense silence in the control trailer becoming almost deafening as the two men monitored their screens.

Then he heard the lieutenant colonel's voice once again over his earpiece, clear and crisp. *Emotionless.* "Captain, you are weapons-free, cleared to engage the target vic. I say again, you are cleared to engage."

Finally, Haskins thought, nearly swallowing the gum. "Understood, ma'am. Going weapons-free."

He turned to Villemont, repeating the authorization as they began to run down their final pre-launch checklist, ticking each procedural box, keeping an eye on the convoy as they did so.

A final nod from Villemont and Haskins reached forward from his stadium chair, pressing the button—marking the perceptible shudder of the cameras as the missile dropped off the Reaper's wing, plunging earthward.

"Rifle!" he spat, keying his mike. "Rifle! Rifle!"

3:14 P.M. Syria Standard Time
The convoy
Douma, Eastern Ghouta—the suburbs of Damascus
Rif Dimashq Governorate, Syria

". . .I'll just have to make a few calls, see what can be worked out—what my employers are amenable to. *Insh'allah.*"

"See that it's done," Abu Firas replied, folding his hands before the belly of his heavy coat, seemingly mollified by the concession.

Mohamed Taferi turned his attention back to the window, marking the muffled *crump* of artillery over the rush of air from the heater, a cloud of dust rising among the buildings far off to the west, probably two to three kilometers out. It was just possible that—

He never finished the thought. One moment they were rolling forward, the Hyundai jostling over fallen rubble from the previous night's bombing, the next, he heard a high-pitched whine, growing in volume, and then—*something* came through the roof, slamming into them with all the kinetic force of Thor's hammer, and everything went black. . .

Chapter 16

"Yeah!" Cole Haskins pumped a fist into the air, watching as the vehicles in front of and behind the target vic came to a screeching halt, the latter nearly colliding with each other and the disabled Hyundai. Rebel fighters spilling out, most of them seeking cover. The braver—or more foolish—of the *mujahideen* running forward to pull bodies from the crumpled wreckage.

Villemont's dark face cracked into a broad smile, and he reached over to fist-bump Haskins. "Introducing warheads to foreheads, sir. It's what we do."

Another terrorist dead, the captain thought, surveying the scene through the cameras with a smile of satisfaction. And no collateral damage.

"Colonel," he began, eyeing the gaping hole literally *sawn* through the roof of the SUV as he keyed his mic, "we have confirmation, target destroyed. No way Abu Firas walks away from that one. How copy?"

A moment's pause, then: "Bravo Zulu, Captain."

3:21 P.M. Syria Standard Time
Douma, Eastern Ghouta—the suburbs of Damascus
Rif Dimashq Governorate, Syria

Shouts, discordant and distant, ringing hollowly through the vacant chambers of his brain. Footsteps, all around, unnaturally loud, seeming to beat against his head like sticks against a drum. Over and over and—

Mohamed Taferi opened his eyes slowly, with painful reluctance—squinting against the light. His ears ringing, his head throbbing, as though someone had taken a sledge to his temples.

Hot air buffeting his face as he realized, abstractly, that the heater was still running, the front windshield still perfectly intact, without so much as a crack in the glass. He was still alive. *But how—*

He looked over to see the driver slumped over the wheel, his face turned toward Mohamed, his blood-flecked lips moving slowly, piteously—a deep, gaping wound visible across his back, even through the layers of ripped, blood-soaked clothing, as though he had been cut apart with a—

Sword. Ears still ringing from the impact, Mohamed glanced down at his left shoulder to see the steel blade there, half-buried in the seat only inches from his own flesh, still smoking with hot blood, dyed a sickly, incarnadine tint.

A nameless dread seeming to consume him as he ventured a look into the back seat—the blood draining from his face at the sight. The Hyundai's roof was crumpled and cut open, the driver's side window shattered from the impact and cold air pouring in to do battle with the heater, a strange cylindrical device with at least five long, wicked *blades* fanned out from its core lying there like a broken, malevolent toy. And where Abu Firas had once sat. . .

What remained could no longer be properly described as a *man*, at all, but a ragged heap of ripped-apart, quivering *meat*, still warm with the life which had so recently deserted it.

His eyes growing wide with horror the longer he stared, unable to tear his eyes away, realizing that the commander's bodyguard was also dead—his left arm simply *gone* below the shoulder, a sixth blade broken off completely and protruding like a spear from his chest—that the interior of the SUV was painted with blood, dripping down upon his forehead from above in dark red droplets.

Something snapped within him, and Mohamed clawed for his door, forcing it open with desperate strength and staggering a few steps from the vehicle before falling to his hands and knees on the broken pavement, retching uncontrollably. Emptying his stomach into the rubble and dust. . .

6:35 P.M. Central European Standard Time
Bruxelles-National Airport
Zaventem, Flemish Brabant
Belgium

Darkness had fallen out beyond the windows of Concourse A, their elegantly curved glass arcing from floor to ceiling as David Shafron moved off the long, flat escalator running the length of the terminal, glancing briefly at one of the myriad banners overhead advertising the services of the Spanish low-cost carrier Vueling Airlines.

He'd had three calls since leaving Helsinki. Two from Nika Mengashe, and one from Abram Sorkin. His two subordinates sharing a common message in their voicemails. *Call in.*

That didn't bode well.

He found a quiet corner of the terminal, near the windows—pushing past a bored, weary-looking pair of parents occupying a couple of seats on the end of the row, their luggage pooled around their feet. A little boy sitting between them, absorbed in a game on the tablet in his hands, his thumbs jabbing away with that childish energy that seemed absolutely inexhaustible until it, quite unexpectedly, *wasn't*. He should know—Shmuel was that age and Aaron not as far past it as his eldest would have liked to pretend.

Out on the runway, a Boeing 737 in the red-and-white livery of *Air Algérie* began its takeoff run, its white fuselage glistening in the lights.

The *Stade de France* attackers had come from here, Shafron realized suddenly, pausing with his phone out in his hand—the sight of the plane triggering something within him. Or rather from Brussels proper, thirteen kilometers to the southwest—Belgian Algerians sowing death and destruction on the streets of Paris in one of the year's more spectacular attacks.

Giving Europe a taste—only a *taste*—of what Israel had known on a daily basis all through the Intifada. The threats that still hung over them, to this very day.

Threats he had given his life to countering. This very airport itself had come under attack by North Africans loyal to the Islamic State, not so very long ago, and yet still. . .he was sure that Belgium would be lined up to condemn the Jewish state the very next time a UN resolution demanded it.

Some things never changed.

"Talk to me, Abram," he instructed as the other end picked up, pressing the phone to his ear as he turned back from the window, scanning the tired ranks of his fellow travelers—searching for anyone showing an undue interest in him or the call.

"Our friend missed his check-in, and no one has heard from him."

"And?" Shafron glanced at his watch. It couldn't have been that many hours—comms windows did get missed, that was a reality of field work, as much as everyone tried to avoid it. Particularly when you were under, the way Taferi was.

"And we're hearing chatter—a piece got taken out of play in his neighborhood this afternoon, by our American friends. He may have been there."

A drone strike, Shafron thought, grasping the situation instantly. Suppressing a bitter curse as he scanned the concourse once more.

The Israeli state had pioneered the UAV technology and laid the doctrinal groundwork for its deployment in the counterterrorism sphere—targeted assassinations—but the Americans, well, it had become their hammer around the time everything started looking suspiciously like a nail.

And now. . .if Taferi had been anywhere near the strike, he was in jeopardy. If not from having become collateral damage from the blast itself, then from the suspicion that was bound to fall upon any relatively unknown quantities in the vicinity of a major Islamist being taken out. Bad news, no matter how you cut it.

"My flight leaves in another hour," he said, checking his watch reflexively once again. "Have Shaul or Shimon pick me up at Ben Gurion—I'll come straight in."

"Already arranged."

9:34 P.M. Syria Standard Time
Khmeimim Airbase
Latakia Governorate, Syria

"Well, that's it, then," Andriy Makarenko said, a faint smile crossing his face as he looked up from the photos displayed on the screen of the GU laptop. "What's that Western rock song? 'Another One Bites the Dust'?"

"The 'man' who sang that song was a *goluboi* pervert," Valeriy Egorov snarled, favoring Makarenko with a sour look.

"This removal of Abu Firas by the Americans will weaken the rebels' hold on Ghouta," Makarenko continued, choosing to ignore the Spetsnaz officer as he glanced over at Major Kulik, leaning against the thick concrete of the listening station's inner walls—his dour countenance lit by the pale light of the nearby screens. "Even if just temporarily, it may give our military and the government forces the opening they need to finally crush the pocket once and for all. God bless America."

It was like stamping out the scattered, still-smoldering embers of a forest fire—dull, sullen coals bursting into fresh flame at the most unexpected moments. But with each one ground under the boot, they got one step closer to putting out the fire. More importantly, to going home.

He was counting down the days until he could see his

family once again, until he could hold his daughter in his arms for the first time. Until he could put the war behind him, a ghastly mirage, fading forever into memory.

Twenty-one more nights. . .

11:07 A.M. Eastern Standard Time
CIA Headquarters
Langley, Virginia

It wasn't the first time he had seen the havoc the new R9X variant of the venerable Hellfire AGM-114 could wreak, Bernard Kranemeyer thought, swiping through the pictures of the destroyed Hyundai on the tablet in his hand as he emerged from the hallway into the main hub of the National Clandestine Service's Operations Center.

Designed as a precision-killer *par excellence*, this missile had just come out of prototype testing back in the early summer, when the QUICKSAND op in the Sinai had gone so disastrously wrong. If they'd had access to it then, it could have saved them a lot of grief.

The R9X was about as far removed from the Hellfire's original tank-killing design as it was possible to get and still be recognizable as the "same" weapon, lacking even an explosive warhead. Instead, moments before impact, six long blades popped from the head of the missile and began spinning, forming a lethal corona.

The media, who had learned of it not long after its first deployment to the Syrian conflict, had displayed their usual hyperbole in dubbing it the "ninja missile," but in this case, Kranemeyer had to concede, they weren't far from wrong. Short of putting a man on a rooftop six hundred meters out with a rifle—with all the problems of post-op exfiltration that entailed—you were never going to truly solve the problem of *only* killing your target, as the images of multiple bodies being pulled from the wreckage of Abu Firas' Hyundai proved.

But this was as close as it got.

"All right, people," he began, raising his voice as he walked out into the center of the floor, "you've all by now no doubt seen or heard about the Air Force strike in Eastern Ghouta. Former al-Nusra Front commander Mohsen Abdul Aziz al-Shaykh is no longer among the living, and this world is a better place with him gone. He was taken out as a part of a DoD program, and we were not involved, but we all know the intelligence which got them on target originated in this building. So, job well done. Give yourselves a hand."

You took your victories where you could find them, the Director of the Clandestine Service mused, tucking the tablet under one arm as he led the applause for his team. And then you went right back to rolling your boulder uphill.

3:04 A.M. Israel Standard Time, December 21
Mossad Headquarters, Glilot Junction
Tel Aviv-Yafo, Israel

Coming back El Al was supposed to have streamlined David Shafron's return to Israel, but his flight had been delayed, and then delayed again—the wait in Brussels stretching out interminably as he pumped his body full of even more caffeine, fighting against the exhaustion that came with not having slept since that thunderstorm had woken him up in the skies over Romania, nearly twenty-four hours before.

Shimon Ben-David had picked him up at the airport, the typically tight-lipped security officer saying precious little as he escorted him out to the waiting Mazda, passing over a fresh thermos of coffee in silence as they set out on the forty-minute drive around the east end of the Tel Aviv metro area before coming back west to the Glilot Junction headquarters.

Abram Sorkin met him at the elevators, a funereal look on the Russian Jew's weathered face. It was clear that he hadn't had much more sleep than David.

"How bad is it?"

"Bad enough that we should save it for the SCIF, David," Sorkin replied soberly, turning and leading the way down the hall. "Welcome back to Israel."

Welcome indeed. It felt as though they'd had a death in the family, Shafron thought as the two of men passed like ghosts through the corridors, past half-lit offices. The hum of a vacuum somewhere deeper in the building assuring him that the cleaning crew was hard at work.

Perhaps they had—once a legend crumbled, a field officer's life expectancy was measured in hours or days, not weeks. If they were lucky.

He was so tired that Sorkin had to remind him to check his phone in one of the small lockers just outside the windowless, soundproofed conference room that served MEGIDDO as a Secure Compartmented Information Facility—or SCIF, another acronym borrowed from the Americans, his subordinate shooting him a sharp look when he tried to proceed without doing so.

Nika Mengashe awaited them inside, lines of worry scoring her dark face. "Welcome back."

"Let me have it," he ordered, taking his place at the head

of the table, and reaching for the bottle of water that had been thoughtfully placed at his seat. "What are we dealing with?"

"Mohsen Abdul Aziz al-Shaykh, aka Abu Firas, a *Jaish al-Islam* field commander in Douma, was taken out in an American drone strike yesterday afternoon, using an experimental guided missile. Mohamed Taferi was in the vehicle with him."

Shafron's face froze, the bottle stopping half-way to his lips. "We *know* this?"

Sorkin nodded and Nika pushed a small stack of photos across the polished walnut of the conference table. "We finally got these out of the Americans a couple hours ago, while you were on the flight back from Brussels."

The destruction spread out before him was at once appalling and. . .*strange*, Shafron realized, flipping through the photos—even when viewed from thirty thousand feet. The interior of the SUV was visibly a charnel house, with blood splattered liberally against the windows, but the vehicle itself was more or less intact, aside from the roof and chunks ripped from the back, driver-side door.

Then he reached the last photo and the breath caught in his throat, the Reaper's cameras having focused in on a body lying sprawled in the dust of the street a meter or two away from the open door of the Hyundai, its clothes soaked with blood. But the face. . .

It was him.

Chapter 17

His ears still rang with the sheer kinetic force of the Hellfire's impact, his head aching until he felt it would split open. A part of him praying that it would, putting an end to the misery.

Mohamed Taferi reached for another piece of the coarse barley bread, shoving it between his lips and forcing himself to chew—aware of the dull throbbing in his left arm even as he did so.

Some of that blood, he'd realized rather belatedly, had been his own, one of those spinning blades leaving a long, wicked gash deep across the bottom of his left deltoid.

No doubt part of the reason he'd collapsed after staggering from the destroyed vehicle, waking up more than an hour later in the basement of a nearby tower block controlled by *Jaish* fighters, still deafened, his beard stinking with blood and bile.

He'd been returned to their own small encampment in

the ruins of Douma after darkness fell, the bandages wrapped around his upper arm already sodden with blood—his head still swimming with noise that had long since faded away.

A rueful smile played at his lips as he swallowed, leaning back against the blankets, the rough bread seeming to stick in his throat. Of all the ways he had thought the previous day might end, with his own plan to kill Abu Firas, finding himself on the receiving end of an American drone strike—and *surviving*—had never entered his calculations. Not for a moment.

But war never lost its ability to surprise you, its chaos at once ever-fresh and unchanging.

He felt, rather than heard, someone enter the room of the ground-level apartment, a shadow falling across the opening in the half-broken masonry.

It was Abu Ahmed al-Golani, the *Fursan Tahrir al-Sham* commander looking even more than usually haggard against the morning light. He seemed on the verge of speaking, but Anas ibn Nadhar appeared at his side at that very moment, a concerned smile playing across the jihadist's face as he brought his hand to his heart, his lips moving inaudibly.

Mohamed pushed himself up off the floor, staggering weakly to his feet out of respect for his guests. *"Wa alaikum as-salaam,"* he heard himself reply, nearly overcome by a sudden wave of vertigo, the sound of his own voice strange and distant. *Alien.*

The last man upon whom he'd wished blessings and peace had ended up dead within the hour—though not, as intended, by his own hand. This business made a mockery of faith.

Ibn Nadhar said something else, seeming to inaccurately assume from his courtesy that he could hear them. Mohamed shook his aching head, putting a hand up to his ear and nearly losing his balance—thrusting an arm instinctively back against the concrete wall for support and cursing as daggers of pain shot through the damaged muscle.

Abu Ahmed hurried forward, clutching him by the shoulders to stabilize him, his lips almost against Mohamed's ear for a brief moment before he took a step back, taking him by the right arm as he guided him into a plastic chair set before a low table to one side of the small room.

Be careful, it seemed as though he—or someone—had said, the whisper seeming to rattle around the passages of his mind, the haunting echo of a warning. He needed to get his phone—send off a message to Qatar, to his "family." Let Tel Aviv know he was still alive. . .what had he missed now? One comms check? *Two?*

Ibn Nadhar sat down across from him, taking the remaining chair and leaving Abu Ahmed to stand awkwardly off to one side. ". . .may Allah. . .praised," he said, reaching across to clasp Mohamed's hand, "you. . .safe, my brother."

"May He be praised, for His protection," he assented dully, shaking free of Ibn Nadhar's hand—his mouth pasty, his own voice indistinct and barely audible.

He gestured toward his mouth and Abu Ahmed handed him a bottle of tepid water, leaving him to screw off the cap with a shaking hand, lifting it to his lips.

"Abu Zuhair?" he began once again, wiping his mouth with the back of his hand. "Have either of you heard from Abu Zuhair, since—since the drone strike?"

Ibn Nadhar and Al-Golani traded a strange look before

the jihadist nodded, his reply inaudible. Mohamed shook his head, and Ibn Nadhar leaned closer, raising his voice. "He will be here very soon. Abu Zuhair demanded a meeting—with you."

10:53 A.M. Israel Standard Time
Mossad Headquarters, Glilot Junction
Tel Aviv-Yafo, Israel

"Thanks for coming in," David Shafron said wearily, gesturing for the former *Sayeret Matkal* officer to take the seat opposite his at the SCIF's conference table, closing the door on the two of them.

He'd gone home, finally, to an empty house—Rahel already gone to work at the Ministry of Justice, the boys off to school—catching a scant couple hours of sleep in his own bed before grabbing a hot shower and coming back in to the office. It still wasn't enough, but he was functional once again, if only barely.

"Of course," his guest replied. "How can I help?"

By way of reply, Shafron pushed a folder wordlessly across the table, leaning back into his chair and taking a long sip of his coffee as the younger man took the folder and began leafing through it.

Looking at Gideon Laner, he couldn't help but be reminded of himself, as he had been at that age, more than a decade and a half prior.

They'd both put in their time in the IDF's reconnaissance units—Laner with *Matkal* in the waning years of the Second Intifada, himself, with *Duvdevan* well over a decade prior—and they'd both ended up at Mossad.

Laner only within the last nine months, though he'd been seconded to Mossad more than a handful of times during his time with the *Sayeret*.

They'd worked together, before, on one of those operations—enough for him to know that Laner's reputation was merited. He was a solid operator who had commanded the respect of the men he led, and who seemed poised to make the transition between paramilitary and intelligence officer more smoothly than most.

This morning, though, it was the instincts of the former that Shafron needed.

"So, you don't actually know if he's still alive," Laner observed then, looking up from the folder.

"No," Shafron was forced to admit, with grudging reluctance. Mohamed Taferi had missed two comms checks now, and was set to miss a third in a few more hours.

It was impossible to identify any life-threatening injuries from the pictures the Americans had sent over, but lying there covered in blood in the rubble and dust, well. . .he had seen dead men who looked more alive than the Druze officer.

"That's why I brought you in this morning. If we need to mount a recovery operation, I need to know what our options are."

Laner grimaced, running a hand over the dark stubble of a day-old beard already showing dull hints of silver. Only twenty-nine, according to his Mossad personnel jacket, he could have passed for late thirties—this job, it had a way of aging people before their time.

"Has Mirit signed off on this?"

It was Shafron's turn to grimace. Gideon Laner, like

nearly everyone else in operations, answered ultimately to Mirit Refaeli. *We've got to get a larger shop.* But that wasn't in this year's budget for MEGIDDO, or likely next year's.

"No," he replied, taking another sip of his coffee, "and as long as this remains hypothetical, she doesn't need to. Work up a plan, pick your team, identify contingencies. Report back to me when you have something viable. And keep this close to your chest. Need-to-know only."

3:03 P.M. Moscow Standard Time
Embassy of Israel
Yakaminka District, Moscow
Moscow Oblast, Russia

The thing which bore remembering about the average end-consumer of intelligence product, the *customer*, truly, was that they were in most circumstances quite content to forget about the individual people tasked with collecting that intelligence in the far-flung corners of the world. Until the moment they needed something, and they needed it yesterday, and found the infrastructure wasn't in place to fulfill their desires. A shortcoming which then became the implicit fault of Collections.

Mordechai Eichler leaned back in his chair, removing his glasses, and breathing on them before polishing them vigorously with a cloth taken from the breast pocket of his dress shirt.

He had never met David Shafron before the previous day in Helsinki, but he knew the man by reputation and had little doubt that he belonged to *that* category of intelligence customers. Shafron had spent his entire career in operations before moving up to management—out on the much-vaunted "sharp end" of the Office's activities, the "bayonet," quite literally. It was hard to imagine how he could be anything but.

He had less doubt that he had any other option than to comply with the man's requests, after a stormy call the previous evening with his own boss Leonard Rosenblatt, the head of Collections, assuring him that Shafron had cleared everything up the chain of command and yes, Tel Aviv *did* hold Moscow responsible for following through.

Fortunately in this case, fulfilling Tel Aviv's desires was only unwise, not impossible.

A view shared by the man currently sitting opposite Eichler's hopelessly cluttered desk—Lev Greenberg, his senior-most field officer here at Moscow Station.

". . .which has been left in the digital dead drop, as you requested," Greenberg shot his sleeve abruptly to glance at his watch, "two hours ago."

"Will anything come of it?"

A shrug. A father of four with a daughter currently pursuing her master's degree at Ben Gurion in Beersheva, Greenberg was in his early fifties and perfectly carried off the air of unassuming world-weariness befitting the underpaid, overworked civil servant his Ministry of Foreign Affairs cover insisted he was.

Well, the underpaid, overworked part was true enough—but behind the mild grey eyes and forgettably average appearance of a middle-aged man whose belt had long since lost its battle with his waistline lay a case officer who had spent seven years working one of the intelligence world's toughest beats, without losing a single asset or compromising his own cover. Greenberg was a seasoned, veteran officer and his palpable unease contributed to the ulcer this particular tasking was giving Eichler.

Greenberg reached over, extracting a dinner mint from the dish on the small endtable at the end of Eichler's worn leather couch before replying. "I couldn't say."

"Of course. But an educated guess? You've handled RUACH for years now."

A nod. "I have. But I've never met him—*no one* has ever met him, or even identified him with any certainty. He simply. . .is."

Eichler pursed his lips. Such was the reality of work in modern Moscow—feinting at shadows, and doing business with ghosts. "Then I suppose time will tell—how long did you give him for a reply?"

"Twenty-four hours."

4:08 P.M. Syria Standard Time
Douma, Eastern Ghouta—the suburbs of Damascus
Rif Dimashq Governorate, Syria

"Very soon" had proven a malleable and highly relative concept, and as the morning had passed into afternoon, and the sun continued its relentless march toward the western horizon, there had been no sign of Abu Zuhair. But such was the reality of life—and work—in the Middle East. *Insh'allah.*

Growing up immersed in Israel's Arab subculture, Mohamed Taferi found it rarely bothered him, and in any case, he seemed to regain a measure of his hearing with each passing hour.

Only his increasing awareness of their circumstances gave him cause for anxiety, the realization that their small encampment was being kept under watch by overtly hostile fighters presumably loyal to the slain Abu Firas.

"Careful," he spat through clenched teeth, grimacing as Nassif changed the bandages swathing the gash in his arm, the boy winding them firmly around the torn flesh.

"Aasifa," Nassif replied, the sincerity of the *"sorry"* belied as he cinched the final bandage tightly around Mohamed's tricep, eliciting a curse.

"Ibn Essam believes we had something to do with the death of Abu Firas," the boy said then, his face earnest in the fading light as he took a step back. "That there was an argument between the two of you and Abu Ahmed, and you betrayed him to the imperialists."

"Ibn Essam?" Mohamed asked, raising a hand, and pressing it against his aching temple. The name sounded familiar, and even so. . .he couldn't place it. Some ice would have helped, for the headache, but despite the chill seeping into the half-destroyed buildings at the retreat of the sun, he might as well have wished for the moon.

"The *Jaish* commander who took over from Abu Firas," the boy replied, looking at him as though he were completely out of it, which he guessed he had been, for the better part of twenty-four hours. An eternity in war.

So much for Abu Zuhair's plan, he thought with grim irony, taking a deep breath before looking the teenager in the eye. "So you're telling me that—"

There was shouting outside, just then—men's voices raised in anger and protest. Then a pair of men carrying rifles showed up in the entrance of the apartment—the foremost recognizable as his driver from two days before, when he'd had that first private conference with Abu Firas' rival.

"You're coming with us," the militiaman announced, his tone brooking no disagreement. "I'm to take you to Abu Zuhair."

5:24 P.M. Moscow Standard Time
Gromov Flight Research Institute
Ramenskoye Airfield, Zhukovsky
Moscow Oblast, Russia

"Again?" *Stárshiy Leytenánt* Yaroslav Svischev asked, the question escaping his lips before the thirty-eight-year-old pilot could recall it, standing at ease before his commanding officer's desk.

The wind was howling outside and around noon the snow had begun to fall fast and heavy from the dense, slate-gray layer of stratus clouds hanging low over the airbase. There hadn't been a prayer of flight ops and he'd spent the day in his office, doing paperwork.

He had been conscious of the increased responsibilities which would come with rank, but he was at the same time keenly aware that his involvement with the new Su-57 was the only thing keeping him in a cockpit at all.

Once its teething problems were worked through and it was rolled out to the line units, his move to a desk would be permanent.

A part of him recognized it was for the best—his youngest would be a teenager in the coming year, and it was past time he settled down and devoted some attention to the neglected parts of his life, the wife and three kids who had put up with his absences so patiently over the years. The other part knew he was going to miss the sky.

"Da," the Russian air force colonel replied, seeming surprised by the question. "Of course. You knew that your testing wasn't complete when they brought you back here."

He had, of course. Yet after those hours spent crouched in a bomb shelter as mortar shells rained down on Khmeimim, he'd struggled to sleep through the night since. It wasn't death he feared, so much—he would never have been a test pilot for the Russian Federation if he was afraid to die, it was the *helplessness* of it all, the feeling of impotence as you sat there in the dark, waiting for your number to come up.

And there wasn't that much they could do in Syria that they couldn't do here from Ramenskoye itself. It wasn't as though they could test the Su-57 air-to-air against a real live adversary— the Syrian rebels had no air force, and unless the Americans or Israelis came out to play. . .he smiled at that thought.

"How soon?" he asked, thinking of how he was going to break the news to his wife. Hoping he would be back in time for Christmas on the 7th of January, when the Orthodox gathered to celebrate the birth of the Christ Child.

"Three days."

4:52 P.M. Syria Standard Time
The tower block
Douma, Eastern Ghouta—the suburbs of Damascus
Rif Dimashq Governorate, Syria

The drafty apartment seemed much the same as it had two nights before, the low, sullen drumroll of artillery fire off to the west, the winter wind still buffeting the stiff plastic of the tarpaulins as it gusted mercilessly around the tower, finding its way in through gaps and cracks in the walls, pouring in at every uncovered window. After years of shelling, there wasn't a pane of glass left in the place.

But the old woman was nowhere in evidence, and no one had offered him tea.

"You got what you wanted," Mohamed Taferi offered, leaning back in his chair and massaging the back of his skull with his right hand. Thankful, at least, to now be able to hear his own voice without shouting. "Now all I'm asking is for you to carry out your end of the bargain, and give us an escort out of the city, through the tunnels."

Abu Zuhair hadn't sat down since he'd first entered the apartment—pacing back and forth, seemingly possessed by restless energy. *Fear.* Now he stopped short, glaring at his guest.

"Seriously? I got what I wanted? Is that what you think, really?"

Mohamed shrugged. "Abu Firas is dead, as you asked. Out of your way."

"Na'am. He's dead. But not at your hand, not in the street out there"—he gestured to the window—"where I could control news of his death until I had time to put things in place. *Fahamit alyee shlon?"*

Do you know what I mean? He did, and wondered now just how delusional the young lieutenant could be, to think he could control something like that. You didn't *control* chaos, and war was nothing but chaos in its purest form.

"And now Ibn Essam has taken over and he suspects you of having been involved in the death of Abu Firas."

"Min sijak?" Mohamed demanded, shaking his head in

disgust. *Are you serious?* "I was *in* the vehicle."

"You were—the only one in the vehicle to survive the strike." That was true enough, the driver bleeding out moments after being dragged from the wreckage. But he'd survived, with a headache and a bandaged arm.

Luck, some would have called it, but Mohamed knew the explanation was far simpler. The time, the *fate*, ordained for him was yet to come. And when it came, there would be no stopping, no escaping it. Only death and rebirth, the gift of new life, ordained by Allah. He wondered if he would remember this life, in the next, like he remembered stray flashes of others which had gone before—fragments of memories, drifting through his mind. A part of him hoped that this life was one he'd be allowed to forget. *Insh'allah.*

"You were the only survivor," Abu Zuhair repeated nervously, "and Ibn Essam believes that to have been no accident. I took a great risk, just bringing you here tonight."

"Then why did you?" That question had been bothering him on the drive over—ever since learning from Nassif of the suspicion hanging over them all. It didn't make sense. *Unless. . .*

"*La,*" he said emphatically, before Abu Zuhair could speak. *No.* "We're not doing that—*I'm* not doing your dirty work for you, not again."

"Ibn Essam will want to meet with you for himself," Abu Zuhair went on anyway, the dull *thump* of an exploding artillery shell a few kilometers to the west punctuating his words, "and when he does, I will make it possible for you to kill him, just as we'd planned with Abu Firas. Simple."

No, no. . .it wasn't simple. It was getting more complicated by the moment, the dangers to his mission increasing exponentially with each hour they stayed here in this beleaguered pocket, riven apart by faction within even as the noose tightened from without. The falling shells from those guns on the slopes of *Jabal Qāsiyūn*, seeming to creep closer by the moment.

"*La.* You'll keep your end of the bargain," he said, gritting his teeth against the pounding headache as he stared the jihadist in the face, "and see us out of the city as agreed upon—tonight."

"And why would I do that?"

Mohamed held up a finger, wincing as he reached into the pocket of his jacket with his left hand, withdrawing his phone and laying it on the table between them.

He tapped the screen a couple times and tinny audio spilled out into the room. "*. . .the aid you've provided to the opposition here in* Sham, *all convinces me that if anyone can kill Mohsen Abdul Aziz al-Shaykh, it's you.*"

Abu Zuhair's eyes bulged at the sound of his own voice, his face purpling through the thicket of beard, standing there listening in rapt disbelief for a long moment before pulling a Beretta from its holster on his hip with a curse. Slamming its butt into the smartphone's screen again and again until the glass cracked and shattered, the self-incriminating voice finally, mercifully, going silent.

He grabbed up the pieces and moved to the apartment's window in two swift strides, pushing aside the tarpaulin and hurling them out into the night.

"Feel better?" Mohamed asked, forcing a smile to his face as Abu Zuhair turned back on him, the pistol now leveled at his head. "But you see, it was already uploaded to the cloud—to be sent to my employers if anything happens to me, or I am prevented from carrying out their mission in Idlib. If they know, your superiors here in Ghouta will soon know as well. And you'll follow my phone through that window. Now please, sit. Let's talk logistics. I want to be through the tunnels by first light."

Chapter 18

2:17 A.M., December 22
Eastern Ghouta—the suburbs of Damascus
Rif Dimashq Governorate, Syria

The concrete was damp in the glare of the headlights, half-frozen puddles of condensation pooling in depressions amid the broken rubble littering the floor of the tunnel. It reminded him of Gaza, of the Hamas smuggling tunnels running back and forth across the border between the Strip and the Sinai, many of them, like this one, large enough for vehicles to pass through. He'd gone into more than a handful of them as a young conscript, enough to know that he'd hoped never to repeat the experience. *Ah well. . .*

Mohamed Taferi cast a glance over his right shoulder at the men riding in the back of the technical, making out the tense faces even in the semi-darkness, weapons clutched in white-knuckled hands. The big *Dushka* usually mounted in the bed had been taken down to reduce the vehicle's profile against the tunnel's low, rough-hewn ceiling, dismounted like the rest of their convoy's heavy weapons.

His own Glock was out in his right hand, the Type 56

slung over his shoulder as he kept pace alongside the lead vehicle, keeping back from the cone of light—his left shoulder was mending, but he knew he'd be slow in bringing the rifle to bear. And in this game, speed was life.

Their trucks were crawling forward, crunching audibly over the rubble, their exhaust choking the close air. There was ventilation, clearly—just not nearly enough of it, and he wondered for a moment how Nassif and the one-eyed man he followed around like a shadow were faring, towards the back.

Perhaps fifteen meters ahead, just at the edge of the light, he could make out the figures of their advance party, a mix of Abu Ahmed's own fighters and their *Fajr al-Umma* Brigade escort. The latter, a not only necessary, but unavoidable, evil.

There was no getting through here without the smugglers' help—no knowing what was waiting for them on the other side without them to clear the way.

He just had to hope that his message had gotten across to Abu Zuhair loud and clear—that the rebel lieutenant was just scared enough to do what he had been told, and not so scared that he'd get reckless. That no one else had decided to betray them, the list of people who *could* far too long for his taste.

Either way, he'd be glad when they were out of the tunnels—the feeling of claustrophobia from the other night in the bomb shelter now returning, full force—building, the longer he walked.

The Israeli felt a draft of cold air against his face and flicked his own light on, making out a round ventilation shaft just above his head, leading up toward the surface beyond the light, large enough for a man to crawl through.

They had to be at least ten meters down.

Far enough, he thought, an involuntary shudder running through his body as he turned the flashlight off, the same brief flash of light having revealed the ramshackle bracing used for the roof of the tunnel—scavenged metal and wooden *doors*, from the looks of it. No doubt torn from destroyed apartments and already of dubious structural integrity long before they ended up down here. *Comforting.*

His pulse quickened as the darkness seemed to open up off to his left and he flashed the light down a long, sinuous side passage, barely tall and wide enough for a single man, stooping, to pass along.

Behind him the technical passed on, a mouthful of exhaust reminding him not to dally. He turned back toward the slow-moving convoy, just as a figure came up behind him, a shadowy silhouette against the headlights of the following truck. The cold muzzle of a pistol pressing hard into his spine.

"Into the tunnel," a low voice ordered in gruff Arabic, emphasizing the words with a jab from the pistol. "And drop the weapon. *Yalla!*"

3:27 A.M. Moscow Standard Time
Moscow Marriott Grand Hotel
Tverskaya Street, Moscow
Russia

The man pushed away the sheets and rose, leaving the warmth of the bed and the warm, supple body which shared it with him, to pad barefoot across the carpet to the window, pushing back the shades to let in the city lights.

He stood there for a long moment, just staring out at the night, his eyes unfocused without his glasses, the beginnings of the headache which always came along with a hangover starting to bite at his brain.

A diminutive, unimpressive figure out of uniform—clad in only a pair of shorts and a worn undershirt, his head crowned only by a lingering fringe of thinning grey hair that seemed to recede further with each passing year—he knew the young redhead who lay back beneath those sheets hadn't been drawn to him for his looks or his personality, any more than she had truly enjoyed the night they had spent together, though she had made all the right noises at all the right moments, in bed and out.

He hadn't all that much either, if he were honest with himself—not beyond the physical release, which he was perfectly capable of achieving for himself. And his hand was rather less likely to give him an STD.

But he had done it, all the same. Maybe for the same reason he had decided to spy for the Jews. *Because he was tired of playing it safe.*

He had played it safe for years—followed all the rules, obeyed orders without question, done his best to be a good husband and father in the stray moments that work allowed—and where had it gotten him?

A career that had ground to a halt for reasons he no longer pretended to understand, passed over for promotion time and time again as he watched far less capable men climb jauntily on past. A wife who loathed him just as much as the young woman he'd taken to bed in her place—and cared far less about concealing it.

So now he was going to do as he pleased—use and abuse

what power his position on the General Staff gave him for whatever momentary pleasure he could derive from it. And cuckold the men who had given him those tastes of power all the while by selling secrets to the Mossad behind their backs.

This latest request from his handler. . .it was risky, getting the information they were asking for now, but he didn't care so much about the risk as proving to them just what he was capable of. He almost wondered if it were a test, of some kind, the way it had been framed—as if even they weren't taking him seriously, didn't believe he could deliver. But he *could.*

He felt anger then, its claws sinking into his brain, along with the building headache. Anger at all those who had underestimated him, all through the years, trifled with him, demeaned him—their smiles, so predictably false.

The redhead would be one of them, he knew that, once she left, laughing tomorrow—no, it was *already* tomorrow—with her little friends on VK about the disgusting old man she'd bedded the previous night, about his pitiful stamina, about the presents she expected him to give her, just for the privilege of seeing her again. *No.*

Turning back to the bed, he ripped the sheets away in a single, abrupt gesture, his gaze sweeping over her body in the moment before he reached up to caress her cheek with thick, fleshy fingers. He saw her eyes come open slowly, still heavy with sleep and bleary with alcohol, that false smile, just beginning to turn up the corners of her pretty mouth as she stretched languidly.

And he slapped her—not hard, just enough to watch those clear blue orbs widen with fear. *"Von!"* he spat as she cowered away from him, his spittle flecking her cheek.

Get out.

2:29 A.M. Syria Standard Time
The tunnels
Eastern Ghouta—the suburbs of Damascus
Rif Dimashq Governorate, Syria

"Keep moving," the heavy-set man said from behind him, prodding him with the pistol muzzle as he ducked his head beneath a rough protrusion in the crudely chiseled ceiling of the side tunnel, the light behind him wavering from side to side, half-obstructed by his own stooped figure, barely enough to light the way.

Well, he now had the answer to his question, Mohamed Taferi thought ruefully. He had, it seemed, pushed too far and backed Abu Zuhair into a corner, panicking the hapless opposition lieutenant.

He shook his head at how smoothly it had all been handled. Abu Zuhair's men—there were two of them, further complicating his situation—had to have known the side tunnel was coming up, had to have been following him along the convoy for the better part of an hour, ever since they'd first descended into the tunnels beneath the site of the abandoned school. And just like a fool, he'd helped them out by pausing to investigate.

It puzzled him why Abu Zuhair had chosen to act now, when he'd had every opportunity to do so right there at the tower block, but perhaps the answer to that was that his people had known where he was, then. Whether either Abu

Ahmed or Ibn Nadhar would actually have stuck their necks out for him was something he didn't know—but neither did Abu Zuhair.

Now, well. . .they'd be out beyond the government lines before they even realized he was gone. And there'd be no coming back for him, if they even cared that much, something he rather doubted. *Well played, indeed.*

Mohamed stooped once again, wincing as his shoulder caught the side of the wall—his pistol and rifle were gone, but he still had the knife, tucked into the pocket of his jacket. He could get it out without trouble in the bad light, and the sooner the better—but there were two of them, and it was hard to say whether his left arm was up to grappling.

Only one way to find out.

2:31 A.M.
The main tunnel

The smell of exhaust hung over the convoy in thick, heavy clouds—seeming barely stirred by the ventilation shafts they passed along the way.

Nassif huddled back against the cab of the technical, his rifle in his lap—his eyes stinging as they struggled to pierce the darkness out beyond the glare of the headlights. His head felt thick and woolen, as though he could go to sleep. One or two of the fighters with him in the bed of the truck already had, though Mamdouh was not among them, his single eye still staring balefully out of the night whenever Nassif looked over at the older fighter.

He had stood up to get closer to the air as they'd gone under the last ventilation shaft, only for Mamdouh to bark at him to get down just before the protruding knob of an old door which had been used as bracing for the tunnel roof could smack him in the head. But it had been worth it, for those precious gasps of clean air, pure and cold.

They had to be nearing the end of the tunnel, the boy thought, not for the first time, wondering if his friend—the Qatari, or whatever he was—was still ahead of them, up with the lead vehicles where he'd glimpsed him as they first went into the tunnels beneath the school.

He started coughing then, a hacking cough that tore at his young lungs until the tears started from his eyes. Wherever his friend was, it had to be better than this.

2:34 A.M.
The side tunnel

The steel of the knife was cold between Mohamed's gloved fingers as he stooped down, putting up his other hand against the wall for support. He pushed himself along, half-turning to pass through the tunnel, keeping the knife concealed, the jihadists' lights dancing across his back.

They had to be at least a hundred and fifty meters down the tunnel now—impossible to say how much farther it would be before it would open out once again, and he would lose his edge. There might even be reinforcements waiting there, and then his fate would be truly sealed.

May Allah give me strength, he prayed silently, watching their shadows play in the lights, deliberately slowing his steps as he tried to gauge the distance.

"Yalla!" one of the men snarled, prodding him with the muzzle of his Kalashnikov to hurry up. "We don't have all—"

Mohamed stumbled, half-turning as he did so, his weak hand closing around the rifle's massive hooded front sight, gritting his teeth against the pain that shot through the arm as he pulled, hard, jerking the jihadist into him.

He saw fear dawn in the man's dark eyes in the half-second before the knife came up in his strong hand, its sharp point stabbing through the flesh and cartilage of the fighter's exposed throat, blood gushing out over his hand, accompanied by a horrible gurgling.

His light clattered to the earth and stone, a panicked shout of alarm escaping the rearmost militant as Mohamed struggled to control the muzzle of the dying man's rifle, to wrest it away, to keep it from being brought to bear—a desperate strength seeming to possess the jihadist in the final, fading moments of his life.

The next moment a brutal, deafening staccato of fire filled the tunnel, muzzle flash lighting up the confined space, a series of heavy blows pounding into the ceramic plate of Mohamed's plate carrier.

Ears ringing, he stumbled backward and lost his balance, going down hard with the now bullet-riddled corpse of the jihadist falling on top of him, driving the breath from his body. Sightless, frozen eyes still gaping in horror, gazing down at him as blood dripped from the dead man's destroyed throat onto his face—his fingers clawing for the rifle, struggling to free himself, to throw off the dead weight pinning him to the earth. Knowing that, trapped like this, his own death was only moments away. *There is no God but God. . .*

He couldn't hear his own voice, if he had even spoken the prayer aloud, his world curiously devoid of sound—the light flickering once more into life back down the tunnel, wavering from side to side as it came closer, his fingers closing around the blood-slick receiver of the Kalashnikov, straining to clear it from between their bodies. *There.*

Another moment, and the light was above him, shining down into his eyes with a blinding glare. He blinked, unable to help himself—saw the light shift wildly, a dark muzzle coming to bear behind it, and he threw all his remaining reserves of strength into the effort, rolling the corpse sluggishly to one side as he brought the weapon up, triggering a long, ragged burst.

The light went out.

Chapter 19

4:34 A.M.
The suburbs of Damascus, north of Ghouta
Rif Dimashq Governorate, Syria

The cracked, broken asphalt beneath Nassif's feet had once served as the parking lot for a modern shopping mall—the tattered remnants of a banner bearing some advertisement in Arabic script still hanging above the main entrance, the bullet-pocked concrete walls of the building looming ominously just to their east, rubble choking the mouth of a gaping hole low in its western wall from the direct hit of either artillery or a tank's main gun. A few panes of glass high above which had somehow, miraculously, survived the shelling, still glinting in the moonlight when it filtered through the scattered cloud cover. Arabic graffiti sprayed harshly across the bare concrete by regime militias. *"Assad or nobody. Assad, or we burn the country."*

A far-off rumbling of thunder from the north and west marking yet another salvo from the guns on the mountain—shells falling on targets somewhere deeper in Douma itself. *Burn the country,* they had.

He remembered having gone to the cinema in one such mall on the south side of Damascus as a child—his father buying him and Talha a small tub of popcorn, and the two of them scrapping over the last handfuls. He didn't remember the movie, strangely enough—all that seeming so. . .*alien* now, as though it belonged to another world, so very different than this one.

A world in which he'd had a father—and a brother—to go to the cinema with. A mother and sister, waiting at home when they'd returned.

The boy pursed his lips. You could go mad, thinking of such a world. But thinking of it wouldn't bring any of it back.

Any more than he could find his friend just by thinking of him. "Where do you think he could be?" he asked quietly, glancing back to where Mamdouh sat on the lowered tailgate of the technical, the RPD light machine gun cradled in his lap.

"The Qatari?" Mamdouh turned his head away, coughing as though he would hack up a lung—the vehicle exhaust which had choked the tunnels, sunk deep into their lungs. "No idea."

Nassif suppressed a grimace, his own head still aching from the fumes as he glanced off to the north, where the Damascus-Homs Highway brooded silent and empty in the night. They hadn't realized the man was gone until well after they'd exited the tunnels, and Abu Ahmed had insisted on stopping here and sending men the three kilometers back to the exit, over the loud protests of both Ibn Nadhar and the smugglers themselves. In the end, it had been the smugglers who had gone, though—sending back three of their own number to investigate, believing they could succeed in dodging Syrian Army patrols.

Mamdouh coughed again, sucking in a deep breath of cold air as his single eye gazed off toward the faded, bullet-riddled sign marking the auto shop just north of the mall. More of the detritus of war. "He probably passed out in that tunnel, same as the others. He just wasn't riding."

It was possible—they'd had to revive three of their own men after making it back out into the open air and Nassif had felt on the verge of collapse himself by the time their truck cleared the exit, his head swimming until it felt as though he were beginning to hallucinate. But the *gunshots* had been real, that familiar hollow death rattle of automatic weapons fire, distant but unmistakable. Echoing through the narrow confines of the tunnel.

At the time, he'd thought little more of it than the distant *thump* of falling shells, but now. . .he found it strangely impossible to escape the thought that it could have been his friend back there, somehow, fighting for his life.

Nassif sighed, exhaling a heavy cloud of steam into the night, casting a critical glance up toward the eastern sky as he shifted his rifle from one hand to the other, the ice-cold chill of the stamped-steel receiver quickly seeping through his ragged gloves. One thing the smugglers were right about—they couldn't stay here for long, no matter whether they found the Qatari or not. Day was coming, and with the dawn would come death if they failed to put sufficient distance between themselves and the Syrian Army lines encircling Ghouta.

He didn't know what, exactly, had drawn him to the man—even before realizing he was a fellow Druze, there in the devastated grove outside his old village of Maghar al-Mir. *Compassion*, perhaps, that rarest, most foreign, of qualities in war. Something in the older man that reminded him of his own father, long since dead, something he had looked for in vain in Mamdouh or even Abu Ahmed.

And now, it seemed, he was gone too. That was the way of war, the boy thought, looking out through the night with dark, dead eyes. You lost everything before the end—your home, your family, your friends. . .everything that made life worthwhile, that made you human, and finally your very humanity itself. You were dead long before Death ever came to claim its own. He—

Movement, out of the corner of his eye, just then, as the moon pierced weakly through the clouds—a figure detaching itself from the countless shadows surrounding the abandoned mall. Walking unsteadily toward the trucks, its steps wavering through the broken asphalt. The outline of a rifle visible across the man's chest, a pistol clutched in his left hand.

"Hold it there!" Nassif called out, shaking his head to clear the fog from his brain as he took a step forward, raising his own rifle.

"Salaam alaikum," a familiar voice replied wearily, the man raising his empty hand in salutation, "little brother."

4:41 A.M. Arabian Standard Time
A gated compound in Duhail
Doha, Qatar

There were only a couple hours remaining before dawn, but Ibraheem Saleh al-Murrah had yet to get to sleep, his eyes burning into the screen of his laptop as his character hacked and slashed away at the giant before him with a sword nearly as long as his character was tall.

And then the giant's fist came slamming down, his thumbs working the controller's sticks frantically as he struggled to block, only to watch as he was pummeled into the ground. *"La, la, la. . ."*

He hurled the controller away from him with a force that ripped it from the laptop's USB port, sending it bouncing off the low shelf across the room. Weary curses exploding from his lips as he shoved the laptop away, clasping his hands together and interlacing the fingers in a futile effort to stop the trembling.

He had to get a grip. He could handle this. He *had* to handle this. But they were still looking—poking around the Special Forces' service records he had so carefully altered last year, when, at his handler's behest, he had gone to work to backstop the legend of Mohammed bin Ammar.

He'd thought it was over and done with—behind him— until an hour before leaving work the previous night, when his supervisor had stopped by and dropped the painfully slender Bin Ammar file onto his desk. Asking that he look into it, and report back with his findings before the end of the week.

Ibraheem reached up, rubbing his knuckles into his eyes, forcing himself to take a deep breath. He had gotten lucky— his supervisor could have easily asked someone else, and he might never have known until they came to drag him out of his bed.

This gave him a chance. But it was only that—a *chance*.

4:43 A.M. Syria Standard Time
The shopping mall north of Ghouta
Rif Dimashq Governorate, Syria

Anas ibn Nadhar and Abu Ahmed al-Golani were standing in the shadow of Al-Golani's weathered Kia Sportage as Mohamed Taferi approached, their heads together with Abd al-Malik, the *Fajr al-Umma* Brigade smuggler who had been tasked by Abu Zuhair with seeing them safely through the tunnels.

Or so they'd imagined. Abdul Latif, standing a few feet off from the leaders, was the first to see him approaching—his guttural exclamation of surprise drawing the others' attention.

"Alhamdullilah!" Ibn Nadhar exclaimed in shock, forcing a smile. *Praise the Lord.* "I thought you were dead."

"No doubt," Mohamed replied grimly, clutching the Glock in his off hand as he stopped just short of the group, his gaze flickering from face to face.

"I thought you might have gotten lost in the tunnels," Abu Ahmed said, genuine concern in his eyes. He might not have truly cared if the Israeli lived or died, but the thought of him simply *out there*, his fate unknown, had clearly been unsettling. He knew too much. "We sent men back to look for you."

"I know." He had crossed paths with the searchers, not twenty minutes before, as he picked his way through the shadowy ruins of the Damascus suburb. Sheltering behind the half-destroyed wall of a compound as they passed, their weapons held at the ready—murmured snatches of conversation reaching him in the night. They had been looking for him, all right.

Only Abd al-Malik seemed to have nothing at all to say, the smuggler's bearded face a study in fear and surprise. Mohamed took a step into him before he could decide how to react, seizing the collar of the man's Western coat in his fist and pushing the smuggler up against the side of the Sportage, the muzzle of the Glock jammed beneath his chin.

"You were paid to kill me," he hissed, his spittle flecking the smuggler's cheek—raw, naked fear in the dark eyes that stared back, only inches away. "By Abu Zuhair."

"That's not true, I swear it by Allah, it's not—"

Behind him, he heard shouts—the rough, metallic sounds of rifles' safeties being flicked off. Glimpsed Abdul Latif out of the corner of his eye, shouldering his own rifle— a rough bellow escaping the big man's throat as he faced down the smugglers. A rough curse breaking from the lips of Ibn Nadhar's young lieutenant, Abu Basir, as he drew his pistol. . .on the other side. *Got you.*

"You're going to tell your men to stand down," the Israeli said grimly, his eyes boring into Abd al-Malik's. "And then you're going to lead us out of here. If anything goes wrong— anything at all—the first bullet's going through your brain."

8:14 A.M. Israel Standard Time
Mossad Headquarters, Glilot Junction
Tel Aviv-Yafo, Israel

". . .which is far from optimal, but it's the only way I see in. Getting out will be even more unpredictable. If *Jaish* figures out who we are. . ."

David Shafron grimaced, reaching for his coffee. Looking over the plans drawn up in the files now displayed on the computer before him, that seemed a fairly massive understatement.

"You're sure this is our best available option?"

"I'm sure it's our least worst." Gideon Laner shoved both hands into the pockets of his jeans. Despite having spent most of the night up working on this, he looked somehow more rested than Shafron. *The benefits of youth.* "Look, David, we're talking about a city under siege, and no confirmed location for our officer. Nothing's optimal about this picture, you know that."

He did. *Had* known it. But they'd gambled anyway, gambled and lost. And now the only way to pull one officer out of the fire was to plunge five more into it.

That was bad business, no matter how you cut it. Like a gambler convinced he could just right his losses with a bit more money. And who was he going to send if the cards came up bad again, and Laner's team found themselves in need of exfil?

"I'll run all this by Mirit," he said finally, kneading his brow with the fingers of his left hand. "Take it to the *memuneh* afterward, hopefully with her support."

That seemed a long shot, but that was clearly becoming a trend. And even Avi might balk at this one, without Refaeli firmly on-board.

"Good luck," Laner replied, a grim irony in the former *Sayeret* commando's voice. "My men and I have a training rotation in the Negev coming up, day after tomorrow, but we'll stand to in preparation to launch, should the decision come down. If anything changes. . ."

"You'll be the first to know. If—"

A knock came at Shafron's office door in that moment, surprising both of them. "Yes?"

It was Nika Mengashe—excitement radiating from his subordinate's dark eyes as she swept into the office, a folder tucked under one arm. "David, we've made contact, we—"

She saw Laner then, and stopped short, her face betraying surprise. "I'm sorry, I didn't realize—"

Shafron shook his head. "No, go ahead, Nika. Gideon is read-in on the Ghouta op. We've heard from Qatar?"

A nod. "Taferi made his morning comms window, with no signs of duress. They've left Ghouta and made it beyond the siege lines, moving north into the mountains."

He let out a breath he didn't realize he had been holding, nodding gratefully. "Thank you, Nika. And thanks, Gideon—I'll be in touch, if needed. Best of luck with your training in the Negev."

It wasn't much—he knew without looking at a map that Taferi was far from out of woods, the territory north and west of Damascus firmly back in the hands of the Assad regime, the last scattered, dying embers of rebellion finding themselves ground out beneath the boot of the Syrian Arab Army and their Russian and Iranian allies.

But you learned in this business to take what hope you got—and make it last.

1:53 P.M. Syria Standard Time
Jabāl al-Qalamūn
Al-Qutayfah District, Rif Dimashq Governorate
Syria

The dawn had never come, the clouds growing heavier and lower with the approach of day. By the time they'd kicked the hapless Abd al-Malik to the curb more than a dozen kilometers north of the city, having already bribed their way past two Syrian Arab Army checkpoints manned by thin, hungry conscripts whose officers had either taken a holiday or been paid to stay conveniently away, an icy drizzle had begun to fall, growing steadier the farther they drove north—soaking the men in the exposed beds of the technicals to the skin.

Now it fell in sheets, drenching the high plateau between the Qalamoun and the Anti-Lebanon, mountains rising all around them.

Mohamed Taferi stood in the entrance of the ancient caravanserai, or khan, gazing out toward the highway not more than two or three kilometers distant, the hood of his jacket drawn up over his head. A thousand years had come and gone, but where the caravan routes of *Sham* had once run, the highways now followed.

These thick, squat stone walls had been new when Saladin had led his army south to the Horns of Hattin, with the Druze of the Lebanon rallying to his banners to expel the Frankish invaders, but still they stood—defying man and nature alike.

A perfect square viewed from above, four walls filled with rooms surrounding a massive central courtyard, the caravanserai offered both shelter and sanctuary. Abu Ahmed had already taken up quarters toward the southern end of the old khan, near the entrance, with Anas ibn Nadhar retreating toward the northwestern corner, as far away as he could get. One of the technicals had parked squarely athwart the main entrance, the yawning muzzle of its big *Dushka* trained on the opening.

The two leaders had argued, apparently, on the drive

up—over Ibn Nadhar's insistence on making contact with some of the fading pockets of jihadist resistance in the mountains to their north, to hear Abdul Latif tell it. Neither man would speak of it to him, and still half-suspecting Ibn Nadhar of having been complicit in Abu Zuhair's attempt to do away with him, he was hardly inclined to press for a private conference in his quarters.

These walls were thick enough to stop a rifle bullet, Mohamed thought idly, surveying the weathered stone—if not a tank's main gun or autocannon. The air would be a different story, of course, but nothing was going to be flying down here on the deck—not today. And they would be gone by nightfall, pressing farther north, along the old caravan routes toward Homs.

He stretched out a hand into the rain, watching as it dissolved the old, dried blood still smeared across his knuckles from the previous night, rust-brown water running in rivulets down the back of his hand and off, dripping to the sodden earth.

And it seemed in that moment as though he could see himself standing in this very place—or something *close* to it—in another time, another age, the sun beating down out of the heavens with scorching heat, the scarred, richly-ornamented stock of a long-barreled *jezail* pressed into his shoulder. The ground trembling beneath the hooves of a charging horse. Sunlight, glinting along an upraised blade. A burning slow match, snapping forward at the end of the serpentine.

An explosion from the pan, a flash of pain as the heavy rifle recoiled into a wounded shoulder—man and horse going down together in a pile of writhing flesh.

A bandit, pinned beneath his fallen, dying horse, his legs broken, begging for mercy. *A flash of steel in the noonday sun.*

Outside, the rain was still falling in torrents—a shudder passing through Mohamed Taferi's body as he came back to himself, taking one last long look down toward the highway before retreating back within the caravanserai.

Mercy had never had any home in these mountains.

2:34 P.M.
Marj al-Sultan Military Heliport
Eastern Ghouta
Rif Dimashq Governorate, Syria

"And they were said to be en route to Idlib," Michael Awad mused, clicking his pen absently in the silence of the makeshift office. There were still bloodstains in the concrete behind his chair dating back to the fierce battle in which the Syrian Arab Army had retaken the heliport from the rebels several years before, and the battered metal desk served as the only furniture, forcing anyone who entered to stand, which suited the Syrian Special Forces captain just fine. "Why?"

"I don't know. To join the rebels there, I imagine. To keep fighting, after the South falls."

Abd al-Malik was a skilled liar if nothing else, Captain Awad thought, his office chair creaking as he leaned back, regarding the smuggler silently—but his words here held the ring of truth, somehow. He let the silence build for another long moment, watching the man shift his weight uncomfortably from one foot to another.

"And you helped them." He saw the smuggler flinch as if he'd reached out and slapped him, the man's face assuming an expression of fawning servility. *Disgusting.*

"Captain Awad, you must believe me—I had no choice in the matter. And I came to tell you, as soon as I could!"

"That's no doubt why you were picked up by a patrol more than ten kilometers away, trying to slip back through our lines and into your maze of tunnels." Awad smiled, allowing his contempt to spill out onto his face. "Because you were coming to see me."

The man now groveling before his desk would have killed him and his family—*everyone* he held dear—without a moment's hesitation or regret, a few short years before, Michael Awad knew well. When this base and its environs had been in the control of *Daesh* scum like Abd al-Malik.

A Maronite Christian who had, before the war, attended mass at the Cathedral of St. Anthony under the Archeparchy of Damascus, Awad had watched as his country was torn apart by revolution—artillery shells falling on the cathedral and into the very bed of the archbishop himself. His fellow believers across Syria, scattered to the winds or martyred by the hundreds as the Islamists imposed their will upon enclaves unlucky enough to fall under their sway.

The church was mostly repaired now, and his family, less his brother who had fallen in the fighting around Aleppo two years before, would celebrate Christmas there in another three days. But he would be here, on the front lines—working to stamp out the last, lingering vestiges of resistance, until every last one was extinguished. Until the threat was no more.

He, very much like his Alawite superiors who dominated the officer corps of the Syrian Special Forces—indeed, much of its rank and file—owed his position as much to his faith and cultural background as to his ability. In a world awash in shifting loyalties, with men like Abd al-Malik changing allegiances and playing all the sides against the middle, *their* loyalty was assured.

If *Daesh*—or any one of the score of other Islamist groups which had risen and fallen throughout the course of the war—actually succeeded in toppling the government of Bashar Assad, they and their families were all dead. The calculus was that simple, that clear-cut.

To keep that from happening, Michael Awad would fight whomever he needed to fight. Kill, whomever he needed to kill. And it had yet to cost him a moment's sleep.

"You're only here at all, Abd al-Malik," he said finally, "you only reached out to us in the beginning, offering information, months back, because you recognized that your side was losing, that neither your false god nor your dead prophet would secure you a victory, not this time. That makes you smarter than your fellow so-called '*mujahideen,*' still cowering in the basements of Ghouta, waiting for the next bombs to fall, but you understand that means very little to me. It's enough to spare your life, nothing more, as long as you continue to be of use. And the next time my men find you actively aiding the enemies of Syria, it won't even suffice for that. Now tell me more about these men, and where you last saw them. . ."

4:03 P.M. Arabia Standard Time
Museum of Islamic Art
Doha, Qatar

The white French limestone of I.M. Pei's last architectural masterpiece glistened like alabaster in the fading rays of the evening sun, shadows playing delicately across the staggered geometric blocks of the museum's structure, drawing the eye toward the five-story tower which formed the central focal point of the building, rising against the harbor and the Doha skyline beyond.

The heat of the day was already abating rapidly, a stiff breeze off the waters of the bay stirring through the heavy fronds of the towering palms lining both sides of the approach to the museum—sending a chill up Ibraheem's spine and raising the gooseflesh on his arms as it cut through the sweat-damp back of his shirt.

"I have to find some way out of this," he exploded nervously, pacing back and forth, hands pressed into the pockets of his dress slacks in an unsuccessful effort to keep them from trembling. "Some way to cover for what I did. I have to—"

"You have to settle down, first of all," the small man replied, his soft voice barely audible over the gurgling of the water running down the middle of the walk from the fountains near the museum's entrance. "Because if you draw attention to yourself, if you walk around your headquarters building with nervous guilt written all over your face, there will be nothing I or anyone else can do to help you. *Fahamta?*"

The Qatari bureaucrat nodded quickly, aware that his outburst had already caused an older woman swathed from head to foot in a voluminous black *abaya* to favor the two men with a suspicious look as she hurried on by, up the walk toward the museum, a messenger bag slung over one thick shoulder. All it would take was one wrong word. . .

He had to get a hold of himself, to trust that his handler knew what he was doing. That he could *help* him.

Because if he couldn't. . .no one could. The shudder that went through Ibraheem's body then had nothing to do with the breeze, and he struggled to focus on the Israeli's next words.

". . .begin again from the beginning, and tell me how these questions came to be raised. Who is suddenly so interested in Mohammed bin Ammar?"

5:28 P.M. Syria
Khmeimim Air Base
Latakia Governorate, Syria

". . .on their way to Idlib, to join in the fighting there. But, sir, it's the same names as before—from the previous intercepts."

"The Knights of Syria, or the Knights for the Freedom of Syria, or whatever they were?" Andriy Makarenko's dinner had been left behind half-unfinished in his quarters, but he'd hurried over to the listening station as soon as the call came in, and now held the intercept in his hand, his eyes scanning across the Cyrillic characters.

"Da, tovarisch podpolkóvnik." The staff sergeant nodded, folding his arms across his chest as he watched Makarenko read. "Abu Ahmed al-Golani is mentioned by name, along with a man they refer to only as 'the Qatari.'"

The GRU officer snorted. That was hardly surprising—the Gulf States were nearly as invested in the overthrow of the Assad regime as Moscow and Tehran were in its maintenance, and while it was a fight they were very clearly, at this point, destined to lose, they seemed no less committed to it than ever. The civil war degenerating, at this late hour, into little more than a proxy conflict between Russia and Iran on the one hand, and Saudi Arabia, the UAE, and Qatar on the other, though by now serious rifts had opened in the latter alliance, with Qatar going its own way almost entirely. There were the Americans, of course, but with the fall of Raqqa and the victory lap their President Norton had taken over the "defeat" of the Islamic State, they were growing less relevant by the day.

The Syrian people? If anyone had *ever* been fighting for them, that seemed all now long forgotten, with those still remaining—those in the path of the warring factions who had somehow failed to flee the country in the early years—finding themselves in the position of the ancient inhabitants of Melos:

The strong do what they can, while the weak suffer what they must.

And suffer they did.

"What else do we know about this Qatari?" Makarenko asked, searching the sheet in vain for any annotation that might give him what he sought.

"Nothing, sir. The intercepted conversation gave no other details to go on." And that wasn't enough, as Makarenko knew well. While Saudi Arabia might have held the predominance upon the international stage, it was Qatar who had the real influence with groups on the ground. Identifying an individual Qatari agent on the basis of. . .just being a Qatari, was a fool's errand.

"Who is this Ibn Essam?" he asked, pointing to one of the conversation headers with a forefinger. Whoever he was, he seemed furious over the group's departure from the Ghouta pocket, his speech laced with a variety of untranslated words Makarenko assumed were typically colorful Arab obscenities.

"The *Jaish* commander who took over the Douma sector after the death of Abu Firas," was the reply. *Oh, yes. The drone strike.* The Americans might not be very relevant, but they still possessed the capacity to shake the scales, even if they themselves didn't always grasp the direction in which they shook them.

"Put a team on this, *tovarisch Stárshiy serzhánt*," Makarenko ordered, handing back the transcript. A vague worry gnawing at the back of his mind. *Idlib.* Maybe these so-called "knights" were headed there, and maybe they weren't. "Prioritize reaching out to our counterparts in the *Mukhabarat* and the Syrian military, see what they can give us."

The idea that a group from the Southern Front could launch a strike against the base had seemed absurd only four days before—with the Knights three hundred kilometers away in Quneitra.

Now, though. . .

Chapter 20

The rain had finally stopped an hour before, but the wind howled down out of the mountains from the north as the small convoy rolled through the silent mountain village, chilling the ragged men shivering in the open beds of the gun trucks to the bone.

Mohamed Taferi leaned back against the seat of the technical, sinking deeper into his own coat as he propped the forend of his Type 56 against the dashboard. The glass served to cut the wind, which meant he was marginally more comfortable than the fighters huddled in the back, but the Hilux's heater had cut out the previous night and the interior of the cab was now bone-cold, a damp, raw chill that sank into the very depths of one's being.

From a forbidding, mountainous crag just visible off to the north in the pale moonlight now bleeding through the clouds, a statue of the Madonna gazed benevolently down upon the sleeping town, her hands spread out as if in

263

supplication for her children.

A futile prayer, in truth, for the prophet's mother had been unable to protect the town when the jihadists of the al-Nusra Front had stormed through this mountain pass years before, looting and pillaging Maaloula's handful of churches, kidnapping nuns from the nearby convent, and blowing that statue's predecessor off the face of the mountain.

A towering Christmas tree stood in the small square in the center of town as the trucks rolled through, a homemade sign affixed to two uprights beside it, its uncertain, flickering lights spelling out "Merry Christmas" in incongruous English. Across the square, beside a shuttered storefront, sat the town's mosque, its spindly minaret standing in mute counterpoint to the spire of its Christian counterpart farther off to the north and west.

From the wall of a building on the west side of the square, the revered image of Bashar Assad stared from a poster at least eight feet tall—smiling out upon his people with all the impotence, if little of the benevolence, of the Madonna. He hadn't been able to protect this town either. *Not when it mattered.*

The Israeli shook his head at the surreality of it all as they rumbled on past, the lights shining bravely in the night behind them, the Hilux's heater randomly choosing to kick back on just then, blowing cold air into his face. War was mad, and war in Syria was by far the maddest of them all. He—

Behind him, over the steady purr of the truck's engine, he heard the sudden squeal of brakes—the shouts of men in the darkness.

"*Qif!*" he ordered sharply, motioning for his own driver to stop—hefting the Type 56 in his right hand as he shoved his door open, stepping out onto the broken pavement and hurrying back toward the square. He plucked the cellphone he had confiscated from Abd al-Malik from a pouch on his tactical vest, dialing Abu Ahmed's number as the lead trucks rolled on out of sight. *Pick up, pick up.*

"Stop the convoy," he said when the Knights' leader answered, sounding half-asleep. Or half-drunk, it was hard to say which.

"What?"

"Just do it."

One of the black-bearded jihadis had knocked the Christmas sign over on its side and was beating at the flimsy wooden frame with the butt of his rifle, the lights breaking and going out in a muted tinkle of glass. Anas ibn Nadhar stood a few feet away, looking approvingly on as another of his fighters shouldered an RPG-7, adjusting his eye to the irons.

Mohamed's eyes followed the line of the launcher, making out the pale outline of the Madonna up there on the cliffs. It was a long shot, but perhaps just within the rocket's maximum effective range, it was hard to gauge in the moonlight. "What do you think you are doing?"

"The will of God," Ibn Nadhar replied, a beneficent smile parting the jihadist's dark thicket of beard, revealing discolored teeth.

Mohamed shook his head. "This is madness. The success of our mission—our very *survival*—depends on our ability to vanish into these mountains and beyond. To leave no trace of our presence, for anyone to follow."

"Our success and our survival are in Allah's hands," the jihadist replied sternly, the smile disappearing. "And idolatry is a blasphemy against His name."

So it was, the Druze officer thought, his eyes never leaving Ibn Nadhar's face, but surely the One could be left to police His own affairs and sort the right from the wrong at the End of Days.

He felt his skin prickle, as though they were being watched from the darkened buildings, the militant with the RPG glancing uncertainly between Ibn Nadhar and himself. "Take the shot."

The man shouldered the RPG once more, sighting in on the Madonna—his finger closing around the launcher's trigger.

Shifting the rifle to his off hand, Mohamed lashed out, shoving the launch tube up and to the right even as the jihadist fired, the heat of the rocket's back-blast blossoming into the cold night air around them, a flurry of curses escaping the man's lips as he struggled to regain his balance. The rocket slammed into the cliffs above the town, more than thirty meters from the statue, triggering a small shower of broken rock.

Mohamed looked up to see multiple rifles leveled at him, Ibn Nadhar's voice an indistinct murmur of protest over the fading sound of the blast in his ears. "We need to move," he heard himself say, putting up a hand. "Before the town comes down on our heads."

". . .fool," was the only thing he heard from Ibn Nadhar, the burly man who had smashed the town's Christmas display stepping in out of the left, the worn butt of his weapon aimed at Mohamed's head.

He threw up his weak arm to block the incoming blow, a faint, distant *popping* suddenly reaching his ears, blood spray flecking the knuckles of his outstretched hand as a burst of rifle fire stitched his attacker across the chest, dropping him where he stood, collapsing heavily to the pavement like a sack of wheat.

Mohamed saw Ibn Nadhar's eyes open wide, heard the shrill whine of a bullet about his own ears and reached out, grabbing the jihadist leader and pulling him forcibly toward the cover of the trucks. "Come on, we have to get out of here. *Yalla, yalla!*"

6:47 P.M. Eastern Standard Time, December 22nd
Quill at the Jefferson
Washington, D.C.

"Seriously?" Olivia Voss glared incredulously across the small table at Jordan Sorbello, her eyes flashing fire. "You brought me here just to tell me this?"

"I'm sorry," the State Department official replied, taking a delicate sip of his cocktail. But he didn't look it. "You understand how these things are."

She did. Had known it was a long shot, from the beginning. But this—this was unbelievable. She rotated the untouched shot glass between her fingers on the tabletop, thankful only that the jazz piano was, tonight, mercifully silent. "This couldn't have been handled over the phone? You know what we're dealing with right now—the Braleys, everything in the Philippines."

He didn't, actually. Didn't—*couldn't*—have known that the Filipino rescue attempt had gone down in flames only a few hours before, that the captive American missionaries were once more in the wind. No one outside a small circle at the Agency—and of course, the Filipinos themselves—knew that.

"I understood you wanted this to be discreet," Sorbello replied, raising the glass to his lips once more. His voice as insincere as before. "I wish there was more I could do, Olivia—but bringing a member of the armed Syrian opposition to the United States, giving him a 'new life' here, that's a non-starter for this administration. You heard the skepticism the President gave voice to on the campaign trail about the "moderate" rebels. Now that ISIL has been shattered, he wants nothing more to do with the region. Assad's going to win, at this point—it's just a matter of time."

That last line, at least, was true. As for the rest, well she had seen the Islamic State "shattered" once before.

"You've done enough, Jordan." Olivia Voss rose to her feet abruptly, ignoring the look of surprise on Sorbello's face as she picked up the shot glass and downed it in a single swallow, the whiskey searing her throat. "Thanks for the drink."

8:03 A.M. Israel Standard Time, December 23rd
Mossad Headquarters, Glilot Junction
Tel Aviv-Yafo, Israel

"So do we know what he had done, back then? To backstop Taferi's legend?" David Shafron asked, raising his coffee to his lips. If Doha had been a source of hope yesterday, it was more than making up for it today.

"We do now." Nika Mengashe looked stricken, glancing over at Abram Sorkin before continuing. "He gave DROR the complete file on a flash drive. It's thin, David."

Shafron put his cup of coffee back down on the conference table, untouched. "What do you mean?"

Sorkin cleared his throat. "Meaning AGUR was lazy. He took our money and did only the bare minimum in return, figuring they wouldn't check, and we *couldn't*. He was half right."

"So Taferi is exposed." You could spend all the time and money in the world developing assets, making sure you had people in the right places, that you had your bases covered. That you'd done what was necessary to protect those you had sent into harm's way. And human nature would get you every time. It was something he hadn't always understood, in his own time in the field. The innate fallibility of the intelligence, of those who collected it.

"He is—as is AGUR, and he knows it. If anyone probes beneath the surface, well, there's nothing there. He's already asked DROR if we can exfiltrate him and his family. He has a wife, and three children—two girls, and a boy."

David Shafron shook his head, incredulous. That an agent would have the gall to demand relocation after a betrayal of this magnitude. . .yet as tempting as it was to simply wash their hands of the Qatari, there was, as ever, a bigger picture to be considered. If the *Lekhwiya* kicked in AGUR's door and dragged him away. . .well, he could identify DROR, compromising their officer's cover within the Gulf kingdom. The Office would be forced to exfil him, too, and ripping an experienced officer out of a well-established network left a hole that was difficult to mend, particularly in a country like Qatar, where Israel didn't enjoy the luxury of a diplomatic mission.

"Have DROR reach out and make emergency contact with Taferi—let him know that he's looking at potential compromise. We'll leave the continuance of the op to his judgment. And send Gideon Laner to my office as soon as he gets in."

They both rose to leave then, but Sorkin hesitated, his hand lingering on the door as Nika preceded him out. "David," he said quietly, his eyes meeting Shafron's, "we both know the planes aren't there. It's past time Taferi knew that as well."

He deserves *that much*—the unspoken subtext of Sorkin's words, full of reproach. Deserved to see all the cards on the table, before he made his decision.

It was a compelling argument for a man who had spent so much of his own career on the sharp end, David Shafron thought, holding his subordinate's gaze. For someone who knew exactly what it was like to be kept in the dark, to be manipulated by someone sitting safe behind a desk, hundreds of kilometers away.

But his days on the sharp end were behind him, and now *he* was the man safe behind the desk, as much as he loathed how that made him feel, at moments like this. You couldn't allow yourself to lose the forest for the trees, sitting here— had to keep your focus on the big picture, on what really mattered. No matter what your heart said.

The former *Kidon* operator shook his head slowly, sadly—feeling the sting of Sorkin's reproach. "No. Not yet."

10:43 A.M. Syria Standard Time
Maaloula, al-Qutayfah District
Rif Dimashq Governorate, Syria

The bullet holes in the walls of the buildings surrounding the town square were fresh, the dome of the mosque itself riddled by an errant hail of fire from a heavy machine gun.

Animals, Michael Awad thought, shaking his head at the irony of it all, looking down into the face of a dead jihadist, young and pale in death, contrasting strongly with the scraggly black of his beard. The followers of Mohammed had always expended so much of their energy fighting each other that it was hard to understand how they had ever conquered the Middle East.

Animals and cowards, as they'd illustrated here—spent steel casings crunching beneath his boots as he turned back toward the trucks. They'd cut and run before a handful of Christian—and yes, some Muslim—villagers defending their homes, a collection of old men and boys and cripples. The leader of that resistance, a hard-eyed, unshaven twenty-eight-year-old named Boutros, was standing not ten meters away, flanked by a pair of Awad's soldiers with the tiger patch of the 14th Special Forces Division on their fatigues, leaning awkwardly on his prosthetic left leg—a cigarette dangling from his upper lip, his AKM clutched in weathered, capable hands.

He'd left his other leg behind in the orchards outside al-Qusayr several years before, as part of the 10th Mechanised's ultimately successful push to retake that city from the Free Syrian Army. Come home to recover, marry, and raise a family, only to be forced to defend his home once again.

"Well done," Awad said, extending his hand. "You say they fled west, toward the highway?"

A nod from the younger man as he shook Awad's hand briefly, taking a long drag from his cigarette before removing it from between his lips, exhaling smoke into the crisp mountain air. "We hurt them, sir—badly. At least eleven or twelve fell, including their leader."

And only the one body, Awad thought, knowing better than to take the former soldier's casualty assessments at face value. That wasn't the reality of war in the Arab world. At best, based on those estimates, the rebels had probably taken four or five casualties, most of them not serious.

But that might be enough. If this was the same group Abd al-Malik had escorted through the tunnels of Harasta—and it seemed unlikely that it was any other—they hadn't had that many fighters to begin with. Yabrud would have been their next stop, like as not—not twenty kilometers up that highway. And that's where he would look for them next—there were still Hizballah contingents in the area, and they might have stumbled across each other.

"May our blessed Mother reward you for your bravery," Awad said with a smile, clasping the young man's hand once again as he turned to leave, casting a backward glance toward the Madonna looking down upon the town from the cliffs to the north.

These days, their faith needed all the defenders it could get. . .

2:03 P.M.
Jabāl al-Qalamūn – the badlands
An-Nabek District, Rif Dimashq Governorate
Syria

Lying flat on his belly against the rocky escarpment, the cold of the ground seeping through his clothes, Mohamed Taferi raised the binoculars to his eyes, glassing down the mountain slope and out across the plateau spread below him—the town of Yabrud just visible against the horizon, seven or eight kilometers away.

The shadows were already lengthening across the rocky slope as the sun descended toward the austere, craggy mountains at their back. Night would be upon them soon, and when it came, they needed to be gone—they were far from safe here, the detritus of war everywhere about.

It had only been a few months since Hizballah, backed by Syrian Army elements, had routed the lingering remnants of the Islamic State and *Tahrir al-Sham* from these barrens—and not everyone was gone just yet.

They'd passed a large poster of Hassan Nasrallah along the roadside not long after turning off the main highway, not far from the charred metal ruins of an early-model BMP—the Hizballah Secretary General's face split by a characteristically smug grin, the Arabic script superimposed over the group's familiar clenched-fist-clasping-Kalashnikov logo proclaiming that *"Our presence will increase wherever it should. . .we will be* everywhere *in Syria."*

He rose, wincing as pain shot through his weak arm—tucking the binoculars back within a pouch on his chest rig. Picking his way back up the narrow box canyon, its sides long since worn down by the elements, toward the shallow caves in which they had taken refuge for the day, the trucks arranged facing the mouth of the canyon in a crude laager, their mounted guns trained outward.

Blast craters from Hizballah artillery pocked the desolate canyon floor, frosted with light snow—legacy of the August bombardment, shells by the hundreds and thousands hurled into these mountains in the effort to dislodge the Islamic State. But like the British Tommies at Verdun, and the American Marines later on Okinawa, the Shiite militias tasked with sweeping Daesh from these mountains had learned the hard way that under artillery fire, men just dug in deeper. And had to be rooted out, one by one, the old-fashioned way—by the poor bloody infantry.

A sharp scream of pain came from within the mouth of the nearest cave, followed by the pathetic, whimpering sobs of a man clinging desperately to life.

Mohamed's face hardened. Three men had been hit in their brief gun battle there in the village square of Maaloula—a fourth left behind in the confusion. Only one of them was seriously hurt, the burly jihadist who had been cut down in the opening burst of fire.

With three 7.62x39mm rounds through his torso, he had no idea how the man was still alive, and after hours of listening to him moan in pain, he rather wished he wasn't. It wasn't as if he or any of the rest of Ibn Nadhar's followers would have shown the villagers an ounce of mercy had the situation been reversed.

Abdul Latif was bent down by the rear wheelwell of one of the Toyotas, a jack shoved beneath the truck, lifting the wheel just off the hard ground. As Mohamed approached, he poured a small amount of water from his canteen over the cold rubber, watching as bubbles popped to the surface.

"We're losing air," he said, looking up as the Israeli stopped short. "Must have picked up something. Won't take long for it to go, out on the road."

"Can you patch it?"

A grimace, distorting the big man's face as he straightened, looking over the side of the truck's bed at the boxed-up UAVs. "Not here. We'll have to either unload and shift the crates to other trucks, or else we take the chance—push it as hard as we can, see how long it holds."

The risks of the latter proposition were too obvious for either man to put into words. "I'll talk with Abu Ahmed," Mohamed said, half-turning away, glancing up to see small pale flakes descending out of the slate-gray sky. "He—"

Abd al-Malik's cellphone pulsed silently against his chest, and he plucked it from the pouch on his rig, running a grimy thumb over the screen to unlock it—half expecting it to be someone on the smuggler's contact list, trying to reach him. That had happened a handful of times in the past forty-eight hours. *Doha.*

He froze, a chill seeming to course through his body as his dark eyes scanned the message. *Your uncle Khalid has fallen and is in the hospital. He's been asking for you.*

They suspected that he was compromised. Suspected—didn't *know.* In some ways, that was the worse of the two, leaving the decision to abort resting squarely on his own shoulders. If they'd known, there would have been no question. As it was. . .

"What is it?" Abdul Latif asked, noticing his expression and the phone in his hand.

"My uncle," he replied reflexively, recovering himself with an effort, looking up to see Anas ibn Nadhar emerge from the caves, a dark, brooding presence. Abu Basir, as ever, at his heels. He couldn't afford to slip up—not here, not now.

"He's in the hospital—his wife says he had a bad fall."

"Tahoor insh'allah," the big man replied sympathetically, bending back to the wheel.

"Shukran." Mohamed returned the phone to his pocket, leaving the text unanswered for the moment—aware of Ibn Nadhar's eyes on him. Aware he still hadn't gotten over their confrontation of the previous night.

Aware that if he suspected. . .*anything*, he was a dead man.

3:47 P.M.
Khmeimim Airbase
Latakia Governorate, Syria

"What I'm saying, *tovarisch generál-mayór*, is that we need more time. A few more days, at least." Andriy Makarenko lapsed into silence, aware of just how insufficient that sounded. He felt Captain Egorov's eyes on him and refused to look his way, refused to give the Spetsnaz officer any more satisfaction than he was clearly already deriving from this. "We've been liaising with our Syrian partners, and they've confirmed the substance of our intercepts. The group we first heard about on the 18th has somehow broken through the siege cordon around Ghouta and has disappeared in the Qalamun Mountains along the Lebanese border."

"And you believe they pose a threat to the base?" the

Russian Air Force general sitting in Moscow asked, his voice clearly betraying puzzlement.

"That was our early intelligence, yes, *tovarisch.*"

"My office received the personal assurances of Colonel-General Khudobin himself that we could now operate from the base in complete security, *tovarisch podpolkóvnik.* Are you saying that he was in error?"

"Nyet," Makarenko replied, more sharply than he'd intended, bridling his anger with an effort. "We have experienced no recurrence of the mortar attacks, but—"

"But *Tovarisch Podpolkóvnik* Makarenko is frightened of shadows," Egorov sneered, more than loudly enough for the conference phone's microphone to pick him up.

"Who is *that?*" the general demanded, seemingly taken off-guard.

"Captain Valeriy Antonovich Egorov," the Spetsnaz officer replied, drawing his shoulders back and flashing Makarenko a nasty smile, "the officer sent here to ensure the security of your airframes by the GU's Second Directorate, before my hands were tied behind my back by personnel in-country. If *Tovarisch Podpolkóvnik* Makarenko is seriously concerned by this 'threat,' he should give me the latitude to do what needs to be done."

4:05 P.M. Israel Standard Time
Beit Shemesh, Jerusalem District

". . .and Papa, the teacher said that tomorrow we would have a documentary on the war of Yom Kippur. Mama says *Zaydee* fought in it—did you?"

A crooked smile crossed David Shafron's face as his

young son clambered into the passenger seat of the Mazda, the uniform shirt bearing his school logo improbably wrinkled beneath his open jacket, talking a mile a minute, pride evident in his studied pronunciation of the newly acquired word "documentary."

"No, I hadn't been born yet." His wife usually picked up the kids after school, but she was tied up in meetings at the Ministry of Justice and had called him two hours before to ask if he could do it today. He glanced at his watch—Laner's team should just be boarding their plane.

"Oh," Aaron replied, seemingly struck dumb by the ineffable vastness of such antiquity. "I—"

"We saw a video about lions and giraffes," Shmuel piped up from the back seat, momentarily distracted from the game on his tablet—cutting his older brother off. "A lion ate a gazelle all up."

Shafron pulled out onto the street, accelerating gently through the quiet neighborhood, past a woman out walking, being tugged along by her small dog, past the Haredi synagogue just down the road from the school. The raven-black form of a man striding away from it, his back to them, long coat billowing out behind him, the December wind plucking at his broad-brimmed hat. *Memories.*

"Did your father fight in the war?" Aaron asked then, startling him from his reverie. *Your father.* His sons had never known him—had never even met him before his death—didn't have the personal emotional attachment that they had to *Zaydee*—grandpa—Rahel's father. They were slowly warming to his mother, but that was taking time— she seemed a stranger even to him, after all these years. "My teacher says everyone fought."

"No," he heard himself say, his mind on the Haredi man still visible in his side mirror, toiling along—an older man, he could see that now, his coat catching the wind like the wings of some great bat. The face was indistinct, but he imagined, implausibly, that it was his own father's. "No, he didn't."

His father had never fought for anything in his life—least of all the survival of the Jewish state, which he had loved more than life itself. No, that wasn't right. . .his father had spent his whole life fighting, only it had been the long-lost wars of long ago, and it hadn't been with guns.

He had himself, after all, been a casualty of his father's wars.

"But my teacher said that. . ."

"Your teacher—" His phone began to ring just then, and he plucked it from his pocket, hitting his turn signal.

"Mama says you're not supposed to talk on the phone while driving," Shmuel observed sagely from the back seat as he answered it, and Shafron suppressed an exasperated curse, recognizing Sorkin's extension. *Kids.*

"Abram, what's going on?"

"We just heard from our friend in Syria, via Doha." Sorkin's voice was heavy, laden down with reproach. "He's made his decision."

But you didn't tell him the truth he needed to make it, he knew his subordinate wasn't saying. He didn't need to. And he knew then what the decision had been. "And?"

"He's chosen to stay on."

It felt as though a heavy weight descended upon his shoulders with the words, nothing of the relief he should have felt at the thought that their mission was still on. That they were still in the game. The odds here were so *long*.

"Any word from Moscow Station?" They still had a chance, if Eichler could come through for them. If they could get the intel they needed.

"Nothing."

6:37 P.M. Syria Standard Time
Jabāl al-Qalamūn – the badlands
An-Nabek District, Rif Dimashq Governorate
Syria

The boxes containing the disassembled UAVs had been shifted from the one broken-down truck into three, and Mohamed Taferi saw the boy, Nassif, perched atop one of them, his rifle in his lap, as he stalked through the billowing exhaust toward the mouth of the nearest cave.

Abu Ahmed's trucks were already loaded and idling in the cold, using up precious fuel, but Ibn Nadhar's contingent was unsurprisingly dragging its feet.

He shifted his Type 56 from his right hand to his left, assuring himself of the Glock's presence on his hip as he entered the cave, the stone floor worn smooth by the millennia and sloping beneath his feet—the interior lit up by the steady light of a Coleman lantern, casting strange shadows against the rock.

The moans of the wounded jihadist were softer now, but he was still, somehow, alive—shifting restlessly against the blankets, the sweat broken out upon his face forming a sickly sheen in the lantern light.

"We need to leave," he announced flatly, halting short of the knot of men gathered a few feet away. *"Now."*

They turned back to face him, and one of them stepped forward to stand protectively over the body, dark eyes flashing above a darker beard. "If we move, my brother will die."

"If we don't, we'll all join him," Mohamed replied, meeting the man's eyes. "What reason does your brother have to fear the Lord of Worlds? *Leave* him."

And Anas ibn Nadhar was there, a sepulchral figure seeming to materialize out of the rock itself, backlit by the Coleman, his eyes opaque and unreadable. Staring at Mohamed for a long moment before turning on his follower.

"He's right," he said finally, the words evidently causing him considerable pain. "We can't take him with us, and we can't stay."

The man's face flushed with anger, curses spilling forth from his lips as he took a step toward Ibn Nadhar. "You go, and may God curse you—I'm not leaving my brother to die alone."

"You won't." Mohamed didn't see the pistol until it was already out in the jihadist leader's hand, the crashing report of a pistol shot reverberating through the narrow confines of the cave.

A shuddering of the body amid the blankets and then it lay still, half the man's head blown away, blood and brains spattered across the rock.

His brother's eyes went wide with surprise and fear—and the jihadist started to slip the sling of his own Kalashnikov off his shoulder, the Israeli's hand flickering to his Glock.

But the rifle sling never made it past his elbow before Ibn Nadhar shot him in the forehead, the man's body seeming to collapse in upon itself as he crumpled to the ground, sprawling heavily across his dead brother.

The jihadist leader was still standing there, weapon leveled, gazing down at the corpses with a strange mixture of disdain and regret when Abdul Latif burst in a moment later, his rifle unslung, followed immediately by Nassif and a couple of older fighters.

Ibn Nadhar looked up and smiled strangely, returning the Beretta to its holster as he took a step forward, over the bodies, beckoning for the rest of his *mujahideen* to follow. "Come—let's be going."

Chapter 21

2:06 A.M. Central European Standard Time, December 24th
Milan Malpensa Airport
Ferno, Varese
Italy

The terminal lights glittered brightly without as Gideon Laner pushed his way along the darkened aisle of the wide-body Qatar Airways Boeing 777, looking for his seat, murmuring a curse beneath his breath as he squeezed past a heavyset woman struggling to cram her overstuffed carry-on in the overhead compartment. One would have thought that the Office could have sprung for business-class, at the very least, but Mossad shared the tight-fistedness of government bureaucracies the world over, and both he and his partner had ended up in economy.

He'd passed Yossi Eiland eight rows back, the former commando's small, stocky frame looking far more comfortable in his seat than Gideon expected to be in his own—already fiddling with his headphones as he settled in to watch the obligatory airline safety demonstration before queueing up a movie.

Eiland had served under him in the *Matkal*, and they'd made the transition to the Office within months of each other, though this was going to be their first time in the field together since coming over.

He found his seat, beside a lanky young American in a hoodie and cargo shorts who had occupied the window seat, his laptop resting on bony knees, already plugged into an outlet.

It seemed impossible to imagine how he could have been warm enough, with snow and ice still lingering on the ground without—but he *was* an American, and there was never any telling with Americans, that much Gideon had learned well enough from hard experience.

He leaned back into his seat, folding his hands across his chest and interlacing the fingers. In another six hours they would be on the ground in Qatar, and then, well. . .getting into the country would be one thing. Getting back out with AGUR—*and* his immediate family—would be much harder.

"What latitude do I have if it becomes impossible to exfiltrate our asset?" he'd asked, taking a sip from his bottle of water before looking down the conference table to where David Shafron and Mirit Refaeli sat, neither of them looking completely comfortable with the direction the briefing had taken.

But though apparently the MEGIDDO chief had equities of his own at stake in this, Gideon himself answered to Mirit—it was her networks under threat in Doha—and she had elected to take the question, her face setting into a hard cast, her voice cold and unwavering.

"The protection of our networks in-country is your primary

objective. The safety of Ibraheem al-Murrah is secondary. Do what needs to be done. Whatever needs to be done."

4:34 A.M. Syria Standard Time
Al-Qusayr District
Homs Governorate, Syria

The night was always darkest in the hours just before the dawn, and it was never colder, the boy thought, wrapping his thin arms about himself as he crouched in the bed of the technical, leaning against the gun mount for support as the truck jounced along through the empty fields, its wheels somehow finding every ridge and rill in the earth.

Mamdouh sat across from him, the RPD's barrel propped up against the side of the truck, one gaunt knee drawn up, that single eye staring out into the barren night, never seeming to rest.

They had passed the industrial city of Hisyah off to the west earlier in the night, its factories still struggling back online after the years of fighting, and now the lights of the government's Shayrat Airbase glowed against the eastern horizon—a false dawn.

They were losing. Nassif realized that, somehow, deep within—knew what the men around him were afraid to put into words, what they chose to ignore, to deny, as the eddies of war swirled around them, ebbing and flowing with each day of battle.

He hardly knew whether to feel regret at the idea. It had been Bashar Assad who had killed his family—the man whose smiling, genial visage had hung as a portrait on his parents' wall in their Damascus apartment, which probably still hung there, amid the ruins—but he could remember the years before, the *good* years, could remember going to school, chanting the praises of the President with the other children all around him. *"With our soul, with our blood, we sacrifice ourselves for you, O Bashar!"*

At one time, he'd imagined Bashar was some kind of god. *"No,"* his father had said, one day after school, his voice hushed to the most furtive of whispers, as though he'd expected a *mukhabarat* informant to leap from within the wall at any moment, *"there is no God but God. And He is One, with no partners beside Him."*

But was even that true? Nassif looked off toward the glow in the eastern sky, lost in his memories. It was hard to know where God had been in all of this—if a god there was—in the years of fighting and slaughter.

Perhaps the violence had become too much for even God to behold—perhaps He, like the rest of the world, had chosen finally to simply look away.

Maybe his parents' death was the fault of Bashar, maybe they never would have died if people hadn't risen up and taken to the streets to defy his presidency. *Maybe.*

All he really knew, huddling there in the bed of the open truck, the cold biting through his thin clothes was that, win or lose, this was all he had left. His world, constricting to these men around him, in these trucks, rolling north toward. . .whatever fate had in store.

By the time the sun rose, they should have reached the illusory "safety" of the rebel lines to the northeast of the devastated city of Homs. After that, it was impossible to say.

6:51 A.M. Moscow Standard Time
Ramenskoye
Moscow Oblast, Russia

It was cool in the bedroom of the small house on Moskvoretskaya Ulitsa, the kind of mild chill that makes it difficult to leave the comfort of one's blankets.

Yaroslav Svischev stirred restlessly, shifting against the pillows as he glanced over at his wife's sleeping form, curled up on her side next to him. It took him a moment to realize her eyes were open, that she was watching him in the semi-darkness, a smile tugging at her lips as their eyes met.

He reached for her hand and brought it to his lips, letting out a heavy sigh as he squeezed it tight. She had put up with so much from him, over the two decades and counting of their marriage—he still didn't understand how she had fallen for him in the first place, a low-ranking, underfed, underpaid fighter pilot in a once-proud air force whose planes were literally being sold off for parts on the black market by corrupt higher-ups looking for a new painting for their dacha in Komarovo or Zelenogorsk.

But she had, and together they'd weathered the years that had followed, as Russia climbed out of the grave of the '90s and began its ascent back to global prominence. He was part of an air force one could take pride in, once again, and while he wasn't as close to their three children as he would have wished. . .there was still time.

"You'll be back for Christmas, won't you?"

"Nadeyus' na eto." I hope so. It was an impossible question to answer—he would be there as long as he was ordered to be, and after all these years, they both knew it.

But that was another two weeks away. Surely, they wouldn't leave the Su-57s exposed in-theater that long.

"When do you have to leave?" she asked then, her voice soft in the darkness.

He rolled over to look at the digital clock on the nightstand, still clasping her hand. "Five hours. I should be at the airbase in three."

The lines of her face crinkled into a smile as she rolled closer to him, her hand playing with the wiry dark hair of his chest. Her lips, meeting his own.

"That should give us plenty of time."

7:03 A.M. Syria Standard Time
Homs District
Homs Governorate, Syria

They had been so *close*.

Mohamed Taferi bit back an angry, bitter curse, gazing out over the flat farm fields of eastern Homs, frozen hard and dusted with snow, a bitter wind sweeping down upon them out of the north.

Above, a high white contrail arced across the roseate dawn sky from west to east, the reverberation of jet engines reaching them only faintly here on the ground—a Russian strike fighter, like as not, on its way to pound lingering remnants of the Islamic State far off to the west. They were sitting ducks here.

Another hour—another fifteen kilometers, maybe less—would have put them within *Hayat Tahrir al-Sham*'s battle lines to the north of the city. "Safe," or at least as close to safe as they were likely to be for the next few days.

The irony of considering al-Qaeda's allies in Syria a safe haven wasn't lost on him as the wind sliced through his jacket, penetrating to the bone. But they had been close.

Until one of the technicals had sputtered to a stop here, in the middle of the open field, its engine seizing and dying.

"Bad gas," Abdul Latif announced just then, the big man's head popping into view from beneath the Honda's hood, his hands stained with grease.

That figured. He saw his own dismay reflected in Abu Ahmed's face and the rebel commander slammed his hand into the hood of the neighboring truck, cursing in frustration. Fuel was a scarce commodity in Syria these days, and much of what was still available was far inferior in grade to what these engines had been designed for. The majority of what they had bought in Douma to top off their tanks had been refined from melted-down plastic.

It was probably a miracle they'd made it this far, and meant the other trucks could start failing them at any moment.

He looked around them once again, shaking his head. It would have been hard to break down in a worse spot—the nearest cover, a compound visible off toward the east, near the actual road, probably six hundred meters out.

And out toward that road. . .his eyes narrowed, his heart freezing in his chest.

"Get the hose," he heard Abdul Latif order, motioning for Nassif to bring him a hose with which to siphon the gas. *And replace it with. . .what?* That seemed an unanswerable question.

But they had no time, in any case—the small cluster of vehicles he had glimpsed out along the road now turning toward them, one of Ibn Nadhar's lookouts raising a shout of alarm.

"Leave it," he ordered, hurrying back along the half-circle of the convoy to the Hilux in which he'd been riding on the drive up, pulling open the door and rummaging in the trash behind the seat, retrieving a dirty green and yellow cloth. "We have company."

7:08 A.M. Israel Standard Time
Bugrashov Beach
Tel Aviv-Yafo, Israel

The sand gave beneath David Shafron's feet as he pounded up from the beach, the cold air stabbing at his lungs—the wind-driven surf crashing and receding from the water's edge behind him, spray rising up to meet the dawn.

Ahead, the high-rises of Tel Aviv glistened white in the rays of early morning sun streaming over the Judean hills. And Paul Keifer, dressed as casually as Shafron had ever seen him, his suit traded in for a bomber jacket, the leather tips of cowboy boots poking out from beneath denim jeans, waited beside a blacked-out Suburban just across Retsif Herbert Samuel Street.

"Mornin'," the American said, extending his hand as Shafron came up, Shaul Litman falling in step behind him as they came across the street.

"What do you have for me?" Shafron asked, more sharply than he'd intended. Night had come and gone with still no further word from Moscow Station, and Mirit's team was now committed, on the ground in Doha. There wasn't an abundance of time this morning for pleasantries, and he could tell from his counterpart's manner that the CIA chief of station hadn't come bearing gifts. Or good news.

"State has shut us down, David," Keifer said heavily, refusing to look him in the eye. "There will be no relocation for Abu Ahmed al-Golani. Not to the United States—nor elsewhere under the auspices of the US State Department. I'm sorry. We've been liaising with State, with the folks at PRM, but the administration isn't budging."

It was hardly unexpected, but even so. . .Shafron shook his head incredulously. "So what is your country's stake, Paul, in all of this? What are you even putting on the table?"

"The Astana talks—"

"Aren't even the beginnings of enough," the Israeli spat, glaring toward Keifer's security. "Walk with me."

"What?"

"Walk with me," he repeated brusquely, turning away without waiting to see if the American would follow. The brown, weathered fronds of the palms overhead rustling in the sea breeze as he walked quickly along the line of low bollards shielding the curb, the chill biting through the thin fabric of his navy-blue tracksuit, his sweat from the run cooling against his skin.

"Listen, David," he heard Keifer begin, the fall of the American's boots audible against the walk as he hurried up behind him.

"No, *you* listen." Shafron's eyes were hard and snapped like black coals of fire as he turned back on the CIA chief of station. "I have an officer out there—exposed—on the point of compromise, for airframes that aren't even in-theater anymore, and now you're telling me your government can do nothing for the one man who knows who he is and who might be able to keep him alive."

Keifer stopped short, putting up his hands in a gesture of helplessness. "Look, David. . .you're angry. I would be, in your shoes. But we both have people we answer to, and when the orders come down, we obey them, like good soldiers, without challenge."

"Maybe in your army." That wasn't the IDF way, Shafron thought, looking the American in the eye. Forced to fight tooth and claw for its very existence from the moment of its birth, Israel's military had never placed any sort of premium on formality, allowing good ideas to be heard and bad ideas to be challenged, no matter from whence they emanated in the chain of command. "And I *was* a soldier. It doesn't—"

His phone went off in that moment and he plucked it from the pocket of his tracksuit, glancing at the screen. *Headquarters.*

"Yes?" He listened for a long moment before replying, *"Toda,* Nika. *Toda rabah leha."*

Thanks so much.

"What was that about?" Keifer asked, favoring him with a skeptical look.

"The Su-57s? They're back in play."

7:12 A.M. Syria Standard Time
Homs District
Homs Governorate, Syria

The captured yellow-and-green Hizballah colors he had shoved into the Hilux back in Quneitra just before their departure now flew above the cab of the nearest technical, snapping viciously in the bitter north wind as the quartet of military vehicles rolled across the field toward them, the lead vehicle, a Russian-built BMP-1, finally pulling to a stop about a hundred meters away. The muzzle of its 73mm main gun pointing threateningly in their direction, a smaller command vehicle nestled in the armored personnel carrier's shadow. Behind them, a GAZ-66 and another heavy army truck of indeterminate Chinese make pulled up short, their engines idling in the cold.

"Steady, steady," Mohamed Taferi breathed through clenched teeth, as if the man on the dual-mounted PKMs above, their muzzles raised unthreateningly skyward, could hear him, forcing a welcoming smile to his face as soldiers spilled out of the back of the GAZ, weapons at the ready, spreading out to take up positions.

The Syrian Arab Army.

The ruse wouldn't hold for long, he knew that—Anas ibn Nadhar, alone, could have served as the poster boy for *Daesh Weekly*—but it wouldn't have to.

A pair of men in heavy winter overcoats detached themselves from the vehicles, soldiers falling in behind them as they advanced. *Command element?*

He had to hope so, hope against hope. If it wasn't, they might well be dead.

And then a diesel engine roared back into full life, the rearmost truck peeling out to take up a flanking position to their north, the clang of metal as its rear gate went down.

He heard the gunner above him begin cursing in a low, fluid stream of vile Arabic, a desperate edge to the man's voice. A handful of loud metallic *snaps* audible in the clear, cold air as rebel fighters now waiting in the shadows of the vehicles slipped off the safeties of their rifles.

Mohamed took a step forward and then another to greet the advancing officers, holding up an empty right hand as he closed the distance, painfully aware of just how exposed he was. *"Shuu ya akhi?"*

The army officer in the overcoat stopped perhaps twenty meters away, a strikingly handsome man somewhere around the Israeli's own age, a thick black mustache adorning his upper lip. He paused, saying something unintelligible to the aide at his side before turning to respond to Mohamed's shouted, *"What's up, brother?"* with a question of his own, "You're Hizballah?"

"Na'am," the Israeli replied, nodding, silently willing them closer, eyeing the squad of soldiers immediately at their back. "One of our trucks broke down, on our way to the front. Do you have a mechanic?"

Come closer. He had seen the Syrians in action enough times to know how well their conscripts functioned without leadership. If this man *was* their CO, if they could take him out of play. . .

Out of the corner of his eye, just out of focus, he could see the gaping muzzle of the BMP's cannon, huge even at this distance. That alone could destroy them all in a trice.

Another murmured aside, then, "What unit do you answer to?"

There was caution in the man's voice, and with good reason. Over the course of the war, Hizballah had executed more than a few Syrian Army soldiers and officers for disobeying *their* orders, the chain of command as muddled as the conflict itself. "Abu Sobhi," Mohamed replied, naming a prominent Shiite commander in the Homs region. "We—"

A shout from somewhere behind him, and he saw the officer's eyes open wide, white and staring, his hand frantically fumbling within his coat. A ragged burst of fire tearing through the crisp dawn.

Mohamed threw himself to one side, clearing his Glock from its holster even as he landed among the snow-encrusted stubble, pain shooting through his injured arm. He brought it halfway up, firing as it came—his first two shots going wild, the officer's sidearm coming out, a cacophony of fire erupting from back toward the trucks.

Then there was a horrible ripping sound—like a buzzsaw—and he saw the officer quite literally. . .come apart in a spray of blood and flesh, his torso disintegrating under a hail of machine gun fire, his aide dying before he could bring his rifle to bear, the dual-mounted PKMs cutting through the nearest soldiers like a scythe through wheat.

Get the tank, get the tank, the Israeli thought, spitting out snow as he came up, putting a pair of rounds into the chest of a wounded Syrian soldier already down on his knees not ten meters away, fumbling with the safety of his rifle.

He saw the Chinese truck on the northern flank eat a rocket, going up in a deathly pall of fire and dark oily smoke, one of Ibn Nadhar's *Dushkas* chewing remorselessly through the dismounts. The BMP lurching into reluctant motion, its turret traversing to find a target. *Get the tank.*

Then a rocket-propelled grenade whirred past over his head, the sound of its motor somehow penetrating the chaos. He stayed down on one knee, unconsciously holding his breath as it flew toward the Russian-made armored personnel carrier, striking the front hull just at the peak of its glacis. And did. . .nothing, the Israeli's eyes opening wide in fear and surprise as the RPG simply failed to explode, rebounding off the BMP's armor like a toy thrown from the hands of a petulant child. *Dud.*

The BMP's cannon barrel seemed to settle for a brief moment before belching fire, a shell screaming above like a passing freight train, the Hilux behind him taking a direct hit, the gunner on those PKMs shredded by shrapnel, the mount itself disappearing as the truck's fuel tank cooked off in a sympathetic detonation.

He had no time to process the reality before rifle bullets scored the air past his head, the GAZ's dismounts slowly recovering, getting into the fight. Mohamed threw himself flat once again, cursing viciously as he unslung his Type 56, bringing it to bear—praying someone back there, whether among Abu Ahmed's men or Ibn Nadhar's, still had an RPG, that they had *focused* on his hurried instructions. *Get the tank.*

If they couldn't, they were dead. All of them, here in this field of frozen, stubbled wheat. *Not for the first time*—not for him, at least, and as he brought his rifle up to his shoulder, triggering a series of short, controlled bursts, servicing targets eighty meters out, he seemed to see himself standing in a field very much like this one, waist-deep with grain, a spear clutched in sweat-slick fingers, shield clasped tightly in his other hand as the ground beneath his feet trembled from the hooves of ten thousand horses, as arrows darkened the sky above, the triumphant cries of the Tatar filling the air.

A villager—his father, maybe, or his son—breaking at his side, panic filling their eyes. An arrow, piercing their back before they'd taken two steps, blooming crimson and red against the white purity of their thawb. He turned to look—

and an arrow came whistling in over his own shield, burying itself to the middle of the birch shaft in the meat of his shoulder. *Searing pain.*

And then another—and another—and he was falling, collapsing into the grain. The staff of life, crushed beneath him even as he died, gazing up at the sun.

His vision seemed to clear even as his magazine emptied and he replaced it with a spare from his belt, low-crawling forward to the nearest bodies. Another round from the BMP's main gun crashing out—a miss, this time, as the shell cleared the top of a nearby Hilux by the slimmest of margins. The firing from the north seemed to have died down, the soldiers up there caught in the open and off-guard, slaughtered to the last man, but so long as that armored personnel carrier stayed up, they were themselves outclassed and outgunned. *Get the tank.*

As if in response to his desperate plea, he saw an RPG slam into the icy ground just in front of the vehicle's tracks, an angry plume of dirt, smoke, and debris blossoming from the earth. But when the smoke washed away, the armored personnel carrier was still moving forward, its coaxial machine gun chattering angrily away as it raked the convoy.

Then two more smashed home, striking almost together just where the turret met the hull, the flash searing across his eyes as the turret flipped end over end through the air, finally falling to earth thirty feet away.

The volume of Syrian fire seemed to waver, then fade— and he saw figures retreating across the blood-drenched snow, saw them fall, lashed by the technicals' mounted guns.

Until their fire, too, ceased, and the field was quiet once more, save for the moans and cries of the wounded and dying. . .

7:54 A.M.
Jabāl al-Qalamūn – the badlands
An-Nabek District, Rif Dimashq Governorate
Syria

The dead men had been *Daesh*, of that Michael Awad had no doubt. Their untrimmed black beards, their dark, austere clothing—stripped in this case of any weapons or ammunition—it was all very familiar, the signature style of the vultures who fed on the carcass of his country, pulling it to shreds between them.

And now they were where they belonged—burning alive eternally in the fires of hell. He wondered what it had been like for them to realize at the last that their "god" was, in truth, Satan himself.

The Syrian Special Forces captain turned and walked from the shallow cave into the pale light of early morning, suppressing a scowl as his eyes fell upon the imposing bulk of Ali Malek Maatouk, the Hizballah field commander known as "Abu Dyab."

That Abu Dyab too would one day burn in hell was another thing of which Michael Awad was certain, but for this moment, the Iraqi Shiite was an ally, one of the thousands of foreign fighters who had poured into Syria at the behest of Tehran, keeping Bashar al-Assad alive and in power when so many of his own soldiers had gone over to the enemy.

The result was a distinct power imbalance in favor of those militias and their leaders, at the expense of those regular army officers who had kept the faith.

I hope to live to see the day when I can put a bullet through your skull and send you to that hell myself, he thought, forcing a grim smile to his lips.

"Your intel was right, Abu Dyab," he said, keeping his voice deferential with a mighty effort, "they were here. Last night, most likely, patching up their wounded from Maaloula."

Or executing *them, from the looks of it.* With *Daesh,* one was as likely as the other. "Headed north, to Idlib, according to the smuggler. Your checkpoints—"

"No one was on the roads," Maatouk replied flatly, transfixing Awad with lifeless black eyes. "My men saw no one."

Which only meant that they hadn't taken the roads— and only a fool would have, given the relatively flat, open terrain to the east. Whatever else these men were, judging by the way they'd slipped through the siege of Ghouta, they were no fools.

They could be most anywhere by now, though, that was the harsh reality of it. He needed air support, but air assets were not simply at the beck and call of a Special Forces captain, and obtaining them would require finding someone with connections above him—finding the person and figuring out what they wanted in return.

It wasn't bureaucracy or red tape, not in the way someone in one of the West's crumbling democracies would have understood it—no, that would have been far too simple. This was Syria, and favors and patronage were ever the order of the day, even on the front lines of a war.

"We will find them, though," the Hizballah commander went on, up-ending his thermos to drain the last of his coffee before wiping his mouth with the back of a grimy hand.

"Sooner or later, we will run them to ground, and—"

"Captain!" a voice called from below them, one of Awad's soldiers hurrying breathlessly up from the mouth of the box canyon—Abu Dyab's eyes snapping angrily at the interruption.

"Captain, we just received a transmission from Homs. They're reporting contact with rebels east of the city, near Zaidal. It's a massacre," the soldier announced, his drawn, swarthy face taking on a paler cast in the morning light, "they're saying a whole unit has been cut to bits."

Awad exchanged a look with Abu Dyab, and he could tell the Iraqi was thinking the same thing he was. It was a long shot, but it might be the best one they had.

"We need to get on the road," he announced. "If we go now, we can be there in a few hours."

"La, la," Abu Dyab replied, shaking his head firmly in the negative. The Hizballah commander plucked a cellphone from the chest rig of his paramilitary uniform fatigues and held it out, struggling to find a signal. "I'll get us a helicopter."

8:42 A.M. Israel Standard Time
Mossad Headquarters, Glilot Junction
Tel Aviv-Yafo, Israel

"So it paid off, your gamble?" Avi ben Shoham asked, flicking on the light switch as he led the way into the SCIF, setting his cup of coffee down before settling into his seat at the head of the table.

David Shafron closed the door behind them and took his own seat a couple places away from the *memuneh*—Sorkin taking the chair opposite.

"Yet to be seen, Avi," Shafron demurred. Shoham had just arrived for the morning and the steam poured off his fresh coffee as he lifted it to his lips, its rich aroma filling the SCIF. Shafron had planned to get his own after the morning run and meeting with Keifer, but the call had scotched those plans and the effects of the crisp salt air were wearing off. "We know more now than we did. But the window. . .it's still perilously tight."

"How tight are we talking?"

"Mordechai's asset was able to get us a copy of the orders." Shafron extracted a sheet covered in Cyrillic from the folder before him and passed it down to the Mossad director. "The planes arrive at Khmeimim in the next ten hours, and once they're on the ground, our clock starts ticking. Three days."

A grimace, as Shoham took another sip of his coffee. "Can he make that timetable?"

"We'll find out when he next makes contact." If there was any way to know. Uncertainty was the order of the day in Syria, as each of the three men knew well. "The *Tachash* will make the first run up the coast tonight, to begin preparing the battlespace."

"And Mirit's team?"

"Landing in Doha within the hour," Shafron replied, consulting his notes. "They'll make contact with AGUR later today and prep him for exfil in the next twenty-four."

"Good. Let's make it happen."

9:37 A.M. Arabia Standard Time
Doha, Qatar

There was construction everywhere Gideon Laner looked, the blue-roofed taxi threading through traffic to the strains of Tamer Hosny's mellifluous voice, coming loudly from the Hyundai's speakers as they drove into downtown Doha, surrounded by a forest of concrete, steel, and glass at every hand. Glittering buildings stretching endlessly skyward, dwarfing man and vehicle alike—the workers on the scaffolding three-quarters up the side of one skyscraper, smaller than ants.

His eyes met those of a Vietnamese migrant just on the other side of a long line of Jersey barriers, working alongside the road as part of a construction crew, dark eyes staring vacantly from beneath the rim of the man's hard hat. A sign just beyond the worker blinked out *Men Working* in orange lights, but it could have read *Slaves* with equal accuracy.

Not unlike the Hebrews in ancient Egypt, the Israeli officer thought ironically, staring out the window. A paradise for some, a hell for the rest—gleaming monuments distracting from a darker truth that the average Western tourist would never pause long enough to see.

He could imagine what Yossi—who had taken a separate taxi, the two of them maintaining the fiction of strangers as long as possible—was thinking, seeing it all. The grandson of German Jews who had fled Europe for Mandatory Palestine under the auspices of the Youth Aliyah in the late '30s, the French-born Eiland had grown up spending his summers with his grandparents on the kibbutz of Beit HaArava in Judea and Samaria, and the socialist heritage of those early settlers still ran strong in the commando's veins.

"*This is what capitalism really looks like when you let it run wild,*" he could hear him saying, as clearly as if he'd been sitting across from him in the back seat of the taxi, "*when you don't have a government willing to regulate business to protect its people. The markets aren't 'moral,' they aren't wise— there's no 'invisible hand,' benevolently guiding affairs. Just a boot, on the neck of the worker—that's what you get, every time.*"

Perhaps. Perhaps it had more to do with the reality that Qatar didn't view the two million migrant workers—most of them from Southeast Asia, like that Vietnamese construction worker—which made up ninety-five percent of the Gulf monarchy's total labor force as "*its* people," at all, just slaves to be used up and thrown away.

But so long as the oil kept flowing, so long as Qatar was content to play host to the sprawling American military base at Al Udeid just outside Doha, so long as it remained a coveted vacation destination for tourists with money to blow. . .few in the West would care. Maybe Yossi had a point.

Gideon leaned back into the seat, keeping a cautious eye on the vehicles surrounding them—a heavy SUV barreling past in that moment, his driver hitting the horn in protest.

Traffic in Doha was very much like any other Arab city, only more so—the monarchy's affluence leading to a proliferation of large 4X4s like the Toyota Land Cruiser and Hilux in its streets, equipped with characteristic treadless desert tires. Colossal, lumbering vehicles driven with the characteristic speed and aggression of an Arab Giancarlo Baghetti. If they did their job right, and the asset didn't

303

manage to screw things up further, this drive in from Hamad International would be the most dangerous part of the trip.

A motorbike—at the other extreme of popular Doha transport—roared up on the right side of the blue-roofed taxi and Gideon felt himself flinch involuntarily, taking in a sharp breath and not releasing it until its helmeted rider had passed them by, disappearing ahead down a side street.

A bad conscience, his rabbi father would have told him—and perhaps he would've been right. He knew far too well what one could do on such a motorbike.

He checked his watch. It wouldn't be long now. . .

11:09 A.M. Syria Standard Time
East of Zaidal
Homs Governorate, Syria

It would have been quicker to drive, Michael Awad thought, ducking low as he ran from the door of the helicopter, the Mil Mi-4's ancient rotors stirring up a tornado of watery slush and stubble all about him, peppering his fatigues with wet debris.

It had taken the better part of two hours just for Abu Dyab's promised helicopter to put in its appearance, as he'd silently fumed over the delay, promising himself, with each passing minute, to make the Hizballah commander's eventual death a slower and more painful affair—and when it had, the sight of the lumbering Soviet relic, daylight visible through a score of bullet holes in its hull, had nearly given Awad nausea.

He'd had no idea that anything as old as the Mi-4—which had seen its first flight in the age of Stalin—was still in service, and he'd ultimately thought it better not to ask how Abu Dyab had conjured one up, the Hizballah commander himself seeming to take on a greenish cast over the course of the flight north as the Mi-4's decrepit airframe groaned and rattled, threatening to shake itself apart.

But they were on the ground safely, the Virgin Mother be thanked.

However "safety" could truly be defined in this country, Awad thought skeptically, glancing about him as he strode forward, his soldiers spreading out behind him, the rotor wash whipping at their uniforms as they brought their rifles to bear. A pall of smoke still rose from the wreck of the destroyed BMP off to the east, the burnt-out wreck of a military truck smoldering farther to their north. The stench of death hung over the field, bodies scattered everywhere, lying just where they had fallen, slowly stiffening in the cold.

Behind him, the Mil Mi-4 dipped forward, wobbling into the air, and screaming by just over their heads in a cacophonous crescendo of protesting machinery, spraying more wet debris in Awad's face.

He grimaced, reaching up to brush it away in an unconscious gesture—his fingers coming away dark and wet with blood, the Special Forces officer's widening eyes falling on the corpse of a young soldier lying in the reddened snow only five or six feet ahead, half-disemboweled by a burst of machine gun fire.

"Massacre" was the right word for this, he realized, noting the single bullet hole in the man's forehead—powder burns around the entry—as he stepped over the body. Executed, where he'd lain—no doubt begging for his life.

Carnage, everywhere he turned his eyes—men lying in

heaps like sheaves of fallen grain. *Butchered.*

There had to have been survivors—he had been in enough battles to know the wounded *always* outnumbered the dead, but no one was now alive in this field of death. *Daesh* had made sure of that.

He saw a crucifix hanging from the neck of one murdered soldier, not so much older than his own Joseph, and paused for a moment to offer a prayer for his soul, knowing there had been no one here in those horrifying final moments to administer last rites.

Abu Dyab was already ahead of him, examining the less-damaged of the pair of Toyotas sitting abandoned in the middle of the field, the one's white paint riddled with dozens of bullet holes, while the other appeared to have taken a direct hit from the BMP's main gun, and it was impossible to tell from the blackened husk which remained what color it had been in life.

"*Daesh* was flying our colors," the Hizballah commander observed angrily, stabbing a thick figure toward the barely recognizable yellow-and-green banner now drooping over the blackened metal of the Hilux's cab, somehow unconsumed by the inferno. "That's how they lured them in."

Michael Awad shook his head, hands resting on his hips—his AK-74 still slung over his shoulders. It made sense—even in the Special Forces, he deferred to their Iranian-backed "allies."

A regular Army unit would have been even more unsure—a hesitation which had cost them their lives.

He scanned the bed of the white Toyota, picking out a small crate lying half-buried beneath debris and cartridge casings in the corner up against the cab. "Get me that," he ordered, beckoning to one of his commandos.

He watched as the man clambered up into the bed of the technical, nearly slipping on the scattered brass—stabilizing himself against the now-empty mount, the heavy machine gun stripped from its mounting, no doubt taken with the retreating rebels.

The commando retrieved the crate and brought it back to the tailgate even as Captain Awad and Abu Dyab moved back—the soldier's hands visibly trembling as he pried off the lid. If years of war against these Zionist-backed gangsters had taught them anything, it was that anything could be booby-trapped. *Anything.*

"It's. . .it's a drone, Captain!" the man exclaimed, and Awad stepped back in, peering into the rag-padded interior of the crate to examine its contents.

The shattered, bullet-riddled frame of a disassembled quadcopter UAV.

2:45 P.M.
Khmeimim Airbase
Latakia Governorate, Syria

Off to the west, through the protective bubble of the Su-57's canopy, the waters of the Mediterranean sparkled in the late afternoon sun, hardly a cloud marring the blue of the sky as Yaroslav Svischev lined up his fifth-generation stealth fighter with the runway for final approach—Khmeimim's tower guiding him in.

It had been an uneventful flight, the pair of fighters lancing south across Azerbaijan and Iran before turning west into Iraqi airspace for the final leg of the route.

Desolate, godforsaken wastes spread out below them as they'd broken the sound barrier over the deserts of eastern Syria, once the playground of the Islamic State, now battered and broken—their radar picking up other military flights, both Russian and Syrian, pounding the scattered remnants of the caliphate into submission from above.

Oil country or not, it seemed impossible to imagine that men would actually *fight* over such a wasteland, but those fanatics had done just that for the better part of half a decade.

Latakia, from the air, seemed a paradise by comparison, but he had been here long enough before to realize that the paradise was only skin-deep. And as the Su-57 came in over the perimeter fence like a striking raptor, its heavy landing gear touching down on the hard asphalt of the runway, *Stárshiy Leytenánt* Svischev began counting the hours until he was gone again. . .

Chapter 22

4:09 P.M. Arabia Standard Time
Souq Waqif
Doha, Qatar

He had left his suit jacket on the seat of his Nissan and replaced his sweaty dress shirt with a loose polo, but Ibraheem Saleh al-Murrah could still feel the sweat building beneath his armpits as he walked deeper into the souq, his eyes darting back and forth, searching for threats—children's sandals festooning a wall of one stall as he walked by, gaily-colored bolts of cloth the next. Ahead of him, a pair of women in wheelchairs, only their eyes visible beneath their enveloping black niqabs, sat in front of a stall selling backpacks emblazoned with the logos of Qatari football teams.

Neither woman so much as met his eyes as he passed, the extremity of their modesty contrasting sharply with the Russian tourist walking just ahead of him, tottering on impossibly high heels, hips swaying beneath an inappropriately short skirt.

The bird market. That's where he would meet his contact,

as arranged. Surely he would have a plan, some way to make all this right.

He had endured another tense, unbearably long day at the Security Bureau, his supervisor stopping by his workstation to inquire into his progress. *"There seem to be some. . .irregularities,"* he'd replied finally, unable to evade the senior bureaucrat's line of questioning without it becoming obvious, *"in the military records. I am making inquiries—it may take a few more days."*

By which time, he fervently hoped—he and his family would be far, far away from here, never to return. He had never dreamed that his desire for a better income—to be less humiliatingly *dependent* upon his wife—would lead to them all fleeing their home.

A youthful portrait of the Emir of Qatar stared out at him from above one of the stalls, those piercing eyes seeming to follow his steps as he unconsciously picked up the pace.

We know you, traitor, they seemed to shout. *We know what you did.*

The sweat was beading on his forehead by the time he reached the bird market itself, passing beneath weathered stone steps that looked ancient but, he knew, dated back no further than the renovation of the souq following the 2003 fire—the shadows seeming to close in on him in the gathering twilight, choking him with guilt and fear. Even the gap-toothed smile of an elderly Arab vendor in a traditional white thobe and checkered ghutra standing before his cages of birds at the entrance, appearing somehow sinister.

He was becoming paranoid, he knew that—the discordant chatter of thousands of rare and exotic birds swelling around him as he entered the market, cages stacked upon cages—a large blue-and-green parrot lashing out at the bars, screaming furiously at him as he walked by. Further on, he saw a pair of very well-fed. . .cats sleeping peacefully in one cage, birds screaming all around. *The peace of the predator.*

"Abu Zaid?" he heard an unfamiliar voice ask, recognizing the name of his eldest son as he turned to find a swarthy, bearded young man standing behind him, wearing the striped blue-and-grey polo shirt and khaki slacks he had been told to expect from his contact. *But it* wasn't *his handler.*

Ibraheem backed away hastily, eyes widening in panic—backing straight into a short woman covered head-to-toe in a voluminous black burqa. He tripped and would have fallen if *she* hadn't reached out and grasped him by the shoulder, stabilizing him with an iron grip.

"*Afwaan,*" he sputtered in apology, regaining his equilibrium, his eyes darting from one to the other.

"Easy there, Ibraheem," the man said, a smile parting his dark, close-cropped beard. He could have passed easily enough for an Arab, but the accent—he wasn't a local, that much was certain. *A Jew?* "He's with me."

He? He glanced back at the "woman," blinking as realization slowly dawned.

"*Na'am,*" the man nodded in answer to his unspoken question, the smile growing wider. "He's so ugly we have to cover him up just to go out in public. Now walk with us, Abu Zaid—the noise of the birds will cover our conversation from any listening ears."

5:03 P.M. Syria Standard Time
Talbiseh
Homs Governorate, Syria

The crackling of automatic weapons fire from off to the south pulsated through the gathering darkness, the sun fading into a liquid puddle of blood and gold across the western horizon.

Mohamed Taferi stalked through the streets, eyes as red as the sky, the barrel of his Type 56 propped back against his shoulder. Across from them, in front of a half-collapsed two-story building, an old man sold oranges from the back of a cart, each of the gleaming orange orbs wiped clean, their perfection discordant, almost surreal in the dirt and chaos surrounding them at every hand.

He had tried to sleep, earlier in the afternoon, but every time he closed his eyes, he saw Ibn Nadhar's killers stalking that field of blood once more, pausing now and then beside the wounded to aim their weapon downward, a short burst or the sharp report of a pistol shot marking the end of a life.

A wounded soldier, driven all but mad with pain, begging desperately for aid, for mercy—for his very *life*. But the only mercy to be found in this country was a quick death.

He had known what would happen, from the moment the guns had fallen silent over that field, had known that he was powerless to do anything about it. They were all safer with no one left to explain what had happened, and far too much blood had been shed in this land for anyone to feel the slightest compunction over a few more dead—on the *other* side.

Abdul Latif strode ahead of him, rolling a truck tire across the broken asphalt of the street, to replace one holed by machine gun fire earlier in the morning. It had taken them close to three hours to limp to the dubious safety of *Hayat Tahrir al-Sham*'s lines north of Homs, down an additional two trucks and running flat on several more, jagged holes punched through the sides of the technical big enough to put a hand through.

"I don't know," he had told the Office earlier, answering their question of whether they could make the new deadline. They had little choice but to try, having gotten this far—as the crow flew, they were now less than a hundred kilometers from the Russian airbase, but the last ninety of those were regime-controlled, and getting through the mountains. . .well, too many of their vehicles were shot up to make it very far, very fast.

They'd lost a half-dozen men in the brief firefight with the Army detachment, that single BMP shell killing two outright and leaving another fighter with his legs sheared off above the knees, begging piteously and incoherently for someone to come and kill him.

Abu Ahmed had obliged him, taking out his pistol and blowing the man's brains out where he lay—the rebel leader's eyes betraying nothing but an ineffable sense of weariness as he turned away, holstering the weapon.

All of this had to come to an end soon, one way or another. . .

5:36 P.M. Israel Standard Time
Mossad Headquarters, Glilot Junction
Tel Aviv-Yafo, Israel

"He hadn't even told his wife yet?" David Shafron heard Mirit Refaeli ask incredulously as he entered the conference room, closing the door behind him. On the television screen at one end of the room he saw Gideon Laner lean toward the camera, Yossi Eiland visible behind him through the open door of the safehouse bedroom, stripping out of a burqa.

Shafron suppressed a smirk with difficulty. That was familiar ground. In another life, as the youngest and freshest-faced member of his *Duvdevan* team, he'd found himself playing that role on more than one op in Palestinian-controlled areas of Gaza and the West Bank.

"No, he hadn't," Laner replied, weary exasperation in his voice. Handling assets had to be one of the hardest challenges of transitioning over from the military to Mossad. Dealing with people who had no concept of discipline or authority, yet whom you nevertheless relied upon to carry out your mission.

"You've made clear to AGUR that we are on the clock here?"

The former *Matkal* officer acknowledged Shafron with a brief nod as he entered the camera frame, before returning his attention to his own boss.

"Of course, Mirit. Abundantly clear. And he's not eager to stay any longer than he has to. He's scared out of his mind, jumpy. If it wouldn't run the risk of tripping alarm bells, I'd advise he call in sick tomorrow. As it is. . ."

"You won't be conducting the exfil tonight?" Shafron asked, only too aware he had missed the first few minutes of the call. *Paperwork*—it was the bane of his existence as head of department, always far too much of it cluttering up his desk.

Laner shook his head. "No. He's asked us to give him another twenty-four hours to get his family ready, to make all the necessary arrangements. We should have him on a flight to Munich by tomorrow night, where he's been briefed to claim political asylum."

Hard to say whether that would be granted, but it wasn't like Germany was really throwing *anyone* out just now, Shafron mused ironically. And Al-Murrah was in no position to demand anything better.

"How are things progressing with the back-up plan?" Mirit asked then, a hard look creeping into her eyes as she stared down the camera.

"They're progressing. We meet our contact within the hour."

6:17 P.M. Syria Standard Time
Talbiseh
Homs Governorate, Syria

The gunfire had largely died away with the coming of night, only the occasional shot ringing out through the gloom—a regime sniper with a nightscope, perhaps—but the southern horizon out toward the cloverleaf of the M5 was aglow with fires from the earlier shelling, eerie flames licking hungrily against the darkness like the fires of hell.

High above, if one listened closely, one could hear the low, threatening rumble of aircraft engines, dark angels of death passing overhead. But passing, at least for this moment. The ground trembling with the fall of bombs farther to the north.

Mohamed Taferi popped a segment of orange into his mouth as he moved through the rude camp in the ruins of the town where they'd been ordered to bivouac by a local HTS commander—hearing Abdul Latif curse loudly in frustration as he and another fighter struggled to put the new tire on the lead Toyota by the light of a dying flashlight in the hands of a third man.

Another day he might have helped them, but he was nearing the end of his own tether this night—stress and exhaustion exacting their inevitable toll. Juice, warm and sweet, flooding his mouth as he bit into the orange—a strangely alien sensation.

They would leave in another hour—two, depending on repairs, striking out for the mountains to the north and west. They needed to be in those mountains by first light.

He found Abu Ahmed leaning back against the hood of the Kia Sportage, staring vacantly south toward those fires, his eyes strangely haunted in the semi-darkness.

Mohamed joined him, wordlessly proffering the remainder of the orange. He'd bought three—given one to the boy, Nassif, and kept two for himself.

The rebel commander shook his head wordlessly, barely looking at him.

"I never wanted any of this," he said after a long moment of silence, the two of them just standing there, listening to the bombs fall off to the north. "I was happy in the army—as happy, at least, as anyone could be in Assad's Syria. Until they ordered us into Da'ara—*my* city—telling us to root out the troublemakers, the agents of imperialism and Zionism. We knew better, knew they were sending us in to clean up the *shabeeha*'s mess—my cousin's son had already been arrested by the *Mukhabarat*, in the early protests. We never saw him again."

Mohamed grimaced, wincing at the familiarity of the story. If the boy had been lucky, he'd died quickly—like those Ibn Nadhar's fighters had executed in the field that morning. But few who fell into the hands of the *Mukhabarat* were so fortunate. . .and fewer still ever returned to their families.

"We left then, stripping off our uniforms and joining the protests. Dozens of officers from my division, and many of the soldiers. We believed, then—believed that if we could raise our voices loud enough, the world would hear. And *respond*. The way they'd responded in Libya, when Gaddafi rolled the tanks. Here, not even Bashar's army was standing with him—men were deserting by the thousands. Was a Syrian life worth less than a Libyan's? And the world heard. But only Bashar's friends responded. Iran and Russia, flooding Syria with weapons and men. Crushing the life out of the revolution while the West looked on, dithering and drawing meaningless lines in the sand."

Abu Ahmed paused, a heavy, ragged sigh escaping his lips—his voice thick with emotion. "My father warned me, said 'They'll do to you what they did to Hama.' That was all his generation could think about—*Hama*, a city wiped out as an object lesson to the rest of Syria. It had cowed them, but we. . .we were too young to remember, and in too deep to back out. But he was *right*. All Syria is now the world's Hama, a place for other tyrants like Bashar to point to and say, 'See, that's what will happen to you.'"

Stability. That had been the world's watchword, Mohamed thought, placing the rest of the orange in an empty pouch on his chest rig, uneaten. Feeling the tremor of the distant bombardment through the metal of the Kia's hood. His own country, among all the rest. A bargain they made with the devils they knew, trading the future for the present until there was no future left.

"My wife was killed by a regime sniper," the rebel commander admitted after another moment's pause, "carrying our unborn daughter. One moment she was crossing the street. . .and the next, she was just gone. My son is gone, I don't know where—they may have taken him to fight in the army. I want to believe he escaped, that he got out, that he might call me one day from Sweden or Germany. But he might have been across from us today even, in that field."

He had wondered why, the moment the firing had died away, Abu Ahmed had climbed up into the seat of the SUV and closed its bullet-riddled door after him, shutting out the world. Now, he knew.

"My father died of a broken heart when the *Mukhabarat* returned my brother's battered body for burial. I look forward to living in America, to finally seeing the land of freedom, of the cowboy, but I will never forgive them for just looking on, as everyone I loved was slaughtered."

There is no America waiting for you, the Israeli wanted to say, thinking back on the latest update from the Office. The knowledge that the Americans had backed out, reneged on their assurances. But he knew better than to speak those words, knew how much depended on keeping this man on-side, on *using* him. Just like everyone else.

He shuddered, feeling the promise of snow in the raw breeze—looked down and saw the Glock was out in Al-Golani's right hand, clutched loosely, muzzle downward.

The rebel raised the weapon slowly, turning it over in his hand and looking at it as though seeing it for the first time. "When they first came to me and said 'Lead us,' I told them 'no.'

Who was I? But then there was no one left to lead. And now I stand here, having killed a man who followed me, with my own hand, to spare him greater suffering. Tell me, where does it *end?*"

6:25 P.M. Arabia Standard Time
A hotel lounge
Doha, Qatar

The lounge was—like most alcohol-serving establishments in the ostensibly "dry" Gulf monarchy—located in one of Doha's luxury hotels catering to, the odd Saudi or Emirati royal aside, an exclusively Western clientele.

Gideon Laner's eyes adjusted slowly to the pale blue-and-purple ambient light as he moved through the lounge—the music pulsating through the floor beneath his feet, the crowd swaying with it. Yossi following him in at a discreet distance. Young Western women in bikinis visible through the massive plate glass windows separating the lounge from the hotel's shimmering pool, preening like models by the cascading waterfall at the other end and taking endless selfies to update their Instagram accounts.

Influencers, they called themselves, but they had no influence over, well. . .anything. Anything real, that is.

They found their man in the dimmest-lit corner of the lounge, away from the pool and the flashing lights—the hypnotic chant of the DJ—a drink in his hand and a raven-haired Filipina in a short sheath dress covered with glittering sequins sitting in his lap. She looked like a teenager, but it was awfully hard to tell.

"Stephen Flaharty?" the Mossad officer asked, extending a hand.

A smile, as the gray-haired man raised his glass of whisky to his lips, draining the last of it in a swallow. He made no move to take the hand. "One and the same, lad. One and the same."

He gestured instead for Gideon to take the seat opposite him on the u-shaped sectional, the rich brogue of Northern Ireland tingeing his voice as he spoke again. "Why don't you have a seat—you and your partner, both."

Gideon shook his head, reluctantly turning to motion Yossi to leave the crowd of dancers and join them. The Irishman was an arms dealer and a terrorist—a *former* terrorist, according to the Mossad file on him, whatever that was supposed to mean—but he was clearly as good as the file had suggested. And right now, they needed him.

"I was told you needed my help with certain. . . acquisitions," he said, the smile widening, his thumb caressing his companion's wrist idly, back and forth. It clearly hadn't been his first whisky.

If he went out on the street like that, he'd be in jail before he could blink, but it seemed as though his plans for the night were already made.

"We do," Yossi spoke up, staring pointedly at the prostitute. She responded by sticking out an impish tongue, snuggling deeper into Flaharty's lap.

The Irishman let out a heavy sigh, pushing her away with evident reluctance. "Off you go, lass."

Her mouth twisted into a moue of disappointment, and she flipped the Israelis off as she stalked away into the crowd, tugging at the hem of her dress. Flaharty laughed. "You lads are going to have to work hard to be near as entertaining company as she was."

"We'll manage."

"So, I understand you need hardware," the Irishman said, getting down to business, "and you need it on a short timetable. Tomorrow, to be exact."

A nod from Gideon, and Flaharty reached forward, examining the bottom of his empty whisky glass regretfully. "You understand, of course, that this limits what I'm capable of supplying. I'm Irish, but I'm not a sodding miracle worker."

"We do." From the stage at the head of the room, the DJ pumped his fist to the beat of a new song, multi-colored beams of light lancing around the room, strobes pulsating to the techno. Here, as in the bird market, electronic eavesdropping would be difficult. "All we're looking for is a pair of handguns, vehicles—and a few pounds of high explosive."

Flaharty's face lit up, a smile of genuine satisfaction spreading from ear to ear. He reached out, grabbing the arm of a passing waitress and motioning for her to bring him another whisky.

"Explosives? Ah, now you're talking my language, old son. . ."

6:29 P.M. Syria Standard Time
The Orontes River, north of Homs
Homs Governorate, Syria

"They have to be up there," Captain Michael Awad observed grimly, lowering the night-vision binoculars from his eyes and passing them back off to Abu Dyab. Beneath the bridge on which they stood, the murky waters of the Orontes flowed sluggishly northward, choked with debris and detritus. Had it been light, Awad felt certain they could have seen a body or two—or a half-dozen—washed up on the mud flats below. They were only a kilometer south of *Daesh*'s lines, the campus of the old military college, its northernmost environs still in jihadist hands, spread out across the bridge to their west.

A grunt of assent was the Hizballah commander's only reply, his own eyes now glued to the binoculars, pointed north. Tracers lancing out suddenly through the night out toward the rebel lines, accompanied by the distant chatter of a heavy machine gun.

After finding the drone and picking up reinforcements which had driven up from the badlands, they had tracked their quarry north from the field outside Zaidal, turning back only when they'd run into heavy opposition about a kilometer and a half southwest of the spiraling cloverleaf interchange along the M5 highway south of Talbiseh, *Daesh* snipers and machine guns dug in deep—prepared positions.

Awad's commandos had taken five casualties before he'd finally given the order to fall back—cursing bitterly in frustration at finding themselves so quickly thwarted.

"Sooner or later," Abu Dyab said, lowering the binoculars and turning to lead the way back off the bridge toward the trucks, "they will have to leave that sanctuary, if your intelligence is accurate. And once they're in the open. . ."

If. He hated the way the Iraqi Shiite said it, as though that it was *his* intelligence placed everything in doubt.

Michael Awad shook his head angrily, wishing he could draw his weapon and kill the man right here and now. His men outnumbered Abu Dyab's, but. . .no. There were too many—the risks of failure, of exposure, too high. His own men might sell him out, for that matter—report his actions to the *Mukhabarat*. There were informants everywhere.

"It's not going to matter if we don't know when and where," he spat, his voice rising dangerously as he fell in with the Hizballah commander. "They could be leaving again this very night, and we'd never know—the front stretches for dozens of kilometers. We need air support—something more than that decrepit old helicopter of yours. *Daesh* has *drones.*"

He knew he had crossed a line, saw the danger in Abu Dyab's eyes as the man turned back toward him, surprise and anger flashing across his face at the challenge. But the Iraqi's reply was never uttered, the distant churn of helicopter rotors—as if in answer to Awad's angry demand—arresting both men's attention.

The throbbing grew louder, attracting a scattering of rebel fire as the Russian Mi-24 gunship swept in from the northwest, making a low pass over the bridge—the rotorwash ripping Abu Dyab's beret from his greasy scalp—before banking hard to bleed airspeed, settling down in an abandoned parking lot not thirty meters from the trucks.

In the semi-darkness, they could see a half-dozen men in camouflage fatigues spilling out of the troop compartment, fanning out to secure a perimeter, weapons trained outward.

Then a single man emerged from within, short and stocky, utterly unprepossessing in appearance but with a strangely unmistakable air of command—the soldiers falling in behind as he advanced toward them.

A shout from one of the Hizballah fighters, several of the

militia raising their weapons to meet the strange new threat, but Abu Dyab bellowed at them to stand down—searching distractedly for his lost beret in the dust and debris of the road.

The man's face was blackened with greasepaint, Awad realized as he reached them—giving the whites of his eyes a strangely demonic cast. His smile, as he drew himself up short opposite them, very nearly feral. *What fresh hell is this?*

"Captain Michael Awad?" the demon asked, in heavily accented English. Awad nodded, and the Russian extended a hand, leaving the Syrian captain unsure whether to take it. Whether to do so might be as much as his soul was worth. *Mother of God. . .*

"Captain Valeriy Egorov, 501st Special Purpose Detachment, 3rd Guards Spetsnaz. I understand you're hunting rebels. . ."

Chapter 23

A cold, westerly wind stirred the surface of the Mediterranean into a rough chop, the moon glistening off the trawler's wake as it edged closer to the Syrian coast. Avigdor Barad stood in the wheelhouse, a hand on the *Tachash's* tiller, gazing warily toward the darkened coastline ahead, the mountains rising steeply into the horizon, far inland, just visible in the moonlight.

The moon was no longer full, but it was close enough not to matter. It lit them up like they were on parade, the former IDF sailor reflected sourly. Reuven Aharoni was for'ard, studying the approaching coast through a pair of binoculars, the scattered lights of Latakia itself visible out toward the north, faint and indistinct compared to what he remembered from naval patrols before the war.

Omri and Marc were deploying the twin trawl net from the port outrigger, the sound of Marc's cursing as he struggled with the netting reaching Avigdor's ears in the

325

wheelhouse. None of his men were cut out for this life, including himself. If they'd had to feed themselves with their catch, like the Gaza fishermen the *Tachash* had been originally confiscated from, they would've surely starved.

None of them were armed, and he'd taken the Kalashnikovs out of the wheelhouse before leaving port. If they were stopped out here, well, anything they could bring wouldn't be near enough, and he wanted nothing onboard that would arouse suspicion, at least any more suspicion than a crew of Gaza fishermen illegally fishing up the coast was bound to rouse.

Tonight—and tomorrow night—would be about establishing their presence in the area. And the third night. . .

He looked out the open door of the wheelhouse, grimly noting the faint shadows cast by his men as they moved about in the moonlight. Murmuring a silent prayer for clouds.

4:35 A.M.
Masyaf District
Hama Governorate, Syria

Snow drifted down out of the heavens above, thick, heavy flakes tossed on the breeze as the open trucks rolled north once more along desolate roads.

Nassif sat with his back up against the cab, one hand on his rifle, the other holding onto the edge of the bed, his fingers numb through the thin, ragged gloves.

They had driven out beyond the "safety" of *Hayat Tahrir al-Sham*'s lines an hour before, just as the snow had begun to fall—out past small knots of gaunt, thick-bearded men gathered around fires fed by broken-up furniture and doors. *None too soon.*

Ibn Nadhar's men were bad enough, but being surrounded by the *takfiris*, in an area under their control. . .it was as though you could *feel* the oppression, at every hand. A weight, pressing one down.

The ghosts of an abandoned strip mall lingered off to one side of the road, advertisements and signs years out of date, faded with the sun and now frosted with snow—the village ahead, like as not Alawite, desolate and deserted, its inhabitants fleeing the area to avoid being trapped between the army and the jihadist scourge.

Syria was no more, a carcass being ripped apart by snarling dogs—the kind he remembered seeing in the village street as a kid, mangy and vicious, half-starved.

*With our soul, with our blood. . .*well, yes, all of Syria's soul and blood had, indeed, been sacrificed to Bashar in the end, and what was left was a broken-down husk, worn out and bombed out.

Once he had thought of leaving, but he had left all that— as he usually left such decisions—to Talha, the older brother who had always had the answers. Who had known how to project confidence in almost any situation, no matter how challenging. Now, alone, he understood how difficult that must have been.

Now, the fight was all he had left, and there seemed nothing to leave for.

The boy leaned the barrel of his Yugo AK back against his shoulder, fumbling in the pockets of his threadbare jacket for the remaining segments of the orange. He had no idea where the Qatari had found them—or why he had decided to share—but it reminded him of something his father might have done. Acts of kindness, so rare in this war.

"Where did you get that?" he heard a rough voice demand as he bit down into the first segment. Looking up to see Mamdouh sitting a few feet away, leaning against a crate containing one of the remaining drones, the RPD across his lap, his single eye focused in on the fruit.

"The Qatari," Nassif replied defensively, swallowing the mouthful of sweet juice. Reaching up to brush a flake of snow away from his cheek.

A grimy, weathered hand extended insistently from the folds of Mamdouh's jacket. "Give it here."

5:17 A.M. Arabia Standard Time
The gated compound in Duhail
Doha, Qatar

"You need to prepare your family. Make sure they have what they need, and that they won't hang back or cause a disturbance at the wrong moment. Tell your children it's a vacation—tell your wife that, if you have to. Just do what needs to be done."

Ibraheem shifted restlessly against the pillows, looking up at the ceiling, the endlessly circling fan, its blades blurred in the semi-darkness, the words of the Israeli officer running as endlessly through his head.

He had *meant* to, had intended to the night before—but his wife had come home exhausted from her work at the bank, frustrated and worn out from a day of dealing with clients. Truly, women weren't meant to deal with such stresses. *In a perfect world. . .*

In a perfect world, he would have been the husband he

needed to be, and she would have stayed home, in the place God had ordained for a woman. And he could have done it all without betraying his country.

He rose and padded barefoot into the apartment's kitchen, retrieving a spoon before rooting around in the refrigerator for a bowl of FAGE yoghurt. One more day. Tomorrow he would wake in Germany, in a new life.

It would be hard, starting over, at the bottom, but they would be safe. He—

Ibraheem looked up with a start as his wife Bahiya swept into the kitchen, her eyes still bleary with sleep, humming tunelessly to herself, the sash of her robe tied tightly about her body as she set out preparing coffee. They hadn't loved each other—not at the beginning—their marriage arranged for them, like that of most Qataris. Their first truly private conversation, taking place on their wedding night—*after* their first hapless, frightened attempt at sex.

Since. . .well, he supposed what they had was love, or something close to it—over the years, he had come by turns to respect and envy her accomplishments, resenting, in some ways, his parents for matching him with a woman who so easily outshone him. But tomorrow—tomorrow they would *both* be starting anew.

She looked up to find him regarding her strangely. "Ibraheem? What's wrong?"

"I. . ." he looked at her, and the words seemed to lodge in his throat. *How to explain*. . .all he had done. "I—Bahiya, there's something I need to tell you."

6:35 A.M. Syria Standard Time
Masyaf District
Hama Governorate, Syria

The Russian Mi-24 gunship was as loud as the older Mi-4 that Abu Dyab had conjured up to bring them north to Homs, but it seemed marginally less likely to shake itself apart.

Michael Awad leaned forward, knee-to-knee with a Russian Spetsnaz commando, peering out one of the small square windows of the cramped troop compartment as the helicopter swept out toward the Nusayriyah Mountains, fleeing the dawn.

It would have been hard to see anything, even if it were light—harder still to communicate it to anyone, the twin top-mounted Isotov turboshafts rendering conversation in the crew compartment all but impossible.

But the Russian seemed to be enjoying himself famously, the wide smile on Valeriy Egorov's face when Awad glanced over seemingly undiminished by the hours aloft or the monotony and apparent futility of their search.

Leaving a pair of Egorov's men with the rest of his own commandos and Abu Dyab's militia to maintain comms, Awad had boarded the gunship with the Spetsnaz captain, accompanied by two of his subordinates, both NCOs of unquestionable loyalty. Their nighttime aerial search taking them first north around the *Daesh* flank toward Hama, before circling around back toward the south and flying a tight grid search pattern between the rebel-controlled Homs exclave and the mountains.

They had found—and lit up—a few scattered vehicles to

the north of the isolated rebel pocket, along the road to Hama, and Idlib beyond—rockets flashing from the weapons pylons on either side of the Mi-24's fuselage, the Spetsnaz officer's grin getting bigger with each flaming wreck left behind in their wake, but nothing that resembled the convoy they were looking for.

"They're coming for us," the Russian had said with utter conviction, contradicting, much to the satisfaction of Abu Dyab, the intel Awad had received from the Ghouta smuggler. *"Their target is our airfield, on the coast."*

With typically Russian arrogance, Egorov had declined to explain his reasons for that belief—or how he had come to learn that they were searching for the *same* rebel group, but clearly the Russians had a direct line to Awad's own command.

Awad heard something—a shout—over the cacophony of the turboshafts and his head came up to meet Egorov's eyes. The Spetsnaz captain extended his arm, tapping his exposed wristwatch and gesturing to indicate their fuel status.

Forty minutes.

6:47 A.M.

Mohamed Taferi leaned forward to blow on his hands, rubbing them vigorously together, the truck's heater continuing to function only sporadically. His eyes scanning the road ahead as they rolled into Masyaf itself, decrepit residential buildings rising three and four stories on either side of the road. They were taking a risk coming here—with a population consisting predominantly of Ismailis,

Christians, and Alawites, Masyaf was regime country and Israel had itself bombed a suspected Hizballah missile factory on the outskirts of town.

But having gotten off to a late start with further repairs of the battered vehicles, they needed to make up time and reach the mountains before the day grew too much older. No one knew they were here, no one knew they were coming—and with any luck, they'd be gone before anyone knew they had passed. *Luck?* No. . .all would be as God willed it, in the end.

The snow had come and gone with the night, leaving behind only the thinnest of coatings on ground and buildings alike—men shivering in the open beds of the technicals as they shook off the flakes before they could melt and soak their thin garments, the morning sun bleeding red and angry through the clouds still lingering behind off to the east.

Just across an empty intersection, innocent of traffic, they passed an elementary school named for the 7th of April—the anniversary of the Ba'ath Party's founding, seven decades prior—winding their way through the narrow streets of the old town, truck after truck. Mohamed's hand clasping the receiver of his Type 56, his eyes alert, searching every window—every parked car.

And there it was, as they turned north before a darkened supermarket, suddenly looming above the hardscrabble little town to which it had given its name, imposing in its sheer immensity—its crumbling curtain walls frosted with snow and bathed in the blood of the dawn. The *castle* of Masyaf.

The sight of it took Mohamed's breath away, though he'd been expecting it, the fortress framed perfectly against the peaks of the distant coastal range, seeming to swell from the very earth like a vast airship in the act of taking flight.

For more than a thousand years, the fabled citadel of Rashid ad-Din, the "Old Man of the Mountain," had looked down upon the surrounding plain from its commanding position atop that limestone promontory, its very base already twenty meters above the level ground, surmounted by walls many meters taller encompassing an inner keep. Itself forming the center of the tenuous Nizari state in Syria at the time of the Crusades, Masyaf had been a sanctuary for Ad-Din and his Isma'ili disciples, the men known to history as the *Asāsiyyūn*.

Assassins.

The trucks rolled north out of the center of town, the buildings growing sparser and lower as the town opened out into fields, passing the citadel along its eastern curtain wall, no more than a hundred meters away—close enough to make out the arrow-slits in the weathered stone which had once formed the castle's barbican—the raw morning air thick with exhaust, the cold, miserable eyes of the men in the technical in front meeting Mohamed's through the dirty glass of the windshield.

Almost through, the Israeli thought, feeling himself begin to relax as the claustrophobia of the tight streets faded away. The mountains, now within sight. Just a bit farther.

That was when he heard it, the insistent throbbing of helicopter rotors, growing closer, his heart nearly stopping with the sound. His head whipping around as his eyes strained to search out its source.

Ahead, the men in the back of the lead technical heard it too, a hoarse shout audible in the cold air—one of the men staggering to his feet and fumbling in panicked desperation with the *Dushka*'s cocking lever.

The next moment, a trio of rockets flashed past overhead, and the Honda ahead disappeared in a pall of orange-black fire. . .

Chapter 24

Senior Lieutenant Oleg Kurbatov saw the lead truck explode into flames, men scattering for cover as the Mi-24 swept by overhead in a high-speed pass, not twenty meters off the deck. The massive curtain wall of the medieval fortress looming over his left shoulder, Maksim's excited voice in his ear as the quad-barreled 12.7-mm in the *Galya*'s chin turret came to life, rounds chewing up the roadway.

He heard a deathly tapping against the fuselage and smiled contemptuously, banking hard over the trees and low residential buildings north of the castle, bringing the heavily armored helicopter back around for another pass.

The sight of an RPG rocketing by thirty feet in front of the helicopter's nose wiped the smile from the Russian pilot's face, a loud flurry of obscenities from his weps officer confirming that it *hadn't* been his imagination.

The *Galya*'s armor would stop anything up to a .50-caliber round, but that wouldn't save it if one of those found its mark.

The next voice over his headset was that of the Spetsnaz captain, confirming that he, too, had seen the rocket.

"Put us down, put us down," the officer ordered, his voice taut, even as Maksim triggered off a salvo of unguided S-8 80mm rockets from the pods slung beneath the helicopter's weapons pylons, plumes of dirt and smoke rising from the fields on the far side of the road, just beyond the convoy. *Two can play that game.*

"Put you down where, *Tovarisch Kapitan?*" Kurbatov demanded, annoyed at the distraction as he jinked right and left, another truck going up in flames below, painfully aware that his maneuver space was limited, down this low. And now this *kretin* wanted him to *land.*

"On the castle wall!"

6:54 A.M.

Flames crackled greedily in the cold, devouring flesh and fabric, blackening metal—the sickening stench of burning skin and hair filling Mohamed's nostrils as he stooped by the rear wheel of the Hilux, his rifle discarded to one side, acrid, oily smoke from the pair of destroyed trucks rising into the morning sky, marking their position as clearly as a beacon. *Come and get us.*

He shouldered the heavy RPG, struggling to ignore the anguished screams of one of Ibn Nadhar's jihadists, not twenty meters away, rolling in the snow in a desperate effort to extinguish the flames consuming him. The screech of brakes as the boxed-in trucks tried to escape the kill zone. *Focus.* That would be him in another moment—that could be *all* of them, soon, if that helicopter couldn't be taken out of play. Their desperate fight, ending here in the shadow of Masyaf.

Taking a deep breath, the Israeli adjusted his eye to the irons—gripping the launcher's crude wooden pistol grips firmly in both hands as the Mi-24 Hind gunship came back around from the south to begin its next attack run, turning sluggishly.

It was a heavy beast, heavy and slow—the very armor that kept it alive, slowing its reactions. *Speed versus armor*, one of the oldest trade-offs known to the fighting man, and often trying too hard to protect yourself just got you killed.

He heard every machine gun in the convoy open up as it came back in over the buildings, hundreds of rounds lashing the incoming helicopter in a futile hail of bullets. *Steady, steady*, he thought, shifting the barrel back and forth in an effort to track the jinking gunship.

Across from him, Abdul Latif took a knee, an RPG on his own shoulder, a grim smile on the big man's face as he glanced briefly back at the Mossad officer. *Together. . .now!*

He pushed to his feet, slipping his finger into the trigger guard just as the Mi-24 suddenly and inexplicably broke off its attack run, darting out low over the buildings to the west and disappearing behind the citadel. *What?*

6:57 A.M.

There were few things Michael Awad feared in life—and none in death—but the prospect of being blown out of the air, of falling helplessly from some great height, was one of them, and he found his palms were slick with sweat beneath the gloves as wind whistled through the now wide-open doors of the Mi-24's troop compartment, Valeriy Egorov's Spetsnaz commandos heaving out two heavy coils of thick synthetic rope as the pilot held the gunship steady not twenty feet above the massive donjon buttressing the western curtain wall of Masyaf.

After a moment, one of them rose, raising a gloved thumbs-up toward his officer. *Ready.*

Egorov smiled that death's-head smile, giving an inaudible command and the Spetsnaz trooper stepped into the door, seizing hold of the rope and stepping out to plummet earthward.

Followed by another and another—bodies sliding down the ropes. "You're up, captain!" Egorov yelled, moving in close enough to be heard. Michael Awad moved to the door, his stomach lurching as he glanced down, visually measuring the distance between the rope and the door—between the door and the ground.

He had done this, in training. *Once.* Rank had its privileges in the Syrian Army, even in the Special Forces, and he had used that privilege to get out of doing it ever again. Sometimes you didn't understand the decisions you had made until long after you had made them.

Awad took a deep breath and seized the rope in a gloved hand, knowing that any hesitation here—in front of his men—was as fatal as that fall. His body swung out over the abyss, the castle of Masyaf spread out below him, and then he was falling, the rope burning beneath his fingers, his gloves growing hot with the friction—his boots braking his descent, another of his men already on the rope above.

His feet impacted against the stone roof of the tower, a sense of relief flooding through his body as he stepped back, tossing his shredded gloves toward the parapet. A trickle of blood dripping from his palms as he brought his AK-74 up, snug into his shoulder.

The first of his own commandos made it down safely—the second. . .Awad knew from the moment he looked up that the man was coming down too hot, the rope whipping in the rotor wash as the pilot above tried to maintain his position in the crosswind—throwing the commando against the crenellations of the stone parapet as he landed, a sickening crunch of bone coming from the man's leg, accompanied by a strangled scream.

He met his captain's eyes for only a moment, then his leg went out from under him and he pitched to the roof, moaning and writhing in pain.

Valeriy Egorov was next and last—stepping over the injured man as he tucked the heavy welders' gloves he'd used for his own descent into a pouch on his chest rig.

"Leave him," he said coldly, meeting Awad's eyes for a brief moment before glancing out across the expanse of the ruined citadel, the rays of early morning sun piercing through the broken stone of the inner keep. "We need to get on that eastern wall."

7:03 A.M.
The convoy

"We stay here, and we *die*!" Anas ibn Nadhar spat, his voice rising tremulously, a bony finger jabbing toward Mohamed's chest. Abu Basir hovering in the background, a greenish cast suffusing the young man's face through the patchy beard as if he were struggling with nausea.

"As Allah wills," the Israeli replied calmly, meeting the jihadist's gaze, the RPG's launch tube still resting heavily on his shoulder. It was true enough, they *couldn't* stay here forever—the noise would bring the local color out soon enough. "We run, and we're cut down on the road, one by one. Like *them*."

He gestured out toward the flaming ruins of the immolated lead technical, still burning down to its tires, seeing Ibn Nadhar's face pale beneath the dark beard. "But it's gone—the helicopter's gone—and we should be too."

It was the first time he had seen Ibn Nadhar openly display fear, even masked as anger, but losing a dozen men in half as many minutes would do that, and he felt the prickle of fear at the back of his own neck, sweat building beneath his armpits in the cold.

"La," he said, shaking his head as he glanced over the hood of the Hilux, toward the looming citadel of Masyaf and the town spread out beyond. You could still hear it, if you listened, over the crackling of the flames, a primal, throbbing sound, pulsating through the very earth.

It just wasn't where they could *see* it, which somehow made it all the more terrifying.

"A few more minutes," Abdul Latif said, raising his voice from where he knelt behind the engine block of the Hilux to their rear. "This, here—*now*—is our best chance to take it down."

They had seven men with RPGs on the line now, sheltered in the shadow of the vehicles—more fighters on the mounted guns, as ineffectual as they had proved.

"He's right," Abu Ahmed interjected, the opposition commander's Kalashnikov held loosely in one hand as he stepped forward, moving in close to the jihadist leader to put a hand on his shoulder, his voice lowering.

"If you want to run, though," the Israeli heard him say, a determined look in those sunken, weary eyes, his voice pitched too low to be heard more than a few feet away, "go ahead and *run*."

Ibn Nadhar colored with anger, and Mohamed saw his hand move closer to the holstered pistol, but finally the jihadist shook his head.

"Good."

Mohamed glanced back to see Abdul Latif leave the cover of the vehicles to move cautiously forward, listening for the distant rotors, an RPG balanced easily on the big man's shoulder—a strange feeling of foreboding washing over him as he looked on.

"Careful, brother," he called out, glancing up toward the citadel. "I—"

He saw Abdul Latif falter suddenly, the flat *cracks* of first one rifle shot and then another ringing out through the morning air. The rebel fighter stopped, seeming to glance numbly down at his chest, and then another round came whistling in from—*somewhere*—and he pitched forward, crumpling into the dust of the road. His RPG sliding from his shoulder to slam end-first into the ground and detonate, shrapnel tearing the big man apart and rattling against the body of the Hilux.

For a moment, Mohamed just stared, struggling to process what had just happened, unable to determine where the fire was coming from—the rebel fighters glancing wildly about as another burst of shots tore through the air, smashing into the gunner on the Hilux above him. Blood spray flecking the Israeli's face as the man went down hard, writhing in his death agonies.

The castle wall. He saw the flicker of muzzle flash from high up on those ancient parapets—opened his mouth to shout a warning, but just then the Mi-24 Hind swept back into view from around the south end of the citadel, catching them off-guard, distracted.

He saw one of the gunners swing round to engage the gunship, saw rockets flash from beneath its stubby weapons pylons—impacting just short of the road, his ears ringing with the thunderous blasts.

"Get the RPGs up!" he yelled, but he could barely hear himself, a ragged salvo rippling off—a rocket here, another there. *Not enough.*

7:05 A.M.
The citadel

Michael Awad pressed his cheek to the buttstock of his AK-74 as he leaned into the ruins of the stone parapet which had once surmounted Masyaf's curtain wall in the days of the Assassins, triggering off another tight burst down toward the *Daesh* convoy, scarcely a hundred meters to their west—watching as a scattered volley of rockets flew out from the smoke hanging low over the trapped vehicles, the gunship jinking to avoid them.

They didn't have much longer, he thought, glancing back to where the Spetsnaz captain knelt by his radio—the Mi-24 would be forced to return to base to refuel in the next few minutes. But back-up was on its way, his own commandos from the 14th Special Forces moving up from the south with Abu Dyab's Hizballah fighters.

Another burst of fire, the Kalashnikov's stock shuddering into his shoulder, and the rifle emptied, a distinctive *click* reaching his ears through the chaos. Awad brought the weapon up, plucking a fresh mag from his chest rig before hitting the mag release and knocking the empty magazine free, rocking the new one into place in a single, practiced motion. *Back and forth.*

The Spetsnaz were spread out along the wall, most of them prone amid the ancient rubble, laying down a cool and disciplined fire—his own NCO with them. Twenty-five minutes, that's all they needed. Just pin *Daesh* in place for that long, and they would be destroyed by his reinforcements—sent screaming back to that hell from which they'd emerged to ravage Syria.

He looked back to meet Egorov's eyes as he reached under the AK-74's barrel, seizing the charging handle with his off-hand and pulling it back—saw the Russian raise a single finger. *One more run.*

7:08 A.M.
The convoy

This couldn't last, the Israeli thought grimly, reaching back as Nassif removed the safety cap from the head of the rocket and handed it over, the boy's face expressionless, strangely devoid of anger or fear.

They were being taken apart, caught between the gunship and suppressive fire from the wall of the fortress— cut to ribbons.

He reached up, inserting the rocket into the launch tube,

as he waved other fighters to where he knelt by the burning wreckage of the lead technical—a couple of scraggly-bearded young jihadists who looked barely out of their teens, along with several of Abu Ahmed's older rebels. Four RPGs among them, little enough.

Out to the north, through the drifting smoke, the Mi-24 was turning back, describing a sluggish turn against the sky. . .a monstrous, predatory insect, glutted with blood and death.

The Mossad officer adjusted the launcher to his shoulder, the stench of burning rubber and flesh choking the air all around as he took a deep breath, aiming through the iron sights—raising his voice to be heard over the rattle of automatic weapons fire. "On my mark!"

7:09 A.M.
The gunship

One more run. Oleg Kurbatov watched his fuel reserves carefully as he brought the heavy gunship around for the final pass—this was cutting it perilously close, his remaining fuel barely more than what would be needed to make it back over the mountains to Khmeimim.

He heard Maksim open up with the chin turret, their rockets exhausted, the stream of fire from the quad-barreled 12.7mm lashing the convoy, a pall of smoke hanging low over the vehicles, obscuring their targets.

His weps officer keeping the gun on target as he took evasive action, the gunship shifting first left, then right—a pair of RPGs emerging from the haze as he banked hard left, the morning sun streaming through the *Galya's* canopy blinding him momentarily.

He heard Maksim's strangled cry of *"Olezhik!"* and saw another RPG flash past just above their nose. . .a split-second before a fourth rocket slammed into the hull of the gunship just beneath the turboshafts, the detonation crushing Kurbatov's eardrums as he lost control, realizing, in a heart-stopping moment as the crippled helicopter hung between earth and sky, that he had come to Syria only to die. . .

7:10 A.M.
The citadel

A cold chill struck Michael Awad to the heart as he heard the explosion off to the north, saw the Mi-24 stagger sideways, smoke trailing from its hull, whipped by the gunship's faltering rotors for a terrifyingly brief moment before the helicopter plummeted to the earth like a falling stone, smashing into the empty fields to the northwest of the castle, off toward the sprawling campus of Masyaf National Hospital, and bursting into flames.

The Russians' weapons went silent, shock written on the grease-blackened faces of the Spetsnaz, every eye glued to the pyre—their own vulnerability hammered home in that moment, their tactical advantage torn away at a stroke.

Naked fury mixed with disbelief in Valeriy Egorov's eyes, an anger too great for words as he stared, the radio still clutched in one hand.

Then Awad felt the stone tremble beneath him, an RPG smashing into the curtain wall of the ancient citadel some twenty or thirty feet below their position—followed by a raking burst of heavy machine-gun fire as they came under fire from a mounted gun, smashed bits of stone blasted from the ruins of the parapet peppering his face, drawing blood from his knuckles as he dove for cover, Egorov's men recovering, spreading out further along the line.

Their turn.

7:10 A.M.
The convoy

"Allahu akbar!" Mohamed heard the fighters around him begin to chant as the gunship fell like a broken bird from the heavens, disappearing from view behind the low buildings to the west—his own voice raised with them as he straightened, the empty launch tube still clutched in his hands. *"Allahu akbar! Allahu akbar!"*

The exultation of the moment, impossible to suppress, even as the men in that helicopter burned—if they had survived the explosion or the fall, which he doubted.

But they weren't out of trouble yet—someone firing an RPG toward the citadel, a surviving gunner on the back of a Hilux opening up with a *Dushka.*

"Keep their heads down," he spat, his eyes red and stinging from the smoke as he turned back toward the surviving remnants of the convoy. They couldn't stay here, not for long, their time already running out, even with the Russian gunship downed—reinforcements would be coming, local militias and perhaps even more air support. No doubt someone up on that citadel had a radio.

He saw Abu Ahmed off through the drifting smoke, his rifle carried in the crook of his arm, rallying his men back toward the remaining vehicles—clearly having come to the same realization. Jihadists and Al-Golani's Knights alike straggling back in from the ditches where they'd sought shelter, forcing open bullet-riddled doors as another couple of the technicals' mounted guns joined in, laying down sustained suppression, the fire from atop the curtain wall nearly dying away as heavy rounds disintegrated the ancient stonework, forcing their attackers into cover.

But where was Ibn Nadhar? For a moment, the Israeli wondered if he might see the jihadist leader come slinking out of some ditch or nearby building, sneaking back in now that the danger was abated.

He retrieved a discarded AKM from alongside the road, unsure where his own rifle had ended up in the chaos, checking the mag as he stalked back down the road to help Abu Ahmed pull the survivors back together.

And that was when he saw a black-bearded figure, huddled and still, lying half-beneath a sieved Honda, just behind the flat, punctured tire.

Anas ibn Nadhar. Mohamed slung the rifle over his shoulder, seizing the man's shoulder roughly as he stooped down. *Nothing.* No.

A low, weak moan escaped the jihadist's lips as the Mossad officer dragged him out from beneath the truck, rolling him over onto his back to unzip his coat. Noting the pair of small holes perforating the heavy fabric, sodden and stained dark, the color of spilled wine. *No, no, no.*

"Get me some help over here!" he yelled, raising his voice to be heard over the staccato of the heavy weapons. *"Yalla!"*

Chapter 25

"And you say, *Tovarisch Kapitan* Egorov, that the rebel convoy was wiped out?" Andriy Makarenko asked, leaning in toward the computer on the desk of the workstation inside the GU listening post. "Despite the loss of the gunship?"

There was a moment of lag in the video connection, but then he saw the Spetsnaz captain nod. Valeriy Egorov had, after the apparent shoot-down of Kurbatov's Mi-24 and the mopping up of the remaining *Fursan Tahrir al-Sham* forces, been escorted by local Hizballah militias to the Russian Army's temporary field headquarters north of Hama, where he'd finally accessed a secure video uplink to report in.

"Da," Egorov replied, hands on his hips in an assertive posture. "Their operational capability was completely destroyed, their leaders killed. What survivors remain are now scattered and in hiding, unable to pose any real threat."

That was, the GU *podpolkóvnik* thought, about the best

outcome it was reasonable to expect in this sort of war, but he found

himself nagged by a vague sense of unease as he listened to Egorov's words. Something...*there*, that he found himself unable to put a finger on. Perhaps it was just his own deep-rooted sense of dislike for the man—undoubtedly, how it would be construed if he made a report based on such ill-defined misgivings—but as Egorov finished his debriefing and both men signed off, Makarenko found himself unable to escape the thought that something was wrong.

Very wrong.

10:04 A.M. Israel Standard Time
Jaffa Port
Jaffa, Tel-Aviv Yafo

"So you weren't challenged?" Avigdor Barad's file hardly did him justice, David Shafron thought, standing on the gently pitching deck of the *Tachash*—glancing out across the small port at the rest of the Jaffa fishing fleet.

Grizzled and weathered by salt and sea, stripped to an undershirt and shorts despite the chill as he sat there on an upturned bucket, the large trawl net spilling out of his lap to cover the nearby deck, Barad looked ten years older than the age given in his Mossad dossier, and yet somehow ageless— as if he was truly the eternal Jewish fisherman, plying these seas back to the time of the Romans, and even before.

The sailor shook his head. "No one came out to take so much as a look—no patrols, that we could make out."

That tallied with their satellite overpasses—but you went and looked anyway, if you could, because there were things that satellites missed. You didn't spend a couple decades in the intel game, even much of it as a consumer, without realizing that.

"And your team is ready for the op?"

"Reuven would be a better one to ask, David," Barad said, paying the net through his fingers, searching for rents and tears. Still clearly a bit uncomfortable with the MEGIDDO head's unexpected presence here at the marina this morning. "I'm just the taxi driver. But they seem to be— we'll be going back tonight, try to work in even closer to the coast. You a praying man?"

The question took Shafron by surprise, its relevance to their discussion, utterly opaque. "Not really," he said, shaking his head. It had been a long time. . .as much as that admission would have appalled his father. *"Lama?"*

Why?

A shrug. "Neither am I, but we were lit up last night like we were out on a stage. If God doesn't see fit to give us some cloud cover, it's going to constrict our operations seriously, closer in-shore."

Shafron took a deep breath, drinking in the raw salt air as he considered his next words carefully. "There's something we need to discuss, Avigdor."

The sailor's hands stopped moving, his eyes meeting Shafron's. "Yes?"

"Do you—" His voice broke off, his phone pulsating insistently with an incoming call. *"Slicha. "*

Excuse me.

"Of course."

Shafron moved toward the bow before retrieving the phone from his pocket. *Headquarters.* "Yes?"

It was Sorkin, his voice thick with urgency and emotion. "David, we've been picking up Hizballah traffic out of the Hama Governorate. You need to get into the office."

10:08 A.M. Arabia Standard Time
A Mossad safehouse
Doha, Qatar

The Irishman had come through for them, Gideon Laner thought, field-stripping the compact Sig-Sauer P320 before him on the kitchen table of the small apartment. It hadn't been cheap—the black market in weapons never was, particularly a rush order—but they had the insurance they needed.

"Do you suppose he's told his wife?" He looked up to meet Yossi Eiland's eyes as the shorter officer sat across from him, hands busy shaping a clay-like substance that resembled nothing so much as children's Play-Doh into a pair of compact charges. Very, *very* angry Play-Doh.

"We can hope," Gideon replied, depressing the recoil spring back into the slide as he began to fit the weapon back together.

"How do you think that went?"

"You're the married man—you tell me."

Yossi laughed at that, a harsh sound, shaking his head. "Meirav would string me up by the nuts if I'd kept anything like that from her."

So she would. . . .the two of them were a good match, Gideon reflected, conjuring up an image of Meirav Eiland, shorter even than her husband, with hair the color of burnished copper and a temper to match. Tough as nails—

a soldier's wife had to be, his own brief, failed marriage testament to how poorly that could go when both parties weren't fully invested in the life.

"Well, then she may well solve all our problems for us," Gideon said with a savage grin, replacing the slide and working it back and forth to check the action before reaching for the Sig's loaded fifteen-round magazine. "If she doesn't, though. . .you about done with those?"

A nod, as Yossi laid the second molded block of Semtex to one side.

"We're due at Ibraheem's at 2100," Gideon said, sliding the magazine into the butt of the pistol and laying it to one side as he retrieved a folded map of the city. "You'll take the SUV there, dressed up as before and pick them up, as arranged, accessing the compound gate with the code he gave us."

That way, he didn't need to say, if anyone had a tracker on Al-Murrah's family vehicle it would stay right where they expected it to be.

"I'll stay outside on the bike and provide overwatch." He unfolded the map, smoothing it out across the table as Yossi dropped the charges into the backpack at his feet. "Here's our route. . ."

10:35 A.M. Israel Standard Time
Mossad Headquarters, Glilot Junction
Tel Aviv-Yafo, Israel

The mood in the SCIF was grim by the time David Shafron walked in, both principals already present along with Sorkin and Mengashe, dancing attendance.

"So, what's the word?"

Avi ben Shoham and Mirit Refaeli traded a look, and Nika Mengashe passed him a tablet, a series of pictures visible on-screen.

"These hit Twitter ten minutes ago," she said, folding her hands together as he took his seat, beginning to swipe through them—a collage of burnt-out, wrecked vehicles typical of the Syrian opposition, bodies strewn across a barren road, "and are being retweeted by all the usual Hizb suspects, supplementing the earlier radio intercepts."

No. He felt the floor give way beneath him, a bitter, gnawing sensation growing in the pit of his stomach. Looked up to meet the *memuneh*'s eyes.

"They're claiming to have wiped out a rebel convoy just north of Masyaf, David," Avi ben Shoham announced quietly. "Abu Ahmed al-Golani is mentioned by name as being among the dead."

"Then Taferi. . ." He had lost men before—men he'd led, men—and women—he'd trained, but this. . .after all the hell through which the Druze officer had passed just to get as far as he had, seemed especially cruel.

"We have no confirmation," Abram Sorkin interjected hopefully, a pained expression etched in the lines of his face. "Nothing at all. Just these pictures, and the reports."

"But they *know* something," Shafron countered, gesturing toward the devastation on the screen of the tablet. Forcing himself to look at it—to *face* the facts, hard as they were. "There's no reason they're suddenly name-dropping a Southern Front outfit in Hama Province. They *know* they're there."

A nod from Shoham. "They do."

"Have we had contact? Early this morning—perhaps before all this went down?"

Refaeli shook her head. "Doha went dark last night to cover for the Al-Murrah exfiltration. The next comms window for Taferi is 0700 tomorrow morning. We won't know anything until then."

Shafron grimaced. Another day—that was an eternity in this world.

"If it is true," Mirit went on, consulting her notes, "then we'll have to notify Taferi's family. I will take care of that. His parents are in Galilee—his brother in Los Angeles. Our own exposure is limited. . .we made sure of that with only one officer. He won't be traced back to us."

"That's it?" Shafron demanded, feeling his face flush hot with anger. "We're just going to write him off?"

"What else would you suggest, David, if he fails to make contact?" Mirit asked, transfixing him with her characteristically steely gaze. "We've known this was a possibility, from the outset of this op. You knew, I knew it. Mohamed Taferi knew it."

As he had himself, so many times, going out into the night. In his own years in the field. And no matter what you knew, you always wanted to believe that someone would come for you, if it came to that.

"We account for the possibility of casualties," she went on, spreading her hands out on the table, "in every operation. And how we will avoid compromising our broader endeavors, despite them."

Casualties. His mind flashed back in that moment to Iraq, to the men he had lost on that night in the desert, so many years ago. *Another lifetime.* Their loss had been "accounted for," too, no doubt, from the moment they'd gone out.

"In this case," Mirit continued, "we've been successful in so doing, despite the failure of the immediate goal. It is contained, and—"

"That's not acceptable," Shafron interjected, cutting her off. Ignoring Avi's warning glance. "We have other sources in Syria—we can *use* them to fill out the picture, determine what happened, and perhaps even recover Taferi, if he's still alive. We *owe* him that much, at least."

"I have not *finished*, David," the Metsada department head replied, her voice turning cold as ice—her eyes flicking out daggers around the conference table. "Give us the room."

Sorkin and Mengashe hesitated for only a moment, Shafron nodding imperceptibly for them to leave, biting back his anger.

Mirit Refaeli spoke once more only when they were gone, Shoham looking on silently from the head of the table. Her voice hard and brittle as a razor's edge.

"You do that. Activate our networks in Syria, to find out what happened to a man likely already dead. But you never move without making noise. . .and what happens when someone hears that noise, and realizes who is making it? That the Jews are showing undue interest in a man killed in an operation against a Russian airbase. And they put one and one together to make two. How many men will you kill, to save one? Those are our stakes, David. And if you weren't prepared to play for them, you should never have become a unit head."

1:21 P.M. Syria Standard Time
Khmeimim Airbase
Latakia Governorate, Syria

It wouldn't be him writing the letters, mercifully, Andriy Makarenko thought grimly, retrieving his cellphone from the locker as one of his security personnel looked on, unsmiling. The afternoon sun struck him full in the face as he emerged from the GRU listening station, a stiff sea breeze sweeping across the runway to tug at his fatigues.

He had only met Oleg Kurbatov once, and his weapons officer never—there were a lot of Russian personnel in and out of Khmeimim, and he was only responsible for a handful of them. But he knew from his file that he had family back in Russia—a wife he'd separated from three years before, and two young daughters.

Not that many years older than Natalyushka. She had started cooing the previous night on video chat, a happy smile crossing her face as she reached out to touch his image through her mother's phone. The thought of such a little girl *losing* her father, a bitter reflection.

Just a few more weeks—that's all, and he would be with them once again, would hold her in his arms for the first time. And this time, when those small chubby fingers reached out to touch his face, there'd be no screen in the way.

At the far end of the runway, one of the Su-57s was beginning its take-off roll, the growing roar of its engines borne to him on the wind.

He paused, watching it roll toward him, breathing barely restrained power. Feeling himself relax for the first time since he'd heard the early rumors of the rebel plan to attack Khmeimim. Perhaps. . .*perhaps*, everything was going to turn out all right.

Just a couple more weeks.

2:45 P.M.
Jabal an-Nusayriyah
Al-Suqaylabiyah District, Hama Governorate
Syria

"He's going to die, if you refuse to treat him," Mohamed Taferi said quietly, keeping his voice even with an effort, looking the short, middle-aged man in the eye.

"Let him," the man spat, a tremor entering his voice. He had to be around the age of Mohamed's own father, perhaps a few years his junior, his grey hair thinning and receding back across his scalp. And here, in this small village in the coastal mountains, he was the only doctor for many kilometers around. "What's it to me?"

There was no way to tell him the truth, to explain how *important* it was that Anas ibn Nadhar live, even if for just a few more days. His forces, now making up most of their remaining strength, bound to this mission by Ibn Nadhar's word alone. If they left now. . .well, it was all over. They weren't going to assault Khmeimim with the dozen or so fighters Abu Ahmed had remaining to his name.

The Israeli looked away, glancing around the living room of the house, noting the scattering of family portraits, weathered with the passage of time, propped up on the endtable at the end of the faded sofa upon which the man sat. A younger version of the man who now sat before him, surrounded by a wife and children.

"If you don't, I can't protect you from his men. They will kill your family, destroy everything you have."

"They already *have*." The doctor's voice dripped with contempt. "Everyone I love is already dead, thanks to their war, everything I built. . .destroyed. And everywhere I go—everywhere *any* Sunni goes now, in Syria—people look at me and suspect that I'm secretly one of *them*. That I somehow sympathize with those dogs."

It was good that Ibn Nadhar's men had remained outside, or else the doctor would likely have been executed on the spot. But Mohamed had the impression that he wouldn't have cared.

Together, the rebels had already swept through the small mountain village of barely two hundred, confiscating cellphones and anything else that could be used to make contact with the outside world. . .along, frankly, with most everything that caught their fancy and wasn't nailed down. That's how they'd found the doctor in the first place.

"You're a Sunni?" That was surprising, in itself. These mountains were Alawite country, with handfuls of Christians and Ismailis scattered throughout. Their very name—*Jabal an-Nusayriyah*—meaning "The Mountains of the Nusayris," from an old slur for the Alawites.

"Na'am," the man nodded bitterly, turning to look at him—proud defiance glittering from his eyes. "Before. . .all this, I had a practice in Hama, I was respected. I lived side by side with Christians, Sunnis, Alawites, all of us alike, all of them my patients. No one knew, no one cared. Now? I'm only tolerated here, and only just, because I can bind up their wounds. Tell them what medicine to take, if any can be

found. You want me to patch up your *Daesh* for you? Just put your gun to my head and kill me now."

It might come to that, the Israeli thought, unsure what else to say—what arguments were left. It would be mercy, compared to the likely alternatives. Mercy, assuming so many strange guises in this war.

The door of the house came slamming open before he could speak again—his hand flickering to the butt of his holstered Glock as he rose. But it was Abu Ahmed who appeared in the doorway of the room, stepping inside to admit the ghastly, one-eyed visage of the fighter they called Mamdouh, together with another rebel, the two of them dragging a fourth man between them.

Blood was dripping from the man's cheek, and the folds of skin above his eye were darkening to a deep, angry crimson.

"We found someone willing to look at Ibn Nadhar," Abu Ahmed announced flatly, his voice devoid of conscious irony. "He's a veterinarian."

3:32 P.M. Israel Standard Time
Jaffa Port
Jaffa, Tel Aviv-Yafo

"What do you mean?" Avigdor Barad asked, stepping into the wheelhouse out of the raw sea breeze as he pressed the cellphone to his ear. "Shafron was here himself this morning, he said nothing of any of this."

"Oh?" He could tell from the surprise in Nika Mengashe's voice that she hadn't been aware of her boss' visit, which raised questions all its own, in light of David Shafron's request. "The situation on the ground has changed, Avigdor. . .I'm sorry, that's all I can say. Your orders are to stand down, and stay in port. Don't go up the coast tonight."

Barad shook his head. *This makes no sense.* Then again, bureaucracy seldom did, in the Navy, or here. "And tomorrow night?"

"You'll be advised," was the Mossad woman's cryptic response, signing off without further pleasantries.

"What was that about?"

The sailor looked up to see Reuven Aharoni standing there in the doorway of the wheelhouse, favoring him with a skeptical look.

He answered it with a heavy shrug and a shake of the head. "I wish I knew."

4:27 P.M.
Gan Ha'Slaim
Park Hayarkon, Tel Aviv-Yafo

A hundred feet or more above their heads, an off-white hot-air balloon drifted lazily against its tether, like a low-hanging, strangely symmetrical cloud. Or a completely out-of-place, white, airborne cactus, David Shafron reflected, bemused by the incongruity of the thought, glancing about them at the plump round barrel cacti littering both sides of the walking path—Shmuel and Aaron charging ahead, as heedless of their surroundings as usual, the energies repressed at school finally unleashed. Seeing the world through your children's eyes sometimes precipitated strange thoughts all your own.

"So, you pulled me away from Christmas dinner with my

family," Paul Keifer observed grudgingly, the American's hands shoved into the pockets of his jeans, sunglasses shielding his eyes against the declining sun. "What are we doing here, David, exactly?"

That was an excellent question, and Shafron grimaced at Keifer's words. He hadn't given the Christian holiday a second thought. "Aaron! Shmuel!"

The boys came back, reluctantly, and he stooped down, putting his hand on Aaron's shoulder, gesturing behind him to his bodyguard. "I want you to go exploring with Uncle Shimon for a while. Listen to him, and look out for your brother, do you understand?"

Big eyes, serious, but impatient, stared back into his own. So much a reflection of himself, at that age. "Yes, *Abba*."

"Then go." He waited until they had disappeared down the sinuous path of the rock garden, Shimon Ben-David's big strides outpacing even the boys' excitement, before digging into the pocket of his jacket for the pack of Camels, extracting a single cigarette and lighting up.

Rahel didn't like him to smoke in front of the boys— didn't like him to smoke at all, for that matter, but such was life. You didn't always get what you wanted, as his morning with Mirit and Avi had more than proved.

"Sorry about your Christmas. But I need access," he said, taking a long drag of the cigarette, "to your country's resources on Syria."

Paul Keifer stopped short, taking off his aviators as he turned to face him. "Are you serious?"

"Completely," Shafron assured him coolly, exhaling smoke into the crisp evening air. He wasn't, of course—but when you had a big request to make, you led with an even bigger one. *Negotiation 101.*

"I'm sorry, David, but that is completely out of the question. Even for an ally as close as Israel."

"Even for the Norton administration?" That was the reality, behind the rhetoric. Barring outright hostility, relationships between nations didn't change that much from one administration to the next, for better or worse—undergirded as they were by hundreds and thousands of lower-level relationships, like his and Keifer's.

"Even for the Norton administration. Besides, your sources are probably better than ours, anyway."

"Dai!" Shafron snorted in disbelief. He had no doubt that was true, on the ground—the American HUMINT capacity in the Middle East, even more than a decade and a half into their vaunted "War on Terror," remained atrocious—but everywhere else. . .well, their resources dwarfed those of the Office. Didn't always mean better intelligence—contrary to common perception in Washington, problems weren't always solved by throwing money at them—but it did guarantee *more* of it. "Technical collection, Paul. I need to know what you're hearing—and seeing."

Keifer paused, the distant towering palms casting strange shadows across the chief of station's face in the setting sun as he glanced back along the path, making sure their security was keeping their distance.

"Is this about our operation?"

"Yes," Shafron replied, amused despite himself by the American's use of the possessive. There had ceased being anything *ours* about this, some time ago. "Our man has fallen off the radar, and Hizballah is claiming a win. I need to find him."

Keifer grimaced. "I wish I could help, David, I truly do. . .but you have to understand that this is being kept under wraps for a reason. Involving the inter-agency, that raises the chances of this reaching the ears of the POTUS to the highly probable. And if that happens, we'll all be answering questions we'd rather not."

Shafron just looked at him, his eyes glittering with the fire of the dying sun. "Right now, Paul, the only questions I'd rather not answer are those his family will ask if they ever find out I could have gotten him back. . .and didn't."

The American swallowed hard, nodded, and replaced his aviators. "I'll see what can be done. No promises."

4:34 P.M. Syria Standard Time
The village, Jabal an-Nusayriyah
Al-Suqaylabiyah District, Hama Governorate
Syria

The sun had disappeared behind the mountain summits long before, leaving the small village in their shadow shrouded in gloom—the electric grid having fallen victim to the ravages of war, the only illumination in the house's kitchen that provided by the glow of multiple cellphones, held over the recumbent form of the man stretched out on the kitchen table, stripped to the waist, gooseflesh rising beneath the startlingly dark hair covering his chalky forearms.

Anas ibn Nadhar was as pale as death itself, slipping in and out of consciousness—thrashing weakly against the men who held him down against the table as the veterinarian probed at his wounds to clean away dirt and fragments of cloth, his gentle prodding eliciting screams of anguish from the wounded jihadist, dying away finally to whimpering sobs as the strength even to scream deserted him.

If there was ever a man who had deserved to die screaming in agony, Mohamed Taferi was reasonably certain it was Ibn Nadhar, might God forgive him the usurpation of judgment. But he *needed* him alive, for another day—no more.

"Bring the light closer," he heard the veterinarian say, motioning for one of the rebels to lower the cellphone in his hand closer to the body, its pale, weak glow providing only faint illumination of the wound site. The man's hands were shaking, his left eye now an angry purplish-black and well-nigh swollen shut.

He had to know as well as Mohamed that any of Ibn Nadhar's men would kill him as soon as look at him for no other crime than being an Alawite. . .let alone their leader expiring on his kitchen table.

The Israeli leaned back into the door of the refrigerator, looking on—knowing the fate of the veterinarian, and that of the man's family, was out of his hands.

He had brought these animals into their lives, into their home, yet he couldn't shield them from harm, no matter how much he would have wished it otherwise. All this fear, this terror—because of *him*. His mission—the orders he had been sent to carry out.

All of it, a burden he would carry long beyond this night.

He lifted the small glass of steaming *yerba mate* the veterinarian's wife had made to his lips, his hands still grimy and smeared with dried blood—thinking of the fear in her eyes, the cowed way she had hurried from the room, pushing their young daughter ahead of her, as if she couldn't get out of their sight fast enough.

Tasting the strong notes of fruit on his lips as he drank the tea down, thinking back to that night on his parents' roof, drinking *halitot,* looking down the slopes of Mount Meron from the village of his forefathers.

The anxious, worried frown on his mother's face. *"Syria. . .you haven't been there, have you?"*

"No." He grimaced at the memory, feeling the folding stock of the Kalashnikov, its barrel hard against his back, wondering somehow what she would think if she could see him now. The tea, leaving a bitter taste in his mouth as he recalled his assurances. *"Of course, mama, I'm always careful."*

And so he was, though he had the feeling that her definition and his would prove quite incompatible—if she ever knew.

His gaze drifted over to the stack of Ibn Nadhar's clothes piled haphazardly on the chair in the darkened corner—his coat draped over the back, the bloodstained shirt they'd had to cut him out of, piled on the seat.

From the table, a low, despairing moan from the jihadist leader reached his ears, thrashing weakly against the men who held him down—one of the fighters cursing as a cellphone's screen flickered off.

Two quick steps, and the Israeli was at the chair, glancing back briefly over his shoulder to confirm that everyone was still focused on Anas ibn Nadhar before rifling through the outer and inner pockets of the heavy coat—one of the warmest garments he'd seen anyone wear in Syria, he reflected idly—his fingers closing at last on the smooth surface of the jihadist's phone. *There.*

There was an unread message displayed on the lockscreen

when he hit the power button, a cold chill washing over his body as his eyes scanned the flowing Arabic script. *The Qatari is compromised, as we. . .*

Chapter 26

4:39 P.M.
Al-Laqbah, Hama Governorate
Syria

The last fading embers of the sun were sinking behind the coastal mountains as Michael Awad pushed open the door of the Russian-built GAZ utility truck, stepping out onto the cracked, weathered asphalt of the town street.

Across from him, low, generator-powered lights still shone uncertainly through the gathering darkness from the window of a pharmacy, in contrast to the darkened windows of most of the surrounding buildings.

Behind him, the brakes of another pair of larger four-and-a-half-ton Ural-375 trucks groaned to a protesting halt, commandos wearing the tiger patch of the 14th Special Forces Division spilling out of the back to secure a perimeter, their weapons held low, prepared to counter threats while not anticipating them.

They were on friendly ground, or what should have been—here along the border of the Orontes River Valley, and across those mountains to the sea, for that matter, was

Alawite country, and what risings had taken place here, stirred up by the agents of imperialism and the Jewish globalist elite, had been quickly quelled in the early years of the war.

Indeed, the second cousin of Al-Laqbah's mayor was Major General Issam Nasif Ahmad, his own superior and the commanding officer of the 14th, with another pair of cousins in the *Mukhabarat*—all of which made Captain Awad anxious that his men demonstrate restraint here, of all places—anxious to *leave*, as soon as possible. But he had to know.

"Take your men and spread out—begin knocking on doors," he instructed his lieutenant as the younger man rounded the front of the GAZ. "Find out if anyone saw anything. And be careful to show respect."

A slow, almost insolent nod—the lieutenant was fifteen years Awad's junior, arrogant, an Alawite, and almost certainly informing on him to the *Mukhabarat*. All the more reason he had to be *sure*, no matter what the Russian had said.

"We cut them apart," Valeriy Egorov had proclaimed angrily, standing beneath the barbican of Masyaf, pacing back and forth before a weathered display in English and Arabic which had once welcomed tourists to the main gate of the historic citadel. *"They are* finished—*no longer a threat."*

The price for failure was clearly as high in Russia as it was in Syria, a price that the Spetsnaz captain, after losing a helicopter to the rebels' fire, was unwilling to pay—but did that make it *true?*

Three vehicles had been left smoldering in the wake of the

Mi-24's attack runs, half-a-dozen bodies scattered about along the road, with more likely dragged away or consumed in the flames. . .but *Daesh*'s heavy guns had still been in action when they'd finally straggled away, a burst of fire tearing one of Egorov's Spetsnaz in half when the man exposed himself incautiously, the curtain wall's rampart growing slick with blood and entrails, bullets and fragments of stone flying everywhere as the rest of them made themselves small, the crumbling ancient parapet reduced to powder. Cut apart they might have been, but they'd retreated in far better order than Egorov had seemed willing to admit.

He could still taste the grit in his mouth, rough beneath his tongue as he ran it across his teeth. The taste of failure. But it didn't have to *remain* failure.

Not if he could find them.

4:41 P.M.
The village, Jabal an-Nusayriyah
Al-Suqaylabiyah District, Hama Governorate
Syria

The rest of the message was hidden behind the lockscreen, a fingerprint scanner coming up when Mohamed Taferi tried to swipe it away. The Israeli suppressed an angry curse, shielding the glow of the screen with his body—knowing all too well the stakes in play here. He could make the phone disappear easily enough, but it had already been an hour since the message had been sent, how much longer until its sender chose to contact someone else?

No, it had to be *answered*, and quickly. *But how?*

Another anguished moan from Ibn Nadhar, a dull *thump*

as his body writhed against the tabletop and Mohamed turned back toward the table, making his decision in a trice.

"Let me help you, brother," he said, looking one of the young, black-bearded jihadists in the eye as he seized Ibn Nadhar's pale, thin wrist, pinning it to the table. "Hold the light for him."

A moment passed, and then the young fighter nodded, releasing his own hold on his leader's arm, leaning in closer with the cellphone in his other hand.

The Israeli waited only a moment for him to turn away before sliding the phone into Ibn Nadhar's limp hand, pressing his thumb against the screen. . .the phone vibrating against his palm as it unlocked.

The Qatari is compromised, as we suspected, the message read in full, each damning word burning itself into his mind, a shudder passing through his body at the thought of how close he had come to destruction. *Deal with him.*

He hesitated only a moment, a choking sob of pain from Ibn Nadhar filling the empty space, before tapping back an answer with the thumb of his free hand. *It's being handled. . .*

10:18 P.M. Arabia Standard Time
South Duhail
Doha, Qatar

Doha sparkled like a jewel in the night behind Gideon Laner as the Mossad officer rode north, the powerful Kawasaki motorbike throbbing between his knees as he wound his way in and out of heavy traffic, the compact Sig-Sauer tucked into a holster inside the waistband of his jeans, the slipstream tugging at the backpack on his back.

Yossi was two minutes ahead, driving the SUV they planned to use for the exfiltration itself—both vehicles, like the weapons, acquired with the Irishman's aid. Untraceable to them, or at least as untraceable as these things ever got.

The glamour, though, soon faded into the rear-view mirror, the buildings growing smaller and far more modest as Gideon left the downtown behind, passing countless storefronts and the entry gates of gated compounds like their destination, leading back off the streets, until at last he saw the Volvo ahead, Yossi's burqa-clad form leaning out the window to enter the passcode into the keypad in front of the gate.

He pulled off to one side of the road, beside a darkened storefront, watching as the gates opened and the SUV rolled on in. *22:24*, he thought, checking his watch reflexively. *Let's make this quick.*

10:26 P.M.
The gated compound in Duhail
Doha, Qatar

Anger had been replaced by tears, only to be exchanged for renewed freshets of wrath, Bahiya's dark eyes still burning with fury as she threw the last of little Zaid's clothes into their rolling luggage.

"They're going to be here, any minute," Ibraheem observed, chewing his lip anxiously as he reached up to gingerly touch the dark, purplish bruise over his cheekbone. A relic from earlier that morning, in the kitchen, when she'd begun throwing other, harder things. His colleagues had given him a hard time about it, at the office—their derisive, contemptuous laughter, one of his last memories of this place.

But they would come to another realization soon—their palpable contempt one of his best assurances that they hadn't *yet*—that the nearly invisible functionary they had so belittled for so long had outsmarted them all. Now he just needed to survive the wrath of his wife.

The words elicited no response from Bahiya, her movements hurried, the folds of her *hijab* wrapped carelessly about her face as if thrown on, her fingers sparkling with every ring she owned, and he added, "We need to be ready."

She paused, Zaid's favorite stuffed lion in her hand, her eyes blazing into fire as she glared at him. "Then *help*. I've had only hours to do—to do all of this, to grasp our life is *over*, thanks to you. To your foolishness, Ibraheem, your *greed* and your lies. Everything we've worked for, our children's future—lost."

The tears began flowing again and she reached up to wipe them away, further smearing her mascara.

"That's not true," he replied, feeling his own anger grow in response to hers. "They'll have a better future, once I can—"

A firm knock sounded through the apartment in that moment, and he cursed, realizing that their time was up—leaving Bahiya behind in the bedroom as he moved to the door, passing his son Zaid sitting on the couch, playing contentedly with a tablet. Anything to keep him occupied—to keep this feeling as normal as possible. His sisters were just old enough to pick up on their parents' tension and doubt the sudden "vacation" explanation, and one of them had thrown her own tantrum earlier after Bahiya had gotten home from work, contributing to the general chaos.

A dark, diminutive figure of a woman swathed in black stood on the threshold as he opened it, the surprise registering on his face for a brief moment before the Israeli pushed his way inside, the brusquely non-feminine voice from beneath the burqa recalling to mind their first meeting in the bird market.

"Are you ready?"

"Almost," Ibraheem said helplessly, gesturing toward his son on the couch. "We just need a few more minutes."

"We don't have long," the Israeli replied, shaking his head beneath the burqa, "we—"

"Who is *this*?" Bahiya demanded, emerging from the back tugging the rolling suitcase to find her husband standing there beside the strange "woman."

"Ma'am, we need. . ." the Israeli's voice trailed off in that moment, a hand suddenly pressed to his ear.

A loud crash from somewhere without suddenly disrupting the quiet of the neighborhood.

10:29 P.M.

"You need to get out of there—*now!*"

From across the street, the Kawasaki idling in the shadow of a deserted storefront, Gideon watched as the lead vehicle, one of the *Lekhwiya's* characteristic red Land Cruisers, hit the gate of the compound at speed—the reinforced steel ram mounted to the front of the truck buckling the gates inward and batting them aside as though they were made of cardboard.

Curses spilled from the Mossad officer's lips as he watched the remainder of the vehicles flow into the community after it, bearing down upon their now-compromised op with all the fury of an avalanche, doors shoved open—armed men in the black riot gear of Qatar's internal security service tumbling out to take up positions.

"Working on it," Yossi replied coolly in Arabic, his voice steady.

"*La,*" Gideon spat, "there's no time. Leave them and move, I'll—"

The radio descended into static, cutting him off, someone in one of the *Lekhwiya* vehicles no doubt activating a signal jammer. Cold, impotent fury distorting the Israeli's face beneath the helmet as he looked on, helpless to intervene. . .

10:31 P.M.
The Pearl-Qatar
Doha, Qatar

Waves lapped gently against the side of the luxury yacht as Makhlouf "Miki" Abecassis leaned against the rail, a fruity mocktail in his hand, resisting the urge to check his watch.

It was happening now, he knew without checking his Piaget wristwatch—maintaining an outer calm starkly at odds with his inner turmoil.

Above, the towers of The Pearl, standing like soldiers all in a row along the circumference of the artificial island's inner marina, shimmered in the night, glittering off waters which seemed themselves to pulse and throb to the beat of the pop music vibrating through the ornate vessel.

No intelligence officer welcomed the thought of losing an asset, but the man Tel Aviv referred to as DROR knew well that far more than that was at stake this night. His own future, hanging in the balance, and that of his network here in Doha.

He lifted the glass to his lips, making a face at the ripe sweetness of the fruit. It was *too* sweet, in his opinion, and missing the bite of the alcohol, but this was Qatar. *When in Rome. . .*

Otherwise, those rules were being observed somewhat more. . .loosely, the middle-aged Algerian-born Jew thought with a wry smile as a young Vietnamese waitress promenaded past on the upper deck above with a tray of the drinks, clad in a teal bikini and displaying more than enough skin to have gotten her flogged a mile or two inland.

Qataris didn't mind their eye candy at all, so long as their people didn't see them enjoying it. The emir's younger half-brother Mubarak, who had parlayed his own youth and rakish good looks into Instagram stardom with a following approaching the quarter-million mark, was himself aboard, partying it up with their American hosts. Christmas, here in the heart of the Middle East.

"You're quiet tonight, Rabah," a tall woman observed, sidling up to him at the rail, her low voice honeyed with the accents of the American South.

His best, most genial smile slid in place over the mask as he turned, taking her proffered hand in his own. "Some nights, work is slow to leave the mind, you know how it is. Forgive me."

"This once, Rabah," she smiled, turning to join him at the rail, the lights of the towers reflecting in her pale grey eyes. "This once."

A year or two his own senior, a stately streak of silver only now manifesting itself in her dark mane of hair, Lori Kerrigan was local general counsel to their hosts—AMPET-McDaniels, a big American oil company based out of the Houston Energy Corridor, with significant holdings in Qatar.

A valuable woman to know, which meant that their own relationship, fleeting as it had been, had, from his end, been more utilitarian than she might have imagined, or wished— a means of establishing himself in his cover as a fellow American expat, the son of Arab-American immigrants, and an entrepreneur neck-deep in the import business of the small Gulf monarchy.

If she harbored any ill-will over its conclusion, she had never given any sign of it—her own husband and nearly-grown children back Stateside likely precluding any longer-term entanglements.

"His Excellency was asking for you," she observed after a moment, meeting his eyes as she leaned back against the rail. "Said he hadn't seen you all night."

A smile, as Miki finally risked a glance at his watch. "Well, we can't have that," he said, raising himself up ever so slightly to kiss her on the cheek as he brushed past, in search of a drink and the emir's brother.

With any luck, Ibraheem Saleh al-Murrah was now on his way out of the country. . .

10:33 P.M.
The gated compound in Duhail
Doha, Qatar

The path back to the SUV was already cut off, Yossi Eiland realized, casting a glance behind him as he hurried along the sidewalk, away from the Al-Murrah residence and the uniformed officers now deploying toward it, his hand tucked within the folds of the burqa, gripping the butt of the Sig-Sauer beneath his feminine outer garments.

Knowing it would do precious little good in a firefight with the *Lekhwiya*.

"You have to help us—to save us—I sacrificed everything for you." Ibraheem al-Murrah's voice growing higher as he'd clutched at Eiland's forearm in the moments following the impact at the gate, cracking with panic. His wife, sobbing through her fury—cursing him and her husband alike.

A chaotic babble from their young children as it sank in that something was wrong—very wrong.

But he *couldn't* save them—couldn't even save himself, if it came to that. *"The safest thing for your family,"* he'd replied—reaching out to grip their asset by the shoulders, realizing he had only seconds to make his own escape, *"is if the* Lekhwiya *doesn't know I was ever here."*

He could sense eyes on him, families in the surrounding houses of the compound peering furtively from their windows into the semi-darkness. The shadow of massive black recycling bins beckoning from a nearby alley. He needed to get off the street, find a way to rendezvous with Gideon and salvage what remained of their op. The Al-Murrahs were past saving.

And behind him, a door crashed inward under the impact of a ram. . .

10:35 P.M.
The Pearl-Qatar
Doha, Qatar

His Excellency Sheikh Mubarak bin Fahad bin Ghanim Al Thani held court on the uppermost deck of the yacht, dressed in an exquisitely tailored pastel blue linen blazer that had likely cost more than Miki Abecassis' salary for his last three years with the Mossad, white pants and a white dress shirt, characteristically left open at the throat to display an expanse of swarthy skin and wiry black hair.

His dark eyes snapped like coals of fire above a dark, pencil-thin Clark Gable 'stache, flickering from one to the next of his listeners as he talked, making eye contact with each man and woman, gesturing expansively, holding each of his auditors in a thrall that went well beyond the kind of polite, semi-bored attentiveness that so often characterized such gatherings.

In another life, Mubarak could have been an actor—a heartthrob of Hollywood's Golden Age, adored by women the world 'round. In this one, well, he had to be contented with being royalty, and the closest he'd come to cinema was his position on the Board of Directors of his half-sister's Doha Film Institute. As for the women. . .well, charm and wealth were as irresistible off-screen as on.

He made eye contact with the Israeli and his smile broadened, waving him in from the outer bands of the concentric circles surrounding him.

"Rabah, *habibi*," the prince smiled, one of his stone-faced bodyguards taking a step back as Mubarak drew the Israeli into a warm embrace, their right cheeks touching briefly in the traditional three kisses of greeting. *"Salaam alaikum."*

"Wa alaikum as-salaam, Your Excellency," Miki replied, placing his right hand over his heart as he withdrew.

"You know Mr. Barnett, of course," Mubarak continued, gesturing toward the white-haired American standing a few feet away—John Barnett, the CEO of AMPET-McDaniels, their host tonight, and Lori Kerrigan's boss. The Texan lifted his lime-green drink in greeting, smiling perfunctorily.

"And Valerie Herrera, the Public Engagement Assistant at your embassy." Blonde, in her late thirties, and well-dressed, Herrera was also CIA, something Miki was relatively certain Mubarak knew, if he did. But there were forms to be observed.

"Of course," the Mossad officer replied, favoring both of the Americans with a warm smile. They, like the prince, knew him only as Rabah Belhadj, Arab-American expat and importer.

But then Mubarak motioned another man forward from the shadows of the deck, perhaps a decade the prince's own senior, his face stern and leathery before its time, a great big black caterpillar of a mustache adorning his upper lip, his starched white dress shirt and tie seeming far too serious for their surroundings.

"Allow me to introduce my cousin, Sheikh Abdulrahman bin Thani, commander of the *Lekhwiya. . .*"

10:37 P.M.
Duhail
Doha, Qatar

From across the street, Gideon had watched as Ibraheem Saleh al-Murrah was shoved, his shirt torn and blood already trickling from a gash on his forehead, into the back of a red

Lekhwiya Land Cruiser, his hands pinioned behind his back. *Just* Ibraheem, not his family, or anyone else—which left Gideon with a flicker of hope for Yossi having managed to escape and evade before the security services kicked down the door.

And then they had torn back out through the battered and wrecked gates of the compound, Al-Murrah in the third truck back from the lead, leaving as quickly and thoroughly as they had come—every last vehicle—no doubt transporting the Qatari bureaucrat to their headquarters, only a few kilometers further north, for interrogation. *Shock and awe*, designed to terrify into submission anyone else who might have pondered resisting the authority of the state.

They had a contingency plan, the Mossad officer thought, reaching back to squeeze the backpack strapped to his back, but it had been set up for two men. . .and time was running short. Once Al-Murrah was ensconced behind those walls, he—

That was when he saw him, Eiland's short figure emerging from the compound's devastated entrance, unceremoniously stripping off the burqa and tossing the bundled cloth aside as he crossed the street.

Gideon met him half-way, revving the Kawasaki's engine as Yossi swung a leg over the back of the bike, retrieving the second helmet from the backpack before wrapping his right arm around Gideon's waist. *"Go, go, go!"*

10:40 P.M.
The Pearl-Qatar
Doha, Qatar

It was all the Mossad officer could do to hide his consternation, dropping the mask firmly into place as he reached out to shake the hand of Mubarak's cousin, mentally searching back through the prince's words for any hidden meaning—any *warning* of his own danger.

Nothing. Which didn't mean it wasn't there. The intelligence officer walked a thin line between caution and paranoia, but it was ever like dancing on a tightrope. Coincidence existed, but this. . .with an operation in progress, it suddenly felt like sighting the dead body of an animal and realizing you had walked into the middle of a minefield.

He wished in that moment for his phone, but everyone had checked theirs with security before boarding the yacht.

"You know sometimes," the prince said, his smile widening as he continued, looking around at the assembled business executives and diplomats, "I think my cousin has the best of it. He's no prince, it's true, but he's better—he's James Bond. He gets to jump out of planes, kick in doors, and kill bad guys. He's like Tom Cruise, in Mission Impossible."

More accurately, Abdulrahman bin Thani looked like he had *eaten* a couple of Tom Cruises for breakfast, and Miki Abecassis doubted that the Qatari royal had personally jumped out of any planes or kicked in any doors in a decade or two.

Killed bad guys, though. . .

Abdulrahman laughed politely, but there was no smile in

the eyes, as though he had heard his cousin's shtick many times before and wearied of it long since.

"I'd like to do all that myself," Mubarak went on, his eyes sparkling, "particularly the car chases, they have to be so exciting—chasing down a foreign spy and forcing him off the road. I'd just like to see one of them try to get away from me."

There were murmurs of approbation all around, and despite his own status as, well, a foreign spy, the Israeli found himself hiding a smile.

If there was one thing Mubarak was known for, it was his fast cars. Indeed, a few years before, he had left the United States hastily after illegally drag-racing his royal-blue Lamborghini through the otherwise idyllic streets of Atherton, California one of the West Coast state's poshest neighborhoods, where the younger set of Al Thanis maintained a residence.

"Indeed," the prince said, a savage gleam entering his eyes as he clapped a hand on his cousin's shoulder, "I understand his men are arresting a spy this very night, isn't that right, cousin? One of our own, a man who betrayed his country. . ."

10:42 P.M.
Duhail
Doha, Qatar

Tears streamed fresh and hot from Ibraheem Saleh al-Murrah's eyes, mixing with the blood now trickling from his forehead as the *Lekhwiya* motorcade sped north in a tight column, wending its way through the darkened streets of Al-

Duhail north toward the one destination he dreaded more than any other—the emirate's secret police headquarters.

He had interrogated men there himself and knew enough to regard disappearing within its walls with a horror for which words were wholly inadequate. *How could he have been so stupid?*

Bahiya had been right in her reproaches—her anger—he realized now, when it was far too late. He had placed them all in jeopardy, risked their future and that of their children, all to stave off his own insecurities, satiate his greed.

Now, they would all pay the price. It didn't matter that they hadn't taken her—*yet*—her life, her career was over. She would never leave the country, would never again hold any position of trust. Condemned, as their children after her, to eking out a meager existence, at the lowest rungs of society.

Because of him.

He curled up into as close to a fetal position as he could manage with his hands cuffed in the backseat of the *Lekhwiya* Land Cruiser, ignoring the black-uniformed, faceless officer sitting across from him, carbine in his lap, drinking in the last sights of the city as the convoy slowed to make another turn, their emergency lights going on as they bulled through a stop light, brushing aside traffic.

His mind racing as he struggled to think what he had to bargain with—what he could *give* them, in exchange for. . .no, freedom, was too much to ask for, but perhaps a better fate for his family. A new lease on life, for himself. Anything to keep them from killing him, to ward off that doom, for as long as he could.

He could give them his handler—he didn't know the man's name, of course, but he could certainly describe him.

And the taller of the Israelis in the bird market—the spokesman. They had to have just arrived in-country, could be tracked down by his old employers, surely.

That had to be worth *something*, he thought, choking down a sob as the convoy picked up speed once again—clutching at the feeble hope like a drowning man slipping beneath the surface for the last time.

He didn't recognize the sound, at first, but then he looked up, blinking away tears. An inexplicable sense of horror washing over him as he saw the motorbike close in from the rear, racing up the side of the convoy, abreast of the Land Cruiser in no more than a heartbeat, a pair of men visible astride its saddle.

It was a sight that couldn't have been more common on the streets of Doha, but even the most foolhardy of Doha drivers gave the *Lekhwiya* a wide berth. Which could only mean—

No, no. . .no. The scream seemed to stick in Ibraheem al-Murrah's throat, his eyes wide with terror as he watched the bike veer closer still, the rearmost rider reaching out to press his gloved hand hard against the door of the Land Cruiser—his eyes, seeming to meet the Qatari's through the tinted glass for a moment in time. . .

And Ibraheem found his voice, struggling helplessly against the bonds. *"No!"*

10:44 P.M.

Gideon felt Yossi's hand squeeze his shoulder and he bent low beneath the Kawasaki's windshield, his body hugging the fuel tank as he twisted the throttle back toward himself, shifting gears as the bike accelerated away and up the nearly deserted highway past the remaining vehicles of the convoy, slowing at the next intersection. *Six. . .five. . .four. . .*

He saw the driver of the lead Land Cruiser begin to put his wheel over, as if to cut him off, and leaned hard into the turn. *Three. . .two. . .*Yossi's arm wrapping tightly around his torso as the bike veered off into the turn lane, heading east toward the sea.

One.

Behind them, the magnetic shape charge's electronic time fuse reached zero, a gout of flame tearing through the side of the up-armored Land Cruiser in which Ibraheem Saleh al-Murrah rode like it was made of tissue paper, reaching the fuel tank a split-second later.

And the night erupted in fire. . .

11:05 P.M. Syria Standard Time
The village, Jabal an-Nusayriyah
Al-Suqaylabiyah District, Hama Governorate
Syria

It seemed an eternity had come and gone since they had greeted the dawn beneath the crumbling curtain of Masyaf, hostile fire raining down from all sides, a deadly predator stalking the skies above.

Mohamed Taferi tilted back the glass of *yerba mate*, draining what remained in a single swallow, aware that it was only the caffeine which was keeping him in action, the exhaustion seeping deep into his very bones.

"You did well," he observed, setting the glass to one side on the kitchen counter—folding his arms across his chest rig as he met the eyes of the veterinarian, washing his bloody implements in the kitchen sink by the light of an antiquated oil lantern someone had finally located in a house on the outskirts of the village.

"He may still die," the man acknowledged softly, looking away after the briefest of moments. As if he was afraid to hold Mohamed's gaze, afraid someone might hear.

"He may. But we'll be gone before the morning."

Shock and dismay chased each other across the veterinarian's face, strangely shadowed in the lantern light, his damaged eye now a ghastly purplish-black. He glanced back toward the recumbent, blanket-shrouded form of Ibn Nadhar, still on the table, now mercifully asleep after hours of agony. "*La, la*. . .that's too soon. The wounds he's suffered, if you move him now, he won't last the week."

He doesn't need to, Mohamed thought, reaching up absently to adjust the sling of his rifle where it chafed his shoulder. "That's not your concern."

"But it *is*," the veterinarian protested, shaking his head vigorously, forgetting himself in his fear. "I treated him. . .if he dies, his men, they'll come back and kill me. They'll rape my wife, and—and my *daughters*."

In that order, if he was lucky, the Israeli thought, reaching for the light. If he wasn't, they'd make him watch.

He extinguished the lantern to conserve fuel, plunging the room into darkness, the voices of the jihadists around the fire outside audible in the silence that followed.

"Don't worry. No one's coming back."

Chapter 27

12:17 A.M. Israel Standard Time, December 26ᵗʰ
The Shafron residence
Beit Shemesh
Jerusalem District, Israel

"*. . .an intersection in Umm Lekhba, devastated by an explosion tonight in what is being described as a terror attack by anti-government subversives.*"

"Are you watching this, David?"

"*Ken,*" David Shafron nodded, the pale glow of the television illuminating his face as the concerned visage of the Al-Jazeera host pulled back to reveal granular cellphone footage of the Doha highway bombing, flames leaping angrily from the gutted wreck of an unrecognizable SUV. He hadn't been able to sleep and had finally given it up for a lost cause, stumbling from the bedroom and into his office, turning on the TV.

Abram Sorkin's call had come only minutes thereafter.

"Have we heard anything?"

"No," was the suitably terse reply, both of them mindful of the limits of what could be said on an open line.

Even if this *wasn't* the doing of Laner's team—and the absence of any comms suggested it was—things were going to be locking down tight in the wake of this. DROR, laying low—avoiding any unnecessary communication, anything that could compromise his own situation. Further hampering their ability to re-establish comms with Taferi in Syria.

And it would be days, if not weeks, before they'd be able to safely exfiltrate Gideon and Yossi. Shafron grimaced, kneading his brow with the tips of his fingers. Getting out was always the hard part, particularly when an operation took an unexpected turn for the kinetic.

How this one had taken that particular turn—to the point of setting off a bomb in the middle of a Doha street—was no doubt going to be the subject of extensive after-action review at Glilot Junction once they'd recovered their operators and begun the debriefing process.

That part, as Shafron knew from hard experience, was about as pleasant as a rectal exam. Especially when an op had skidded this far off the mark.

Right now, though, sitting in front of the muted television with Sorkin's foreboding voice in his ear. . .he only hoped they would get that far. *All of them.*

2:36 A.M. Arabia Standard Time
A penthouse apartment
Doha, Qatar

There were two kinds of people who were afraid of heights, Miki Abecassis had determined, after years of pondering the subject. Those who were afraid they might fall. And those who were afraid they *wouldn't*—who heard the void crying out to them and lacked the courage to answer its call.

He'd always recognized himself in the latter camp.

The Israeli reached out, running his fingers over the glass—such a *fragile* barrier, to stand between a man and a fall—all of Doha stretched out below him, thirty stories down, a city a-glimmer with light, his bare toes sinking into the thick pile of the carpet, cool in the air-conditioning.

Behind him, Lori Kerrigan stirred restlessly beneath the sheets, as though disturbed by the light now streaming through the floor-to-ceiling window from the city without.

Abecassis wasn't sure, if he were honest, just how he had ended up back at her apartment, back in her bed, after so long—but John Barnett's Christmas party had come to an abrupt end as word spread of the bombing and Mubarak's security team whisked the prince away, leaving the rest of them to their own devices.

"It's been too long, Rabah." Her hand, caressing the inside of his wrist as she finished her mocktail, her eyes boring into his own.

"I really should be getting back. . ."

But she'd been clearly rattled by the bombing, and while he suspected he could have allayed all her fears on that note with a word, it was a word best left unspoken. Tonight, her needs were his. Anyone suspecting him of involvement—and he was no longer sure the presence of Abdulrahman bin Thani at the Christmas party had been anything but a cosmic accident—would expect him to go to ground. Go to the airport and buy a ticket out. Not follow a wealthy American back to her penthouse and spend the night.

He had checked his phone as soon as he was able to do

so without drawing notice, but there was nothing from either of Mirit's officers, and he personally hoped it stayed that way.

There was little he could do for them, and after watching one of his assets go up in a flaming pyre in the middle of a Doha highway, replayed over and again on the television news, even that little was more than he had any inclination to do.

Ibraheem Saleh al-Murrah had been no hero—he'd been venal, corrupt, and cowardly, with an ego so vastly in excess of his competence that it had left him vulnerable to manipulation. But this was no game for heroes.

And he had deserved better than a fiery death.

Now, well, the whole operation was exposed—*very* exposed—and as Miki Abecassis turned back toward the bed, he knew he stood on the edge of another precipice, even more real than the one which lay outside that window.

Without even glass to stand in the way. . .

3:19 A.M. Syria Standard Time
Jabal an-Nusayriyah, Jableh District
Latakia Governorate, Syria

High off the road, the squat concrete shape of the abandoned forest observation tower sat atop the barren crest of the ridge, cast into stark relief by the moonlight, standing watch over a shifting hellscape of ash and snow, guarding a forest that remained here only as twisted, blackened ruin.

Fires, many of them set by incautious charcoalers or farmers deliberately blazing their lands during olive-picking season, had devastated the coastal range in the past few years, as Syrian society had broken down and normal safeguards were thrown to the wind as the struggle for survival became truly desperate. There had been a forestry service, once, manning towers like the one on the ridge, but they were outnumbered and outgunned by the gangs, filled as they were by battle-hardened men, many of whom had once fought for Assad and now answered to corrupt businessmen with ties to the regime.

And still Syria burned.

"Assad or we burn the country," indeed, Mohamed Taferi thought, remembering the graffiti sprayed luridly on the bare concrete wall of the shopping mall on the outskirts of Ghouta, near the front of the shifting battle lines. It had been a promise kept, as the regime set out to ensure that if they found themselves unable to retain power. . .anyone else would rule only over a desolated waste.

He ran a hand over his bearded face, struggling to stay awake as the trucks, what was left of them, rolled slowly down the mountain road, a worn, battered procession, supplemented by what vehicles they had managed to requisition from their "hosts" on the other side of the mountains, family cars taking their place scattered among the bullet-riddled technicals, drone crates thrust into car trunks to clear more space for the fighting men in the trucks.

Another four hours and he would reach out to make contact with Doha. In another twenty-four, he'd be on his way back to Israel, along with Abu Ahmed, toward whatever uncertain fate awaited the rebel commander, now that the doors of America were closed to him.

Promises betrayed. It came no easier now than it had in the beginning, and there was a bitter taste in his mouth as he contemplated the moment when Al-Golani would learn the truth, even knowing that he likely wouldn't be there to have to look into his eyes, his involvement with the rebel commander, itself coming to an end with the end of this operation.

Abu Ahmed. . .*and perhaps Nassif,* Mohamed thought, just able to make out the dark form of the boy huddled in the bed of the truck as he glanced back through the spider-veined glass of the Hilux's rear window. He was a *brother*, and watching over one's brothers was among the pillars of Druze faith.

Surely, he could get him out, at the last. Bring him to safety, see that he had a future, of some kind. He had spoken once of family in Germany, perhaps he could ensure that he got to them. Or supply his own, in their place.

Do something *right*, for once. *Balance the scales.*

For the moment, though, they needed to find cover, somewhere in these mountains—before the dawn. A place to lay-up and wait for the coming of night.

To rest, one final time, before their assault on Khmeimim itself, now just out of sight beyond yet another twisting, sinuous mountain ridge, twenty kilometers to the west.

Almost there.

6:56 A.M.
Khmeimim Airbase
Latakia Governorate, Syria

The first weak, cold rays of the dawn were just straggling over the peaks of the coastal range as the Mi-8MT transport spiraled in for a landing on the airbase's main helipad, settling heavily onto its tricycle undercarriage like the great, ungainly beast it was.

It had only been sixteen days since the President himself had landed here, Andriy Makarenko thought wearily, the downwash of the rotors kicking up a choking hurricane of dust, fine particles of sand and grit whirling through the air all about.

It felt far, far longer, the stresses of the mortar attacks and the threat from the Southern Front wearing him down, making it almost impossible to sleep.

Now, though. . .

*D*espite his lingering doubts, he found that he *wanted* to believe, more than anything else. The danger in that desire, one he knew all too well—but the knowledge made it no less compelling, the thought that the threat could be over, that he could close out the remaining weeks of his deployment in—well, if not *safety*, as close as one could get to it in Syria.

Close it out, and get home to his family.

Valeriy Egorov emerged from the dust as the helicopter's turboshafts shut down, looking as worn and. . .*defeated* as Makarenko could ever remember seeing him, the last word striking him with a terrible incongruity, and yet he found himself unable to get away from it.

"Tovarisch Kapitán!" the GRU officer greeted sharply, raising his voice to be heard above the sound of a Su-24 taxiing out on the nearby runway, offering Egorov his hand as his Spetsnaz disembarked, their clothes dirty and disheveled.

Some of the men were lugging body bags, four of them, long and black, carrying the remains of Kurbatov and his weps officer, along with a pair of Egorov's men who had died in the firefight with *Daesh*. By nightfall they'd be on a transport back home, to what families they had.

"Welcome back."

"Spasiba," the Spetsnaz captain replied, his tone clipped and short—his eyes seeming to look everywhere but Makarenko's face as he accepted the proffered hand. Perhaps it was the sense of guilt over losing men he had led into battle, perhaps. . .

"The Knights, their force has been destroyed?"

"Da. As I indicated in my report, *Tovarisch Podpolkóvnik."*

"Yes, but you indicated that—"

Egorov stopped short, anger flaring in his eyes as he turned back toward Makarenko, leaning in close—his voice low and menacing, nearly lost as the Su-24's turbojets roared to full life, sending it racing down the runway and into the dawn. "I lost good men out there, Dryusha. Don't think for a moment that I would have come back if those who killed them were still alive."

7:39 A.M.
The foothills of Jabal an-Nusayriyah
Jableh District, Latakia Governorate
Syria

Thirty-five minutes. And no reply from Doha. No acknowledgment of the message, no sign that anyone still knew he was out here. Still alive, still driving forward—prosecuting the mission that had been given him.

Just. . .*nothing.*

Mohamed Taferi shoved the phone back into the pocket of

his chest rig, unable to banish the sense of disconcertion that overcame him at the absence of contact. Behind him, through the trees covering this long ridgeline running down into the coastal plain, an area which had, mercifully, escaped the forest fires, he could hear the low murmur of voices—the remaining fighters, Abu Ahmed's men and Ibn Nadhar's jihadists alike, completing the last of their bivouac before hunkering down for the day. He should be with them, getting some sleep, but the tension pervading his body was impossible to ignore, a restless agitation refusing to release its hold.

He had understood that Doha was going dark for twenty-four hours, but. . .not beyond. Anything longer was fraught with hazard on an operation of this sort, and surely Tel Aviv would have reached out, if something had gone amiss.

If they could, he realized—if Doha had passed along his updated contact information after he'd started using the smuggler's phone, four days earlier.

Only three days before Doha had gone off the net.

If they hadn't, well there was a possibility that he was truly alone out here. No one waiting for him at the coast—the longest of possible roads home.

The Israeli drew in a deep breath of icy mountain air through his nose and released it in a heavy sigh, steam billowing from his lips into the cold light as he raised the binoculars to his eyes, aiming them through the trees scattered along the lower slopes, out toward the airbase in the distance, still thirteen kilometers or so off, its runways just visible in the growing light of the morning sun, still laboring to clear the mountains looming to their east as it climbed higher into the sky.

They were close now—so *very* close.

9:47 A.M. Israel Standard Time
Tel Aviv Station
The Embassy of the United States
Tel Aviv-Yafo, Israel

"Look, I'm not talking about giving the store away." Paul Keifer leaned back in his seat, his bagel still lying half-eaten and abandoned on the plate at his fingertips—irritation creeping into his voice as he stared into his computer's webcam. "But we're going to have to show them something, support them in *some* way, if this is to move forward. If we're to have a prayer of salvaging this. We've got to show a little skin."

It wasn't the first time the Good Idea Fairy had descended upon Headquarters only to depart leaving everyone concerned stumbling around the next morning, holding their heads and looking for their clothes, anxious to pretend that the previous night had never happened.

But much like virginity, field ops weren't something you simply put back into the bottle.

"I understand that, Paul," he heard Olivia Voss reply, a weary edge to her voice, "but what you're asking, there are other equities involved. The inter-agency remains as messy to deal with as ever. All the more so, over Christmas."

That was a fact. He was rather surprised that Voss herself was in the office, though he suspected the Clandestine Service's senior leadership was still processing the fall-out from the Braley rescue on Jolo the night before and sorting out how best to conduct damage control.

"I know," he said flatly, unwilling to back down. "I spent an hour last night on the phone with Palochak's watch officer at Fort Meade, unable to reach anyone senior enough to handle my requests."

Keifer murmured a curse of frustration at the memory, shaking his head. "Olivia. . .you know how this works, all I need is enough to convince Shafron we're working with him. Whether we are or not. And if we actually locate his missing officer or proof of life, so much the better."

10:51 A.M.
Mossad Headquarters, Glilot Junction
Tel Aviv-Yafo, Israel

The tension pervading Avi ben Shoham's office was palpable, building in the silence—relieved only by the faint buzzing of a fly trapped in one of the pale fluorescent light panels above.

Trapped, David Shafron reflected, looking up and finally locating the insect. *If that wasn't a familiar feeling. . .*

"So I'm to understand," the *memuneh* began finally, taking off his glasses and laying them to one side as he looked up at David and Mirit, "that we've had no contact with our officer for a day and a half now?"

"Ken," Shafron replied, nodding reluctantly, "that's correct. And it's been more than twenty-four hours since the first reports began to filter out from Hizballah groups in the region around Hama that Abu Ahmed's convoy had been ambushed and destroyed near Masyaf, with photos of burning, charred vehicles posted to the group's social media accounts."

"And Doha is still off the grid." That was the sticking point, in all of this—the variable they'd been unable to predict or plan for. *Uncertainty*. You could have the best intelligence in the world, but human beings were notoriously unpredictable, always capable of surprising you.

"*Ken.*"

"As per standard operational protocols," Mirit Refaeli interjected, not looking Shafron's way, "in light of what happened. DROR's safest course of action is to do nothing that could call attention to himself. Al-Murrah's former colleagues in State Security are almost certainly monitoring all comms traffic in and out, in the wake of the bombing."

It was rare to see Mirit on the back foot, but that's where this morning found her—her voice far more subdued than normal, if lacking none of its usual ice. Her officers had. . .well, it remained unclear what, exactly, they had done—or what had led them to do so—but Qatar had turned into a mess, and visions of Dubai a half-decade before, of a network rolled up and assets thrown into prison, had to be dancing in her head, never mind the impact on the Syria op.

"Understood, Mirit," was Avi ben Shoham's studied, patient reply. "No one is blaming DROR, at least, for his actions. We simply need to determine where to go from here. Specifically, what actions, if any, to take tonight."

"We need intel before we do anything, otherwise we're just groping in the dark. Risking more assets in the effort to recover those already lost."

"If we've received intel confirming Mohamed Taferi's death," Shafron countered acidly, "I'd like to know the reason it has yet to reach my desk. If we haven't. . ."

"You want to keep to the plan. Send in Barad and the *Tachash*." Shoham, and they weren't questions. The older man shook his head. "There's more here to consider than simply whether Taferi is still among the living. If the Knights' fighting force was shattered, the mission is at an end. If he was captured and tortured, Barad could be sailing straight into a trap."

"And if he's still in the fight? If he makes it to that coast, and there's no one there, waiting for him?"

There was a long silence once more, as the fly above made another desperate effort to break free. A cascade of emotions playing across Shoham's face. He was an old warrior, and he knew—or had once known—all that Shafron knew. But when he spoke again, his voice was strangely gentle, yet unyielding as granite.

"I think we always knew, David, that these were long odds. And they've only gotten longer."

1:03 P.M. Syria Standard Time
The foothills of Jabal an-Nusayriyah
Jableh District, Latakia Governorate
Syria

It was the sound of a chainsaw that brought Mohamed Taferi fully awake—his hand clawing for the rifle at his side as he sat bolt upright in the dirty, debris-strewn bed of the Hilux, his head coming off the pack and folded jacket he had used as a pillow.

And still the sound continued, carrying through the stands of remaining timber, a high-pitched, metallic whine, oscillating in volume. *Not far off.* Not far at all.

The Israeli glanced around, realizing he wasn't the only one who had been startled from sleep—the pickets they had thrown out, already reacting, their weapons unslung and leveled. Nassif visible down on one knee, his battered AK tucked into his shoulder.

Their trucks were sheltered among the towering Turkish pine which covered the low ridgeline running down out of the mountains, pulled in just off a narrow road that might well have been little more than a goat path. Concealed from an aerial search, but these mountains weren't empty. Far from it.

Falling asleep had taken him forever, or so it had seemed, cries of pain and anguish from Anas ibn Nadhar keeping them all awake as the jihadist fell deeper into the fever-drenched delirium into which he had slipped overnight, the movement and exposure of the trip taking its toll on his weakened body. *The doctor had been right*.

Mohamed levered himself over the side of the truck and leapt to the ground, feeling the impact shudder through his stiff, aching limbs, nearly taking him to his knees. He could have slept for a week.

Abu Ahmed was just extricating himself from the faded blue Chang'an sedan he had commandeered back at the village, worry etched across his weathered face, his Glock already out in his hand as the reality sunk in. "Charcoalers."

The Israeli nodded grimly. *Like as not*. Their choices, becoming only too clear, a bifurcated path. They could stay where they were, hole up—hope against hope that the men cutting down trees wouldn't wander up the ridgeline, wouldn't stumble across them.

Risk shots being exchanged, if they did—one or more men getting away, in the confusion.

Or they could go out after them. . .

Chapter 28

Dappled sunlight filtered through the Turkish pine to cast strange shadows across the grim, weary faces of the rebel fighters as they picked their way down the slope, weapons already raised, moving over snow-encrusted outcroppings of rock and around dense pockets of underbrush.

Mohamed Taferi kept his AKM at the low ready, aware that he only had another three mags for the rifle, even after scavenging for spares before their retreat north from Masyaf. Glancing over his right shoulder to glimpse the scraggly-bearded, youthful visage of Abu Basir, Ibn Nadhar's young lieutenant, an American Beretta drawn in his hand, leading his men forward through the pines.

Whispers, flickering back and forth among the dozen or so fighters that had followed them down the slope—the scrape of metal against wood as someone's rifle swung against a tree.

The crash of a falling tree resounded from ahead, shuddering through the forest—the chainsaw revving suddenly, its throaty roar tearing through the clear cold air before dying away completely.

Careful now. The Israeli slowed his advance, taking his left hand off the forend of the AKM to gesture for silence, for caution. They were close now—the crash of the tree couldn't have been more than thirty meters to the front, the sound of voices drifting through the trees toward them.

He took another careful step forward, his booted foot breaking through the crusted snow, edging past a small outcropping of rock nearly covered in scrub—and it was in that moment that he knew, he *felt*, that they were no longer alone.

The Israeli's head came up and to the left, meeting the eyes of a young man standing not more than fifteen feet to his left, half-concealed by an overgrown boxwood, but staring straight at him.

The fly of the man's faded blue tracksuit was wide open, warm urine now streaming forth unguided into the cold air as their eyes locked, shock and fear chasing each other across the Syrian's face. The two of them just staring, as if frozen in place, time itself seeming to slow down.

The young Syrian reacted first, letting out a yelp of surprise—fumbling desperately with himself as he turned, Mohamed's shout of *"Stop!"* going unheeded as he darted away.

Cursing viciously, the Israeli forced himself into motion, hearing the sharp crack of Abu Basir's pistol off to his right, a flurry of shots ringing out through the woods.

The man seemed to stagger, then trip over his feet, going down hard—moaning and writhing pitifully against the earth.

"Come on," Mohamed bellowed, pushing his tired body into a run, all use for caution evaporating with those gunshots. Their chance for surprise, lost. Violence, all that was left them. *"Yalla, yalla!"*

He stepped over the body, catching a brief glimpse of the fear and agony written on the countenance of the dying man before he pushed on—hearing someone else coming along behind finish him off with a single shot.

They burst out into the clearing another ten meters ahead, catching the gang of charcoalers scrambling for their guns—a ragged burst tearing from the muzzle of the Israeli's AKM, cutting down a man in a military coat on the other side of the mounded pile of wood forming the makeshift charcoal kiln, just as he picked up his own Kalashnikov.

Mohamed heard a ripping sound tear through the air to his left as Mamdouh opened up with his RPD, bullets chewing harmlessly into the tree trunks on the opposite side of the clearing before finally finding their target—a man stooped down by a string of donkeys loaded down with processed charcoal, his guts spilling out onto the cold ground as he collapsed. *"Allahu akbar!"* ringing out savagely as the woods echoed with gunfire.

He saw one of the animals go down as well in the hail of bullets, its hooves thrashing and kicking, a terrifyingly pathetic bray of pain and terror filling the air, saw the rest buck and start—but first one and then a second bullet cut through the air past his own head and he turned to see a young man cowering in the shadow of the kiln, holding his pistol sideways like a gangster in an American rap video as he squeezed off panicked shots.

A half-step forward, the muzzle of his rifle swinging to

bear as he squeezed off a burst, a tight grouping tearing through the man's upper chest, his body jerking as he fell back against the wood, staring blankly into the Israeli's eyes in the final remaining moments of his life.

Silence descending once more over the clearing, punctuated by a single shot as Abu Basir stalked toward one of the wounded desperately trying to crawl off into the underbrush and shot the man in the back of the head.

Mohamed walked forward, his ears still ringing with the gunfire, stooping down beside the body of the first man he had shot, his military coat stained with blood and torn by bullets.

The man was still alive, pain distorting his rough features, his burly chest rising and falling with each labored breath—hatred in his eyes as he met the Israeli's gaze, struggling to speak.

The Mossad officer ignored him, instead turning over the man's limp arm to reveal the logo emblazoned on the right shoulder sleeve of the coat—an eagle, gold and white against the desert camo, talons outstretched as though descending upon its prey. Flowing white Arabic script on a backdrop of black and red, just above.

Liwa Suqur al-Sahara. The Desert Hawks. The man was part of a private pro-Assad militia, or had been, once—the line between militia and criminal mafia in Syria, never exactly clear.

He straightened, shaking his head as he glanced around at the devastation—bodies sprawled among the fallen trees, now riddled with bullets. Blood spattered across the snow.

It took another moment to realize what *wasn't* there, anymore, the realization sinking home with a jolt.

The string of donkeys. Bolted in the mayhem and panic of the gunfire, untied or breaking free from their tethers.

Like as not. . .already on their way home.

1:57 P.M.
The village, Jabal an-Nusayriyah
Al-Suqaylabiyah District, Hama Governorate
Syria

"I did *not* treat them! They are dogs, they—"

The doctor's voice broke off suddenly as Captain Awad's clenched fist crashed into the side of his face, rocking the kitchen chair to which he was bound unsteadily on its wooden legs, blood mixing with his spittle as he hacked and coughed, spitting out a broken tooth—his indignation subsiding into a feeble moan.

"This is the way the *Nawasib* are," Michael Awad observed conversationally, using a derogatory term for Sunni Muslims, a smile of satisfaction on his face as he leaned back in the opposite chair, glancing around at his gathered men. "As treacherous as Jews. When *Daesh* is around, oh how they love them—they hail them as their saviors and dream of their reborn caliphate. But when *Daesh* runs away like the cowards they are, then their courage deserts them and no one has ever *heard* of *Daesh*, no one could *possibly* support such murderers, how could one accuse them of such a thing? You can never think for a moment of trusting them."

Or any *Muslim*, Awad thought, but it would have been unwise to have added that in front of his men, even with his Alawite lieutenant out of the room, ransacking someone else's home, deeper in the village. There were ears everywhere, as every Syrian learned from birth.

The Christian special forces captain leaned closer, putting a gentle hand on the doctor's knee, feeling it tremble beneath his fingers. "I know, Mustafa, that he was treated in this village. Your neighbors, your *friends*, have told me as much. And they all say you did it."

It had crossed his mind that they could have been lying, scapegoating their Sunni neighbor in an effort to save themselves, but he would have started with him in any case, for the same reasons. . .there was no one around with any interest in defending him, and he would serve as a convenient example to break down the resistance of the rest.

"Then there's you. . .and you say you did not. Your word, the word of a *Nasabi*, against all of theirs. So tell me, Mustafa, if you didn't treat him—where would he have gone?"

Another moan escaped the doctor's broken, bleeding lips, his eyes seeming to struggle to focus as he looked back at Awad, his voice thick with anger and pain. "Where all dogs go—the *vet*."

2:05 P.M. Israel Standard Time
Mossad Headquarters, Glilot Junction
Tel Aviv-Yafo, Israel

The paperwork, David Shafron had learned, never truly went away. Even with a secretary—a perk he'd never enjoyed in any of his previous positions at the Office—there was always *something* that needed his attention as head of unit, his decision, his signature. It was endless.

He took off the glasses that had, reluctantly, become a

part of all his desk work and laid them to one side, reaching up to pinch the bridge of his nose wearily as he considered the morning meeting once again.

"You've heard nothing from the Americans?" Avi ben Shoham had asked after Mirit had finally departed, leaving the two of them alone with their thoughts. The two men who bore more of the responsibility for this operation than anyone else.

"No," he'd replied, adding *"not yet"* as a barely conscious afterthought. It wasn't likely—hadn't been.

Keifer's demeanor had made it clear that whatever had prompted the Americans to put forward this operation, their commitment to the idea had. . .waned. *Typical.* Follow-through had always been a weakness of American foreign policy, and it was one that bled through into the intelligence arena as well.

"You understand, don't you?" the *memuneh* had asked after another long moment, seeming to pick his words with more than usual care. *"This decision. . .it's not an easy one. It may not even be the right one. It's not, certainly, the decision we would have considered right, when we were ourselves in the field. But you and I, David, are no longer in the field—and the bigger picture we now see comes with responsibilities broader and in some ways more difficult to bear than even those we once shouldered, out there. Because the consequences of our decisions no longer concern the fates of one man or a dozen, but hundreds, and even thousands. The state of Israel, itself. That is the weight of what we do—the* choices *we make."*

He understood, all right, Shafron thought, rising from his chair and turning toward the window. The Mediterranean, sparkling in the afternoon, just visible from his office, through the scattering of tall apartment buildings that grew thicker the closer one got to the beach.

And right now, it was a weight that bid fair to crush him beneath it.

2:27 P.M. Syria Standard Time
The village, Jabal an-Nusayriyah
Al-Suqaylabiyah District, Hama Governorate
Syria

"Please. . .captain, they *threatened* me, if I didn't operate on their leader. They threatened to kill me, to rape my wife, and my daughters."

"They threatened you, did they?" A faint smile tugged at Michael Awad's lips. "And because they *threatened* you, you saw fit to betray the President, to turn your back on all that Bashar has done for us, in his mercy and benevolence."

He reached forward and took the veterinarian's chin in his hand, lifting his head and forcing him to look him in the eye—one of his eyes swollen shut, the flesh discolored an angry purplish-black. He had resisted, clearly, but it hadn't been enough. "That makes you either a traitor or a weakling—or both. How long have you dreamed of betraying Bashar?"

"I'm. . .I'm not a traitor," he sputtered in feeble protest, blood trickling from his chin as he stumbled over his words. *"Allah, Souriya, Bashar wa Bas."*

God, Syria, and Bashar only. Awad smiled at the panicky repetition of the slogan. *But it hadn't worked out that way, had it?*

"A weakling, then. Maybe your wife, your daughters, deserve to be raped, if you're too weak to protect them. And when they bring *our* children into the world, maybe your sorry little village will finally have some men in it, after all."

The man refused to meet his gaze, his head drooping toward his chest when Awad released his chin. Not an ounce of defiance left in him. *Pathetic.*

"If you're no traitor, if your loyalties are truly still with Bashar, then you'll have no objection to telling me where *Daesh* went when they left. Otherwise—"

"I don't *know*! They told me nothing. *Nothing.*"

"Otherwise," Awad repeated calmly, as if the man hadn't spoken, "we can drill out your kneecaps. . .and start with your youngest daughter."

"La!" The man was sobbing now, tears streaming down his bloodied face, sniveling out his protests of innocence. *"La, la. . ."*

The captain turned toward one of his NCOs, standing there looking impassively on, hands clasped behind his back. "Ali, get the drill."

The veterinarian let out a wail, his voice cracking as he struggled to speak. "They. . .he, he said no one was coming back. That's all he said, I swear it before Allah."

As if oaths to a false god had any meaning. It was amazing, though, how the memory cleared. He turned to the sergeant, who had hesitated at the door. "Go ahead, get the drill—we'll see what else he remembers before it reaches bone. Or after. We—"

"Captain!" Awad turned to see his lieutenant enter the room, hauling their radioman behind him. "It's headquarters—they've received a call from a former militia commander in Latakia. A group of his men was wiped out, in the mountains. . ."

3:49 P.M. Israel Standard Time
Tel Aviv Station
The Embassy of the United States
Tel Aviv-Yafo, Israel

"And that's as far as we've gotten with him," Steve Bollinger acknowledged, reaching for the bottle of water in front of him as he looked up from his laptop. "If it's more money he wants, he's given no sign."

Paul Keifer acknowledged his deputy's words with a short nod, forcing his mind back to the meeting, and the potential asset under discussion in the West Bank.

Recruiting in this part of the world was ever fraught with hazard, and never more so than here, with the added risk of treading on Israeli toes. Legend had it that the Agency had once recruited a high-ranking member of the Palestinian Authority's hierarchy, only for him to end up on the Mossad's hit list after plotting a terror attack. The legend went on to claim that he had been found dead in a villa on Elba, in bed next to his young wife, shot through the head, but legends tended to grow in the telling.

Still, an incident like that, however it might have been embellished over the years, was enough to precipitate institutional PTSD, and recruiting in the Palestinian Authority was something the Agency still approached with more than usual caution. *Gaza? Forget about it.*

"Let's keep talking with him, keep the lines of communication open. Reel him in if we can, if we can't. . .let's at least try not to make any new enemies." He closed the folder, reviewing the notes on his screen. "Do we have any fresh numbers on Hizballah fighters in Syria? We had a request from Dodson at Beirut Station."

With no CIA presence in Damascus itself, the quixotic task of estimating Iran's contribution to the "Keep Bashar Alive" cause had fallen to no less than four CIA stations— Tel Aviv, Beirut, Baghdad, and Amman—all trying to track thousands of fighters belonging to dozens of confusing variations on the Party of God, and no doubt double and triple-counting people along the way.

"No estimates more recent than November, no," his ranking analyst, Tim Molstad, replied, pushing his glasses up the bridge of his nose with a forefinger. "We—"

A knock on the door interrupted Molstad's reply, and Keifer looked up to see his secretary standing in the doorway of the conference room. "You have a call from Headquarters, sir. Olivia Voss."

"Put her through, please," the Tel Aviv chief of station replied, reaching for the phone in front of his seat and waiting for a moment for the connection to complete. "Yes, Olivia?"

"Palochak's boys and girls came through, Paul. You're going to need to check your e-mail."

4:03 P.M. Syria Standard Time
The skies over Idlib Governorate
Syria

Fifteen thousand feet below, angry flame-black flowers bloomed amidst the trees on the edge of the desolated Syrian town in the fading sunlight, immolating *Tahrir al-Sham* fighting positions. . .or what were reported as such by Syrian and Russian intelligence, Yaroslav Svischev thought, banking hard as his Su-57 described a sharp arc above the devastation, sun glinting off his silvered wings. His radar accurately tracking the flight of Su-25 *Grachs* as they pulled up from their low-level attack run, barely visible streaking out across the farmland to the east.

Chasing the ground rush, like as not—he had been a young pilot himself, once, and it was a temptation that never left even the oldest. The feeling of *speed* that you got down on the deck like nowhere else in flight, the heady knowledge that the slightest malfunction, a reaction timed scant tenths of a second too slow, and your life would be over. Only the steadiness of your hand standing between you and the grave.

The feeling of immortality that came over one in such moments.

Below, he saw flashes of impotent fire lance out after the fleeing aircraft as the jihadist fighters recovered, firing from whatever positions had escaped the bombing, seeking to bring down their tormentors.

His own jet—and that of his wingman, the latter taking up position once again off his left wing as he followed him into the turn—was unarmed, their role in this strike mission strictly that of observers, testing their systems. Staying above the fray. *Out of danger.*

And everything was functioning as it should—the Su-57's radars had been able to pick up the flight of *Grachs* against the ground clutter, maintaining lock for the duration of the run. If they'd been hostile attack aircraft, he could have dispatched them with no trouble from stand-off range.

Likely before they even knew they were being targeted. Down on the deck, there wasn't much room for maneuver.

Svischev was too old of a test pilot to believe that the Su-57 was revolutionary. It wasn't a game-changer of an airframe, and while it was difficult to truly gauge its effectiveness against its American counterparts—*adversaries*—without the opportunity to go head-to-head in the real world, he was left with some qualms as to the outcome of such an encounter.

What it *was* a competent fifth-generation fighter, and so far, the radar techs at Khmeimim had proven unable to detect either of them until they were nearly on top of the base. That had to count for something.

He tracked the Su-25s on his radar until they were nearly a hundred and thirty kilometers away, striking more assigned targets near Raqqa, and then glanced back over his shoulder to where his wingman rested calmly off his left wing. A quiet, satisfied smile crossing the Russian pilot's face.

Time to return to base, refit and get ready to do this all over again. *One more day. . .*

4:13 P.M. Israel Standard Time
Mossad Headquarters, Glilot Junction
Tel Aviv-Yafo, Israel

It was thin. David Shafron knew that, knew it all too well, looking at the map now spread out over the cluttered surface of his desk, his computer's keyboard shoved away to clear space. *Perilously thin.*

Syria was a country riven by war, filled with dozens if not hundreds of armies, militias, and armed gangs, any one of which would have slit the others' throats at the drop of a hat—and been the ones to drop the hat.

A single intercepted report of a massacre in the

mountains, former militiamen still answering to their old commander, a businessman and regime loyalist, cut down in a hail of fire—it wasn't much to go on. Even supposing he could trust the Americans without seeing the raw intel for himself.

But. The site of the massacre, near as he could establish it from the NSA intercepts, was only thirty to forty kilometers northwest of Masyaf as the crow flew. Over the mountains, *yes*, but close, for all that. And close enough to Khmeimim to have served as a lay-up position for whatever remained of the rebel force to hunker down for the day—stage for the night's assault.

It's what he would have done, staying up in the highlands until the last possible moment, avoiding population centers. But in the field, even the safest bets could prove uncertain.

He took his seat once again, his eyes drifting across the map, lost in his own thoughts. Avi was out of contact, having left the building early for a work dinner with Damien Ardouin, the local DGSE chief of station, no doubt discussing Syria—the French, always the most invested of the European powers in the affairs of Damascus. Mirit was still in her office, so far as he knew, but. . .*no*.

No, this had to be his decision and his alone—the declining sun washing in through his office windows to bathe his desk and the folds of the map in a ruddy glow.

The risks Avi had outlined were real, and far more certain than this ELINT from the Americans. But he had been out there far too many times, run far too many of these operations himself, to rest easy at the thought of dismissing it.

After a moment, he retrieved his cellphone from beneath

the unfolded map, scrolling through his recent contacts to find Rahel's number. *"Motek,"* he began, when his wife finally picked up, *"silchi li,* can you get the boys from school? I know it's late." *Sweetie, forgive me.* "Lo, lo. . .everything's okay, but I won't be home tonight. Something's come up here at work. Of course, *motek*, you know I'll be careful."

Shafron ended the call after another moment, a strange sense of guilt nagging at him as he searched once again through his contacts, selecting another number. The knowledge that what he had told her was a lie.

He lifted the phone to his ear once more, listening as it began to ring, knowing he was about to cross a bridge from which there could well be no return. "Avigdor, listen to me. . .are you at the port?"

Chapter 29

"He's dead."

Mohamed Taferi grimaced as Abu Basir rose from beside the now-still body of Anas ibn Nadhar, stretched out on blankets beneath a towering Cilician fir, its branches dark against the gathering dusk, a chill wind sweeping across the hillside.

The dead man's face was just visible in the half-light thrown by a carefully shielded lantern, pale and distorted beneath the wiry scruff of the black beard, now set in the anguish which had tormented his final hours.

Not long enough, the Mossad officer reflected, turning away. Anas ibn Nadhar had deserved all the torments this life could imagine, and his had been cut far too mercifully short, a few hours of half-conscious delirium in exchange for years of cruelty and bloodshed, a country torn apart by him and his kind.

The only consolation lay in the knowledge that his settling of accounts with Allah yet remained, but that didn't solve the Israeli's problem of the moment. *Not nearly long enough.*

He stalked back to the vehicles, finding Abu Ahmed leaning against the hood of the Chang'an, hugging himself against the cold. They had shifted position after the debacle with the charcoalers, moving another four kilometers north through the twisting roads and hard-packed dirt paths, made treacherous by half-melted ice and snow, that wound their way through these foothills.

A move which had likely hastened the death of Ibn Nadhar, but it had been necessary. Even now, from the crest of the ridge above their vehicles, the lights were visible—search parties, out looking for them. Their hours were numbered. And *still* silence from Doha, his line of communications with the Office, severed at the worst of moments.

"Is he dead?" Abu Ahmed asked, his dark eyes meeting the Israeli's. A nod, serving as his reply.

"Good."

"We need to pull everyone together," the Israeli said, watching him closely. *Something was. . .wrong.* "Go over the plan of attack, make sure everyone understands their role."

The surviving drones had already been unpacked and were being fitted with their explosive payloads, though darkness had fallen before they could risk any test flights. One of the control laptops had been shot to scrap in the ambush outside Masyaf and they'd been forced to slave multiple drones together to a single controller to take up the slack.

"I'll do it," the Southern Front commander responded, and pushed himself away from the Chang'an, putting a hand on Mohamed's shoulder as if to steady himself, his breath foul and reeking. . .*with alcohol.*

Ya Allah. Anger surged within the Mossad officer, nearly overcoming him. Al-Golani had to have found it in the village back in the mountains, one of the houses his men had looted. *But even so. . .*

"Min sijak?" he demanded incredulously, seizing the man's arm, a sullen light flaring in Abu Ahmed's eyes as he turned to meet his gaze.

"Does it matter?" A morose shake of the head. "In another few hours, we'll all have joined Ibn Nadhar in the fires of hell. *Jannah* is not for the likes of you and I, my friend. Only a fresh hell awaits us in the next life, not unlike that we've created for ourselves in this one. And tonight, we go out to meet it."

"La!" Mohamed spat sharply, gripping the commander's shoulder and shaking it, Abu Ahmed's breath washing over him as he looked the man in the eye, mustering himself for the last, the great, lie. "Tonight, *you* go to America."

5:07 P.M.
Beit Yashout, Jableh District
Latakia Governorate, Syria

Ice clung to the flat roof of the two-story concrete block house and Michael Awad scuffed at it with his booted foot, moving back to firmer footing as he adjusted the Russian-made night-vision monocular to his eye, scanning the darkening slopes of the ridges surrounding the small town.

Beit Yashout, tucked in a valley between the foothills descending toward the coastal plain, was home to the Hadadeen tribe of Aniseh Makhlouf, the President's now-deceased mother, and he'd found no difficulty in swelling his ranks with volunteers to search the surrounding foothills.

So long as the light lasted, that is. After seeing the bullet-riddled bodies of the charcoalers brought back into town, no one was any too anxious to go up into the hills after that particular bear in the dark, and Awad had barely a dozen of the NODs for his own men, not enough to mount his own patrol. He'd resorted to throwing out checkpoints as a compromise, covering the roads down to the coast—and back toward the mountains, in case *Daesh* chose to retreat, instead. Their annihilation could wait for morning.

Out beyond those ridges, where the plain met the sea, lay the Russian base, and as many soldiers with night-vision as he could have asked for, but Awad remembered far too well the look on that Spetsnaz captain's face as he'd insisted that the rebels had been *destroyed* there beneath the curtain wall of Masyaf, despite the evidence of everyone's eyes to the contrary. Madness lurking there in their depths, as though the demon within screamed to be unleashed.

Embarrassing such a man would come at a cost far greater than Michael Awad was willing to pay. He might himself end up stood up against a wall, his brains blown out like those of the Sunni doctor he'd executed with his own hand before leaving that village back in the mountains.

No, it was abundantly clear that the best—the only *safe*—approach was to handle this discreetly, on his own. Without involving, or embarrassing, his superiors' Russian patrons.

Awad lowered the monocular, turning back toward the steps leading from the roof. Time to make sure those checkpoints were where they needed to be. Throw out the net, and in the morning they would draw it shut.

5:16 P.M.
The foothills of Jabal an-Nusayriyah
Jableh District, Latakia Governorate
Syria

". . .while your detachment will come in from southeast, here." Mohamed Taferi reached out, marking a slashing arrow across the map with a grease pencil, as he glanced up at the faces of the men surrounding him, half-concealed in shadow—the light barely enough to render the map visible. "We'll breach the wire *here*, and move against the revetments."

He glimpsed Abu Ahmed nodding his approval—sensed rather than saw a disturbance among the jihadists as Abu Basir shoved his way to the fore.

"The drones," Al-Golani said, leaning toward the map and extending his hand for the pencil, "will take out the towers here, and here, drawing their QRF toward this end of the base—"

"We're leaving," the young man announced, towering over Mohamed in the darkness. Behind him, the engine of one of the Hiluxes came to life, sputtering in the cold, the *Jaysh* fighters slowly beginning to drift away from the semi-circle around the Israeli. *No.* If they pulled out, it was over.

"So soon?" Mohamed asked, keeping his voice even with an effort as he rose to confront Abu Basir, brushing his coat back to clear his holstered Glock. "If you're detected moving in before the rest are in position, you could compromise the attack."

Abu Basir shook his head, seeming to puff himself up as if in an effort to reclaim his lost height. "We will take no part in any attack—this is madness, all of it. You will all die."

The Israeli nodded, his voice growing in volume as the younger man started to turn away, seeming to consider their conference at an end. "And do you fear death so much, Abu Basir? Does the thought of martyrdom fill you with such terror that you would run from it? Flee away, into the night?"

He saw the young jihadist quail, felt every eye turned on the two of them in that moment, silence seeming to fall all around, broken only by the sound of the truck engine, and the moaning of the wind as it whipped up the ridge through the trees. *"La,"* Abu Basir replied, shaking his head uncertainly, "I'm not afraid of death, I—"

Mohamed took a step past him, as if the younger man was no longer worthy of his attention, raising his voice to be heard by those among the *Jaysh* fighters who had begun to straggle toward the trucks. "The Russians came here, to your land, to oppress the faithful, to bomb your homes, kill your families, and keep the doctor's boot on your throat. Tonight—we're going to kill *them*. May all who have sworn to fight in the way of Allah join with us. *Allahu akbar!*"

5:21 P.M. Israel Standard Time
Jaffa Port
Jaffa, Tel Aviv-Yafo, Israel

Night had fallen over the city and the sea, but lights sparkled from the apartments overlooking the port and the sound of music filled the streets of Old Jaffa, small knots of tourists visible moving to and fro.

A cold breeze sweeping in off the moonlit sea, sending a shudder of premonition down David Shafron's spine as he stood on the deck of the *Tachash*, hands shoved into the pockets of his jacket.

"I can't order any of you," he said, looking around him into the young faces of men who reminded him of what he once had been. "I'm not a part of your chain of command, and to do what I'm asking will require you to go *outside* your own command as possibly never before. To bend the rules so far, they may well break. And there will be consequences. . .consequences I likely can't shield you from, no matter what responsibility I accept for my own, and I'm prepared to accept it all. Still, the risks you're taking go well beyond the immediate dangers of hostile action tonight, and I wouldn't hide that from you."

"But one of ours is in harm's way." This from Reuven Aharoni, leaning casually against the wheelhouse, arms folded across his broad chest.

"Ken." Shafron paused a moment before adding, "He may even be dead already. We've lost comms. But if he's still alive, if he reaches the rally point on the coast and finds no one there waiting. . ."

His voice trailed off, letting the implications sink home.

Needing to say nothing more. They'd all been there, waiting for exfiltration—fearing, irrationally, that it might not come. Knowing that their lives were measured in scant hours if it didn't.

"I'm willing to take us there," Avigdor Barad announced, rising from his seat on the upturned bucket and laying aside his nets. A hard, sober look in the sailor's eyes. "You'll be wanting to go along, as we'd discussed?"

"If you'll have me. It's been a few years, I'll grant, but I can still handle a gun when need be."

Reuven took a step out of the shadow of the wheelhouse. "If you go ashore, David, it will be under my command. My team, my rules."

"Of course." He'd have expected nothing less—have *done* nothing less, when it had been his team.

The younger man nodded slowly, glancing around at the remaining members of the team, as if giving space for them to comment, to object. But neither was forthcoming.

"All right, then," Reuven said, a grim smile creasing his face as he extended his hand, clasping Shafron's firmly, "let's go bring him home."

7:09 P.M. Syria Standard Time
Khmeimim Airbase
Latakia Governorate, Syria

The Su-57's engines glowed hot against the night as it began its takeoff roll, the penetrating whine of its turbojets growing in volume.

Andriy Makarenko paused at the door of the listening station to watch it go, shaking his head as if to clear it of the noise. The fighter jet pulling up well before the end of Khmeimim's runway, climbing steeply into the night sky, moonlight glistening off its wings. Night operations, the final phase of this round of testing. They'd be back in a few hours.

When all this was over, he was going to take Zinaida and their daughter and go somewhere very far away from any planes, from the incessant commotion which had dominated his life for the last year. Only a couple more weeks.

He nodded briefly to the guard before entering, placing his cellphone in one of the small lockers immediately within and shrugging off his coat under the eye of the bored soldier behind the desk, who was playing something on his own phone, whiling away the hours on duty. His PP-19 submachine gun, its stock folded back along the receiver, lying neglected on the desk before him.

There was no stopping it, not with the younger generation, Makarenko reflected, closing the door of the locker and accepting his badge from the soldier before entering the facility proper. Keeping up with family and—mostly—friends on VK was everything, and it was all they could do to keep sensitive information from getting posted along with everything else. *Kids.*

"So, what's going on?" he asked, finding the officer who had called him huddled amid the maze of glowing screens, bent over his keyboard.

"This," the young lieutenant replied, scooting his chair back and standing to offer it to Makarenko. *"Prosti, pozhaluysta, Tovarisch Podpolkóvnik. . .*it came in hours ago, early this afternoon, but it was only translated just before I called you over."

That was ever the danger, the GRU officer thought, his eyes scanning over the rows of Cyrillic characters on-screen as he took the proffered seat. There was so much raw intelligence out there now, it was overwhelming. And the worth of so much of it, impossible to even determine until it had passed through the painfully bottle-necked process of translation.

But this—his eyes bounced up to the header, realizing it was a radio intercept off the Syrian Arab Army comms network, their allies, whom they monitored as a matter of course.

The initiator of the transmission was a known lieutenant of Mohammad Jaber, a prominent Latakia businessman, former general, and friend of Maher al-Assad, the President's younger brother, who had commanded the private militia known as the "Desert Hawks Brigade" up until their disbandment earlier in the fall, and who still retained many of them as his own personal mafia-style enforcers.

The recipient, Brigadier General Burhan Khalil, the head of Damascus' Branch 235 of the *Shu'bat al-Mukhabarat*— military intelligence. *Interesting.*

"He lost men in a firefight in the mountains?" he asked, glancing over his shoulder at the young officer.

An anxious bob of the head. "*Da, tovarisch.* They were charcoalers, illegally logging the coastal range to obtain fuel— criminal gangs, most of them, these days. But—I'm sorry, you don't need all of that. . .they were attacked this afternoon— "massacred" is the word he uses, by a rebel group in the hills northeast of Beit Yashout, a village in the—"

"I know where it is, *Tovarisch Leytenánt*," Makarenko replied, half-lost in his own thoughts. There was no reason for such an incident not to be violence as all-too-normal for even this part of Syria—it wasn't even two weeks since the mortar attacks and someone with a rifle had taken a few wild potshots at their guard towers only the preceding night. Even so, he felt the return of that nagging unease he'd experienced several times since the loss of Kurbatov's gunship, since Egorov's after-action report had first reached him. "Go over the rest of our intercepts from this afternoon—task whatever people you need, find me *anything* else relating to this. And have someone reach out to Damascus, I want to talk with General Khalil. *Tonight*."

8:13 P.M.
The foothills of Jabal an-Nusayriyah
Jableh District, Latakia Governorate
Syria

Above, the moon shone down through the needles of the pines, obscured only rarely by the infrequent clouds, casting the ridge into shadow. The soft, low voices of men singing, drifting through the trees.

Nassif leaned back into the rear wheel of a Hilux, his rifle propped up beside him as he shoveled cold cooked rice into his mouth with his fingers, wiping plump kernels away from the corner of his lips with the back of a grimy hand.

The words of the *nasheed* reaching him now and then from where the *Jaysh* fighters gathered, snatches of song torn away by the breeze as it moaned through the trees. *". . .then where are those who want martyrdom, for God's sake, for surely . . ."*

The boy jammed another handful of rice between his lips, shifting his position restlessly. It wasn't martyrdom he sought, but oblivion. An end to everything, beyond which lay only the endless void.

He knew not what lay at the end of this night, but he suspected he was more likely to find his oblivion than the jihadists were to reach paradise.

". . .they fight in the cause of Allah, they kill and are killed. . ."

The *nasheed* was familiar, one he remembered hearing around the cooking fires back in Quneitra, a lifetime ago, or so it seemed—and he found his own mind supplying the words, without conscious thought. ". . .has purchased from the believers their lives, for that they will have Paradise. . .and who is truer to his covenant than Allah?"

Who wasn't? If there was a God, the boy mused, he was far more interested in taking away than in giving. A trickster god, who cheated and stole, toying with the wreckage of men's lives, making bargains with mortals, with no intention of following through.

Perhaps it was true, after all—God *was* a Jew.

He heard a footstep and looked up to see the Qatari round the back of the truck, reaching out to put a hand on his shoulder as he squatted down beside him.

Nassif reached into the knapsack, seizing another handful of the cooked rice he had looted from the village back in the mountains and extending it toward the man in his clenched fist.

"La, la." A shake of the head, the man's face shadowed in the moonlight.

"They believed you," Nassif said after a moment, still listening to the singing, "that you are one of them. But you aren't, are you?"

A pause. *"La.* You and I, we were raised to know the truth they only grope for, like blind men, in the dark. *La illaha illa Allah, wahdahu la sharika lah."*

There is no God but God, He is alone, with no partner. The words he remembered his parents repeating to him, as a child. *But was there any truth to them?*

"What would you have done, if they hadn't believed?"

"Died, probably." The man shook his head. "We all must, sometime. Die, to be reborn, to carry on anew."

The soul, in death, leaving the body to enter that of another Druze being born in that very hour. The circle of life, unending, spinning on and on down through eternity.

Once, as a child, the boy thought, chewing slowly on the last grains of rice, that had all sounded like hope.

Now it felt more like a curse.

"But not tonight," the Qatari said, reaching over to squeeze Nassif's shoulder once again. "Tonight, I want you to—"

He felt, rather than heard, the intrusion, the man's words breaking off as he looked up to see Mamdouh round the front of the Hilux, his single remaining eye shifting restlessly back and forth between the two of them for a moment before he addressed himself to the Qatari.

"We're getting ready to roll out. . .Abu Ahmed was looking for you."

8:37 P.M. Eastern European Time
The Tachash
The Mediterranean Sea

The AKM's receiver felt cold against David Shafron's hand as he sat in the boat's stern, re-assembling the weapon, sliding a fully-loaded mag into the mag well of the rifle—the foam of their wake glistening white in the moonlight as the trawler forged steadily north.

Down below, Avigdor Barad was coaxing every ounce of speed he could out of the engine, the lights of Beirut just visible in the distance off to their northwest.

He had operated there a handful of times over the years, in both peace and in war, but he'd never grown to like the city. Polished, sophisticated, *Western*, even—it was far too easy to relax in such an environment and forget Beirut could slit your throat in the least unguarded moment, with more suspects than one could begin to enumerate.

It might not be that dangerous for the average tourist, but the Jew would find no friends there—there were reasons Lebanon didn't even let anyone with Israeli stamps on their passport into the country—and if your cover became compromised, you were a dead man.

Of course, that last held true far beyond Beirut. *Death to spies*, a maxim old as the business itself. A fate Mohamed Taferi might well suffer, if he hadn't already, if they failed to exfiltrate him from the coastline of Latakia. *If.*

It had become clear to Shafron years ago that if you wanted certainty in your life, you didn't go into intelligence.

He heaved himself to his feet, the rifle now clasped in his right hand, grimacing as his muscles protested stiffly against the exertion. An unwelcome reminder of the reality, that his place was truly no longer *here*, alongside these men.

Shimon Ben-David had dropped him off at his house after leaving headquarters, and he'd bid the head of his security team a good night before changing into street clothes and retrieving a Beretta from his safe. Watching the clock, all the while—knowing that Rahel would be home soon, with the boys. That he had to be gone by then, if his story were to hold.

The same doubts plaguing him on the drive to Jaffa which haunted him now. Why was he here, why was he doing this, truly? Was it really about Mohamed Taferi, about coming to the rescue of an officer in danger? Or was it about himself?

His own need to throw off the restraints and responsibilities which had so chained him down in recent years, to take *action* once more, rather than sitting behind a desk.

And if the latter were true, it begged another question. . .*at what cost?*

Chapter 30

There were moments, in this part of Syria, when you could almost convince yourself there wasn't a war—houses unscarred by bullet or shell sleeping peacefully alongside quiet country roads—groves of olives and orchards of citrus covering the gently rolling hills as they descended to the coastal plain.

Mohamed Taferi leaned back into the threadbare seat of the Hilux, his hand clutching the receiver of his AKM as they rolled into one small village at the head of their small convoy, an electronics store, shuttered for the night, coming up on their left—farm fields, visible in the moonlight through the scattered houses to the right of the road.

Almost there. They needed now only to turn north and move into position around the airbase itself, another seven to eight kilometers. Still nothing from Doha or even Tel Aviv, the Mossad officer thought, checking his phone guardedly.

431

Something had to have gone wrong. . .something clearly *had* gone wrong in Doha, judging by the message Ibn Nadhar had received—but did that mean their entire network in-country had been rolled up? He shoved the thoughts away with an effort, recognizing their futility—forcing himself to focus on the present, take the problems as they came.

He could do nothing about Qatar.

Right now, they needed to stage, perform the final recce of the target and settle in for the last few hours before the assault. They'd strike in the small hours of the morning, and—

The Hilux braked suddenly, jerking the Israeli forward in his seat. Men in military fatigues visible in the intersection just ahead, a truck pulled out, half-blocking the road.

"Keep going!" Mohamed spat, punching the driver in the shoulder to emphasize the command—pushing his rifle's safety down and off, the Toyota's wheels burning against the pavement as they accelerated once more toward the checkpoint. *"Yalla, yalla!"*

He saw the enemy fighters hesitate but for a moment, the technical's windshield disintegrating and falling inward in a cascade of glass as someone got off a wild burst, the Israeli bringing his own rifle to bear.

The Hilux hit one of the men head-on even as he turned, too late, to run—bowling him up and over onto the Toyota's hood. Mohamed shot him as he lay there, broken, dazed, and gasping in pain, his body jerking with the impact of the rounds at point-blank range.

A ripping sound tearing open the night as the machine gun on the back of one of the following trucks opened up, cutting down the men at the checkpoint. The technical veered around the blocking truck at the last moment and into the turn, wheels squealing as the Israeli shot another militiaman in the back, dropping the man where he stood, his rifle clattering to the pavement—the Hilux accelerating on down the road.

Behind them, the gunfire ceased as rapidly as it had begun, the Hilux braking to a halt, seventy meters down the road, as their gunner swiveled the *Dushka* to cover the remaining trucks as they rolled through the now-devastated checkpoint. Men jumping down from their beds to rifle the pockets of the dead and finish off the dying.

The Israeli let out a weary sigh, shaking his head—realizing only then, as the adrenaline ebbed, that fluid was dribbling down his cheek and dripping onto his chest rig. He put a gloved hand to his face, finding a shard of glass protruding from his cheek through the beard, a curse escaping his lips as he pulled it out, prompting a fresh trickle of blood.

He safed his rifle, brushing more glass from his lap as he leaned forward, poking his head into the open air through what had once been the windshield, reaching for the arm of the dead man lying splayed out across their hood. The corpse was dressed in worn military fatigues, but that meant nothing—so were half their own men. He seized hold of the man's arm, struggling for a futile moment against the dead weight to turn him over.

Then he looked down at the arm in his hand and began cursing once again, plucking a small tac light from his chest rig with his free hand and shining it upon the round insignia stitched to the upper sleeve of the man's uniform.

The face of a tiger, fangs bared, stared back from the roundel, the truth sinking home with terrifying certainty.

Syrian special forces.

9:23 P.M.
Abu Rummaneh neighborhood
Muhajirin, Damascus
Syria

All the children should have been asleep long before, but instead the uppermost two floors of the ornate old Mandate-era apartment rang with their laughter and the insistent beat of Lebanese pop, nearly drowning out the low, distant rumble—like summer thunder—drifting down upon the city from the summit of *Jabal Qāsiyūn* to the north.

Artillery, as Brigadier General Burhan Khalil knew well, but the shells were falling far from his home and his children, and so long as he could ensure that remained the case, it was no concern of his.

And it was his son Majid's eleventh birthday—a celebration which had been postponed until he could return home from a long day of work at the Damascus headquarters of the *Shu'bat al-Mukhabarat,* where he served as a branch head.

He'd had to personally supervise an interrogation earlier in the day for the first time in months—a prominent Damascus businessman, an Alawite like himself, with family ties to the Assads. A man whose young son had nearly been invited to this very party, Khalil reflected with a shudder. *What a mistake that would have been.*

He had been caught trying to flee the country for France

three days prior, his wife and children already gone, under the pretext of visiting relatives in Toulouse. Rolling around, helpless and naked, on the wet concrete of the cell trying to curl into a ball to protect himself from the batons and booted kicks, his heavy body grotesquely pale in the harsh glare of the utility lights, he hadn't seemed nearly as powerful as Khalil had once remembered him—or as arrogant. *You fool.* To leave now, when they were so close to victory.

Though if the reports were true that he had embezzled money from Bashar. . .victory wouldn't have saved him.

The general felt his wife's eyes on him and pushed the imagery from his mind with an effort, forcing a smile. Tonight—he could enjoy tonight.

And it *was* time to get on with it, he thought, smiling as his young son scooped the last of what had been a heaping bowl of *booza* into his mouth, smiling in delight as he savored the chewy ice cream. Khalil pulled a wrapped present from behind his own chair and stood, passing it down to Majid. "Enjoy."

His son descended on it with a crow of delight, nearly elbowing one of his small friends in the face as he tore into the packaging, the familiar maroon, blue, and gold colors of Barcelona FC emerging from the box as he held the large football jersey up to display the No. 10 on the back. *Messi.*

"Lionel Messi himself signed it," the general announced, feeling a glow of pride, of achievement, swell within him at the coup, "as well as Ronaldinho—"

His phone began to pulse, and he felt the pride bleed away into frustration as he glanced at the screen, recognizing an unknown number which had tried to reach him no less than four times in the previous hour.

He cursed, rising from the table, and stalking into the next room of the apartment, electing finally to answer it. "Yes? Who is this? How did you get this number?"

"General Khalil, this is Lieutenant-Colonel Andriy Makarenko," a man's voice replied, "of the GRU. I've been trying to reach you about a call—"

"Lieutenant *Colonel?*" Khalil demanded incredulously, barely even hearing the reference to Russian military intelligence. *The audacity of the Russians.* "I am at home, with my family. If you have something to ask me, it can wait until tomorrow."

"General, it is import—"

"It can wait," the general hissed, his voice rising, the frustrations of the day pouring into the phone. "If you try to call me again tonight, I will take it up with your command."

9:36 P.M.
Khmeimim Air Base
Latakia Governorate, Syria

Ever he found something sobering in those first moments of returning from the sky, earth reasserting its surly bonds once more as man became man yet again, his wings no longer a part of himself.

There was an audible *hiss* as the canopy's seals opened, the cockpit depressurizing. Yaroslav Svischev pulled off his helmet, placing it in his lap, his eyes reflective as he stared out toward the runway lights.

Everything had checked out—short of actual combat ops, he had done everything he could do. Pushed every limit as far as he dared.

It was time to go home. And in the morning, their planes refueled, he and his wingman would do just that. *Home in time for Christmas.*

A harsh metallic clang against the fuselage broke in upon his reverie, and he glanced up to see his ground crew maneuvering the boarding ladder into position.

"Good flight?"

"Ochen' khorosho," Svischev replied, seizing the sergeant's hand as he descended the ladder, a smile lighting up his face. *Very good.*

A good flight, he thought, walking away as the ground truck maneuvered their tractor into position, towing the jet into the shelter of the revetments. And a good night. Time to get some sleep.

9:42 P.M.

Mohamed Taferi lowered the binoculars, the moonlight glistening eerily off the serried roofs of greenhouses on the rise behind him, a loose tarpaulin somewhere snapping and cracking in the breeze. The sound of the Russian tug tractor's diesel engine in the distance to the west drowned out by the whine of jet engines as an SU-25 taxied out to the main runway, turning south as it began its ground roll.

They were going to have to launch their attack early, come what may, another hour for their diversionary elements to finish maneuvering into position around the north end of the base, at the most—that checkpoint hadn't been random, not with a 14th Special Forces commando backing up the militia fighters.

It wasn't that Syrian SF was that good—it wasn't much

more than glorified light infantry, in truth, but having it *here* meant that someone knew they were in the area, had followed them over the mountains, most likely.

And that gave them very little time. He focused in on the Su-57s being towed into their revetments on the eastern side of the base, suppressing a shudder at the thought of how close his mission had come to failure. *If they had still been in the air. . .*

"You and your men will cross the runways toward that structure, there, near the terminal," he said quietly, passing the binoculars to a subdued Abu Basir and pointing toward the large, squat concrete-block structure positioned on the western side of the base, just across from the main terminal which still served Bassel al-Assad International Airport, though commercial flights were few and far between in these days. "Your primary target—the Russian military intelligence listening station."

Diversions within diversions, he thought, toying with the radio in his free hand—knowing the *Tachash* should be out there, waiting. *If things hadn't fallen through completely.* Knowing he dared not attempt to raise them, not now.

Not with the Russians monitoring everything in hundreds of kilometers.

He checked his watch, shielding its luminous dial with his hand as he did so, the pain from his cheek subsided to a dull throb, his close-cropped beard now stiff with blood.

Not much longer now.

10:13 P.M. Eastern European Time
The Tachash
The Mediterranean Sea

They should just reach him in time—*if* Taferi stuck to the plan. Shafron pursed his lips, leaning back against the wheelhouse as the *Tachash* breasted the chop, plowing north, a northwesterly wind kicking spray over the bow.

The odds of a days-old plan still holding down to the timetable, well. . .he'd run far too many of these ops to count on it.

Nothing ever quite held together or went according to plan. *Nothing.*

He could be preparing to launch even now, with their rescue hours yet away, Shafron reflected, glancing toward the dark coast of Lebanon. Willing the ungainly old trawler to sail faster, only too aware, in this moment that he should—somehow—have found a way to launch earlier, to convince Avi, to overcome his objections, in some way. Even knowing, as he did, that the *memuneh* had always been immovable when he put his mind to it.

Reuven and Omri were both within the wheelhouse, playing cards and whiling away the journey. He'd joined them for a hand or two of *Yaniv*, but found himself utterly unable to focus on the game.

Marc Harel, the team's medic, stood in the stern, smoking a cigarette, and Shafron dug his own pack of Camels from the pocket of his pants as he moved to join him, lighting up.

He could imagine Rahel's look of disapproval, knew even better than she did the detriments of the habit on his fitness.

But he could feel the stress begin to ebb away with the first drag, the nicotine creeping into his system—calming him, at least for this moment.

Off in the distance to their southwest, he could just make out the lights of a large ship, not far from the horizon, sea and sky melding together in the darkness. A tanker, most likely—or perhaps even a livestock carrier, sailing south to the port of Beirut.

"You were with 669, *ken?* Lebanon?"

"Ken." Shafron just nodded and took another drag of his cigarette, recognizing the volume of meaning in the simplicity of that *"yes."*

Lebanon had been a war with no victors, no glory—only frustration and death, the kinds of wars the IDF had found itself increasingly tasked with over the years.

The great heroic wars of national liberation—of *preservation*—seemingly consigned to Israel's history books, replaced by the clinging murk of low-burning insurgency. And the old men moaned that the new generations of conscripts lacked the zeal of their own youths, unable or unwilling to recognize all that had changed.

He had trained men—and women—who had fought in that war. Had watched them go out to kill, to die, and when it was all over and the ceasefire signed, the troops withdrawn. . .the rockets had come flying right back over the border, just like before.

These were the wars that broke men's souls, not just their bodies.

But still they fought, because they had no alternative, because if they failed to, then one day it *would* be about survival once again. And when that war came, they would need every edge they could get.

That was what this operation had been about, from the beginning—*keeping* that edge. And now they had to recover the man who had sacrificed so much to preserve it.

Or failing that, if possible. . .his body.

10:33 P.M. Syria Standard Time
Jableh District
Latakia Governorate, Syria

This was becoming a bad habit, Michael Awad thought grimly, crossing himself as he rose from beside the battered, broken body of the special forces corporal—*his* corporal— who had headed up the contingent of former Desert Hawks tasked with manning this particular checkpoint.

Wiped out, to the last man, several of the men clearly executed as they tried to crawl away from the carnage. From the field of blood outside Homs, to here. . .he was getting far too used to arriving at the scene in the wake of *Daesh*, picking up the pieces. Ever just too late.

It had to end. *Tonight.* He grimaced, thinking once again of the Spetsnaz captain as he stared north, into the darkness—of the dangers he would run in exposing his deception. All of them, still so very real.

But with them slipping the net, he was out of options. And if the Russians had been right, he knew where they were going.

"Bring up the radio," he announced quietly, turning to the NCO standing there a few feet away. Lights flashing across the roadway as militiamen moved about, collecting their dead. "And raise the Russians at Khmeimim."

10:37 P.M.
Khmeimim Airbase
Latakia Governorate, Syria

". . .but she was fussy, and we didn't stay long. I think she just wants her father."

It was strange how you could want something you'd never even had, Andriy Makarenko thought, smiling only faintly as his gaze flickered between the webcam and his fiancée's image on the screen of his laptop. Like he wanted his daughter, now.

"Are you okay, Dyusha?"

"Konechno," he replied, nodding quickly, feeling embarrassed that she could tell. *Of course.* "It's just been a long day, that's all, *kroshka.* I'm fine."

Long and *maddening*, he thought, suppressing a grimace at the memory of his abortive call with Burhan Khalil. He *knew* somehow, deep down, that the general could have given him valuable information, if only he'd been willing to listen, but the call had ended before he'd gotten anything of relevance out, and his further attempts to ring the number had gone unanswered.

"I can help with that, *kotya,*" she said, a smile in her eyes as she shifted closer to the camera.

He smiled, a weary, grateful smile, finding himself unable to refuse her, to resist this escape, however illusory, from the dirt and grime of his surroundings. From—

The hard rap at his door startled them both and he saw her start, her shirt falling back in place. *"Da?"*

"Tovarisch Podpolkóvnik," the muffled voice of a soldier replied, "you're wanted at the station. A call from a Captain

Awad, *tovarisch*. Syrian Special Forces."

He swore in irritation, turning back to his screen to see his own disappointment mirrored in Zinaida's eyes. *"Izvini, kroshka.* I have to go. I will call. I—"

Another, more distant sound reached his ears in that moment, subsiding as quickly as it rose, and he hoped she hadn't heard it through the microphone. *Small-arms fire.*

"Get *Kapitán* Egorov," he said suddenly, striding to his door and flinging it open as he buttoned his uniform blouse. "I want him there."

10:40 P.M.

Mohamed Taferi heard the short, violent outburst of fire from the north and swore viciously, lowering the binoculars. He traded a glance with Abu Ahmed, seeing the older man's grimace in the darkness. They had known the chances of getting everyone into position without discovery were perilously small.

It would have been hard enough even for professionals and their own *ad hoc* force was anything but.

But now they were compromised, their chances of surprise flowing away like blood, hemorrhaging from a wound.

Their only hope was to go *now*—hit the Russians hard and fast, do as much damage as possible before they recovered. He brought the radio to his lips, toggling the mic. "All strike elements, execute. I say again, execute. *Yalla, yalla!*"

There were a series of squelches in acknowledgement, and behind him, near the trucks, he heard a low whirring—turning to watch as their heavily-laden quadcopters staggered into the night sky. . .

10:43 P.M.
Khmeimim Airbase

"It's just more probing," Valeriy Egorov said dismissively, buttoning his jacket against the cold as he emerged from the barracks behind Makarenko. "Testing our responses. That's all, nothing more serious—they do it every night, *tovarisch*."

The firing *had* already died away, Makarenko thought, leading the way out across the apron toward the listening station. Still, the timing left him uneasy, with the events of the day, and now this summons.

"This call," he said, glancing back into his fellow officer's face to read his reaction, "it's from a Syrian special forces captain. A Captain Awad. Do you know him?"

Egorov stopped short, the shadowy, hulking form of an Antonov An-32 transport looming in the moonlit semi-darkness behind him, the expression on his face indicating more clearly than words that he most certainly *did*. "*Da*. He was leading the Syrian unit at Masyaf when we destroyed the. . ."

His voice trailed off, strangely, the moonlight casting odd shadows across his face. Another long, tearing burst of fire rippled through the night from somewhere off to the north, arresting both men's attention.

They had to have troops in contact, somewhere, and Makarenko plucked the radio from his belt, squeezing the switch—just as explosions hammered his ears, a nearly simultaneous flare of light emanating suddenly from both towers flanking the main gate.

He swore, reaching with his free hand for his holstered pistol. Hearing Egorov's curse of surprise behind him, a dull *boom* emanating from a low hill to the east of the base. The next moment, an RPG slammed into the right engine nacelle of the Antonov not more than twenty feet away, and the night erupted in fire. . .

Chapter 31

Yaroslav Svischev was out of his bunk at the first explosion, grabbing for his pants and pulling them on hurriedly in the dark, reaching for his holstered *Grach.*

He reached over, shaking the shoulder of his sleeping wingman even as the barracks building shuddered with another, closer explosion. "Come on, Filya—wake up!"

He cursed angrily, buttoning his shirt as he reached down, squirming into his flight suit. He had to get out there, see if he could somehow get his jet refueled and back in the air.

Before it was destroyed.

10:46 P.M.

The perimeter fence fell away with the last metallic *pop* of the bolt cutters, and Mohamed Taferi watched as Abu Ahmed stepped into the breach, his lean, gaunt figure stark against the

446

runway lights—his rifle tucked into his shoulder. Al-Golani's remaining men following him in, the one-eyed fighter, Mamdouh, glancing in the Israeli's direction before ducking through the cut fence, his bandoliers of ammo for the RPD hanging away from his chest. Nassif following after, another long belt of ammunition slung over his shoulder.

Mohamed pushed the wire fencing aside, keeping his own rifle raised as he followed—eyeing the ground between their position and the revetments. Open terrain, two hundred meters at least, but quiet—so far at least.

Behind them, Abu Basir's men swarmed through the opening in the fence, streaming out toward the runway and the Russian listening post beyond. Secondary explosions lighting the night as the big Antonov across the airbase went up in flames, the banshee wail of alarm sirens ringing in his ears. He ran forward, toward the revetments, his booted feet pounding against the hard ground, the cold knifing into his lungs.

He saw a Russian BMP rumble out toward the main gate, the flickering figures of its infantry escort backlit against the glare of the fires, the long snout of its main gun probing the night as it responded to the diversionary attack.

The next moment, an RPG slammed into its rear armor, and it vanished in a roiling pall of dark, oily smoke lit by flashes of fire. Someone's machine gun opening up to cut down what escorts remained standing, savage cries and shouts of *"Allahu akbar!"* vying with the small-arms fire.

The Israeli shook his head, willing his legs to move faster, holding his AKM close across his chest as he ran, a small knot of rebel fighters following on behind as he closed the distance across the open ground. *Well, they know we're here.*

10:48 P.M.
Jableh District
Latakia Governorate, Syria

"How soon will they arrive?" Michael Awad demanded, glaring at his young Alawite minder in the shadow of the dark Toyota SUV, all concern over what he might think, what he might report back to Damascus, lost in that moment. The dull *thump* of explosions off to the north— that spectral glow, dancing against the horizon to the accompanying chatter of small-arms fire—confirming his worst fears.

"Ten to fifteen minutes, captain. They're still loading men into the trucks."

Awad swore, lifting the radio to his lips and once more, without success, attempting to raise the Russians at Khmeimim—to re-establish the connection which had broken off so abruptly. He had been so *close* to making his report. To covering himself against all that was to come.

Now he had no choice but to ride to the rescue with his own men and whatever Desert Hawks he could pull together—and hope the Russians didn't shoot *them* in the confusion.

"Tell them to hurry it up. We're not going to have all night."

"*Na'am*, sir, of course," the lieutenant stammered, seeming unusually deferent, as though he realized his power had evaporated in this moment.

Perhaps he would kill him tonight, Awad thought, staring balefully at the younger man as he got back on the radio with Beit Yashout. It would be easy enough to do, in the chaos. And *satisfying*. But Damascus would simply send him another—if there was one thing of which Syria had no lack, it was informers.

He left the lieutenant relaying his message, shaking a cigarette out of his pocket as he circled the hood of the Toyota—staring off through the night toward the airbase. They needed to get up there.

10:51 P.M.
Khmeimim Airbase
Latakia Governorate, Syria

Fire everywhere, angry, hellish tongues of fire licking out into the welcoming night. Fire. . .and pain. Andriy Makarenko lifted his head from the concrete, disoriented and unable to focus his thoughts, nearly deafened by the force of the blast. Something warm and wet trickling down his face.

It seemed as though only moments had passed since he'd been on the call with Zinaida, watching her begin to undress, already anticipating the warmth of her soft body against his own—counting down the days until there would no longer be a screen between them. Until they would be a *family*.

Now. . .he raised a hand to his face, and it came away wet and sticky with blood—the glow of flames from the burning Antonov destroying his night-vision, blanking out everything more than four or five meters ahead of him.

Death, lurking out there in that darkness, unseen, unheard—a desperate moan of fear escaping his lips, his eyes wildly searching the void. He struggled to rise, but his legs refused to work, and he collapsed back against the concrete, gritting his teeth against the pain—his heart racing. Its beat, heavy in his ears, the only sound he could hear, that rhythmic, darkly ominous *thump-thump, thump-thump.*

He glanced around, recognizing his service pistol laying a few feet away. Searching in vain for any sign of Egorov, unable to determine whether he had been consumed in the explosion or survived it somehow, only to run off and abandon him here to—to *die.*

"I will call." His last words to Zinaida, his *promise*—tears mixing with the rivulets of blood running down his cheeks as he lay there, gasping out his pain and trying to gather what strength remained. He *would* live, would make it back—would *call* her. But if he stayed here, it was only a matter of time before Death came for him. He raised himself up on one elbow, biting his tongue against the agony that shot through his weakening body.

Raised himself up and put out a hand against the cold, desolate concrete, beginning to crawl forward with his hands and elbows toward the welcoming darkness, dragging his useless legs after him. . .

10:51 P.M.
The listening post

The private behind the desk was already dying by the time the remnants of the RPG-blasted door were kicked in, slumped in his chair with a jagged, nine-inch shard of steel protruding from his abdomen—his submachine gun lying uselessly out of reach, his cellphone, its screen shattered but still pumping music through the broken earbuds, fallen to the floor.

Abu Basir was the second man through the door and blew his brains out with a pistol shot, putting an end to his sufferings. The inner door collapsed inward under a flurry of rough kicks—shouts of alarm and a flurry of shots echoing from within until one of the jihadists began tossing grenades among the clustered workstations, screams of pain echoing through the deafening hammer of the explosions as the building lights flickered on and off, surreal flashes of illumination lighting up the madness, the carnage.

Fierce cries of exultation ringing out as the bearded figures of Abu Basir's *mujahideen* slowly stalked through the nightmare, dragging office employees out from where they cowered beneath desks, shooting them in the head or slitting throats. Every movement drawing a burst of fire, or another tossed grenade. Blue electrical flames licking out from a destroyed workstation to blossom to life in an overturned wastebasket, flaring up toward the ceiling.

"Allahu akbar! Allahu akbar!"

10:52 P.M.
The revetments

Mohamed Taferi bent over in the open cockpit of the Su-57, the canopy pushed back, the penlight clenched between his teeth as he took picture after picture, doing his best to photograph everything in the low light.

He was still breathing heavily from his run across the open field—the sweat now chilling on his body, a strange sense of euphoria filling him as small-arms fire crackled across the airfield—explosions lighting up the night as the rest of the rebel quadcopters found their targets.

They were here. After all they had gone through, all they had *survived*, they were here.

And *they* were dying, he thought grimly, the flat staccato *crack* of an autocannon pounding away from the south as another BMP rolled into view, its 30mm gun blazing. The Russians, shaking off the paralysis of the initial moments of the attack and lashing back, struggling to find targets in the confusion, but finding them all the same—pinning down small knots of rebels and eliminating them, one by one.

He was alone in the revetment, the small handful of fighters who were supposed to have maintained watch as he worked, drifting north to join in the fight now raging around the hangars. Abu Ahmed was up there too, still leading his men—his voice, audible in the crackling static over Mohamed's radio, shouting orders.

This was never going to have ended any other way, he reflected grimly, extracting a small screwdriver from a pouch on his chest rig and reaching down to the bottom of the instrument panel. His rifle, leaning abandoned back against the seat. They were nothing but a lion's paw, after all, and expendable so long as the objective was achieved.

That objective, now within reach, all that mattered. It was just a matter now of getting what he had come for, linking back up with Al-Golani, and getting both of them to the coast. The *Tachash* would be waiting.

10:54 P.M.
The hangars

Automatic weapons fire tore apart the night, shells exploding in the night above in flashes of orange-black fire as Nassif stooped down on one knee behind the massive front wheel of a parked Russian military truck, uncoiling a belt of linked ammo from around his shoulders.

"Yalla, yalla," Mamdouh snapped impatiently, cursing him to hurry up, a scowl distorting what remained of his destroyed face in the half-light. The feed cover of the RPD open and waiting as Nassif handed him the belt, his fingers moving quickly—careful not to twist its links, his work lit by the flames leaping from the Russian helicopter gunship destroyed on the ground not sixty meters to their east. Bullets screaming wildly by overhead as fuel stores cooked off in a warehouse back toward the terminal, chaos and fire consuming the night.

Their small group had been tasked with watching over the Qatari as he sabotaged the Russian fighter aircraft, with maintaining security outside the revetments, but as the fighting intensified, Mamdouh had snarled at him and the others to follow, and follow they had—forging north into the maze of hangars and warehouses that covered the base's northeastern quadrant. And straight into the heart of the battle. The other two men were dead now—cut down as they crossed between the buildings, one rebel simply ceasing to exist as a 30mm shell slammed into the ground at his feet, vanishing in a savage mist of meat, metal, and blood.

Mamdouh slammed the feed cover shut and clambered to his feet, a bony hand outthrust against the wheel of the truck as he steadied himself, his remaining eye glittering horribly in the light of the fires.

He brought the battered wooden stock of the RPD to his shoulder, the linked belt swinging free as he stepped out from cover, bringing its muzzle to bear—and then his head snapped back, the light going out in that eye as he toppled to the ground, shot in the face, the back of his skull blown half away. His weapon, unfired, clattering uselessly against the pavement.

Nassif had been reaching for his own weapon, but froze, staring at the suddenly lifeless body of the man at whose side he'd fought for so long, a strangely frail, crumpled heap of rags and bones sticking out at bizarre angles. He had never liked the man, had been on the receiving end of his kicks and curses far too many times. But together, they had *survived.*

He had never even heard the shot that killed the older man, one shot impossible to pick out among the chaos of the night. But he heard shouts, the fire shifting ever closer. His hand closing around the receiver of his rifle as he staggered to his feet.

He couldn't stay here.

10:55 P.M.
The revetments

The cold night air bit at Yaroslav Svischev's cheeks as he hurried across the tarmac toward the revetments, his pistol out in his hand. He had given up any thought of getting into the air upon exiting the barracks and glimpsing the chaos now reigning across the base. Organizing a ground crew to fuel the plane would have been impossible, even if he could have successfully taxied to the runway. No, the best thing he could do was secure it, best he could.

He called out to a passing detachment, waving them over, but their noncom ignored him in favor of pressing on north, toward the fighting, and he swore, regretting again that he hadn't picked up a rifle on his way out. But they were nearly there now, his wingman Filipp hurrying along behind, still fumbling with the zipper of his flight suit—hustling to catch up.

Pandemonium reigned across the airfield, tracers lancing out across the night sky as automatic weapons fire built into a deafening crescendo, accompanied by the duller backbeat of autocannon. He saw a ground crewman lying dead not fifty feet from the opening of the revetment, sprawled in a pool of blood, a curse escaping Svischev's lips at the sight.

And that was when he saw the light, flashing briefly across the windscreen of the jet from *within* its cockpit. The SU-57's boarding ladder, propped up against the jet, its canopy incongruously open.

Hissing at Filipp to keep quiet and cover him, he brought the Grach up awkwardly in both hands, stepping forward past the revetment wall until he was within feet of the plane, taking aim at the hunched-over figure visible within. "Show yourself and keep your hands up."

Chapter 32

10:56 P.M.
The terminal

Their night-vision was almost worthless, the flames rising up from around the beleaguered airbase flaring madly across the lenses. Valeriy Egorov tore his monocular away from his face, hurling it to the ground with a savage curse, bringing his rifle up to one shoulder as he moved, still conscious of the pain in his crudely bandaged side—shrapnel from the Antonov's explosion having torn through meat and muscle, lodging deep in his body. His Spetsnaz spreading out behind him as they advanced on the listening post where *Daesh* was now holed up, Kulik's QRF finally rolling into action—the massive bulk of a T-90 tank lumbering out from behind a warehouse a couple hundred meters to the east, the long barrel of its main cannon probing the darkness.

He was going to need serious medical attention before the night was over, but for this moment, the painkillers were outpacing the shock, keeping him in the fight. And he was better off than Makarenko—who had looked dead, unresponsive, his legs mangled beneath him when Egorov had staggered away from the apron.

Duty had demanded he rescue the GU officer—*attempt* it, at the very least, but he'd heard the suspicion in his voice, in those last moments before the RPG flew past their heads. *Suspicion?* No, *knowledge*. He *knew* what had been done, knew the Knights hadn't been crushed beneath the walls of Masyaf as Egorov had indicated in his report. And Awad, apparently, had followed the remnants of that force across the mountains to. . .*here*, his own hubris and desire to avoid humiliation leading to all of this. This could end his career, were it ever known, the Spetsnaz officer reflected grimly, pushing forward at the head of his men. *Were it ever known*.

His radio was alive with chatter, barked commands and contact reports in brusque, tension-laced Russian as Khmeimim's garrison struggled to recover, to fight back. Someone with a radio still alive inside the listening post itself, feeding out reports of the carnage within, their voice tinged with fear bordering on panic.

He glimpsed movement out of the corner of his eye and glanced back over at the tank to see a lone figure in a tracksuit clamber up onto the rear hull of the T-90 as it crawled glacially forward, crushing debris beneath its ponderous tracks. The rebel swayed unsteadily and for a moment, Egorov thought they might fall, but *no*. Another moment and they were kneeling on top of the turret, pulling desperately—if futilely—at the hatch cover.

A sharp command escaped the Spetsnaz officer's lips as he dropped to one knee, switching his AK-104's fire selector to semiautomatic, acquiring the rebel fighter through his reflex sights. The trigger broke beneath his finger, shots crashing out all around him as his men opened fire, and he saw the figure jerk spasmodically before crashing to the ground like a broken toy, disappearing beneath the treads of the tank. His grenade falling to explode harmlessly against the tank's armor.

Egorov grunted in pain, pushing himself aright, the noise of the shots fading from his ringing ears as the comms traffic came back over his earpiece. A voice in thickly accented English, now joined with the rest, demanding a reply and going unanswered. *Captain Awad.* The one man who could ruin him, even yet.

He raised his hand for a halt, still a hundred meters south of the GRU listening post, his men fanning out around him as he reached up, keeping his voice level with an effort as he keyed the mic. "Captain, God be thanked that you're here. We can use your men—where are you?"

There was a moment's wary hesitation, as if Awad, recognizing his voice, suspected a trap—then, "Just south of the base—I have fifty men."

"Come to the west gates," Egorov replied, his mind racing. "My men and I will meet you there—guide you in."

He ended the transmission, waving to his men to close the circle around him even as, across from them, the T-90's barrel swung toward the squat concrete outline of the beleaguered listening post—flame belching from its rifled throat.

The tank shell slammed into the eastern side of the GRU building, blowing great chunks of concrete out of its wall, and the transmission from the officer trapped within went strangely silent. . .

10:56 P.M.
The revetments

Mohamed Taferi froze at the sound of the harshly-barked Russian, his fingers still tugging at the panel holding the internals of the Su-57's avionics package in place, his ruck pulled open to receive the electronics.

He didn't understand the language nearly well enough to know what had been said, but the pistol now aimed at him from a scant couple meters away was more than clear enough.

The man holding it was perhaps eight or nine years his own senior, dressed in a flight suit—as was the second man who appeared from the opening of the revetment, tugging his own weapon awkwardly from its holster. *The pilots?*

The Druze officer shook his head to indicate his incomprehension, letting the panel fall back in place as he stood, nearly banging his head against the edge of the raised canopy, raising his hands. He'd be dead before he could reach the rifle, and they were too close to even draw his pistol from its holster on his hip, half-concealed by the jacket.

To have come so far. There was a brutal irony in it, to think of dying, of *failing*, after all the hell through which he had waded to get here. He'd raised Abu Ahmed on the radio a few moments before, urging him to fall back, but the heavy bursts of fire making it through the static had told their own story.

There was no way he'd make it back in time.

Beneath him, the plane shuddered with the force of yet another explosion off to the north, and he saw the Russians flinch, the nearest pilot raising his voice in another command.

"Ana mob afham," Mohamed replied in incomprehension, shaking his head once again. He could see the hesitation in the Russian's eyes—the uncertainty, the *unease* with which he clasped the pistol. It was one thing to drop bombs from thirty thousand feet, to flatten houses, to blow apart women and children, along with the odd *Daesh* convoy.

It was quite another to look a man dead in the eye and pull the trigger. He'd spent three years as an IDF conscript, fired his weapon plenty of times—but he hadn't had to do *that* until he'd come to the Mossad. And if he'd been given any time to think about it, he wasn't sure he could have.

More Russian, and this time the pilot gestured with the pistol for him to descend the ladder, his tone of voice brooking no further delay. Mohamed nodded, turning half-away from the man as he lifted his left leg over the side of the cockpit and set foot on the boarding ladder, knowing the darkness to be a friend. If he could just clear his Glock from its holster, he—he lowered a hand as if to steady himself as he took another step down, his fingers brushing against the butt of the pistol. If—

A shout of surprise echoed through the air, and he turned, the Glock coming out in his hand as he saw both Russians look away, responding reflexively to some fresh threat.

The long burst of automatic fire raked the night almost before the Russian's shout had faded away, bullets going wild, ricocheting dangerously off the reinforced walls of the revetment. The rearmost officer got a pair of shots off at the newcomer before the incoming rounds found their mark and he went down in a heap.

Mohamed brought the Glock up and around, seeing the

look of surprise and chagrin on the face of the first Russian in the half-second before he put two rounds in the man's chest.

He fell backward, collapsing hard into the pavement, and the Israeli was down the ladder and over to him in a heartbeat, kicking the Grach away from the man's outstretched hand as he lay there, dying.

Fortunes of war. He moved on to the second pilot, finding him already dead, before ducking under the nose of the Su-57 to greet his savior.

Nassif lay crumpled back against the wall of the revetment—his rifle lying useless beside him, his face twisted in pain as he clutched at his wounded shoulder, blood seeping through his fingers. A curse exploding from the Israeli's lips at the sight of his young friend.

"Stay with me here, *habibi*," he breathed, peeling Nassif's fingers away from the wound—the bullet had smashed through his left shoulder and straight out the back, through and through, likely breaking the shoulder blade. The boy was breathing heavily, fighting off the shock, but he nodded as Mohamed moved away, kneeling by the corpse of the nearest Russian and unzipping his flight suit. He reached in, ripping the dead man's undershirt half away and tearing it into wide strips.

He wouldn't be able to use that shoulder for a while, but he should live—*if* he could get all of them out of there, the Israeli thought grimly, scooping up the pilot's pistol before returning to Nassif's side, winding the torn shirt tight around the damaged shoulder, the tan fabric soaked instantly with blood.

"Hang in there," he admonished, dropping the pistol

into the boy's lap before rising to return to the plane. "And keep an eye out."

11:03 P.M.
The western gates of Khmeimim

The battle was fading, Captain Michael Awad thought, running the beads of a rosary idly between his fingers as he murmured out a prayer to the Holy Mother beneath his breath. The Toyota's engine idling as he waited at the head of the convoy—his men already fanned out to either side of the road, taking up positions outside the west entrance to the base. The crackle of small arms slowly dying off to the north.

But flames burned angrily, all across the base, the dull *thump* of cannon punctuating the sporadic bursts of remaining fire.

Flanking the gate, the guard towers stood silently in the glare of the truck's headlights, a wrecked searchlight hanging drunkenly down the sand-bagged façade—sand running in rivulets down from a torn bag ripped apart by the explosion which had shredded the tower's occupants, the mangled, disembodied remnants of an arm lying only meters in front of the Toyota's front tire.

Lights appeared in the darkness, on the other side of the gate, and he felt his breath catch. *Finally.* They were exposed out here, vulnerable to a *Daesh* counter-attack, if there was one. The burly, mustachioed Desert Hawks commander in the seat across from him, growing more fidgety by the moment as they waited, fear reeking off him, along with a nauseating body odor.

He very nearly hadn't come himself, after hearing Egorov's voice over the radio. Hearing the danger, lurking there beneath the Spetsnaz captain's seemingly relieved tones.

But there was a far more certain danger in staying away. If he were accused by the Russian command of abandoning them, in their hour of need.

That was a quick ticket down a very dark hole, and having sent more than enough men there himself, Awad was particularly anxious not to follow them.

The gates rolled back, and he saw Valeriy Egorov walk forward into the headlights, his Kalashnikov held across his chest. There was a hesitancy in the Russian's gait, as though he were favoring a wound—and blood matted the hair over his left temple.

He extended a gloved hand as Awad stepped from the Toyota, his dark, soulless eyes meeting the Syrian's even as another explosion erupted into the night off toward the far side of the base. "Welcome to Khmeimim, Captain. You're just in time to help us sweep out the rest of the scum."

11:03 P.M.
The clinic

Chaos. Pain. Lights, shining brightly in his eyes. Commands, barked harshly in Russian, ringing hollow and distant. The sound of the gurney's loose wheel, discordantly *loud* as it rumbled down the hall, reverberatingly madly through the chambers of his mind as he wavered on the edge of consciousness.

Andriy Makarenko felt the nurse's hand on his arm, the

man's face looming only inches away from his own as he was wheeled through the building. A hideous face, strangely like Death itself, dark and cowled against a halo of light.

Coming for him. He felt himself cringe away from the specter, no longer able to feel his legs or even crawl—pain lancing like fire through his veins, the gurney seeming to race faster and faster, accelerating as though it could never stop. And then everything faded away in a wash of ethereal light. . .

11:04 P.M.
The revetments

It was past time they were going, Mohamed Taferi thought, only too aware of the ebbing fire from the north as he zipped up his ruck over the components of the Su-57's avionics package, hefting it onto his back as he stepped back down the boarding ladder.

The men he had brought here were dying, one by one, as Khmeimim's garrison recovered and fought back. As had been inevitable all along—twenty minutes from their breach of the wire, and they were pushing it. Across the runway toward the terminal of Bassel al-Assad, the square concrete building which had once served as the GRU's listening post for this end of the Mediterranean was being demolished, with Abu Basir's jihadists and whatever remained of its hapless staff still trapped inside as tank cannon pummeled the building from short range.

Mission accomplished. And in another five minutes, the explosive charge he'd deposited in the cockpit of the Su-57 would blow, destroying all evidence of his work. Just another of the dozen or more planes left in flaming wreckage all across the airbase.

Nassif was waiting for him at the base of the ladder, casting an anxious glance back toward the mouth of the revetment, the Russian's pistol clasped loosely in his good hand. His dark eyes, radiating pain, but otherwise fathomless as ever.

But no sign of Abu Ahmed, even as another long, lashing burst of machine-gun fire tore through the night off toward the hangars before fading away almost completely. Leaving behind a haunting silence, broken only by the pounding of the heavy guns. *Death.*

Mohamed plucked the radio from its pouch on his chest rig, lifting it to his lips. If he couldn't raise him now. . .

A dark, armed figure appeared in the opening of the revetment just as he keyed the radio, and he raised his Glock to cover the threat before recognizing Al-Golani. The rebel commander was limping, favoring his right leg—his breath steaming heavily into the cold night air as he approached, rifle clutched in both hands.

His weathered face was streaked with blood—his own or that of someone less fortunate—his hollow eyes betraying fear and pain, grief dulled only by the lingering residue of the alcohol.

"Where are the rest?" Nassif demanded, speaking up before Mohamed could open his own mouth. A raw edge to the teenager's voice as it rose, nearly breaking.

"Dead," was Abu Ahmed's brusque reply, the renewed, harsh staccato of automatic weapons fire from the area of the hangars in that moment, belying his words. "Those who remain. . .are beyond our help."

Chapter 33

Dead. Al-Golani's words hit Nassif with the force of a hammer blow, and as the teenager stood there, his fingers wrapped loosely around the polymer grips of the pistol, he could see Mamdouh crumpling once more into a heap in the shadow of the truck, his frail, lanky body seeming to collapse in upon itself.

His brother Talha, disappearing off through the maze of rubble and craters in the seconds before the rockets hit, that disembodied *boot*, raining down out of the sky, the bone glistening and white.

Abdul Latif, Abu Ahmed's big, genial right hand, back there along the road beneath Masyaf, simply. . .*vanishing* in a crimson haze. A score or more others, all along the way. He hadn't known all their names, but together, they'd represented all that he had left in this life. *Oblivion.* Reaching out to claim them all. One by one.

All that was left was to share their fate, to *join* them in that abyss. All of them together at the end of all things, the

466

slayers and the slain, broken at last.

"We need to get you out to the boat," he heard the Qatari say, the words ringing hollow and discordant in the boy's ears. *Boat?* His dark eyes settling on Nassif's own. "Come with us, *habibi*. I'll see to that wound, once we're safe—you'll be among your own once more. But we need to get away from here. *Now.*"

"*La!*" The word came bursting out from between his chapped, cracking lips, the boy's eyes shifting from one man to the other. More firing punctuating his words as men fought and *died* off to their north. "No, we can't just. . .*abandon* them."

But he saw the truth, written there in the weary, deep-ringed eyes of his commander. He had given up, he was *running*—just like so many before him, all across the years of revolution, leaders who had sold out. *Fled.* Turning their backs on the men they had led, on the men that had followed them into battle. Choosing to save themselves from the hell into which they'd helped lead everyone else.

No.

The pistol came up as if of its own will, trembling in his outstretched hand, its sights wavering as they settled on the commander's face. "*La, la, la.* We're not going anywhere. Not without the others."

He glanced over at the Qatari to find himself looking down the barrel of his friend's pistol, aimed steadily at his own head. A slight tremor in the man's voice as his head shook back and forth behind those iron sightposts. "Come on, *habibi*. Put the gun down."

11:08 P.M.
The listening post

His head was splitting with the reverberation of the bombardment as shells hammered the building to powder, his ears ringing madly—his eyes, gritty with dust and tearing in the haze and smoke, blood trickling down his cheek from where a falling chunk of concrete had bit into his scalp.

Abu Basir pushed himself aright, coughing through the smoke of the electrical fires as he stumbled toward the door of the server room, past the bodies of his men, the dead and the dying. A Russian officer lying just outside the door, face-down in a welter of blood.

Some of his men were still alive in the building, or what remained of it—they *had to be*—but deaf and disoriented by shock, the young jihadist no longer knew how to find them, how to regroup. His hands still gripped his rifle, but they shook uncontrollably when he tried to raise it. Death's icy fingers, seeming to close around his throat in a vise-like grip. *I seek refuge in Allah. . .*

He struggled to remember the rest of the *dua*, but found the words refused to come, fear seizing hold as he realized he didn't want to die. Not here, not *now*. The Qatari's eyes, seeming to bore once more into his own, stern as those of the Questioners. *"Do you fear death so much, Abu Basir?"*

And he knew in that moment, the truth. *He did.*

The figures of armed men loomed out of the smoke through one of the few still-standing doorways of the crumbling building and he threw aside his rifle, falling to his knees as a plea for mercy struggled out of his raw, choking throat. *Don't shoot.*

His eyes met those of the lead Russian, a short, stocky man in full kit, eyes blue and cold as ice. *Implacable.*

His lips parting in a final desperate cry, just before a 122-grain bullet smashed through his forehead and through his skull.

And all the lights went out.

11:08 P.M.
The revetments

"Don't make me do this, *habibi*," Mohamed Taferi breathed—more a prayer than a request, his finger curled around the Glock's double-action trigger, already taking up the slack. "You saved my life, now just put the gun down, and kick it over to me. We are brothers, you and I—I will make sure you come to no harm. But neither must this man."

"You don't understand," was the bitter reply, the boy shaking his head—tears shining in his eyes. "You could *never* understand."

He understood more than Nassif knew, the Israeli thought—had seen too much of it in his own years in and out of the war. Opposition commanders had faded away like dew in the summer sun, many of them choosing to run for safety as soon as the tides of war turned against them, many more exploiting the very people they had once vowed to free, growing fat and wealthy in the midst of the devastation. *Corruption, at every hand.*

But the boy had his own losses, his own griefs. And he'd been a fool not to see the danger before. He glanced over at Abu Ahmed, standing silently there a few feet away, beneath the nose of the Su-57, making no move to raise his own weapon.

Resignation—*acceptance*—written on his weary face.

"Just put down the gun," the Mossad officer repeated, knowing only too well that their clock was running out of sand. The fire growing ever more scattered off to the north, the timer of the explosive charge in the cockpit of the jet, ticking down. The moments, streaming by. Another shake of the head. "We can all get out of here together, we—"

"*La!*" It was an anguished, soul-rending cry, nearly drowned in the pair of pistol shots that followed it, ringing out together almost as one.

Mohamed felt the trigger break beneath his own finger—saw Abu Ahmed reel backward, nearly going down. Nassif's head snapping back under the impact of a bullet, the pistol falling from nerveless fingers as the boy collapsed, sprawling across the concrete like a broken toy.

Dead before he hit the ground. The Druze intelligence officer walked forward, anger and grief distorting his features as he stood over the body of his young friend, looking down into that youthful face, lifeless eyes still staring upward, older than they would ever be. The face of a *brother*.

A brother he had killed, for the sake of his mission, and it seemed as though he could feel the wound in his own body—the taste of bile, hot in the back of his mouth. The bitter taste of self-reproach. *Kinslayer.*

But the mission wasn't over yet. He turned to see Abu Ahmed take a faltering step forward out of the shadow of the plane, his face strained and ashen, a bloodied hand pressed to his chest. "Can you still travel?"

A nod and labored grunt of assent and Mohamed draped

the opposition commander's free arm across his shoulders, wrapping his own arm around the man's gaunt waist, supporting him as they staggered out of the revetment and into the night. . .

11:09 P.M.
The Tachash
The Mediterranean Sea

Inside the trawler's wheelhouse, the games of *Yaniv* had blurred one into another as the men continued playing, passing the time as best they knew how.

Outside on deck, David Shafron shook another Camel loose of its pack, lighting it off the dying ember of the burnt-down cigarette dangling from his lips. The coastline, slipping sluggishly by as though they stood still in the water. The lights of Tartus visible far off the starboard bow, almost on the horizon as they stood out to sea, the Russian naval facilities there, sheltering just behind the breakwater. Ships from the Russian Navy's 5th Operational Squadron, as Shafron knew well. Corvettes and offshore patrol vessels, a *Ropucha*-class landing ship or two, providing logistical support. Perhaps even a couple *Kilo*-class diesel subs, as controversial as that was under the provisions of the Montreux Convention.

He had failed to pull the latest TecSAR imagery from the base before leaving the office and he regretted that now. It was the kind of omission that could come back to haunt a man. He—

"David, you're going to want to hear this." It was Reuven Aharoni, standing there in the door of the wheelhouse for the briefest of moments before disappearing back inside. Shafron flicked the burnt-down Camel into the churning froth of their wake, taking a long drag off the new one before following him inside.

The cards still lay scattered about, but no one was playing—the tension written clear in the faces of the men gathered around. Avigdor Barad was at the wheel, but he had the radio's headphones cupped to one ear. At Shafron's entrance, he extended a second pair wordlessly toward him.

He slipped them on, struck immediately by the volume of the chatter. Arabic and Russian, intermixed—the latter predominating as he listened. He only understood a word here and there, his Russian only rudimentary on his best days, but the urgency in the tones was palpable. Equally clear was a single word, repeated over and again: *Khmeimim.*

The certainty of the truth sinking home like a lead weight.

"What are we looking at?" he asked, removing the headphones as he glanced from Reuven to Avigdor.

It was Marc Harel who took the question, though, sparks spinning from his lighter as he lit up another cigarette. "Based on what we're hearing off the Russian unclass networks, Khmeimim is under heavy, sustained attack."

Shafron suppressed a bitter curse. It was happening, and they weren't in position for the pick-up. *Wouldn't* be, for another couple hours. At the earliest.

"How much longer before we can raise Taferi on the net?"

Avigdor shrugged, shaking his head. "Another eighty, ninety minutes."

11:09 P.M.
Khmeimim Airbase
Latakia Governorate, Syria

He was dying. Yaroslav Svischev knew that, deep down, feeling the cold crawl deeper and deeper into his body as he lay sprawled against the blood-wet concrete, his brain drifting through the ether of delirium and pain, soaring higher, ever higher—higher than he had ever dreamed of flying in life. Earth's bonds, not only slipped, but shattered now for once and all. Snow, falling down soft and white upon the house on Moskvoretskaya Ulitsa as a woman made ready for Christmas.

But he was a stranger there now, somehow. His presence, but a memory. The price of those broken chains. And as the cold claimed him, the night above burst into fire. . .

Chapter 34

11:39 P.M.
The coast, Jableh District
Latakia Governorate, Syria

"*Sakr* calling *Zulfikar*. *Sakr* calling *Zulfikar*. Come in, *Zulfikar*." Mohamed Taferi's voice died away, the highway overpass casting long shadows in the light of the moon as he stepped from beneath its shelter, holding the radio aloft before keying the mic once again. "*Sakr* calling *Zulfikar*. . ."

There was no answer but the raw winter wind, moaning through the trees on the slope above. Covering the weaker moans of the man lying beneath the overpass, a hand pressed to the rough dressing against his chest, his lung slowly filling with blood.

He was losing him, the Druze officer thought, glancing back to where Abu Ahmed lay—he had to face that, no matter how bitter the truth.

And the *Tachash*. . .Allah alone knew. Not within radio range, apparently. It was impossible to think that they had come and gone—they would have expected him to attack later in the night, if they expected him at all. Which left only

474

the most unwelcome of conclusions.

They weren't on-station, and hadn't been.

Whatever had gone wrong in Qatar, it had compromised him clearly enough, and they'd cut their losses. Him among them, along with how many others? He grimaced at the thought, wondering if Doha had been rolled up entirely. The long-term ramifications, if that were the case, hardly bore contemplating.

He shook his head, forcing the raw emotion away with an effort. Betrayal had so many faces, but this, at least, was one he could understand. Looked at coldly, the Office's decision made *sense*. What he very well might have done, in their shoes.

But as it was written in the Qur'an. . .they had planned, and God had planned, and God was the best of planners. *Where now?* He felt himself ask, staring up into the moonlit sky. But then, as before—as he turned back into the shadow of the overpass—there was no answer but the wind.

11:57 P.M.
Khmeimim Airbase
Latakia Governorate, Syria

"I don't have the men to spare." Major Kulik's face was drawn in the pale electronic glow suffusing the command center, grimy and worn—his fingers darkened with gunpowder residue. "We'll spend the rest of the night just resecuring the perimeter—making sure no one is still lurking inside."

The need for that was obvious, Valeriy Egorov thought with a grimace—the explosion which had claimed one of the

Air Force's prized Su-57s had been a nasty surprise. Finding the bodies of both test pilots littering the ground not far from the burning wreckage had been worse. Heads were going to roll for this, and it was his principal concern to ensure that his wasn't among them.

"Tovarisch Generál-mayór," he began, turning toward where the Khmeimim base commandant stood, still in his shirtsleeves, his greying hair hopelessly mussed from rudely-interrupted sleep, "I can take my own commandos out. Reinforced by Captain Awad's soldiers," he said, gesturing to the Syrian officer on the opposite side of the table, "and supported by the Orlans, we can sweep the countryside for any stragglers."

One of the interpreters translated his comments to Awad and he saw the Syrian stiffen briefly before nodding in agreement. "Yes, I can do this. My men are at your disposal."

"Khorosho." Yury Kovpak nodded, his face grim and set. "A lesson must be taught, after tonight. See that it's done."

"Da, Tovarisch Generál."

The general looked around, glancing from face to face as if to ensure that his words were sinking home. "Where's Makarenko?"

"Tovarisch Generál, I am sorry to say that *Tovarisch Podpolkóvnik* Makarenko did not sur—"

"He was seriously wounded in the attacks, *Tovarisch Generál,*" a staff officer interjected, cutting Egorov off. His surprise and anger at the interruption, bridled at the sight of the colonel's stars. *He had survived.* "He's in surgery in the clinic's trauma center, his condition critical."

Kovpak pursed his lips together, shaking his head. "May Our Lady watch over him."

He looked up then, as if surprised to find them still standing there, the unruly tuft of mussed grey hair over his forehead giving him the aspect of a startled owl. "Go cast your nets, *Tovarisch Kapitán*. Hunt them down and make them pay. Leave no one alive."

12:08 A.M. Israel Standard Time, December 27ʰ
Tel Aviv Station
The Embassy of the United States
Tel Aviv-Yafo, Israel

It was happening. Paul Keifer leaned back into his office chair, running a weary hand over his eyes. The whine of vacuums droning in his ears as the Arab cleaning crew worked away in the nearly deserted offices without. *It was really happening.*

The partially translated transcripts of NSA intercepts from Russian forces at Khmeimim pulled up on the screen of his SIPRnet-connected computer, each of them telling their own story of a base under assault.

Assault. This wasn't the kind of probing attack the Russians dealt with on a weekly, if not daily, basis, the sniping at outposts—the shelling. This was the real deal, casualties mounting as the stunned garrison struggled to recover, to fight back.

This was *their* attack. The Israelis, following through on their end of the bargain.

He'd suspected it, from the urgency in Shafron's voice earlier, when he'd passed along the intel of the communications picked up in Latakia—had made the decision to come back into the office after dinner in Tel Aviv with his wife.

To see through what he'd started, come what may.

Now, as the carnage distilled itself into stark black-and-white lines of alternating Cyrillic and Roman script on his monitor, the CIA chief of station realized that sleep was going to be a distant memory for some days to come.

He was far too old a hand to be surprised by anything this part of the world had on offer—or so he'd thought. But the Middle East somehow never lost its capacity to shock, and as Keifer read the panicked transmissions—some sent out in the clear—from GRU analysts watching their colleagues being dragged out from beneath their desks and butchered one by one, he found himself grateful that his dinner had been digested hours before.

This—this *horror* was his doing. The blood of those men and women, on his hands, as much as those of anyone else.

Somehow in the beginning, he supposed, he'd conceived of this operation as something of a throwback to the old days of the Cold War, military espionage against the Soviets. Straightforward, and clean-cut. The kind of thing he might have read about in a Clancy novel as a kid.

But this war was very, *very* hot.

And in this war, deniability sometimes meant using a sledgehammer instead of a scalpel. . .just so it wouldn't be attributed to the kind of people known to use scalpels.

What a mess. Well, the Israelis had hit Khmeimim with a sledgehammer, that much was clear. What they might have succeeded in recovering from the wreckage remained to be seen. . .

12:11 A.M. Syria Standard Time
Jableh District, north of Jableh
Latakia Governorate, Syria

The pharmacy window smashed under the impact of the rusty crowbar in Mohamed Taferi's hand, the broken glass cascading down onto the sidewalk in a crystalline shower as he reached a gloved hand through, unlocking the door and pulling it open.

If there was an alarm, it gave no sign, but they'd still best not linger.

He took a step back, glancing around them at the apartment buildings scattered along the road on both sides—towering four and five stories into the moonlit sky. Darkened, forbidding monoliths—lights showing here and there, enough to indicate that this part of Syria, at least, still had electricity, but clearly most of their occupants were abed. With luck, they'd stay that way.

"Come on, come on, let's get you inside," he said, moving back to where Abu Ahmed leaned against the wall of the building, nearly the opposition commander's full weight collapsing into him as he offered him his shoulder, half-supporting him, half-dragging him within, out of the wind.

Abu Ahmed coughed spasmodically, his whole body trembling, bloody spittle flecking the Israeli's cheek as he propped him against the counter and flicked his tac light on, scanning the cabinets for antiseptics, tape, dressings—painkillers—anything that could be used to keep Al-Golani in the fight a little while longer. If he could hotwire a car—he had seen a dusty old Lada up the road—perhaps they could drive. . .*where, exactly?*

There weren't any good options, really, and no doubt the Russians and their Syrian allies would be mobilizing even as he rifled through these cabinets. Throwing out roadblocks.

He saw a couple bottles of Tramadol behind the glass of the middle cabinet and smashed it with the butt of his AKM, brushing away the glass as he retrieved the precious opioids. Perhaps driving on into Jableh proper would be their best bet—there were bound to be boats riding at anchor within the breakwater. And the Russians would no doubt be expecting their assailants to try to fade back into the mountains instead.

"He was right, you know." It was a weary sort of grief that filled Abu Ahmed's voice as he leaned heavily into the counter, his words dissolving into a horrifically wet cough, blood spattering over the cash register. A hissing sound escaping his chest as he struggled to catch his breath. "To abandon the men I led, like *this,* it's everything I once despised, it—"

"Save it," Mohamed replied, finding a roll of wide, heavy tape beneath the counter. He needed to get that wound sealed, before they did anything else. Stabilize him, somehow. "You're going to need your strength."

What there was of it.

"I'm dying," Abu Ahmed replied, shaking his head wearily. "We both know that, Mohammed. . .whatever your name is, truly. He killed me, and—and you should have *let* him. My life, what there's left of it, wasn't worth his."

The life of a brother. He had once heard one of the *uqqal* describe the body of Druze society as a bronze platter. Struck in one place, the shock reverberated through every member.

And he could *feel* that wound, as clearly as if he'd turned the gun on himself instead.

"La," he replied simply, shaking his head as he moved back to the Syrian's side, beginning to peel away the torn, blood-soaked fabric of his shirt. "I'm going to get you out of here yet."

Al-Golani didn't resist his hands, but shook his head slowly, that rasping, sucking sound coming from his chest as the Israeli stripped a length of tape from the roll, the fresh blood around the entry wound foaming a ghastly pink in the glare of the tac light. "For what? So I can die tomorrow? The day after that? If God were just, I would have died with my wife and—and our daughter, in that street. A *quick* death, instead of this slow one. Twisting and dying within, until there's nothing left. Until you *are* all that you once fought against. But God. . .wherever He is, whoever He is, hasn't cared about Syria in a very many years. He—"

And his voice broke off suddenly, at the sound of a shout from the street.

12:15 A.M.
The Tachash
The Mediterranean Sea

The Camel dangled from between David Shafron's lips, its tip glowing briefly cherry-red in the darkness, as he went over his kit once again, checking and rechecking each piece of gear with all the obsessive care he remembered from his days in *Kidon* and later, supervising training for those units. Leading by example, as he'd always tried to do. . .until that had become all but impossible, the higher he'd climbed.

As he was attempting to do, however futilely, tonight. To redeem the *mess* that had been made of this operation.

He raised the Kalashnikov in both hands, the bulky suppressor at the end of its muzzle looming large in the night as he pulled the charging handle back just far enough to catch the glint of brass in the chamber—extending its folding stock back against his shoulder. Checked his chest rig's mag pouches, each of the larger ones holding a single curved AK magazine. Sixty rounds, plus the thirty in the gun. It was well short of a full combat load, but as with so many other moments in his career, if they had to fire their weapons at all, things had already gone very wrong.

He rose to his feet, ducking into the wheelhouse to find Reuven and Omri doing the same thing, removing equipment from its pouches and replacing it, cementing the muscle memory—making sure they could put their hands on anything at a moment's notice, in the dark.

Avigdor Barad had bummed a smoke from him earlier and now the cigarette smoldered between the gnarled fingers clutching the wheel, a curious look of contentment on the sailor's face. The confidence of a man perfectly at home.

He raised the Camel to his lips and glanced over, seeing Shafron standing in the door.

"I want you to start trying to raise Taferi in another ten minutes, Avigdor. Then every five minutes after that. Until we hear something back."

If they heard anything back.

12:15 A.M.
Jableh District, north of Jableh
Latakia Governorate, Syria

They had seen the light. That was the only explanation for it, Mohamed Taferi thought, cursing himself in the stillness as he pressed his back up against the wall—the only sound in the desolate pharmacy that of Abu Ahmed's long, ragged breaths, masked by the bitter moan of the wind as it increased in strength, whipping around the corner of the building. The crunch of footsteps in the gravel without, coming closer.

And the broken glass. The rough shout of surprise giving them away. There were two of them at least, a hand on the door—pushing it open cautiously, moonlight glinting briefly off the barrel of the long rifle leading the way. A hand, groping for the light.

He wished in that moment for the crowbar, but he'd tossed it to the ground after breaking the window. *Another mistake.*

Then Abu Ahmed drew in another painful, rasping breath, and collapsed in a fit of coughing—a sharp exclamation coming from the man in the door as the rifle barrel swung toward the sound.

The Israeli came out of the darkness, catching the outlines of a heavyset, balding man in a worn tracksuit—*the pharmacist?*—in the moment before he seized control of the bolt-action rifle's long barrel, catching the man off-balance as he jerked the weapon forward, sending him crashing to the concrete floor, cursing and moaning in pain. Mohamed put a knee between the Syrian's shoulder blades, bearing down with his weight as the Glock came out in his hand, aimed toward the door.

He looked up into the scared eyes of a boy, barely in his teens, clutching a Tokarev as he stood framed in the entrance, his whole body trembling. *Father and son.*

"Khalaas, khalaas," the man on the ground wheezed, struggling to get his breath. "Just *stop*. I'll give you whatever you want, I have medicines, I—"

"Tell your son to put down the pistol, or I drop him where he stands. *Do it!*"

The man stammered out his repetition of the command, the boy's voice quivering as he replied, raising a hand as he stooped down, placing the pistol on the concrete floor between them, rising with both hands held aloft.

He saw the warning in the boy's eyes—too late to react, too late to stop him as he bolted from the door, disappearing from sight before he could even raise the pistol. He brought the butt of the Glock down hard into the back of the pharmacist's skull, feeling his body go limp as he sprung for the door—eyes searching the moonlit street. But there was only the sound of running feet slapping hard against the pavement—a small figure draped in shadow, running pell-mell for one of the apartment towers.

Too far for a shot, even if he'd dared take it.

He spared a glance toward the slumped, unconscious form of the store owner before snatching the painkillers off the counter, stooping down beside Abu Ahmed. "Come on, *yalla!* We've got to go—they could be down on us any minute."

"La," the rebel commander replied weakly, putting a hand on Mohamed's wrist, his fingers unnaturally cold. "I'm. . .I wouldn't last another kilometer, and with me, you'll only be taken. Give me my pistol."

He fumbled with the holster beneath Al-Golani's coat, extracting the Glock and placing it into the man's right hand, wrapping his fingers around the grip. A weary *"shukran"* serving by way of reply.

Abu Ahmed looked up as he started to rise, his fingers falling away from his wrist. "Just tell me this. . .was it real? Any of it? Was I ever going to California, truly?"

The Israeli paused, unable to look away from his hollowed eyes. Unable, in that moment, to tell him anything but the truth. A man in his death deserved that much honesty. He shook his head slowly. *"La."*

The eyes closed, but for the briefest of moments. Then, "I knew it, somehow, all along." Abu Ahmed drew in a deep, hissing breath, blood bubbling around the wound as he shook his head in resignation. "The America of John Wayne is dead anyway. They stood by and watched as everyone I loved died. Why should I think I would be any different? Because I'd helped them? There's no one they're as likely to forget as their friends."

He seemed almost amused by that, his harsh laugh breaking off in a bloody fit of coughing. "Now *go.*"

The Israeli rose from his side, unslinging his rifle as he pushed through the door and out into the still-desolate street, hurrying toward the faded brown Lada he had seen a hundred meters or so further south, in the shadow of yet another looming tower.

He'd made it half-way there when, behind him, he heard the muffled sound of a single pistol shot.

12:21 A.M. Israel Standard Time
Mossad Headquarters, Glilot Junction
Tel Aviv-Yafo, Israel

Abram Sorkin and Nika Mengashe were waiting in the SCIF when Avi ben Shoham arrived, tossing his phone into the equipment locker before pushing open the door.

He had been asleep when the call came in—as had Sorkin, from the look of him, only Nika appearing fully awake—her dark fingers tapping away at the keyboard of the laptop set up before her.

"We're still picking up traffic out of Latakia, Avi," she announced, not looking up. "The Russians appear, from the chatter, to have regained control of their base, but—here— you can see the TecSAR imagery from the overpass thirty minutes ago." She spun the laptop toward him. "There were still fires everywhere."

So it appeared, the *memuneh* thought, adjusting his glasses on the bridge of his nose as he bent toward the screen. His gaze drifting instinctively across the runways of Khmeimim toward the squat concrete structure just across from the Bassel al-Assad terminal.

The *ruins* of that structure, he corrected himself, looking at what could be seen on the satellite imagery. It appeared to have been leveled, rather completely, leaving him to wonder what, exactly, the Syrian rebels had hit it with. What—

"Where's David?" he asked, struck suddenly by the conspicuous absence. His question leaving Sorkin and Mengashe looking at each other as if uncertain which of them should take it.

Finally, Sorkin cleared his throat, looking at once

embarrassed and troubled. "We haven't been able to reach him."

12:29 A.M. Syria Standard Time
Jableh District, north of Jableh
Latakia Governorate, Syria

It was a hollow, sunken face, still frozen in the moment of death, and the back of the head was a mess, blown half-away, presumably by the Glock fallen haphazardly into the man's lap. But he knew the face, for all that.

Captain Michael Awad rose from his crouch, picking up the pistol and placing it on the counter of the pharmacy. "Abu Ahmed al-Golani," he announced, looking Valeriy Egorov in the eye. "A Southern Front battlefield commander and the last known leader of *Fursan Tahrir al-Sham.*"

"Are you sure?" the Spetsnaz captain asked, his voice sharp as a razor. Those dark eyes, hard and pitiless. Awad glanced over at his minder, who had stepped in the spattered brain matter and was doing his best not to retch. A nod.

"I'm sure. It's not his real name, of course—as near we've been able to determine, he was an Army officer who deserted in the early years of the war. But it's him. Come on, let's be going. . .the boy said there was another with him."

"The drones will be with us soon enough," Egorov replied, referencing the Orlan-10s. "They'll pick him up—he can't have gotten far. But you're sure that this is Al-Golani?"

*Mother of God. . .*Awad bit back the sarcastic response that rose to his lips, concealing his weary irritation behind the mask he usually assumed in dealing with his superiors as he glanced from Egorov to the Spetsnaz NCO at his side and back again. "Yes."

He turned for the door, beckoning for his lieutenant to follow as he scuffed his soiled shoes against the concrete. One of the Desert Hawks militiamen was helping the pharmacist up from where he'd lain by the door—moans, complaints, and invective escaping the heavy-set man's lips as he rose, holding the back of his head.

He'd get over it, Awad thought, shaking his head in disgust. He was lucky to be alive at all.

The pistol shot behind him echoed loud as a cannon blast in the narrow confines of the pharmacy and he turned to see the pharmacist pitch forward, Al-Golani's pistol in Egorov's outstretched hand.

Betrayal. The Special Forces officer swore, seeing the demonic light in the Russian's eyes, realizing through the exhaustion and the fatigue that he had allowed his guard to slip—his hand flying to his own sidearm, fingers closing around the grip.

But the Glock's muzzle belched fire once again, and oblivion claimed Michael Awad. . .

Valeriy Egorov turned and put two bullets into the chest of Awad's young lieutenant, smiling in satisfaction at the horrified look on the kid's face as his legs gave out from under him and he collapsed to the floor. The bewildered Desert Hawks' militia fighter froze for a split-second, standing over the body of the slain pharmacist, his rifle only half-raised. A split-second too long, as Egorov shot him in the head, and he joined the civilian on the floor.

"Bring in the can of gasoline from the truck," the

Spetsnaz captain ordered, turning toward his NCO. "And set the place on fire."

He tossed the Glock on the floor and stalked from the building, pleased to see that only his own men remained without. The rest of Awad's commandos dispatched, on his orders, to search the towering apartment buildings. By the time they returned, it wouldn't matter.

"How long until we have the Orlans, *Tovarisch Leytenánt?*" he asked as one of his junior officers emerged from the shadow of the Russian military truck which served as his command post. He'd expected them to be overhead by now, providing support. Searching out ahead of his own ground units—serving as, what did the Americans call it? *A "force multiplier."*

"Fifteen to twenty minutes yet, *Tovarisch Kapitán.* Maybe more—the KAMAZ command truck was destroyed in the attack and they're still working to bring other systems online. And in this wind—"

"Enough, *tovarisch,*" Egorov snapped, glaring at his subordinate. "I don't want excuses, I want eyes up above. See that I get them."

And behind him, a sheet of flames leapt skyward from the pharmacy, billowed ever higher by the wind. . .

12:36 A.M.
The Tachash
The Mediterranean Sea

High above, feathery bands of cloud scudded like will-o'-wisps across the face of the moon, the north-easterly wind whipping the sea into an ever-heavier chop as the trawler forged north, breasting the waves. "*Zulfikar* calling *Sakr. . .Zulfikar* calling *Sakr.*"

On the other side of the *Tachash*'s small wheelhouse, Marc Harel lowered the radio microphone from his lips, listening patiently in the ensuing silence. The medic's dark face set in grim, hard lines beneath the greasepaint.

He was thinking what they all were, David Shafron realized, keeping his own face neutral with an effort as Reuven Aharoni leaned in closer with the paint stick, applying the finishing touches to Shafron's camouflage. What they were all thinking and none of them dared voice. That there was a good chance that the silence on the radio was that of the grave—that the Druze officer hadn't made it out.

His death, just another among the many of this night— the Russians' casualty reports mounting steadily over the unclass net until they'd finally managed to re-establish comms discipline thirty to forty minutes earlier.

Avigdor Barad had one hand on the wheel, another hand smoothing out the crinkled folds of his charts, his face half-obscured by the drifting smoke of his third cigarette. Two calls had come in from the Office on the *Tachash*'s satphone in the previous twenty minutes, but he had ignored both of them, on Shafron's orders, and if it bothered the sailor, he gave no sign.

"Once we pick him up, we're going to stand out to sea," he announced, looking up. "Toward Cyprus. Exfiltrating him immediately post-attack was one thing. Now? They've had nigh on two hours to mobilize a response. There's no way Tartus doesn't deploy, and I'm not taking the *Tachash* straight back down the coast into the teeth of that. If the exfil turns hot. . ."

Then all the more so, Shafron thought—and the odds of a successful exfiltration went down for everyone. They were playing for heavy stakes.

He simply nodded as Reuven took a step back, recapping the stick. He was a passenger here, and he recognized that—but it was a solid plan.

"*Bedyuk,*" Reuven replied, nodding his agreement. *Exactly.* "It would also put us on the outside edge of their unmanned aerial surveillance capability." The former *Shayetet-13* operator shrugged. "We have enough rations aboard to spend a day or two at sea, if we have to. And if Avigdor has his nets mended. . .we can always catch some fish."

The captain laughed at that. "If your men can use them properly, you mean."

"*Zulfikar* calling *Sakr,*" Marc intoned once again, reprising his efforts to raise the missing officer. "*Zulfikar* calling—"

The radio crackled suddenly with a burst of static, followed by an unexpected voice. "*Zulfikar,* this is *Sakr.*"

12:41 A.M.
The coastal road
Jableh District, Latakia Governorate
Syria

The rows of nursery greenhouses lined the sides of the road like soldiers along a parade route as the battered old Lada rolled south on balding tires, its gas tank needle wavering dangerously ever closer to empty. Their green plastic coverings taking on an otherworldly cast in the moonlight, throwing off strange, wavering shadows as the wind buffeted the fragile structures.

". . .we're still five kilometers south of Map Reference Point 14," *Zulfikar* announced, their voice coming calm and clear through Mohamed Taferi's radio as he drove, his eyes searching the road ahead.

Baniyas, the Druze officer thought, recalling the briefings to mind. It was a small city along the coast to the south in Tartous Governorate. They weren't on-station, weren't even close to it. He shook his head, overcome for a moment in his weariness and exhaustion by incredulity at the folly of it all. But there wasn't time to consider the circumstances that might have led to such a screw-up. Not now. He needed to get off this road and out of Syria and, late or not, they were his ride.

"Say again your pos, *Sakr*?"

"Driving south from the primary exfil," he replied, bringing the radio to his lips with his free hand. "Approx six klicks northwest of MRP 16."

It was a *rough* approximate, he thought grimly, guiding the Lada into the turn of the road. The countless twists and turns he had taken driving south, dodging a thickening web of Syrian Arab Army checkpoints flung out across the roads—no doubt at the behest of their Russian masters—disorienting him. But the sea was there, not more than a kilometer to his west, its dark gulf visible here and there in gaps between the buildings.

There was a moment's silence before *Zulfikar* transmitted again, then, "Can you make the southern alternate?"

He waited a moment before keying his mic, knowing the reason for the question. In a car, he could cover the ground in less than half the time it would take the trawler, and they could be waiting for him on the beach at the alternate exfil by the time he arrived. And he should have enough fuel, even if only just.

"Affirmative, *Zulfikar*. The roads are getting thicker with OPFOR, but I should be able to reach you. I—"

He came around a bend in the road past yet another squat row of greenhouses, his voice breaking off as he saw the military truck pulled half-across the road in a blocking position not forty meters ahead, the shadowy figures of soldiers or militiamen gathered about. No chance he was going to get through, the way they had done earlier in the night. Not in a little car like this.

The Israeli slammed on the brakes and put the wheel hard over left, the Lada's bald tires squealing against the pavement as they clawed for a purchase, his hand reaching down for the manual gearshift.

His windshield dissolved in a shower of glass, a rifle round creasing the air only inches away from his head. Another bullet, blowing out the front right tire. The car lurched and he lost control for a moment, the wheel shuddering beneath his hands as the car skidded off the road and smashed into the entrance of a nearby greenhouse, nearly bringing down the flimsy structure on top of it, the impact knocking him back into his seat.

He dropped the radio into a pouch on his vest, grabbed his rifle and pack off the seat beside him and shoved open the door, ducking low as he heard harsh shouts fill the night, a scattering of further shots tearing through the Lada's light metal frame.

Keeping his head down as he ran across the road and into

the maze of greenhouses on the other side—the moon seeming to glare down from above as he ran past shelters filled with orange and olive seedlings, slinging the pack containing the Su-57's avionics onto his back as he stumbled along, summoning up his last, flickering reserves of energy.

He made it through the greenhouses and into the open, windswept fields beyond, the shouts of men pursuing him into the night. The dark shelter of a hedgerow seventy or eighty meters ahead, beckoning to him. And beyond, well beyond—he could hear a dull, roaring sound, booming in the darkness.

The crash of the surf.

Out of breath, his legs burning, he collapsed into the shadow of the hedgerow, lifting the radio once more to his lips. "*Sakr* calling *Zulfikar*. . .cancel that last."

Chapter 35

Smoke was curling from beneath the Lada's crumpled hood as Valeriy Egorov dismounted painfully from the Russian Army Haval SUV, stalking toward the small cluster of Syrian soldiers gathered around the crashed car.

The painkillers were slowly wearing off, the Orlans were still grounded, and while his fury at being forced to rely on their Syrian "partners" to run the attackers to the ground had spent itself on Khmeimim's technicians, it flared to new life at the sight of the soldiers.

"What are you all standing around for? Have you already caught him?" Egorov demanded angrily, waiting impatiently as his interpreter repeated his words in annoyingly calmer Arabic. He might just have saved himself by eliminating Awad—if the Syrian captain's commandos had suspected his story, none, at least, had dared challenge him—but now he was the instrument of Kovpak's vengeance, and the general

495

would expect his orders to be carried out. *To the letter.*

"No," his interpreter said, translating the reply of a Syrian non-com standing by the blown-out right front wheel of the Lada. "He says they've sent out patrols, but have been unable to re-acquire him."

"Then get back out there," the Spetsnaz captain spat, but he shook his head wearily, indicating that he wasn't to translate the order. A lesser race, if there had ever been one, the Arabs never liked to operate at night, even when they had the kit—and here, it was nowhere in evidence. This was a job his men would have to do for themselves.

He reached up to his helmet, flipping down the monocular NOD over his left eye before turning to his own NCO. "Get the men deployed and start running a grid search south along the coastline. *Find* him."

1:23 A.M.
The Tachash
Off the Latakia coast

Sheltered in the lee of the trawler, the Zodiac rocked uneasily in the gathering chop as David Shafron descended the boarding ladder into the boat, feeling it give beneath his feet as he stepped off and immediately went prone straddling the port gunwale, rifle clutched in both hands, his knees gripping the hard rubber.

Omri Tishman was already at the tiller, serving as coxswain, with Marc Harel stretched out on the starboard gunwale across from him, his dark outline melding into the black of the raft.

It brought it all back, Shafron thought, remembering

more than a few nights like this in his life. Lurking in the darkness off the coasts of Gaza, Lebanon. Libya. . .

He didn't, though, remember his joints feeling quite this stiff, the cold of the night sinking deep into his body as he laid there, waiting as Reuven Aharoni took his place at the bow, his weapon trained forward. The broad-bladed paddles they would use for their final approach to the pick-up lying on the deck between them.

It was a young man's game he was playing at, a reflection that made him feel no better as the outboard roared to life, the Zodiac emerging from the shadow of the *Tachash* and into the moonlight, the wind tossing icy droplets of salt spray against his cheeks as the boat plunged through the waves, gathering speed.

His breath catching in his throat as they crested one wave to drop into the shallow trough below, that strangely heady frisson of fear and excitement coursing once more through his veins. *Going into battle.*

That most deadly of all intoxicants. He hated it and he loved it, with all the hate—*all the love*—that a man knows for an addiction which he knows could be the death of him.

Their odds were getting worse by the minute, as he knew all too well. The chances of pulling this off smoothly—*silently*—fading away down to near-zero with an active search going on for the Druze officer on-shore.

He glanced back along the gunwale, the churning froth of their wake pale and glistering in the light of the moon—the peaks of *Jabal an-Nusayriyah* looming large against the horizon ahead, picked out in ominous relief.

Tense, blackened faces all around him as the boat surged forward, the shock of the waves shuddering through his body. A grim smile creasing Omri's face as he sat at the tiller, conning them in toward the shore, but the eyes. . .the eyes gave it all away. They all knew what he did.

That this had every chance of going hot. *Very hot.*

1:32 A.M.
Jableh District
Latakia Governorate, Syria

The dog had barked as Mohamed Taferi passed, a mangy, ill-fed, half-savage creature scuttling in between the pair of apartment towers that nestled atop the rocky promontory jutting out into the Mediterranean, picking its way through the trash and detritus that now littered their grounds.

And the dog was barking now, a prolonged string of rapid barks that died away abruptly in a high-pitched yelp, no longer of alarm but of pain. Followed only by silence.

They were up there, the Israeli thought grimly, pressing himself closer into the rough scree littering the beach, the precious backpack beside him, checking his rifle for what seemed like the fiftieth time. He was down to his last mag, but he knew if he brought them down on him now, all the ammunition in the world couldn't save him.

The surf boomed against the rocks to his west, tossing ghostly white fountains of spray high against the night, deadening all softer sounds. A few meters off to his right, beached in a softer patch of sand, lay a rusting jet ski, testament—like the apartments themselves—to the affluence this part of Syria had once enjoyed. But now, this many years into the war, the utter breakdown of life and public services was felt even here, in the homeland of the Assads.

Farther along, left similarly stranded by the outgoing tide, lay a small, open wooden skiff, but his hopes of floating it and getting out of reach had been dashed by the discovery that someone—a malicious soldier or power-hungry militiaman, most likely—had long ago stove-in its bottom.

So he sheltered against the scree, the rifle hugged to his chest, praying quietly for them to pass the beach by. . .

1:37 A.M. Israel Standard Time
Mossad Headquarters, Glilot Junction
Tel Aviv-Yafo, Israel

The lights were low in Avi ben Shoham's office, the glow of the computer screen illuminating the *memuneh*'s weathered face as he leaned back in his office chair, nursing the last of his brandy.

He had known, the moment that they'd failed to raise Avigdor Barad and the *Tachash*—no. He'd known far earlier than that—*suspected* it, when David Shafron had sat before him in this very office, only the morning before. Suspected that he might act rashly to assuage the recriminations of his conscience. To save the man he'd sent into harm's way, whatever the cost.

And he'd done his best to warn him away. *"The consequences of our decisions no longer involve one man, or a dozen. . ."*

That was the truth of it. He knew what David was feeling—had felt it himself many times over, through the years. Once, in the Golan, in a war that was even now sliding into the mists of history, he had acted on those feelings and helped drag his fellow crew members out of their burning Centurion.

They'd called him a hero for it, but he'd known then that he had simply done the right thing. The *only* thing. Back when the right thing had been clear, unmuddied by the responsibilities of position and power.

But the decisions were much harder these days, the consequences more far-reaching and difficult to divine. And a clear conscience was a luxury anyone at their level could ill afford.

He tossed back the remaining brandy and set the empty glass on the corner of his desk, turning off his computer screen to sit alone in the semi-darkness.

Tapping David Shafron to head up MEGIDDO had been his idea—he'd known the man for years, from Shafron's own days as a young operator onward. Known him to be an incisive and skilled leader of men, a talented instructor, and an excellent operational commander.

But there was such a thing as promoting even the best of men past their level of ability, and as the moon drifted in and out of the light clouds above Tel Aviv, throwing its pale rays through the window of the *memuneh*'s office, Avi ben Shoham began to wonder if that's exactly what he had done. . .

1:42 A.M. Syria Standard Time
The coastal road, Jableh District
Latakia Governorate, Syria

"Anything?" Valeriy Egorov demanded, the pain from his bandaged side driving a raw edge of irritation into his voice as his NCO re-emerged from behind the abandoned seaside restaurant.

A shake of the head, the man's monocular swinging back and forth like a wagging finger. *"Nyet."*

Movement from behind one of the overflowing dumpsters tucked along the southern wall of the restaurant, and one of his men moved back, startled—his rifle coming to his shoulder as a scrawny cat darted from its shelter for the bushes.

Several of the other Spetsnaz laughed, but it was the harsh, grating sound of men on edge. *Nervous.* Fatigue and the exhaustion of the night, taking their inevitable toll.

He turned his back on his men, looking out toward the sea and the apartment towers back on that rocky promontory to the north as he popped another pair of Nurofen into his mouth, willing the pain to subside—a wave of dizziness washing over him even as he did so. He *had* to see this through, come what may.

And that was when he saw it, away toward the north, a flash of movement—*something*—dark against the moonlit chop of the Mediterranean. "What's that?"

1:44 A.M.
The Zodiac

The blade of David Shafron's paddle bit into the waves in time with those of Reuven's team as he sat upright on the gunwale, buffeted by the wind, his arms burning with the unaccustomed effort. Their combined impetus thrusting the boat forward through the final line of breakers toward the waiting beach, a stranded skiff washed up on the scree just visible in the strange shadows cast by the moon, not more than twenty meters off their starboard bow and near enough to the water that the next high tide would likely lift it off.

Foam boiled around their small craft as the next wave swelled behind them, shoving the Zodiac closer to the water's edge and Reuven and Marc were over the side in knee-deep water, the former pulling security, his rifle raised—the latter holding the boat steady, keeping it off the stray rocks.

Shafron saw Omri working the IR strobe from his position at the tiller and flipped his own NODs down over his face just in time to see an answering pulse of light, a dark figure detaching itself from the shadows surrounding the beached skiff and hurrying into the water toward them.

The water's chill knifed through Mohamed Taferi's legs as he plunged into the surf, soaking him to the bone and slowing his progress as he forged toward the waiting Zodiac, his rifle slung across his back, the backpack lifted as high as his weary arm could sustain it, keeping it above the waves. *Escape, so close now at hand.*

He responded dully to the challenge of the man at the bow, lofted the precious pack up and into the Zodiac, the avionics package of the Russian Federation's new stealth fighter landing against the aluminum deckplates of the inflatable with a dull thud. A strangely familiar figure moving off the opposite gunwale, extending a hand to help him up into the boat.

"Welcome back." It was David Shafron's voice, but *no. . .*there was no way, his weary brain struggling to process the thought as his eyes searched the grease-darkened face. The boat rocking beneath him as the other paramilitary officers climbed back aboard, shoving the Zodiac toward deeper water.

He felt relief wash over him, relief and a strange sense of *loss*, the adrenaline seeming to drain from his body as he slumped against the gunwale, the exhaustion of the night—of the previous two weeks—finally sinking home.

An odd hiss reached his ears in that moment, audible even through the crash of the surf, the harsh sibilance of escaping air. A strange, insistent *tug* at his side—a split-second before he heard the crackle of small-arms fire from somewhere off to the south.

And he was falling, toppling from the deflating gunwale and into the breakers, his kit unbalancing him, weighing him down. The cold waters of the Mediterranean closing over his face. . .

The fire from the heights to the south took them all off-guard, the Zodiac lurching drunkenly to one side as one of the raft's airtight chambers collapsed under a burst of incoming rounds.

David Shafron snapped his rifle to his shoulder, picking out in the glow of his night vision the scattering of figures spread out along the road, more than two hundred meters out. He heard the suppressed bark of Marc's weapon as the former pararescue opened up in response, heard Reuven bellow *"Take us out of here!"* to Omri at the tiller as the outboard roared to life.

They'd planned to paddle back out as quietly as they'd come in, but all that was in the wind now. *Speed*, their only ally in this moment.

He pushed his AK's safety lever all the way down, the trigger breaking beneath his finger as he squeezed off a flurry of single shots—realizing only then, as the Zodiac came sluggishly about, backing away from the shore, what the tunnel vision of his NODs had blinded him to. *Mohamed Taferi was no longer across from him.*

Shafron glanced out into the churning surf, glimpsing a dark figure among the foam—stripping his rifle away from his tactical vest and dropping it to the deck as he moved forward, squeezing Reuven's shoulder and shouting into the former *Shayetet-13* operator's ear, pointing toward the beach before leaping into the water.

He sank up to his thighs in the wind-lashed waves, the cold numbing his stiff muscles as he plowed back toward the Druze officer—bullets slapping at the surf about him, answering bursts of fire rippling out from the Zodiac as the three paramilitaries laid down covering fire.

He reached Taferi even as the man came up sputtering once again, choking on seawater and struggling to find his footing—a breaking wave slamming into Shafron's back, soaking him to the skin and nearly taking him to his knees.

"Come on," he spat, straining to lift the man aright, his water-soaked weight threatening to pull them both down into the embrace of the sea. A sharp pain knifing through his lower back even as he did so, but he ignored it with an effort, wrapping Taferi's arm around his shoulder as they staggered back out of the shallows. "*Yalla zazim*, let's go!"

And the Zodiac was there at their side, Reuven's strong arms reaching down to help first Taferi and then Shafron up into the boat. Shafron collapsed against the deckplates, struggling to catch his breath as the outboard thundered once more to full power, the Zodiac describing a 180-degree arc as it roared back out to sea, toward the waiting *Tachash*. He saw Marc bent over the Druze officer, doing a blood sweep—Reuven leaning against the still-intact gunwale near the bow, still returning fire.

David fumbled for his own rifle, started to roll over on his side to retrieve it, to join Reuven. *Started.*

His face distorting in agony as pain shot like liquid fire through his back, his involuntary cry drowned out by the outboard as he collapsed back against the deck. . .

1:46 A.M.
The coastal road

"I need the air support *now, Tovarisch Leytenánt*," Valeriy Egorov spat, watching darkly from the heights as the damaged Zodiac sped out of range of his commandos' rifles, turning south, the roiling foam of its wake glistening in the moonlight. Realizing in that moment, at the sight of the military craft, that this had been about far more than a simple rebel raid. The thought of all that he had overlooked—of what he had inadvertently *allowed* to happen—chilling the Spetsnaz captain to the bone. "Get the Orlans up."

"*Izvini, pozhaluysta, Tovarisch Kapitán,*" the technician replied stolidly, his apology sounding utterly insincere, "but in this wind—"

Egorov shook his head, venting his rage with a curse. "I am ordering you to put them in the air. *Immediately.*"

Or a helicopter gunship. That would be all he needed. Another wave of dizziness hit him, and he put out a hand to steady himself, clutching his NCO's shoulder for support as he struggled to remember if any of Khmeimim's gunships had survived the attack intact.

"*Tovarisch Kapitán,*" the technician replied, this time not even bothering with the form of an apology, "you are not in my chain of command, and—"

Whatever else he went on to say, Valeriy Egorov never heard him—the earth seeming to suddenly revolve unsteadily beneath him as he lost his grip on the commando's shoulder, staggering a couple feet away before his legs went out from under him.

The ground rushing up to meet him. . .followed only by darkness.

Epilogue

Eight thousand feet below the orbiting Orlan-10 UAV, a fishing trawler lay rocking in the gentle swell off the southeastern coast of Cyprus' Karpas Peninsula, her nets deployed out behind her in the crystalline sea, men visible on her decks.

Valeriy Egorov leaned back in the spare chair in front of the command console, watching the screens through narrowed eyes. He'd woken up in the base clinic, six hours later, his collapse precipitated by fatigue, dehydration, the side effects of the Nurofen, and of course—the wounds themselves. The doctors had pulled half a dozen jagged pieces of metal from his side, and left nearly as many in place, too deep to retrieve. But he'd be fine, in time, and able to stay in the field—which was more than one could say for Makarenko, who would be on a flight back to Russia before nightfall.

"Take it down closer," he ordered, ignoring the nagging pain in his side as he leaned toward the monitors.

"Pochemu?" the technician demanded, but Egorov shook his head. "Just do it—I want to see how they react."

They had been here for hours, scouring the sea from north to south, a hundred to a hundred and fifty kilometers out, pushing the envelope of the drones' operating range. Passing over container ships and oil tankers, fishing boats and pleasure yachts.

But this one, something felt different for reasons he found impossible to articulate as the small aircraft slid into a steep dive, the ocean filling its cameras for a long, interminable moment before leveling out a hundred feet over the wavetops, passing over the trawler from bow to stern before coming back around for another pass.

He saw a man just outside the trawler's wheelhouse glance up unconcernedly as the Orlan went overhead the second time, seeming to regard the drone curiously for a long moment before lifting his hand in a casual, almost mocking wave.

Egorov swore beneath his breath at the insolence of the fisherman, unable to make out any reason for suspicion as the man casually watched the UAV circle once more over the trawler.

"All right," he announced with grudging reluctance, "let's look elsewhere."

2:41 P.M. Eastern European Standard Time
The Tachash
Five kilometers off Cape Apostolos Andreas, Cyprus

Mohamed Taferi watched the Russian surveillance drone disappear into the low-hanging clouds off to the north before turning to go inside, a grimace distorting his face as pain flared from his side. The rifle bullet had gone in and out, missing one of his lower ribs by scant centimeters as it punched straight through the meat and muscle.

As clean a wound as they got, but that didn't mean it wouldn't take time to heal.

"We had company, but it looks like they got bored," he announced, ducking into the wheelhouse, his eyes adjusting to the gloom, the pungent aroma of cigarette smoke filling the confined space.

Avigdor Barad was behind the wheel, a Camel between his lips as he guided the trawler slowly south along the Cyprian coast, David Shafron flat on his back among the blankets in the lower berth of the trawler's only bunk, shaking another cigarette out of his almost-empty pack.

"The Russians?" David Shafron asked, looking up at Taferi's entrance, grimacing in pain as he tried to sit up, only to give it up for a bad job and fall back against the blankets—flicking his lighter until flame spurted from the tip.

He had pulled a muscle in his lower back, trying to pull the Druze officer out of the water, and it had laid him flat—helpless as a baby, the inflammation making it difficult to even stir from the bunk.

A helpless old man, he groused ruefully, placing the cigarette between his lips and taking a heavy drag—Reuven hadn't let him hear the last of being more thoroughly incapacitated than the man who'd actually gotten shot, and the good-natured raillery showed no sign of ending anytime soon.

Taferi nodded. "Looked like. A light military surveillance drone, definitely. Maybe Turkish, but I'd say Russian. Flew back away to the northeast."

"Sababa," Shafron grunted approvingly, wincing in pain as he shifted position, trying and failing to get comfortable. "Avigdor, take us home."

7:03 A.M. Moscow Standard Time, January 3rd (Six days later)
N.N. Burdenko Main Military Clinical Hospital
Moscow, Russia

It was still pitch-black outside the military hospital, the sun yet to push its way above the cold horizon, but Andriy Makarenko was awake, stirring restlessly against the sheets.

Zinaida had been in the night before, once again, bringing their little Natalyushka—the warmth that the baby's contented chortling brought to him as her pudgy fingers played with the rough stubble of his unshaven face washed away by the look in his fiancée's eyes. Weary eyes, from which the horror—the *shock*—had yet to fade. She'd borne up through his absence, or so he believed, but now. . .he'd failed to come back to her, somehow—all of him, at least.

His legs were gone, both of them, below the knee—the stubs healing, but slowly, as his body battled off infection and he sank deeper into depression. His military career was over, and with it, his ability to support the woman he'd intended to make his wife, the daughter he had fathered.

And there was to be an internal investigation into the circumstances surrounding the attack on Khmeimim. *"Lapses in security"* was the official word going around, which told him clear as day whom they intended to scapegoat for their failures. He'd be lucky to stay out of a very dark hole.

Russia Today was on the television screen, and he looked up just in time to see a stock shot of Khmeimim itself, looking away out toward the sea past the terminal building. Clearly taken before the assault—maybe during the President's visit weeks before. *Weeks?* It felt like a lifetime.

He reached for the remote against his better judgment, turning the volume up, even as the footage cut to uniformed soldiers standing at attention, Yury Kovpak appearing on-screen, leaning close to yet another familiar figure.

" . . .Air Base, where *Kapitán* Valeriy Egorov of the 3rd Guards Spetsnaz has been decorated for his role in thwarting *Daesh*'s vicious but unsuccessful attack last week. The newest recipient of the Order of Kutuzov, *Kapitán* Egorov's bravery and fidelity to. . ."

On-screen, Egorov's face turned toward the camera, and it was as though his eyes met Makarenko's, that cool assurance radiating from their fathomless depths, bile rising in the GRU officer's throat at the sight. At the mad folly of it all. *You won.*

10:46 A.M. Israel Standard Time
Mossad Headquarters, Glilot Junction
Tel Aviv-Yafo, Israel

David Shafron shifted against the cushions of the couch in Shoham's office, grimacing at the twinge in his lower back as he waited for the *memuneh* to finish up his paperwork.

Ice had helped reduce the inflammation, once he'd gotten home, but it would take several weeks for a full recovery. Rahel's distress had been palpable, all the more so when he'd proven unable to answer any of her questions, her anxiety turning to anger and frustration at the suspicion, which he knew approached a near-certainty, that he'd found his way back out into the field.

"You can't be doing this to me," she'd said the previous day, after taking the boys to school. *"To us."*

Aaron and Shmuel were too small to understand, though Shmuel had tried to help, sitting by the couch and reading aloud to him in a humorously sing-song voice. But they could feel the tension, and deep down, he knew she was right. *He couldn't.* A foot or two to the left, to the right, in those waters, and it could have been a bullet that brought him down, not a strained muscle. Death, wading beside him every step of the way through the surf, its dark robes stained with salt.

And yet he'd never felt more alive than in that moment, the crack of rifle bullets in the air, Mohamed Taferi's weight heavy against his shoulder. Life so very immediate, so *vital* just then, filled with color, with fire—even in the shadow of Death.

But it wasn't just his home life that was in turmoil— things at the office had been strained ever since his return, and Gideon and Yossi's long-overdue return from Doha had done nothing to uncomplicate matters.

The Su-57's avionics had been turned over to the technical wunderkinds of *Maf'at* and—presumably—the Americans, and while it was possible that the technological intelligence gleaned might make its way back to Mossad at some point, it was unlikely to do so in any way that would be recognizable as their work. Such were the realities of this life—if you wanted credit, commendation, and a sense of accomplishment, you went elsewhere.

Avi ben Shoham cleared his throat just then, laying his glasses to one side as he rose from behind his desk. "You realize the risks you took, don't you?"

"*Ken.*"

"I don't think you do," the older man replied, settling heavily into the chair opposite. "If you'd died, if your body had washed up on the coast of Latakia. . .our odds of exposure would have increased exponentially. We could have denied Taferi, easily enough, if he'd been killed. But you—that would have been a far greater challenge, and one we might very well not have weathered. This is what I meant, David, in speaking of that 'bigger picture,' the consequences of our decisions, far-reaching often even beyond our own ability to comprehend them."

He was right, and that was the worst of it. He and Rahel, both. His actions had put them all in jeopardy. But it had been the *right* thing to do.

"I owed it to him—to bring him back," he replied stubbornly, looking the *memuneh* in the eye. "I sent him out there."

Shoham took a deep breath and closed his eyes, shaking his head. "You serve the state, David, not your men. And if you want a clean conscience, you need to find another line of work."

"You're firing me?" Shafron demanded, ignoring the pain in his back as he sat up straighter, taken off-guard by the edge in the older man's voice.

"Mirit has asked me to," Shoham acknowledged quietly, opening his eyes once more. "She's furious, David, and she has every right to be. You utilized her personnel, her equipment, in a high-risk, unsanctioned operation. The successful recovery of Taferi, and his success in retrieving the avionics of the Su-57, doesn't change that. Avigdor is being sacked for his part in this whole affair, and Reuven's head is next on the chopping block."

"They acted on my orders, and I take full—"

"Is that why you went out there, David? Because you thought in so doing, you could protect those who had followed you, against their own chain of command? *Chai B'Seret.*" The *memuneh* shook his head incredulously. *You're living in a movie.* "But no—your job is secure, for this moment, even if theirs is not. Perhaps that's the most fitting punishment, after all. You can't protect your people from everything, David, not at this level. They are *tools* to be used, in the defense of Zion. If you're going to continue to run MEGIDDO, you need to come to terms with that reality."

Avi ben Shoham rose from his seat to signal an end to the interview, extending his hand as Shafron struggled to his feet, making a futile effort to mask the pain. "I understand why you took the course you did—once, I might have even taken it myself. But no longer, and that's a point you must reach for yourself. Or get off the road."

He gripped Shafron's arm firmly, dark eyes boring into his face. "Now get back out there, we still have a war to fight."

11:37 A.M. Moscow Standard Time
Zhukovsky International Airport
Moscow Oblast, Russia

The winter wind whipped mercilessly at the hem of Vera Svischeva's heavy woolen skirt as she waited in the cold at the lowered rear ramp of the Russian Air Force Antonov An-72, arms hugged close to her body. The salt trails of tears, long since dried unheeded against her cheeks.

The tall, gangly figure of her son, towering over her at her side, hands shoved awkwardly into the pockets of his tracksuit.

"*Mne ochen' zhal,* Vera Vladimirovna," the stocky Air Force captain announced, his bluff, open face betraying far more discomfort than genuine compassion. *I feel so sorry.*

And then the soldiers emerged from the bowels of the transport, four young men not much older than her own Anton, carrying the zinc-lined coffin between them. She staggered forward, placing a hand on the box, looking in through the small window at the top—a groan escaping her lips at the sight of her husband's face, eyes closed in death, her tears flowing fast and free once more to spatter, freezing on contact against the glass. "*Oh, Yarik.*"

He'd come home. *Just in time for Christmas. . .*

1:07 P.M.
Beit Jann
Northern District, Israel

The previous night's light snow was melting away from the slopes of Mount Meron as Mohamed Taferi made his way up the street toward his parents' house, a raw tinge to the air, defying the weak mid-winter sun.

A new apartment building was going up at the end of their street, a backhoe backing noisily away from the site, its exhaust spewing hot into the air. Its operator, Samir Qablan, the kid brother of a boy he'd grown up with—calling out to him as he passed.

He raised his hand in mute reply, passing on without a word, leaving the younger Samir staring after him in surprise. He'd visited the village shrine on his way in, laying a silk scarf he had purchased in Tel Aviv on the resting place of Al-Nabi Haydar, and lighting the candles in their niches by the tomb of the holy man.

A soldier's way to express his gratitude, to God above, for his safe return—but in his heart and mind, he was still there, in Syria, and suspected he would be for some time to come.

He could still see the desperation in Nassif's eyes as he stood there, the pistol in his outstretched hand—the pressure and fatigue of the years at war wearing him down until he'd snapped at the last.

The quiet reproach etched in the lines of Abu Ahmed's face as he'd taken the Glock from his hand, intending even then to end his own life.

He hadn't been able to save either one, in the end. That failure, eating away at him, far overshadowing anything else his mission might have achieved. He'd likely never know what had happened to the avionics components he'd lugged out in that backpack, but *Nassif*. . .he'd intended, however improbably, to bring him back here, if not Germany, to Beit Jann. For his parents to take him, as their own, if they would have him. His, if not.

The Druze looked after their own. But he had *killed* him instead.

His father opened the door, a broad smile dawning across his face. He reached out and drew Mohamed inside, wrapping his arms around his younger son in a fierce embrace.

Mohamed grimaced, biting his tongue to avoid crying

516

out—the wound in his side still far from fully healed.

"I was so disappointed to hear that I had missed you when I got back from Boston," his father said warmly, taking a step backward. "You've been well?"

"*Na'am, ya Abbi,*" he replied, forcing a smile. "*Shukran.* I was sorry I had to leave without seeing you, but you know. . .government."

"Of course, of course." There was a wise, knowing smile on his father's face, but he didn't know the half of it, Mohamed thought, unable to find words for the irony.

"Where's mother?"

"On the computer, video-chatting with Amin and Nadia," his father replied, referencing his older brother and sister-in-law in California. "It's her first time to see their newborn son. She'll want you to go right in."

"They named him Farid, yes?" he asked, following his father through their sparsely appointed home. His father was a wealthy man, but in keeping with the Druze antipathy for opulence, one would never have known it from his residence.

"Yes. He was born eight days ago—your mother and I almost flew out there to see him, but I am glad we didn't miss your return. Go on in."

Eight days. The night of the attack—new life being born, even as he had been taking it. *Blood on his hands.* His mother was chatting away in rapid-fire Arabic to his brother's wife, her shawl removed, and a pair of headphones perched incongruously atop her thick, greying hair, but she looked up at his entrance, waving him anxiously over to the monitor. "Oh, Nadia, Mohamed is here—he'll want to see Farid."

A weary, good-natured smile crossed his sister-in-law's face and she bent down, jostling the camera as she lifted the small bundle on her lap, a squawk erupting from the folds of fabric as she turned it toward the camera to reveal the ruddy face of a rudely awakened baby boy. His dark eyes opening to stare straight into the camera's lens with abnormal focus, his cries slowly abating.

Mohamed's face went ashen, the room around him seeming to fade away to a dull roar in his ears as he stared into his nephew's face and his newborn nephew stared back, strangely knowing.

They were the eyes of Nassif.

An author lives by word-of-mouth recommendations. If you enjoyed this story, please consider leaving a customer review(even if only a few lines) on Amazon. It would be greatly helpful and much appreciated.

If you would like to contact me personally, drop me a line at Stephen@stephenwrites.com.

For news and release information, visit www.stephenwrites.com and sign up for the mailing list.

Stay in touch and up-to-the-minute with book news through social media.

On Facebook:
https://www.facebook.com/stephenenglandauthor

Join the Facebook group to discuss the series with other fans: Stephen England's Shadow Warriors

On Twitter:
https://twitter.com/stephenmengland

Read more from the Lion of God *series!*

Lion of God: The Original Trilogy

Also by Stephen England

The Shadow Warriors Saga

NIGHTSHADE
Pandora's Grave
Day of Reckoning
TALISMAN
LODESTONE
Embrace the Fire
QUICKSAND
ARKHANGEL
Presence of Mine Enemies
WINDBREAK

And the stand-alone alternate history:
Sword of Neamha

Author's Note

When I sat down to write the acknowledgements at the end of the final episode of the original Lion of God trilogy toward the end of 2016, I wrote that "all good things must come to an end." The sentiment was true enough, but my delivery was premature. And I came to realize, in the years that followed, that David Shafron's story wasn't quite as complete as I had imagined. That his service to the state of Israel had, in fact, continued beyond his retirement from the field.

The only question was what part of his story, precisely, to tell next, and while it would take me another couple years to answer that question, the result is the novel you hold in your hands. Shafron is older, and the years have left their mark, but his commitment to both his nation and the men he leads—now, sends—into battle remains as unwavering as ever before. And now, the future of Israel is the future of his own sons.

The enormity of the Syrian Civil War proved difficult to condense into a novel, but I trust that I have managed to convey in some small way the raw humanity of the conflict, and the devastation wrought by the Assad regime's desperate attempts to maintain power at any cost. Syria was a massive stage on which to set a story, with the scenery at times dwarfing the cast, and I found as the story progressed that, in the absence of a central antagonist or "villain," it had become something of "man versus the environment" story. The environment, in this case, being the creation of one man and the dozens of hostile factions struggling to dethrone him.

Bashar Assad truly has made a desolation of his country and, in victory, called it peace.

In the extensive research for this book, I owe a special debt of thanks to the journalism of Sam Dagher, most notably his 2019 *tour de force, Assad or We Burn the Country: How One Family's Lust for Power Destroyed Syria.* Also of note: Wendy Pearlman's moving collection of refugee accounts *We Crossed a Bridge and It Trembled: Voices from Syria.*

Special thanks are also due to my colleague Russell Blake for providing the original impetus for *Lion of God,* back in the day. And to his artist, Jun Ares, for continuing to provide top-notch artwork for the series.

To my colleague Steven Hildreth, Jr., for his friendship and advice along the way over the years, and for his willingness to give this manuscript the once-over before publication. Having the perspective of another top-notch author is always valuable.

To my learned friend Raymond Stock, a noted writer and translator in his own right, for his patience in walking me through the complexities of the Arabic language. Any mistakes which remain are mine and mine alone.

To friends, new and old, in Israel for providing countless

bits of insight on the developing story.

And to the members of the beta reading team for *The Lion's Paw*: Bodo Pfündl, Joe Walsh, Diane Goldhammer, Jack Patterson, Paula Tyler, Michael Schuette, and Yuval Cohen. I couldn't do this without you all, and I appreciate the time and diligence you displayed in helping me polish the final product.

And last—and most—of all, thanks is owed to my readers, whose enthusiasm for David Shafron's debut in no small part precipitated his return.

May God bless you all.

Made in United States
Troutdale, OR
06/08/2025